Eternal Seas

by

N. Christine Samuelson

This is a work of fiction. Names, characters, places, events and incidents are the products of the author's imagination or are used fictitiously. Any resemblance to actual persons living or dead, business establishments, events, or locales, is entirely coincidental.

Eternal Seas

Contact Information: info@thewildrosepress.com

Cover Art by *Debbie Taylor*

The Wild Rose Press, Inc.
PO Box 708
Adams Basin, NY 14410-0708
Visit us at www.thewildrosepress.com

Publishing History
First Champagne Rose Edition, 2018
Print ISBN 978-1-5092-1979-7
Digital ISBN 978-1-5092-1980-3

Published in the United States of America

"I promise, when I leave on a ship to fly jets, I will always come back to you. In one way or another, I will come back. In time, all ships must return to port. Ella, you are my home port."

In that moment, his words were truer than any she'd ever heard. But with eyes closed, her spirit lifted into another realm and through the potent energy passing between them, she detected a whisper. As had happened before, it did not emanate from her brain like a thought; it came from outside herself and drifted in. Just as she knew the light from a star took a thousand years to reach her eyes, she sensed this message was spoken long ago in some ancient time and had just reached her ear on this day. It was the familiar voice of a man who had loved her, and when he'd held her, he smelled of the salt air and the sea, and he had said, *I promise I will come back to you.*

She heard the words now, but her lover in that ancient time had never returned. And now the loss of him drifted back through time as well—it still had a home in her heart, a grief so deep and pervasive it would never leave. The pain was not just felt; it'd been imprinted on her, like a brand on the soul, marking her for life and obviously beyond it. There was no getting over that kind of pain.

Dedication

Dedicated to Scott,
for every good thing about him.

Acknowledgments

Thank you to first reader, Eve S., for insight and contributions. Many thanks and love to all those who read, supported, critiqued, and encouraged my writing, especially Ariel H., Salli G., Lisa V., Susan N., and Carol O'C.

Many thanks to friend and career Navy veteran of Desert Storm, Skip H., who assisted with Navy information and inspired part of the story. Any discrepancies or errors are mine alone.

With deep gratitude to skilled editors and teachers who improved my writing and helped shape this story and my life.

Finally, in memory of the first person to believe in my writing. Thank you and rest in peace my friend, Jacquie H.

Chapter 1

Soaring through a world of infinite blue, of sky and sea with no horizons, no beginning or end, was like flying off the earth into the arms of God. It was as close to heaven as Daniel Ellsworth imagined it to be. There was no greater thrill than catapulting off a carrier flight deck in a Navy fighter jet with engines roaring, cutting through the air at insane speeds. He entered *the zone*, as he called it—defying nature, commanding the space above the Atlantic Ocean and loving every minute with his senses tuned in razor-sharp to every sight and sound in the cockpit. But today there was something wrong. An odd sensation tugged in his gut. Approaching cruising altitude, he did another flight check: no problems; the sea was calm, the sky was clear and welcoming in this routine flight. His rational mind knew there was no basis for concern, but Daniel's trusted inner voice said, *Something is coming, and this is fair warning*. He knew he'd have no control over whatever it was, like going in for a landing into destiny.

****

With a death grip on the steering wheel after an hour's drive from the tip of south Florida heading toward Key West, Ella Rowe saw a bridge in the distance. It was seven miles long and suspended over open water with not a speck of land in sight. It was Ella's idea of hell—driving over ocean and sky through an endless blue nightmare, trapped in a car with no way to get off but over the side. Even worse was an hour and a half more of driving through the Florida Keys mostly over water, over forty-two islands connected by forty-two bridges. As much as she had tried to suppress it, the war inside her between the fear, love, and hate of the sea raged. The longer she drove, the stronger it got, and the fear was taking over. But there was no place to escape as she approached the Seven Mile Bridge with no exits, just road and sea. *An accident here would send you to a watery death,* she thought. *I've heard Key West is a paradise, like heaven on earth, but driving through hell to get there doesn't seem worth the trip.*

She'd never been to Key West before, let alone driven there. On a map, the Keys appeared as tiny dots of land slung over the water like a strand of pearls. Just the sight of them on paper gave her chills as she imagined how quickly the ocean could swallow them up. Janie, her best friend and a photographer at the newspaper in Tampa where Ella worked as a reporter, had assured her the actual drive couldn't be as unnerving as the aerial view on a map. But the reality was worse for Ella. Even driving over what little land there was, the water was so close on both sides of the road that there was no doubt she really *was* driving out in the middle of the ocean.

With over an hour of driving and about twenty more bridges to go, her fear grew exponentially, wrapping her in a suffocating grip. Ella needed help, but all she had was Janie asleep in the passenger seat. Attempting to calm herself, she thought, *This is not happening. I'm a sane, rational person. I must rise above this. I can do this.* But that only made her feel worse, as if she were talking herself down off a ledge.

The fear ignored her pleas, consuming her, spilling over an invisible edge of what she could handle. In the distance, she saw the road climbing gradually up the arch of the bridge, higher and higher until it disappeared beyond the apex. From her perspective, it seemed the car would drive straight off into the sky. Every nerve in her body trembled with a fear she couldn't contain. Even as she gripped the steering wheel, knowing her body was solidly in the car, something inside her rose and took over. She felt as if her spirit lifted, up and away from the crushing fear, almost as if she could fly.

Ella looked to the sky and saw a jet flying high, gracefully suspended above the earth, free from its confines and fears. As if sitting in the cockpit, she knew what the pilot must've been feeling as he gazed down at the turquoise seas from above. *How peaceful and soothing to be so far removed from the limitations of life on the ground*, she thought. The sensation of flying over the earth was so real. It was visceral yet comfortable, eerie but familiar.

Unwittingly, she'd swerved and an oncoming car blasted its horn, snapping Ella back to reality, bringing the familiar gnawing in her gut—not just the fear of being surrounded by the sea, but something else—a haunting feeling of the past catching up to her, colliding with destiny. Running away to a new place had always been her escape from the past. Even though she dreaded the upheaval, if this feeling continued to resurface she'd have to uproot her life again. But a small, silent voice played in the background of her thoughts, saying, *Running away won't work anymore*. There truly was nowhere to run, figuratively or literally, expanding her fear into terror.

Maybe praying would help, she thought. *This is the kind of situation where people do that.* But with it not being a regular habit, praying out of desperation seemed wrong. God might say, "*Ha!* I never hear from you unless you need something." And the last thing she needed was to have God ticked off at her. Ella was spiritual in her own way, but tended to keep her thoughts about the nature of God and life to herself. It made for cleaner relationships. Her private beliefs were nobody's business, especially since no one could wrap their minds around her life's mysteries and secrets. They were so inexplicable, even she couldn't fathom their depths.

And then there were the losses—to the sea—her ghosts of the past rendering her a pitiable, haunted being—a person she did not want to be seen as. So she never talked about the issues surrounding her past. She never explored or understood them beyond the obvious facts on the surface. Like oil floating on water, the events of her past would never sink or disappear, but she could move around them. Denying their existence allowed her to carry on through life as a seemingly normal person without a curse, even though its presence rippled through her life. For the last fifteen of her twenty-seven years, she'd managed to evade her dark history. Until now, on this bridge, the unrelenting fear triggered Ella's memory of the first time the sea had terrorized her, setting off a series of foreboding events for the rest of her life.

****

Near Cape Elizabeth, on the coast of Maine

At nine years old, Ella walked almost every day along the shoreline of the rocky coast of Maine where she'd grown up. She'd stop at the same place on the beach to look atop a bluff at a dilapidated Victorian house. It cast an ominous pall over the land below, not just with its decaying state and overgrown weeds, but with the air surrounding it—heavy air, burdened with secrets and sadness. Something inside that house seemed to be alive. It frightened her, yet Ella had been inexplicably drawn to it.

One scorching August afternoon, Ella had worked up a good sweat by the time she'd reached the house. Even though she was a good swimmer, she rarely swam in the ocean because she struggled with an unidentifiable lifelong fear. But that day, with the sun burning her skin, she stared out across the endless sea and was mesmerized by the rhythmic sound of the waves stroking the shore. The navy-blue water lured her with the promise of a cool, soothing bath. She could feel the brilliant white froth of the crashing swells like ice in her mouth, and on her parched body. Entranced, she felt as if she was inside a glass dome, set apart from present time and space.

Kicking off her sandals, she took one step toward the water. It invited her in farther, so she took another cautious step. Walking slowly, she looked down, and it seemed her feet were not part of her, like she wasn't really there. She halted as the first cold water rushed around her ankles and up to her calves. Gazing back at the ocean, the fresh salt air cleansed her thoughts and promised good things, a friendly seagull called out above her head in agreement. The wind picked up and gently hit her from behind, a nudge that seemed to come from the old house, pushing her to move deeper into the sea.

Feeling pulled by a tide of destiny, Ella's common sense evaporated into the sea mist. The first cold wave hit her middle, shocking her. She jumped over it, refreshed by the chill. Jumping over two more waves, she moved past the breakers and faced a rolling sea, her feet still on the bottom, floating over each new wave. The cold water numbed but invigorated her, lulling her into a peaceful place, floating on her back, looking to the sky. A large swell, several feet above her head, approached. She glided easily up and over it, but when she came down the other side, her feet no longer touched the bottom. She turned around to look at the shore. She'd been carried far away. Panicked, she turned her back on the open water to swim toward land. Getting closer, chin deep in water, she felt sand under her tiptoes and relaxed. But then a huge wave hit from behind and broke over her head.

As she went under, she remembered her grandmother, Hannah, cautioning, "Never swim alone, and never turn your back on the sea." But it was too late. She'd tumbled head over heels, briefly breaking the surface again. But as she tried to plant her feet firmly on the bottom, the sea came up and grabbed her with cold arms, clutching her legs, pulling them out from under her. With her head submerged and being sucked out again, for a moment she sensed this had happened before—a feeling of powerlessness against the sea. Pumping her arms toward the surface, she got a quick gulp of air before another wave crashed over her. Somersaulting violently, she lost all orientation of up, down, top, or bottom. Panicking, she tried desperately to hold her breath, so long she thought she'd pass out, when a lone thought passed through her mind. *I've drowned before*.

With that, scenes flashed before her closed eyes, like lightning flashing at night in the distance, illuminating the landscape and her mind for mere seconds: images of a ship, a violent man, a woman falling overboard—and Ella felt herself falling into oblivion. Her head hit the sand as a wave tumbled her like clothes in a dryer. Then something seemed to wrap around her legs. It felt like a long dress, soaked and heavy, pulling her further down. Another vision flashed before her—a woman in a Grecian gown threw a ring into the sea, then succumbed to it as Ella was now.

Knowing her next breath would be water, she recognized the feeling of surrender, of looking death in the face. She screamed inside her mind, *I don't want to die!* In the next moment, the ocean spit her out and threw her onto the shore. Gasping for air and choking out water, Ella's small body lay sprawled on the beach while she let the sun revive her enough to crawl away from the water like a crab escaping an encroaching net. Weak and trembling, she collapsed with her eyes squeezed tightly shut against the world and her cheek resting on the prickly, hot sand.

Shaken, the scenes she'd just seen while under water burst through her mind again like a movie fast-forwarding through her head. She felt connected to them, like this was supposed to happen; she knew those people and the feeling of dying at sea. *But how? Why?* Her head was spinning and bloated with water as she dug into the sand with open fists, clinging to solid ground. The space around her fell still and quiet, except for the sound of her breath going out, in, out. She was alive. Exhausted, she let herself drift into a twilight place—conscious of her surroundings while letting her mind go empty and tranquil. In that relaxed state, one question emerged. *Why did this happen to me?*

An answer came, not as a thought from her own mind, but rather it drifted in from the outside like it was carried on the wind from the sea: *Secrets, lies, and murder*. The message shattered her calm, making her fully alert, and she pushed her body up to kneel in the sand. Dark clouds had filled the sky. As she rose to stand on wobbly legs, the air grew thick and crackled around her. It was charged with those words, as if the old house echoed them back from a long-ago past.

Ella looked all around. Maybe someone was playing a joke on her, but the long stretch of beach was empty with only her footprints in the sand. She stood, got her bearings, and wondered, *Whose secrets? What lies? Whose murder?* The house, now shrouded in fog, appeared briefly out of the mist like a ghost and stared down at her with two huge windows glaring like eyes. Thunder clapped overhead. Ella felt the vibration through her body and its echo resounded through her mind: *Yours—all yours.*

Terrified, she ran for her life with legs that had never moved faster, running to escape the mysterious message of her life's own secrets, lies, and murder. The message didn't seem to be as much a forewarning as it was a light cast back onto a mysterious past, one that might determine her future. She'd run like the wind that day and every day since, away from the haunting past, into the distance, and into a future away from the sea, from death, toward home.

Chapter 2

The Road to Key West

As Ella's car approached the Seven Mile Bridge, the sun shone brilliantly, and the sky was a safe, clear blue, but the fear from that day in Maine still gripped her. Then, she'd gone home to tell her grandmother about it, who'd made her promise never to swim alone in the ocean. As for the rest of it, her grandmother Hannah said it was most likely shock and imagination gone wild. Ella knew the experience had to be more than that, but didn't argue. Her nine-year-old brain couldn't fathom any of it, so she stuffed it in her subconscious as something to forget. Her fear of that house and the sea lingered, but the mysteries they posed were buried deep within forever, or so she thought. Gram Hannah had soothed her then with love, a warm bath, and a hot dinner. Today Ella relived the memories but had no mitigating comfort—only more driving ahead and Janie sound asleep in the seat beside her.

Surrounded now by only water, sky, and fear, Ella's imagination went into overdrive. If only the situation could be solved as simply as it had been when she was nine. But nothing had been simple in Ella's life since then. Today she was still running, and there was no escape from the small car and the past catching up to her. She couldn't do this alone, so she silently asked anything or anyone who would listen for help, to dissolve the fear and get her through the last leg of this journey and back onto solid ground. Ten minutes went by, but no help came. In desperation, she called out to Janie, but she didn't wake up. Ella called louder. Nothing. Nudging her shoulder, she yelled, "Janie!"

Janie jumped in her seat and woke up, startled. "What? Where are we? What's happening? Are you okay?"

Ella calmed immediately now that Janie was awake and talking. "Not sure. I'm glad you're conscious. I'm getting loopy from this drive and all this water."

"Jeez! You scared me. What's going on?" Janie asked through a yawn, rubbing the sleep from her eyes.

"*You're* scared? How do you think I feel driving on this thin ribbon of road with nothing but ocean surrounding us? It's freaking me out." Ella explained in detail the feeling of lifting out of her body and sensing the pilot's feelings in the jet overhead.

"You *are* getting weird, and you're scaring me even more. Are you sure you're okay?"

"Yeah. It was a fleeting sensation…probably my brain's way of getting me out of a scary situation. I'm feeling better now that you're awake and talking to me. I need a diversion, so I don't get wrapped up in my head."

"And your wacky love/hate thing about the ocean. That's what all this fear is about, isn't it?"

"Of course. And it's not wacky. There are good reasons for the way I feel. And I don't hate the ocean. I hate what it took from me."

"I've never quite understood all of that. But then, I don't know the whole story. I know you have things you don't talk about. Regardless, here you are in this predicament." Janie looked around in every direction. "I'd say, 'Pull over and I'll drive,' but that's impossible. There's nowhere to stop."

"Exactly. Hence, my anxiety. It's like panicking in an airplane and feeling as if you'll die if you don't open the door to escape, but you can't open the door. I'm powerless to do anything. I'm trapped."

"I think it's called claustrophobia."

"I'm not claustrophobic. It's complicated."

"*I* guess. You look awful." Janie pulled up the map on her cell phone. "This is the Seven Mile Bridge. Then we have another hour or so until we reach Key West. I only had three hours of sleep after taking photos of that accident for the paper, then drinks with the guys, and I really don't think it's safe for me to drive. Can you hold out?"

"Just keep talking to me…about anything. My mind has to think of something other than where I am."

"Oh, how unusual for my rather tight-lipped friend, who is now a willing subject, ready to talk. How tempting. Let's see…"

Ella glared sideways at her. "You know what I mean—just gab, gossip, nothing too heavy."

"Okay, okay." Janie put on a sly smile while arranging herself comfortably, and grabbed a bag of popcorn, settling in for a good, long conversation. "There's something I've always wondered, and you never really talked about it. What was the real reason you moved so far from Maine? Was it really just to take this job in Tampa? I mean, there are plenty of newspapers up there that need good reporters. Did it have to do with your relationship with Peter ending? It was sudden and unexpected, right?"

Ella straightened in her seat, took a deep breath, and focused on her answer. She absolutely did *not* want to talk about the details, but talking meant occupying her mind and getting it off the ocean waiting nearby to swallow her up. "Yeah, that was part of it, along with all the other endings in my life. It was time for a complete change of locale." She went silent for a while.

Janie waited patiently for Ella to sort out her thoughts, but the words never came. "You said *endings*, plural. What else was there besides the breakup with Peter?"

Ella fidgeted, clearly uncomfortable.

Janie tried to be understanding, despite her predominantly Type-A, impatient self. "I know your anxiety level must be through the roof, but, hey, I can't give you a glass of wine to relax 'cause you're driving, and you said to keep you talking. I'm doing what you asked. The least you could do is give me an honest answer."

"I'm always honest with you, but this subject is hard to talk about. I guess I'm afraid of judgment, or if you knew the whole truth, you'd think I was crazy and walk away from our friendship. I've never wanted to risk it."

"Are you kidding? I've shared everything with you about all my exploits in the Navy. I've trusted you with all the down and dirty stuff of my life. C'mon. Trust me and spit this story out."

"I'm trying. It's just scary, dredging up things I've kept buried my entire life. It's new territory. Risky."

"That's exactly the reason why you can't get close to anyone, especially men."

"I'm close to you…and Hannah." Ella sorted out her thoughts. She figured, if she admitted to what Janie perceived as her main fault, she'd let Ella off the hook and quit questioning her, so she conceded that one point. "But you're right about men. I just can't seem to break through the fear of getting close."

Unfortunately, her plan didn't work. Janie continued with her questioning. "What's that about? Why can't you just let yourself feel what you want to feel?"

Exasperated, Ella let out a heavy sigh. "You just won't let it go, will you?"

Janie grinned. "Of course not. You know me. I'm like a bulldog with a bone. I'll hang on until I get answers. So?"

Feeling defeated, but still needing to talk to keep her mind off the long bridge she now drove over the middle of, Ella gave in. "Okay. But this is difficult. You know, I just get to a certain point and I shut down. All the past experiences come back to haunt me, and I get consumed with the fear of losing a loved one to something I have no control over. It's safer not to risk getting too close in the first place."

"I don't understand. As a reporter, you're not afraid of anything new or risky when it comes to getting a story. I know you got it in you, so get talkin', sister, and start at the beginning. This secret is probably not as bad as you think, and most likely you're blowing it out of proportion. I mean, you're a solid, stable person. Are your issues and losses so bad they debilitate you?"

Ella, agitated, struck back. "I'm not debilitated. I simply make a choice, the best, most reasonable choice for my life at any given time."

"Sorry for the unkind word. But your life *right now* seems kind of stuck with no way to move forward. Your past is holding you back."

To Janie, Ella's past was black and white, simple. But Janie could never fathom all of what had shaped Ella's emotions and actions or why she'd never be in a serious relationship again.

The last five years, working as a reporter in Tampa, had been fairly calm and fulfilling. She dated but never, ever got serious, mainly because, when it came to love, Ella felt jinxed or, more accurately, cursed. It started with the terrifying experience at nine years old, which she'd tried to forget until it came back to haunt her once she'd reached adulthood, manifesting when she lost the only two men she'd ever loved. The sea had played a large part in those losses, turning her inside out, sending her tumbling inside of her life as sure as if she'd been hit by those same waves breaking over her head.

The fear of losing everything, even her own life because of the sea, was not imaginary as Hannah had suggested; it felt ingrained in her on a cellular level. She knew she'd been born with the fear because it'd been part of her psyche from as far back as she could remember. The terrifying experience at nine had reinforced it. Even while fighting the fear of the ocean, she was simultaneously drawn to its immense beauty and power, knowing it somehow played an integral part in her life's most tragic events. Most times, the fear won. She was no different than anybody else when it came to danger. She avoided it yet was oddly attracted by it, like when passing the scene of an accident, knowing you shouldn't look but feeling compelled to anyway. Along with that came an aura of death. It hovered in the periphery of Ella's awareness, always reminding her that loss surrounding the sea was real and close by if she let her guard down.

Janie, knowing the bare minimum about Ella's ambivalence toward the sea, had once asked her why, then, would she choose to live near the coast in a state surrounded by water on three sides. She'd answered honestly, "Because, after growing up on the coast of Maine, living near the ocean is familiar; it feels like home. I love the sea, but I don't trust it not to turn on me, not to hurt me or cause loss."

Therefore, Ella swore she'd never have another serious relationship. Having to explain her past to suitors would be a relationship killer anyway. *So,* she'd thought, *why waste the time and effort?*

A huge impediment to this strategy, though, was her looks. Her wholesome, blond, blue-eyed features were classically beautiful. Standing five feet, eight inches tall with a statuesque form and shapely legs, she drew men to her like a magnet. A few times, her natural instinct for love had tempted her to fall for someone, but invariably she'd feel like a black widow spider, luring in innocent male victims who surely would meet a dark fate if they were to fall in love with her. Ella's compassionate heart wouldn't let her put some unsuspecting nice guy in harm's way, in her way.

That was why work and career became Ella's entire life and kept her on an even keel. She kept her secrets buried, never unearthing them, not even for herself, let alone anyone else. Distancing herself from her own life meant distancing herself from most people. Even with Janie, she'd never divulged the whole story or the details. Ella didn't even know the answers to some of her personal mysteries, and she didn't care to ever find out. Her grandmother would say, "Don't ask questions about the past, or you'll open up a Pandora's Box. Let what's done and gone rest in peace. Life is for the living. Just keep moving forward."

Ella had lived her life trying to do just that—never looking back, except when the past crept in and caught up with her, reminding her that her present was affected by it, just as it was now.

****

As they sat in the car talking, some of what Janie said about Ella's past holding her back made sense.

"I don't know," Ella said. "Maybe I've kept my stories to myself so long they've taken on more significance than what is real. Maybe it's not as bad as I think." But even as she spoke the words, her intuition defied them. Her anxiety grew as every loss and mystery caught up to her. She had no place to put all the emotional garbage she'd been suppressing her entire life. Something inside her was approaching the limit of how much she could push down, like filling a closet with so much junk the door strained to close. She was afraid to open that door. Things would be exposed that she didn't want to see, and baggage would spill out that she didn't want to deal with.

Therefore, Ella planned to edit her conversation, withholding what she couldn't share and elaborating on the rest, weaving bits and pieces together to save her sanity, to get through the drive. Janie sat quietly, mostly just listening, waiting for any new revelations.

"Well, you already know my parents died when I was a kid and I was raised by my grandmother Hannah near Cape Elizabeth on the coast of Maine. I met Peter in college. We were serious, but it didn't work out. I was so heartbroken I wanted to get out of Maine. When the job in Tampa came along, I figured it was as far away as I could run from the loss of him."

Janie shot her a disgusted look. "I'm bored already. I know all that stuff. Get down to the dirty details, this thing you have about the ocean."

"All right. I should've known you wouldn't be happy with the short answer." Ella realized she had an iron grip on the steering wheel, beads of sweat forming on her face. Thinking this level of stress was ridiculous given she was starting a vacation, she relaxed her grip, grabbed a tissue, patted her face, and took a drink of water along with a deep breath. "Okay. The truth is I don't remember a time when I didn't have some kind of weird, conflicted feelings about the ocean. Growing up on the coast, I was constantly near the sea and loved it for the most part. I'd walk the shore for hours at all times of the day during every season. I watched it change from calm to storm, from sunrise to sunset. At its worst, it raged and roiled, frothing all green and gray, pounding at the shore, gouging out deep handfuls of sand. At best, it was a restful blue, the waves curling gently on land in summer. Even in winter, with waves violently crashing against the cliffs, I appreciated the beauty in its raw power and came to respect its constantly changing nature."

"Well, that all sounds idyllic, but you're avoiding the connection with the not-so-great parts of your life."

Ella looked sideways at Janie, who stared out the front window while tossing popcorn into her mouth. *Good*, Ella thought. *Maybe she's given up on me and isn't really paying attention.* She felt safer divulging information thinking it might not be completely heard.

"You know, with my being so afraid just before you woke up, I remembered something that happened as a child. I never told anyone about this. Can I trust you not to tell anyone?"

Nonchalantly, Janie said, "Yeah, sure."

"Janie, look at me. I mean it. You promise, if I share this with you, it won't go beyond us?"

Looking at Emma now, her big brown eyes wide with curiosity, accentuated by her shortly cropped, dark, tousled hair, Janie realized this must be one good story. "Of course, I promise. Jeez. Now spill it."

Ella proceeded to carefully recap the experience of the old house, her near-drowning, and what she'd seen and heard.

Janie not only paid close attention, but her jaw dropped open with a gasp. "Are you kidding me right now? I mean, almost drowning is bad enough, but then that creepy old house, seeing people drowning and dying, and hearing those scary words." She shuddered. "What could those words have possibly meant?"

"I don't know. When I told my grandmother, she was shocked at first—upset enough to drop and shatter a glass she'd been washing. But then, quick as a chameleon, she calmed and turned into her usual, sensible self. She'd assured me that I'd never lied to anyone, that I wasn't old enough to have any secrets to keep, and there hadn't been a murder in our town for as long as she could remember, so it certainly would've had nothing to do with me. Her reasoning made sense, and I needed common sense then, especially when she chalked it up to being my imagination."

"Passing the whole thing off as your imagination? That's really strange. Don't you think?"

"I did at the time, but I was too young to argue, and too afraid. I assumed if I left it at 'my imagination,' then I wouldn't have to deal with the true meaning, so I guess it was a good thing."

"But how have you lived with it following you over the years?"

"I told you—I pretty much buried it and tried to forget what happened, but it all came back today with a vengeance ."

"Yeah, lifelong denial will do that. Now I know why it takes an act of God or a ninety-nine degree day at the beach to get you into the water and why you won't swim alone."

"Yes, and now you know one of the reasons for my love-hate of the sea." Ella winced, realizing she'd slipped and let out there was more behind it. Maybe Janie didn't hear her.

No such luck.

"What? There's more? Oh, this I gotta hear. C'mon. Tell me now."

"Nope. I can't. Because…look." Ella pointed at the long-awaited land ahead, diverting Janie's attention. "We're over the last bridge and coming into Key West."

Janie brightened and clapped her hands, a wide smile spreading across her face. "We're finally here! We made it! Good for you. You did it. I knew you could. Now let's find our cottage and get down to partying."

Indeed, Ella thought. *After a couple of drinks, Janie will forget about asking more questions, and I can forget about the parts of my life that are best left hidden and unexplored.*

Chapter 3

Arriving in the small, tropical island of Key West, the southernmost point in the United States, they made their way to a beach-front rental cottage. Pulling into the sandy driveway, the cottage looked even better than the website photos. Tall coconut palm trees framed the front door, and Bahama shutters tilted away from the bottom of the windows to let in light and air. Ella felt she'd stepped back in time to a more rustic era where simplicity, vibrant colors, and ocean breezes welcomed them. Large flowering bushes and palm trees grew between the cottages, giving privacy and filling the air with fragrance.

The cottage was decorated with casual furniture and plenty of Key West beach charm. Inside, the living area was spacious with a kitchenette on one side and a view of the beach and ocean at the far end, facing the front door. There was a small bedroom for each of them with a shared bath in between. The walls were painted turquoise with white trim and decorated with starfish, shells, and nets. A watercolor painting of an ocean sunset hung in the living area. All the furniture was white-washed wood and wicker. Potted palms sat in the corners of a living room filled with sun streaming in through the large glass sliding doors. The place had a light and airy feel, an extension of the beach outside. Ella loved that the beach was just out the back door.

She could walk onto it without having to drive. With opening the patio doors wide, warm ocean breezes and salt air floated in, and every night the sound of the waves would lull her to sleep.

Janie liked that the cottage was close to good local cafés and bars with music. She was ready to party, but Ella was tired after driving eleven hours, so they compromised on drinks and dinner at a restaurant within walking distance. Janie was determined to get Ella out to meet men on this trip, to change her attitude, so she'd be more positive about relationships, about her life.

Ella decided to pretend to go along with Janie's plan and keep the vacation status quo. But with opening the door to this cottage, she opened the door to a new start in life. Secretly, she planned to update her resume and research jobs to relocate, maybe somewhere out west. There was definitely the feeling of a new beginning steeped in the air. If something worked out, it would appear unintentional to Janie, just a coincidence. Ella's survival had always depended on moving, running, keeping one step ahead of the things that haunted her. She wouldn't tell Janie until it was a done deal because she knew Janie would try to stop her.

Ella never shared her belief of not staying attached to any one place, job, and especially a man and a relationship for long, meant she couldn't be hurt. She wouldn't be abandoned and would never feel that pain and loss again. The truth she never shared with Janie was that the men she'd loved most didn't leave her; they were taken by the sea in one way or another. And here she was surrounded by the sea in Key West and by a friend determined to find her a man.

****

The next day, still recuperating from the traveling, they lounged on the beach, sunbathed, read, and did very little talking, at Ella's insistence. That evening, exhausted from the trip and the day in the sun, Ella got take-out meals and talked Janie into not going out by bringing margarita fixings and tequila back to the cottage. They sat on the patio with their drinks, watching the sunset, and all seemed right in the world. Feeling good, Janie thanked Ella for getting them there safely, for facing and overcoming her fears.

"Ella, I know you'd rather not talk about this, but I still can't get that picture out of my mind of you almost drowning, having flashes of people somehow connected to you, lying on that beach, and hearing those cryptic messages. It's just too weird. When you became an adult, didn't you ever want to learn more about it? Especially now, being a reporter, with your curiosity and innate sense of investigating a mystery, didn't you ever want to look into the history of that house, find its owners, or any stories that might connect you to it?"

Ella got a far-off look in her eyes, fielding the question. "As a kid, I blocked it out because I wanted to fit in and be 'normal.' I never shared the story with childhood friends, and I didn't want to know the facts because it would make it real and validate the experience. I've never wanted to dredge up the past, so I took Hannah's advice to leave it alone. What I don't know can't hurt me, right?"

"But maybe there's more to it or more behind it that might give you some insight or clues into your fears."

"Nah, I don't think so."

"But now, in the present, aren't you curious at all about your past?"

Ella hated being badgered about anything, especially this, and her annoyance showed in her tone of voice. "Janie, just drop it. It's my past. It doesn't affect me now and it never will. Okay?"

"Fine. Sorry I pushed you. I won't bring it up again unless you do." She lifted her glass. "Let's toast to a great, relaxing vacation."

"And a new start in life," Ella added while she thought, *I'm not kidding her or myself. I'm still affected by the past. Those fears go with me everywhere. Hopefully, I won't have to deal with any more of them on this vacation or anytime in the future*. But with another drink and her boundaries down, Ella's mind drifted into the ethers where secrets lay buried. She wondered if Janie had been right, if maybe finding out more about the mysterious happening and the old house would bring clues to uncovering the source of her lingering fears and constant losses surrounding the sea; maybe *not* knowing was hurting her more.

****

The next day, they drove all over the island to get a feel for the layout of the town, beaches, and top tourist spots. Key West charmed them with its casual beach atmosphere, local color and laid-back, friendly people. There was nothing about the place they didn't like. They had great fun soaking up the ambiance—equal parts Victorian, Gothic, Cuban, and Bahamian mixed with an air of the history of pirates and famous writers and artists who had lived and vacationed there. The heady scent of tropical flowers filled the air; turquoise water and white beaches everywhere lent an otherworldly feel to the island.

With the sunset closing down the day, they passed a local church in the historic area of downtown. Looking to be straight out of the last century, it had a white steeple, tall stained-glass windows, and was framed with lush, tropical shrubs and palm trees. Billowy clouds turned a deep rose color in the mauve sky behind the church. Ella stopped across the street after Janie pleaded to take photos. As they got out of the car, people emerged from the church.

"They're all dressed up, at least, for Key West," said Ella.

The men sported colorful, large floral-patterned shirts, long white trousers, and loafers with no socks. Most of the women wore long, silky dresses with sandals.

"Beachwear with class," Janie chimed in. "This must be a wedding, you think?"

"Probably. We should probably leave."

"Heck no," Janie said. "Let's gawk. They won't even notice us. I love weddings."

After five minutes with nothing happening but people milling around, Ella was ready to go, but Janie said, "Wait…look! The bridal party's coming out. Hey! They're Navy."

"How do you know? They could be Marines or Air Force."

Janie looked at her like she was crazy. "Are you kidding? I was *in* the Navy. I know what the summer dress whites and the insignias look like."

Totally uninterested, Ella replied, "If you say so."

Janie was about to make fun of Ella's ignorance when she saw the bride's white gown moving out the door. Excited, she pointed, yelling, "There she is, the bride!" A slender young woman in a flowing gown and long veil emerged with a dashing naval officer groom on her arm. "I just love brides," Janie cooed. "Just look at her, so beautiful, glowing, so happy." She got a wistful look in her eye. "Do you think we'll ever have weddings?"

"You, probably. Me, I doubt it. I just don't know."

"Yes, you do. Use that super intuition to check in on the future. What do you think?"

Willing to placate her and have a little fun, Ella closed her eyes and held her hands, palms-up, like a fortune teller might. Mockingly, she said in a deep, monotone voice, "I see a wedding in the future. Don't know whose. Don't know when."

Janie laughed. "Oh, you're no fun. What good are premonitions without faces and dates?"

"My sentiments exactly. Can we go now and get on with our night?" They got back in the car, but an inner voice urged Ella to turn and look back. She was drawn to the men in their uniforms, so handsome. One of them looked familiar, even though it wasn't possible because she didn't know anyone in the service. At the same moment, he glanced in her direction, and they locked eyes for an instant just before she turned away, uncomfortable with the pang of unidentifiable emotion inside her. The man, however, continued to hold his gaze on her until they drove away. She saw him in her rearview mirror, watching them, and it made her uncomfortable.

"Hey," Janie squawked. "You-who-was-so-hot-to-move-on, what are you looking at?"

"Nothing," Ella said. "Just one last look at happy

people. Maybe we *will* have this someday. Stranger things have happened."

"Stranger things have happened in your life…*literally*."

They shared a good laugh and drove off, up and down the coast, looking for a casual place on the water to have drinks. There were some fancy hotels, but they finally stumbled upon a ramshackle bar on the beach. It looked like a dive on the outside, but good music and the scent of barbeque drifted out. Janie noticed the worn wooden sign above the door: Sailors Rest. "It has a nice ring to it. Sounds like my kind of place."

"Of course, it does, Miss Navy. But to me, it sounds like a place for sailors to get drunk and make trouble."

Janie elbowed her. "You're so negative. We're in this tropical, romantic place, full of folklore about ships and pirates and the sea. This place is just what we came here for. I'm going in. You can stay in the car if you want, but you might have a long wait."

"Okay," Ella relented. "I'll go in with you, but if I get a bad feeling about it inside, we're leaving. Agreed?"

Janie was already out of the car. "Sure. C'mon."

The closer they got, the rowdier the crowd sounded. The front porch creaked, its paint was peeling, and its wood floors were worn and warped by the salt air. Raucous laughter erupted, and male voices shouted as chairs crashed to the floor. Janie grew hesitant. "I don't know about this after all. It looks kind of dilapidated, and the crowd sounds a bit out of control, even for sailors."

Oddly, Ella got a better feeling about it, despite the

look and sound of it.

Janie was closest to the door, but didn't want to go inside. "You go first," she told Ella.

"You were the one who was so fired up about this place. Just grab the door handle and go in."

They argued for a minute about who would take the first step in the door and be exposed to who-knew-what on the other side. Finally, Ella grabbed the handle. "Oh, for cryin' out loud, let's go." She opened the door and saw a small bar with its stools full of people. Everyone looked happy and like typical Key Westers. No tourists or college kids. Most likely serious drinkers and partiers. A band was set up at the far end, and a deck was perched on the beach with tile-top tables and thatched umbrellas. With the sun mostly down and the sky ablaze, it looked to be a calendar page for the best of Key West. No one stared or even looked their way, except the bartender, who said, "C'mon in. It's ladies' night. Two for one drink specials. Join the fun."

Ella turned to Janie who stood behind her. "Well, there you go. And you were afraid to come in."

Janie playfully swatted her arm. "Okay. You got me. Now, let's go in and party."

After two shots of tequila and a beer, Janie was dancing with anyone who asked. Ella, however, turned down requests, preferring to take her first drink out to a beachside table on the deck. The black night swallowed the ocean view except for ragged lines of white surf rolling in. Torches were lit all around the bar's perimeter, making the beach glow with golden light; palm trees swayed, and a million stars burst through space. *Magical*, Ella thought. Happy to sit alone and enjoy a little piece of paradise, she sipped her margarita, feeling giddy.

But as she gazed out over the ocean, she felt herself move back in time to the beach below the old Victorian house, overlooking the sea. In a single moment, her real surroundings dropped away, and Ella, almost in a trance, sensed something calling to her, drawing her to the house, up to the widow's walk. She felt herself rise there as she stared at the sea with longing and sadness. Silent words drifted into her mind from a faraway place…*Something is coming, and this is fair warning.* She closed her eyes, hoping to shake it off; instead she felt a gentle presence suspended in the soft breeze against her cheek and asked, *What's coming?*

The presence, ethereal and all-knowing, filled her mind with a silent message…*You'll know when it happens. Not long now.* The words drifted into the ethers, hushed by the darkness. Fear crept into her heart with yet another cryptic message from who-knew-where-or-what. Then the presence disappeared as quickly as it had arrived. She opened her eyes and looked around. Nothing had changed. Her drink waited, the torches glowed, the waves crumpled and dissolved against the shore. Music drifted out from the bar as her senses came alive in the present. People were talking and laughing, and from behind her, a deep, male voice spoke.

Chapter 4

The next thing Ella heard was a man speaking to her back. "Excuse me, but you look very familiar to me, like I've met you before, or maybe I know you from a past life."

It wasn't the best pick-up line she'd ever heard, but it was offbeat enough to get her attention, while thinking, *You've got to be kidding*. But if a guy was going to use a line like that, she supposed Key West would be the place.

She didn't want to turn around because her mind conjured a long-haired, hippie-looking guy or a bearded Hemingway look-alike in a faded T-shirt and flip-flops. But sitting here in a place like the Sailors Rest, more likely he was just a laid-back local, a writer or artist or musician looking for a good time. She prepared to brush him off nicely yet quickly when his arm reached alongside hers from behind. He was so inappropriately close, she felt the heat rise from his body, giving off the subtle scent of very nice, not-cheap cologne.

This was definitely a move, and she was annoyed until she noticed his well-muscled arm as he laid his hat on the table—a formal, white and black with gold trim, military-looking hat. Ella turned in her chair to face the interloper, and found in front of her a not-an-ounce-of-fat midsection, decked out in a starched white shirt and trousers. Looking up, she noticed colorful ribbons above the shirt pocket and black shoulder boards with gold insignias. Carrying the impressive uniform was a tall, broad-shouldered body and a nicely tanned face set off by a perfect white smile. Even with the short-on-the-sides, tousled-on-top military haircut, he was oh-so-handsome—dark hair, piercing green eyes, male-model handsome.

The disparity was so huge between who Ella thought she'd see and the real man standing in front of her, it threw her off guard. She let out a nervous giggle and was immediately embarrassed.

"I'm not who you thought I'd be, right?" he said with a confident grin on his face.

"You could say that." Ella looked him up and down, thinking he was too good to be true. "Are you really in the service, or are you a model or an actor here on a movie set?"

"Oh, man, I don't know whether to be flattered or insulted. Let me respond with *you're not even close* on the second guess."

"Hmm…so you're in the service, huh? What branch? Marines? Air Force?"

He put a hand to his stomach and groaned as if punched. "Ugh, you're killin' me. Marines? Air Force? You sure know how to hurt a guy." His grin told her he wasn't really upset as he pointed to a small anchor tattoo on his left arm and the anchor insignia on his hat.

"Sorry. I guess that means Navy?"

"Very observant. Right. Navy. Fighter pilot."

"Oh, impressive. Sorry about the mix-up. I didn't know you guys were so touchy about that kind of thing."

"It's not touchy. It's territorial. It's pride in who we

are and what we do. And of course, competition. Every branch of the service thinks they're the best."

"I see. I suppose that goes with the job."

"Yes, it does. Didn't you see the movie *Top Gun*?"

Ella laughed. "Yes, I did. A classic. Loved it. So, you're one of those egomaniacal, cocky pilots, huh?"

He grabbed the chair next to hers. "Some are, not me though. Not in my nature. In fact, I'll be a gentleman and ask if I may join you."

"Help yourself. So, what are you doing here, sailor?"

"Well it *is* the Sailors Rest. How could I not come in?"

"Oh, right. Except you look like the only sailor in here."

"My buddies are in the back of the bar playing pool."

"Why in the back?"

"Well, this is a locals' bar. We look a little out of place in these uniforms."

"So why bother? Why not go somewhere else?"

"Because this is a great place with great food and a nice spot here on the beach. And of course, because it *is*…" They spoke the next words exactly in unison, "…the Sailors Rest," laughing easily together. He added, "We just came from another buddy's wedding and the night is young."

"Earlier, I saw a bunch of men in formal Navy uniforms just like yours in a wedding downtown," Ella recalled. "That couldn't have been you and your friends, could it?"

"Probably was. Unless there was another wedding at the same time. Was it near Duval Street?"

"I don't know the streets that well. This is my first time here."

"Do you happen to drive an older model white BMW with Florida plates?"

Ella looked at him suspiciously. "Maybe. Maybe not. How would you guess such a thing?"

"Because when we came out of the church, my attention was drawn across the street to a white BMW parked there. Briefly, before she drove off, I saw a gorgeous blonde, who happens to look a lot like you. There was someone else in the car, but I couldn't see them. It was you driving, wasn't it?"

"It might have been."

"This is amazing, isn't it? Fortune, fate or destiny has brought us together."

Nervous, she said, "It's not all that mystical. I was there. You were there."

"And here we are. I had a feeling when I saw you at the church, I'd run into you somewhere. If this isn't fate, what is it?"

Not wanting to venture down that road, Ella sloughed off his comment. "It's just a coincidence. Nothing more."

"Okay. If that's what you believe. I happen to believe it's more. Our meeting was meant to be."

"I think we were both looking for a casual place on the beach to have a drink, and came upon the Sailors Rest. No more unusual than anyone else in here."

He wasn't about to argue with a woman he'd just met and wanted to know better. He knew positively they were meant to meet. But he went along with the conversation, thinking he could always revisit the "destiny" discussion later. He continued with his original train of thought. "True. We did come in here wanting to prolong the festivities of the wedding into the night, hopefully into early morning."

"Why are you sitting here with me then? Hoping I'll be part of the festivities?"

"You just never know. Thought I'd give it a try."

"Listen, I know it's cliché, but your uniform is the only thing that got you a seat here. I was ready to rebuff you after that opening line."

"What line?"

"The 'past life' line, the new-age version of the 'haven't we met' line."

"Well, I'm obviously not a weirdo or old hippie, and it wasn't a line. What *is* silly, though, is we haven't properly met." He extended his hand. "I'm Daniel. Daniel Ellsworth."

With a wry smile and still not completely convinced he was what he appeared, she shook his hand. "Ella Rowe."

"Ella. As in 'Cinder'?"

"As if I haven't heard that one before. My mother was from Maine—no pretense—so it's just Ella."

"I see." The look he gave was of admiration and fondness.

His laugh warmed her, mingling comfortably with her own. She'd never before let a perfect stranger in a bar sit down with her. But he seemed perfect in some odd way; the feel of his hand as she shook it was comforting, pleasurable, and he did seem vaguely familiar. It was why she'd been drawn to look at him as she watched the wedding party. And now, reluctantly, she had to admit it felt like she really *had* met him before.

Ella sipped her drink. "So if your ice-breaker line was not a line, how does someone of your conservative vocation come up with something so unconventional? You couldn't possibly believe in something like that, in past lives."

"Actually, I do." The mellow tone of his voice reached into her, setting off a bell of intimacy, like she'd heard it before and felt safe inside its genuine quality.

"I don't see how that's remotely possible. None of this is logical." Doubtful of his intentions and who he really was, she smirked and played devil's advocate. "I'm not stupid. The probabilities are great that it wasn't you in that wedding. You could've rented the uniform. Maybe you went to a costume party or something."

With not a trace of anger at her insult, his amazing grin resurfaced, warming her entirely. "Yeah, right. On Key West? Every night is a party, costume or otherwise, and anything goes as far as clothing. If I was going to dress up, it wouldn't be as a naval officer, not here. Now what kind of brain would suspiciously conjure up a scheme like that? What are you? A detective? CIA?"

"I'm a reporter."

He belly-laughed. "Oh, that explains a lot. You must be a good one and a good writer because you've got a great imagination, accusing me of all kinds of vocations except my true one."

"I'm just cautious, so don't evade the subject of whether you're the real thing. I see no other Navy guys anywhere."

Daniel put his fingers to his mouth and blew a loud

whistle into the bar. Within minutes, three more Navy "hotties" came from around the corner where they'd been playing pool and huddled around him. "Guys, this lovely lady here thinks we rented costumes to party and maybe to pick up women. Could such beauty and brains be so insulting?"

Ella recognized them from the wedding and was truly embarrassed, realizing she'd pushed the forgery questioning too far.

The three of them tossed out their credentials, laughing. The tallest one bent down close to Ella's face, put his arm around her shoulder, and whispered seductively, "Missy, we're as real as it gets. How would you like us to prove it?"

Daniel stood up. "Okay, that's enough. I just needed proof. You guys can hurry on back to whatever trouble you were brewing over there."

They taunted him as they walked away, laughing and yelling, "Danny-boy, you must have it bad callin' for backup. Woohoo! Go for it, Daniel! Dan-the-ladies-man!"

"I'm sorry about that," he said to Ella, "and, no, I'm not a ladies' man. What can I say? They're the typical Navy pilots you were eluding to. And you did ask for proof."

"I certainly did. But you still didn't explain your 'past life' comment."

He called to the waiter and ordered a beer. "Better yet, make that a martini, very dry with a twist of lemon." Facing her, he added, "I think I'm going to need a little more reinforcement than a beer." Pointing at her almost-empty glass, he asked, "Margarita? May I buy you another?"

"Yes, thank you." Ella figured one drink was okay, but she didn't intend to encourage him further. She held firm to her conviction of not getting involved with men on this vacation, especially now with contemplating a big change in her life situation. But she was intrigued by him; he was different from the average guy, certainly very different from any man she'd ever met. *What can it hurt to spend a little time talking and learning something new?* At the very least, the reporter in her was curious about his background. "Talk on, sailor. Explain how you came to believe in such a far-out concept."

Daniel grinned. "Far-out, huh? I'm not laughing at you. I'm laughing because that's something my mom and grandmother used to say."

Ella shot him an insulted look. "I sound like your mother and grandmother?"

"No. I didn't mean it that way," he said with a sheepish smile. "I don't mean you're acting 'older' like them because you're young. Young and gorgeous, I might add. It came out wrong."

She knew very well what he'd meant but kept up the feigned look to tease him, to get insight into his temperament. "So, saying I was 'young and gorgeous' was not your intent either?"

His grin turned serious. "Oh, no, I didn't mean the 'young and gorgeous' comment came out wrong. I meant that as a compliment. The 'mother/grandmother' part was what I didn't mean."

Still faking being upset, Ella didn't respond and stared at him.

Running his hand through his hair, embarrassed, he tried to explain. "I only meant to say your choice of words brought back a memory, a pleasant one of Mom and Gramma." He looked down at the table, twisting up his napkin. "There are those 'mother' words again. Man, I'm burying myself here."

Ella burst into laughter and let him off the hook. "Relax. I'm teasing. I'll bet those women were terrific people, and I'd be flattered to be compared to them. I didn't mean to insult them; it's just that most guys I've known have used those labels in a negative way about women who are bossy or domineering or whatever reflection of their terrible childhoods. So, I should be apologizing to you."

Daniel shook his head. "You're amazing. No woman has gotten me that nervous in a very long time—like when I was fourteen and attempted my first kiss."

"Well, settle down, because there'll be no attempted kisses tonight, or any night for that matter." Her eyes betrayed her words as she looked at him with warmth and attraction.

"You're something else, you know?" He returned her look, seeing her as a long-lost friend who was happy to simply sit and chat. "Okay, to answer your question about how I could possibly believe in past lives and since 'Mom' has already come up, I guess I'll start with her. And by the way, yes, she was a wonderful person who was also really cool.

"My mother was strongly influenced by her mother, my grandma, who had been a hippie back in the sixties, did the Haight-Ashbury scene in San Francisco, and even lived in a commune for a time. So, my mom grew up with a lot of far-out people. Then in her teens, she got caught up in the new-age scene, given her rather 'alternative' upbringing. She met my dad, who was a sculptor and artist, at a metaphysical conference. So, by the time they had me, they were fully immersed in their alternative lifestyle, even though both had very respectable, mainstream careers as teachers. And my grandma lived with us until she died. Therefore, I was raised around a lot of very unusual people with far-from-conventional ideas."

The waiter placed their drinks down, and Daniel took a couple swallows of his martini. "Okay, I'm ready to elaborate, if you wish."

"I do," Ella said with a coy smile.

"Well, I spent much of those formative years wondering what was real and what wasn't, and questioning my parents and their friends about their belief systems. With collecting various answers, I learned a lot, but had my own questions and so began to research. I read and tried everything from traditional religion to eastern, from Buddha to Yogananda, from Cayce to Castaneda, new age to Native American teachings—basically anything I could get my hands on to sort it all out.

"My parents and grandmother shared their rather expansive, alternative and new-age beliefs with me, but encouraged me to explore and make my own assessments. I finally settled into a personal set of values, my own commonsense version of life, afterlife, God, and karma. I admit, my beliefs are much more avant-garde than the average career military guy. I call that part of my life 'the other me,' and keep it pretty close to the vest. You won't catch me talking to my boys over there about *this* kind of stuff."

Ella was intrigued. "I understand completely. I

have 'another me' from a strange part of my life that I don't share, especially at work with conservative editors and inquisitive reporters. So why are you sharing your 'other you' story with me?"

"Because I have a feeling we're kindred souls, you and I. That's not a line—my gut feelings are pretty right-on. I believe our meeting is kismet." He flashed back to being in the cockpit last week and the odd feeling he'd gotten in his gut then. Daniel's heightened intuition and gut feelings had always proved right in the past: when his father died in a car crash, when his mother was diagnosed with cancer, and a year ago, a forewarning of a mechanical problem with the jet he was flying. It had hit him the same way—after taking off and reaching cruising altitude when every sensory perception was in overdrive. Those feelings had been strong and fierce, clear and immediate, telling him something was wrong then and there.

But last week it had been a vague, slow gnawing deep inside, silently saying, *Something is coming, and this is fair warning.* He'd been obsessively careful landing the jet and felt greatly relieved to be safely back on the ship's deck. The feeling lingered long after, though, and was still with him. He'd push it down and ignore it, but it always resurfaced, warning him of something lurking in the future, reminding him not to let his guard down. He was trained to be unemotional, rational, and level-headed in any circumstance or crisis.

But since that day, he'd found himself on edge emotionally, waiting, watching, in a constant state of vigilance. It wore him down even as he embarked on what was supposed to be a relaxing vacation. Daniel knew, whatever waited for him, good or bad, would be life-changing.

And here he sat with this woman, relaxed and comfortable, and wondered, *Is this it? Could this be what was coming at me?* But he questioned his intuition: *This meeting seems to be a good thing, though, nothing to be warned about.* He lifted his glass to toast. “Here’s to knowing you, Ella, maybe for a long time, longer than just this night.” But a small doubt made him think twice about pursuing her, especially if karma was involved—karma he’d suspected caused him to die at sea many times before, karma he refused to obsess on or let control his life.

With his pilot training, he had great focus and willpower to cancel out all negative or intrusive thoughts, and his own karma was one of them, especially since revealing it had abruptly ended a relationship in his early twenties. He’d learned his lesson and wouldn’t make that mistake again. If a woman came along whom he felt strongly connected to and knew intuitively was meant for him and they fell in love, then karma wouldn’t deter him from pursuing her. Besides, the karma he recalled couldn’t be proved for sure, and it wasn’t anybody’s business but his own.

Ella tapped her glass gently against his. “I’d rather toast to the start of an interesting evening, probably just until midnight. That’s as much as I can commit to.”

Daniel’s gaze grew endearing as he spoke. “Okay, *Cinder*-Ella. At midnight, you go back to your BMW pumpkin and ride away, huh?” He took a long swallow of his drink and winked at her. “But I’ll be coming around with that glass slipper until I find you.”

Ella didn’t expect such an answer. He certainly had a quick wit and a creative comeback. “Really? Well, good luck with that, Prince Daniel. I'm no princess, and this is no fairy tale. This is an enjoyable conversation so far. Let's leave it at that with no talk of stalking me with a glass shoe." She sent him a coy smile while she sipped her drink, hoping he'd get the message that she appreciated his inventiveness, but he better not dare to try to find her.

Ella and Daniel talked the night away. She couldn't remember the last time she'd been so charmed by a man. She was usually too smart for that. This was refreshing and challenging, and he sure was easy on the eyes. At the very least, she was flattered by his attention. After all, he could obviously pick up any woman he wanted. She resolved to give it a go for the evening because under the good looks, the obvious intelligence, and unusual life, there was something about him that was captivating and familiar. The feel of him was like opening a seldom-used closet and finding a beautiful coat buried in the back, waiting for you to remember it was there, waiting to be wrapped around your body again to warm you and keep you safe.

They talked about their childhoods and worked up to the present, how they'd gotten through life and chosen the paths they had. Daniel Ellsworth was born in San Francisco, but starting at five, grew up moving around every few years all over the southeast, mostly to towns near the coast. His love of the ocean and traveling came from that experience. Living near a small airport and making friends with the owner and then working for him found him catching free rides, and so grew his love of flying; hence, his career combined both his passions as a Navy pilot.

Ella shared only the basics with him, the necessary

information to piece together her history. She'd have to know him much better to share more than that. But she could envision being frank and honest with him because he was so genuine and open-minded, and so non-judgmental. Just not now, some other time, if there ever was another time with him.

****

Just before the Sailors Rest closed, Janie, who was ready to drop from dancing and partying all night, yelled out to Ella as she stumbled toward the door that she'd be waiting in the car.

Daniel took Ella's hand. "Looks like the night is over. Thanks for a great time. I'd like to see you tomorrow if you'd like. Can I have your cell number or email?"

She wore a friendly smile while courteously turning him down. "I'm afraid not. You seem like a really nice guy, but I'm sorry, I just can't give out my personal information."

"I understand. So how about if we meet somewhere neutral for coffee or breakfast?"

A small fear kicked in, of getting close, of how she could possibly fall for him, of how she knew for sure he'd be leaving at some point to go back to his life, his life at sea. "I don't think that's a good idea. Maybe we should just be thankful for a wonderful night and leave it at that. According to your idea of fate, if we're meant to run into each other, we will somehow."

At first, his face registered disappointment, but then he seemed resigned to her wishes. Cupping her hand in both of his, he politely said good night. "Okay. But I've never had such an interesting, fun time with a woman I just met. Thank you. I really don't want the night to end, but I'll respect your wishes."

When he let go of her hand, she felt a shift in her heart, like it missed a beat at possibly never seeing him again. She wondered if she was making a mistake but decided to indeed leave it up to fate.

He escorted her to her car, looked through the open window, pointed at Janie, who was sound asleep, and said, "Who is this passed out? Your fairy godmother?"

Ella laughed. "Not likely. Janie's more like the teasing stepsister. But she *is* a great friend. She does love to party, having served two years in the Navy. I guess it goes with the territory, huh?"

"Certainly does." Daniel reached in and put his hand on Janie's forehead. "She's warm and breathing." Then he affectionately smoothed his hand over her head as if to soothe her. "She's a cutie. Must've driven those sailors wild."

"You got that right," Ella said, noticing his genuine interest in and tenderness toward a perfect stranger simply because she was Ella's friend. Here was another wonderful, endearing thing about him. There was something innate in his character that showed compassion and depth. Ella felt her heart start to slide down a caring slope, but she stopped it.

Daniel opened the car door. "Well, your carriage awaits, Miss Ella. I knew you'd disappear at the end of the night." She felt bad then, bad and sad. But she didn't know what else to do but leave. He waved into her rearview mirror.

Watching him while she drove slowly away, she was overtaken with a feeling of leaving him before, of being forced to say good-bye, knowing she'd never see him again. Her heart broke slightly as she rounded the corner, and he was gone from sight. The feeling washed over her enough to scare her. She pushed it away, but still wondered how her brain could recall something that had not actually happened with him. *I must be remembering Peter*, she thought. *My God, will the pain never go away?*

Ella fell into bed that night, still shaken from the memory, yet holding a warm place in her heart for Daniel while struggling to let him go. "Just let him go," she whispered to herself, hoping to embed it into her subconscious as she slept, so she'd wake with no regret or longing.

Chapter 5

A brilliant morning burst through the cottage windows waking Ella early, jarring loose thoughts of the night before, making her think it had been a dream. Knowing Janie wouldn't become conscious for another couple hours, she walked to the café down the street and grabbed coffee and breakfast-to-go for them. With a book, coffee, and a bagel, she settled herself on the patio overlooking the beach.

Much as she tried to focus on reading, she was mesmerized by her surroundings. Her eyes wouldn't move off the infinite field of turquoise sea in front of her and the cobalt sky above. As palm trees swayed with the gentle breezes, her lungs filled with fresh sea air and the scent of jasmine, lifting her into euphoria.

Ella's longest experience of coastal living had been on the rocky shores of Maine, but the energy surrounding Key West was so vastly different, even from the sleepy gulf coast of Florida where she lived now. The sea in Maine was cold and raw, constantly, powerfully beating against the land as if in battle with it. Sitting here on a warm, white sand beach with golden light all around was gentle and forgiving, a paradise. Fresh beginnings, so delicate, lush with life and palpable beauty, enticed her into a new world. Her spirit stretched out to the horizons, expanding her senses and intuition as never before. The odd experience on the bridge driving here, she realized now, had been a precursor of how magical life could be in a place like this.

Things were already starting to change in inexplicable ways, and she wondered if there really was something predestined about crossing paths with Daniel. But she reminded herself that being drawn to a person or situation was the easy part. Living out what you create from there was the hard part, the complicated and scary part. At least, that was how Ella's life had always previously played out.

She'd only read a couple pages of her book and taken a few sips of coffee when a knocking sound came from inside. Ella didn't move. She waited. Silence. Ten seconds later, more urgent knocking came. Then, after half a minute, very loud knocks rang through the cottage. This time it woke Janie, who shrieked, "Who the hell is banging on the door so early?"

Ella thought it might be the management and went in to answer the knock. "I'll get it. Go back to sleep." Obviously, whoever it was needed something, and they weren't going away until they got it.

She peeked out the front curtains and saw a man with his back to her, looking across the street. He was dressed in shorts, a T-shirt, and sandals. Under her breath, she whispered, "I'm not opening this door until I know who you are and what you want." Then she yelled through the closed door, "Who is it?"

A deep, somewhat familiar voice answered, "How soon you forget."

"Who are you? What do you want?"

The man turned around as she peeked out the window. "It's Daniel…from last night…remember?"

Feeling her privacy invaded, Ella got upset and flung open the door. "Are you kidding me? What are you doing here? You scared me half to death. I thought you were the management, coming to kick us out for a bad credit card…uh, Janie's…Janie's card or something…or the cops for something that happened in the middle of the night…you know, a theft or something." Embarrassed by her ridiculous excuses, she blurted out, "What do you want, other than making me feel like an idiot?"

Daniel laughed. "Man, you really do have that writer's imagination going, don't you?"

Ella gave him a nasty look. "More like I never expected to see *you* here at my front door first thing in the morning. How did you find me? Are you a stalker or something? You sure look like one in those casual clothes without the formal dress uniform."

Trying to make light of the situation, he explained, "Technically, they're summer dress whites. Formal dress has a jacket with long sleeves. Way too hot for this climate."

Ella was not amused. "You must have followed me. That's stalking and I'm shocked. What are you doing here?"

"I'm very sorry to have upset you," he said sheepishly, and she could see genuine sincerity on his face. "I really am sorry. I didn't follow you and I'm not a stalker. I was hoping you'd be pleasantly surprised. When you left last night, I was just so sad and kept thinking as I watched your car drive off, 'There goes Cinder-Ella, back to her life.' I knew your car, had noted your plate number last night, and being this is such a small town that I know well—and you'd told me all about the place you were staying—I had a pretty good idea of where you were. I got up early, wanted to see you more than anything else I could do, came to the place I thought you were staying, saw your car out front, and voilà. Here I am." He threw his arms out to his sides as if to say, *"Aren't you thrilled?"*

Ella's emotions were conflicted. She was impressed by his detective skills, upset at his barging in on her morning, yet weirdly happy to see him. All she could think to say was, "Terrific. Great. If I had wanted you to know where I was staying, I'd have told you."

"You're so right, and again, I apologize. But you lost something and I just had to return it."

"What? I didn't lose anything."

"Yes, you did. That is, if it fits you." From under his shirt in his back shorts' pocket, he pulled out a flip-flop. "It's your glass slipper. If it fits, then you're the woman of my dreams who ran out on me last night."

Ella looked at the sad flip-flop in his hand and burst into laughter. "You fool! I don't believe this. Where'd you get that? In a dumpster?"

"No. It's new, from the convenience store. But like I said. It's yours. Are you going to let me in, so I can try this thing on you and see if you're the one?"

She started to say, *I guess I have no choice*, when he walked through the doorway, picked her up, and set her down in the nearest chair.

Janie had come out of her room, rubbing her bleary eyes, then ran her hands through her spiked hair. Her clothes were disheveled, and her wiry, petite body slouched, obviously hung-over. She stood in a stupor, watching, unable to speak with her mouth gaping open as this gorgeous man knelt on one knee in front of her friend. He took hold of Ella's foot and slipped the flip-flop on, beaming up at her like a boy on Christmas morning opening his best present. "See. It fits perfectly."

Ella couldn't help but feel affection toward him. In fact, she felt more than that—beyond charm, attraction, and good looks—he was creative, funny, and was really pursuing her. She didn't know if she had the power to resist the hugely magnetic force he exuded that drew her in almost against her will.

Giggling, she twirled her foot around. "Well, it sure does fit. So, what does that mean?"

"It means I found you after I thought I'd lost you for good. I warned you last night I would find you."

Hearing the word "warned" snapped her back to last night just before she met him, when she'd heard, *Something is coming, and this is fair warning.* Chills went down her spine, especially recalling the rest of it: *You'll know when it happens, not long now*. The next thing to happen was meeting Daniel.

"I'm not going to let you go as easily as just walking away," he declared. "This is destiny." That word "destiny" caused him to flash back to last week in the cockpit, with the feeling of something coming at him, coming in for a landing into destiny, and he fell silent.

They both got lost in their thoughts and inability to comprehend what was happening.

Janie broke the silence. Looking at Ella, she asked, "Am I dreaming? Because if this is real, then that's the last time I party all night and leave *you* alone. Look at this—you've got a crazy man stalking you." She then turned to Daniel. "So, are there any more like you where you came from?"

They all laughed hard, and Daniel joked back. "Nope. They broke the mold with me."

Ella watched him, listened to him as he bantered with Janie, and knew he really was one of a kind, at least for her, and she could so easily fall for him—like falling off a cliff—one foot over the edge, losing balance, no going back, free falling with loss of control. In a split-second, her mind transported her to another place, suspended in space. She was lying on her back, and he was above her. She saw his face clearly and felt his embrace as he made love to her. It was natural and familiar. It was…what did he call it? *Kismet.* She was over the cliff now, falling, falling. It scared the hell out of her. Somehow, she'd have to make it stop.

****

Daniel wanted to spend the day with her and thought, after his Cinderella routine, she'd certainly agree. But he didn't know Ella and the power of her fear to override happiness, especially when it came to possibly caring about a man, especially a man as tempting as Daniel.

Ella told him *no*; she appreciated the offer, but she and Janie had plans.

Later, after he'd left, Janie verbally kicked Ella around the room for turning him down. "You must be nuts. A gorgeous guy pursues you and you say you have plans with *me*? And we don't even have plans! What's wrong with you, Ella?"

"You know what's wrong. Besides, I just met him. I'm not going to fall into his arms and spend the day with him. And I'm not going to ditch you. Now get cleaned up and we'll have a great day."

"I'm all for having a great day, but don't you dare blame me for not going with Daniel."

Ella called after Janie who sauntered into the bathroom and slammed the door. "I'm not blaming you. I just want to chill with my best friend and relax. No guys today, not even great-looking ones, okay?"

Janie opened the door with a toothbrush dangling out of her mouth. "No, it's not okay. You're just too weird for words. But you're my friend, and since I'm stuck with you, why don't you whip up a Bloody Mary for my hangover?"

"No way, not at eleven o'clock in the morning. Let's go lie on the beach and soak up the sun. You can sweat last night's drinks out of you."

Janie turned back to the bathroom sink and looked into the mirror. Seeing Ella's reflection behind her, she said, "You are absolutely no fun. If you don't go find Daniel, I will."

Ella grabbed her arm as she tried to walk by. "Oh, no, you won't. We came here together; we're staying together, at least, for our second day."

Headachy and not up to arguing, Janie caved. "Okay. Okay. Okay. You stubborn woman. I'll get my bathing suit on. No drinks. Just sweat. Let's go."

After initially putting up a fight, Janie realized she truly hadn't been up to much more than doing nothing but lying on the beach, soaking up some sun, and recuperating. Around two o'clock, they decided to head in, clean up, and go out for lunch at Sloppy Joe's, one of Ernest Hemingway's favorite haunts. The place had jalousie doors opening onto the street, allowing sweet salt air to float in while live jazz music drifted outside. Inside were a few casual bars and lots of tables and chairs filled with tourists and locals alike. Old photographs were hung of Hemingway and his literary, drinking, and local illustrious buddies. The walls were filled with all kinds of memorabilia—huge ocean fish, flags, and just about anything having to do with pirates, boats, fishing, and the bar's and Key West's famous clientele and its unique past. It was steeped in so much history that Ella could sense the presence of spirits everywhere—the sailors and writers and locals who drank there, shared stories, laughter, and tears. She supposed their spirits lingered because this place was as much a home as their boats and the sea.

If she closed her eyes, she could almost see Papa Hemingway sitting on a barstool, toasting and gulping down drinks, telling tales of deep-sea fishing and big game hunting in Africa. The others would reciprocate with their own stories; then all would laugh, not realizing they had created memories that would linger seventy years or more into the future. Ella envisioned them now and was ensconced in their world, allowing the timeless charm of Key West to fill her own spirit, wondering if a piece of herself would be left behind as well.

She and Janie ordered martinis in Hemingway's honor, while listening to music and stuffing themselves with seafood. After a couple hours, they walked away completely satiated. Feeling full and giddy, they walked around town, window shopping for the rest of the day, peeking into expensive but exquisite boutiques and art galleries until their heads cleared up.

After taking naps back at the cottage, Janie suggested they go to the Sailors Rest again for dinner and drinks, and to watch the sunset.

Ella's response was immediate. "You really think I'm going to fall for that? You're guessing Daniel will be there, which he probably will. So, no, I'm not going there. You can go alone if you'd like."

Caught with her plan to run into Daniel, Janie got irked and played into Ella's hand. "Fine. I *will* go alone. What will you do?"

"I'm not even hungry after our late lunch. I'm tired. I'll hang out here, read a good book, and turn in early."

"Well, now that sounds like a blast. Too bad I'm going to miss it."

"You're really going alone?"

"Hell, yeah. I had a great time last night. I'm hoping maybe I'll run into that cute guy Eric, who I danced with most of the night. Or maybe one of Daniel's buddies."

"Great. Just be careful. Be safe and call a cab to take you there and back, will you?"

Janie headed toward the door, not quite believing Ella wouldn't go. Already on her cell calling the cab, she yelled back, "Yes, mother, I'll take a cab. You be careful, too, with all that reading," she said, chuckling as she walked out the door.

****

Ella couldn't believe Janie had left alone. But looking around at the quiet cottage with only the sounds of the ocean and palm trees swishing in the breeze, she was glad for the peace and quiet. After a glass of wine, she took a long walk by the shore to watch the setting sun. The clouds streaked across the sky in shades of orange and gold, the sky blue and pink, reflecting off the water and spinning Key West into a celestial world.

The air swirled, moist and salty, on her skin. Her feet tingled as they sank into the soft sand, like walking on air.

Lost in thought, Ella didn't realize how far she'd gone, and it was getting dark. Her intuition nudged her to get off the beach for the walk home. She went across a small wooden bridge over dunes, then walked a block more onto a street lined with older beach houses and the safety of street lights. Not that it was dangerous to walk the beach at night, but she didn't feel comfortable walking alone.

The town was beautiful at night with palm trees lit in tiny white lights. Festive lanterns glowed softly, strung here and there, and small globes twinkled, brightening the dark with golden orbs. Walking closer to the historic district, she admired the restored Victorian-era homes lining the streets. Further down were more restaurants with music drifting out and people laughing. She hummed to these sounds of happy life around her, feeling sensuous, soaking up the hot night filled with tropical fragrance and the distant sound of ocean waves pounding on the shore.

A small tavern drew her interest with a band playing Jimmy Buffet tunes. *Maybe I'll go in and grab a nightcap*, she thought, but a group of men were getting rowdy inside, so she decided to head back to the cottage. As she turned to walk away, several men tumbled out of the bar, obviously having had a lot to drink, and one bumped quite hard into her back.

From behind her, the man reached for her arm to steady her. "I'm so sorry, miss. Are you okay? My friends here are getting a little unruly."

Ella turned around to face him to say she was okay,

and went pale.

"Oh, my God! Ella!" Daniel yelled as he hugged her with one arm around her shoulder. "I can't believe it's you. I can't believe I just literally ran into you."

Stunned and still disbelieving, she mumbled, "Hmm…how about that."

She could tell he was tipsy with slightly glassy eyes and sloppy mannerisms.

His reply was, "Hey! You weren't stalking *me*, were you? A little payback for this morning?"

She pulled away from him. "No, of course not." She explained how she'd happened to be there.

Daniel's eyes grew wide with amazement. "Don't you see? It's destiny at work again, putting us in the same place at the same exact moment. This isn't just a sheer coincidence."

He tagged along, uninvited, as Ella continued walking. "I hate to disappoint you," she said, "but it probably is just that—a coincidence."

Very animated now, he took her hand. "No, no. The island is small, true, but there are probably a hundred places to drink and eat, and we bump into each other at the same place at the same exact time. You yourself said, if we were meant to see each other again, we'd meet somehow. And we did. Now you *have* to go out with me tomorrow. We can't slap destiny in the face now, can we?"

Looking straight ahead, she flatly told him, "I do it all the time. So, if you'll excuse me, I need to be on my way."

"Alone? No, let me walk you to wherever you're going. Hey! Where's Janie?"

"I'll give you one guess."

Laughing, he said, "Gotta be the Sailors Rest, right?"

"Yup."

"She's too much. I bet she thought she'd get you there and I'd be there, right?"

"Right again."

"Well, see? Her plan didn't work because you can't plan fate. It just happens the way it's supposed to. And here we are."

"Yes. You certainly are clever tonight. But I can see you've had more than a bit to drink, and I really need to get back."

As she walked away, Daniel stood perfectly still, alone, holding his hat by his side, speechless in the middle of the street. Glancing back at him, she saw his face, sad and crushed, and felt a twinge of regret. She didn't mean to hurt his feelings, so she offered an apology. "I'm sorry to burst your bubble of excitement. Really, I am. And I'm sorry that I don't share your reasoning. It *is* nice to see you though, Daniel, very nice and—"

He interrupted her. "If you're truly sorry, then make it up to me."

"Uh-oh. You know I can't promise anything."

"Yes, you can. Promise me this…"

Ella looked at the ground with her arms crossed in front of her, knowing another invitation was coming, and now she was stuck. She hated being manipulated, even by a gorgeous hunk of man.

Daniel walked over to her and tilted her chin up to meet his gaze. "Promise me, if we run into each other tomorrow accidentally *again*, because of fate or destiny or whatever you want to call it…promise me you'll see it as a sign we're supposed to spend time together."

Caught off guard by his non-invitation and the logic behind it, she understood completely and agreed. "It's a deal. And you promise me this: no stalking or following me, *and* if we don't run into each other by chance, then you'll give up this notion. It'll be proof that we are *not* supposed to spend any more time together. We had our one night; it was wonderful, a great vacation experience, and we'll let it go at that. Okay?"

He agreed to everything a little too quickly, like he was sure events wouldn't happen as negatively as she anticipated. Walking backward to look at her as he moved away, he saluted her. "Good night, Miss Ella. 'Til we meet again, hopefully tomorrow. Be safe now."

Ella smiled and saluted back, admiring his confidence and respectfulness, feeling waves of emotion coming through the air in her direction. It felt amazingly good. And he looked even better. *Oh, those female hormones, or is it his pheromones?* Regardless, she blamed them for the level of heat surging through her body. Now she wasn't sure if she didn't want to cross paths with him after all.

****

After Janie's late night, Ella let her sleep until noon the next day, then dragged her out of bed with the promise of a great story and even, yes, a Bloody Mary. After hearing the events of Ella's night, Janie was a willing accomplice to do something unpredictable that Daniel wouldn't suspect them to do. There'd be no running into him walking downtown through the tourist spots, lying on any beach, or hanging out at any bar, and most certainly not the Sailors Rest.

They decided to take an afternoon cruise on a tourist boat. After that, they'd go to a fancy hotel for dinner—a place they figured Daniel and his buddies would not gather. As much as Janie wanted Ella to hook up with Daniel, she was excited by the thrill of the chase or, in this case, the non-chase, and by Daniel's insistence that fate was at work. She couldn't wait to see how it would all play out.

Everywhere they went, they kept a vigilant look out for anyone suspiciously following them or keeping tabs. Leaving Ella's car at the cottage, they took a cab to the boat and had a great cruise with no sign of Daniel. It was terrific fun to be out on the open sea in a safe boat with exquisite views of the island and harbor, listening to the lively history of Key West.

Of course, sharing a bottle of champagne helped Ella relax and enjoy herself despite her uneasiness about being on the water. There was something very freeing about it—like when she imagined the pilot as he must've seen the sea from above. Thinking of that made her think of Daniel, and she was almost sad they hadn't run into each other.

But next up was dinner at an expensive hotel on the beach. This was their big splurge for their vacation. It had originally been planned for their last night there, but they were both flexible enough to change plans for this little adventure. No stalkers, no sailors, no pilots, just great drinks and food, and an amazing sunset view of the ocean. After dinner, indulged in every way, they headed out to catch a cab. But on the way out, they passed the gorgeous hotel bar at the pool's edge, complete with waterfalls, towering trees, private tables with candlelight, and soft music coming from a baby grand piano. They looked at each other and knew they had to stop in for a nightcap.

After two brandies each, with lots of good talk and laughter, they felt no better night could be had and called a cab to head home. Outside they waited and wilted in the heat of a steamy, tropical August night. They waited and waited, but the cab never showed up. Finally, a different taxi came toward them and turned his light on as he approached the hotel entrance. Giving up on the first one, they ran to the cab door, waiting for the current ride to get out. Ella, relieved the night was over with no sign of Daniel, was a little let down. She realized fate had played its hand, and Daniel would have to accept it.

The cab windows were darkly tinted, and it was dark inside. The door swung open and a very inebriated but lovely young woman stepped out, or rather almost fell out, slurring her words, "Are you sure this is my hotel?"

"Yes," a man's voice answered.

The woman stumbled to her knees, and Ella took her arm to help her up, while the man inside the cab put his leg out the door to get out. The leg was dressed in bright white trousers that could only be…Janie said it first, "Navy summer whites. Jeez! We can't get away from them, huh?"

As the tall man crouched down to get out of the cab, his hat fell off. Ella picked it up and handed it to him as he started to straighten.

As his face came into view, Ella couldn't believe what she saw. Her tone of voice was accusatory. "Daniel!"

His eyes wide, shocked, he replied, "Ella, what are

you doing here?"

The drunk girl lunged for Daniel's arm. "Hey! He's with me."

Ella felt as if she'd been punched in the stomach. She didn't expect to see him, or the girl, or to feel the way she was feeling now. She turned to run down the street and get as far away from him as possible, when he came up behind her and grabbed her arm.

"Wait! Ella. Listen."

Looking at him with daggers in her eyes, she said, "I'm listening."

Then he began to laugh. "Look at you. You're jealous. That means you must care about me." He took her hand to pull her closer.

She yanked it away. "I'm not jealous. I'm just shocked and disappointed in you. So much for fate, huh, and kismet and all that other crap?"

Pointing toward the girl, Daniel said, "My buddies and I were at a bar having a good time, minding our own business, when I saw this girl slumped over the bar, half off the barstool. She was so drunk she couldn't even remember her hotel, let alone how to get there. Since I needed a cab home anyway, I told her she could share mine and I'd make sure she got to her hotel safely."

"She said you were with her."

"Look at how drunk she is. She barely knows her own name, and tomorrow she won't remember how she got into her room alive. All I did was give her a cab ride here—just being a good Samaritan. If *I* was that drunk, I'd want some honest person to help me out."

Ella was embarrassed, mostly at the depth of her emotion when she thought he'd been out with a gorgeous, albeit drunk, woman. This was not lost on Daniel either.

By now Janie had helped the woman into the hotel, and the concierge was making sure she got to her room. Janie stood at the open door of the cab, hot, sweaty, tipsy, and yelled, "Karma's a bitch, isn't it? C'mon, Cinderella. Your chariot awaits. I'm dyin' here."

Daniel walked Ella to the cab. She slid in back with Janie. He got in the front seat. Janie called out, "Oh, Prince Charming's coming, too? This should be good."

Daniel dropped them at their cottage, opened the door, and before getting back into the cab, he pulled Ella close and kissed her forehead. Relieved he didn't go for her lips, she put her arms loosely around his waist and drew him close. He let out a sigh and said, "I can't even believe how good you feel."

"I'm so exhausted from everything that's happened the last couple days. I don't know how I feel."

"But you *are* going to keep your promise, aren't you?"

Ella backed away slightly. "Oh, that."

"Uh-huh. *That*. The fate thing. Do you believe in it now?"

"Do I have a choice?"

"No."

"Good, because I'm too spent to argue," she said.

"Great. I'll pick you up tomorrow at noon. Okay?"

Ella smiled knowingly. "I do keep my promises. Noon it is."

He kissed her hand as she walked away from him. The feeling from it lingered in the air between them as they parted.

Janie waited inside at the kitchen table. "Oooh,

buddy, you're in trouble now."

****

The next day, Daniel showed up on time, and the first thing he did was bring out the matching flip-flop to the one he'd put on her foot two days before.

Laughing, Ella couldn't believe he had the mate.

After looking around the living room, he wanted to know where the other one was. She pointed under the coffee table. He retrieved it and insisted she wear it.

"You expect me to wear them?" She giggled.

"I thought you'd want the set, your beach version of the glass slippers. I have a feeling we're going to remember this for a long time."

Ella stood and slipped them on. "Let's not get carried away. Let's just enjoy the day." Changing the subject, she asked what he had planned.

"I just want to enjoy you and get to know you better."

****

They spent all day on the beach, sunning and playing, talking, laughing and thoroughly enjoying each other's company. That night, they met Janie at the Sailors Rest again.

Janie didn't mind being alone and doing her own thing, even if it were to be for the remainder of their vacation. She was thrilled with Ella's going out with a great guy and hoped it would continue beyond the one date she'd promised.

After dinner, Ella and Daniel walked along the shore, holding hands and talking. She was curious to know why he chose her out of all the women in the bar that night.

"I didn't choose you. You chose me. You drew me

in like a laser beam."

"But I was outside on the beach with my back to the bar. You couldn't even see me."

"You forget I was inside in the far back corner. You didn't see me, but I saw you the minute you walked in." He hesitated as if deliberating whether to tell her the whole truth.

"And?" she prodded.

They were sitting in the sand at the water's edge. He stood up and pulled her up to face him. He moved a strand of hair off her face. "It wasn't this silky blond hair that drew me."

"It's only blond in the summer. In winter, the hairdresser helps out."

Grinning, he said, "Will you stop? I'm trying to be serious here."

"Sorry. I'm not good at serious."

He pulled her close and looked into her eyes. "Loved those eyes the moment I saw them, the color of the ocean on the clearest blue day, full of goodness and emotion, comforting as deep pools of cool water on a hot day. I wanted to jump right in. The way you walked in the front door, with confidence, no hesitation, unlike your timid friend who trailed behind you."

"Don't talk about Janie like that. You don't know her; you misunderstood."

"See that? You're loyal, too. I just knew that about you, that you are a really good, genuine person. You have that air about you. And don't argue with me because I'm a great judge of character. Almost never wrong."

What he didn't tell her was that on the night they met, in the back of the dark bar, right before she walked in, he had stopped playing pool, overcome with a feeling, a compulsion to look toward the front door. Waves of deep emotion ran through him, so much so he felt lighter, the room seemed brighter, and all at once, he knew without a doubt that someone special was going to walk through the door. His buddy noticed him acting oddly and asked what was wrong. "You're gonna think I'm crazy, but this feeling just came over me—intuition, I guess. The next person to walk through that door is going to be a woman. I'll recognize her and feel connected to her. In some way, I think I'll know her for the rest of my life." His friend had told him he was nuts and drunk. But Daniel was neither. He'd had one of his premonitions.

Little did he know, Janie and Ella had been arguing at that moment over who would walk in the door first. And in came Ella. As soon as he saw her, he recognized her as the woman outside the church. They'd been drawn to each other then, if only for a few minutes. And now with her walking through the door, it was like walking into destiny, their destiny, like being reunited with a long-lost lover or best friend.

But he couldn't share this with Ella on the first full day of getting to know each other. Their friendship was too new, too delicate, and she was too afraid. She couldn't handle it now. Someday he'd have to tell her.

****

Never before had Ella gotten so close, so quickly to a man. Despite trying to keep her distance emotionally, her body betrayed her, and it wanted him to touch her, hold her, and kiss her. Her intuition urged her on, as if to say, *Yes, it's okay; he's a good one. Go for it.*

Daniel, however, acted in a respectful and gracious

manner, even though she sensed he was really controlling himself. The eastern horizon lightened a bit, reminding them dawn would follow soon.

"I'm having a great time, but I need to get back before Janie wakes up and starts calling the police."

"C'mon. I'll take you back." As he opened the door to his car, he said, "Your carriage awaits, Cinder-Ella. No pumpkins tonight, though. No disappearing into the night. And I hope you'll spend more time with me, even though your promise was for just today."

Ella smiled in her heart and agreed to see him again. She decided to let him in, to give him a try. After all, they'd both be leaving soon. There'd be a natural end to this beginning they'd started. And if it continued to work as well as it had the last four days and continued to blossom? Well, she'd worry about that if and when the time came, but she doubted it would. She could always put the brakes on. For now, she was exhilarated—a rare feeling in her life—and she was caught up in the magic of this tropical paradise, feeling like the heroine of a great romance novel, inside a dream, and she intended to make the best of this unexpected gift of pure pleasure. But with all dreams, there always comes the time to wake up to reality.

Daniel dropped her off and they made plans to meet again for drinks and dinner later that night. "I would ask you to lunch, too, but we need to get some sleep. And I'm sure you need some down time."

"I do. But I doubt I'll be able to sleep much. How about a late lunch?"

"Love it," he said. "If I pick you up at two, is that enough time to recover?"

"Yes," she said, lying, thinking, *I don't know if it's*

possible to recover from you. But she confirmed anyway, "It's a date."

He drove off, and she walked into the cottage, realizing it'd been a long time since she'd had a real date, and even longer since she had really looked forward to one.

Chapter 6

Janie was waiting to interrogate Ella about her date with Daniel, wanting every detail. Ella shared only the basics, wanting to keep him private, all to herself. Janie didn't care. She was so thrilled Ella actually *liked* him and wanted to see him again, although she worried how long it would be until the old fears kicked in. "So, when does he leave to go back to wherever he's stationed?"

Ella looked like she'd been hit with a brick. "My God, I didn't even ask him that question. We were so busy talking about all kinds of things and having a good time. It never occurred to me."

"Wow, that's new. The whole *when-are-you-leaving* question is usually the one you ask first."

"True. I guess there's something different going on, something unusual about him."

"Well, he certainly is resourceful in his pursuit of you, and with the whole fate thing he believes in…you gotta give it to the guy. Not only is he smart and creative, he's great fun and he *really* likes you."

Twirling her long hair in her fingers, almost in a trance, Ella said, "I know. But it *is* kind of scary."

"Hmm…'scary' means you must think this thing with him could be serious."

Ella snapped out of her daze. "Oh, please. I just met him." But as she changed into a T-shirt and slipped into bed, half-asleep, she made a slip of the tongue. "I guess it could be. He's a serious guy—thirty years old, already traveled the world with an accomplished career flying jets. He says he's looking for something real. But who knows?"

Janie closed the curtains on her way out of the room and thought, *He does, and so do you. Even though you can't admit it, you know*. And she thought of the church and the wedding where Ella had first seen him and wondered what kind of premonition Ella had really had then.

****

Daniel picked her up promptly at two, and after a quick lunch, they toured the Ernest Hemingway House, then drove around the island, stopping in Old Town, the historic district. They discovered they both loved the quaint, unique architecture so prevalent throughout Key West. Most of the historic homes had been beautifully restored, and they felt as if they were walking back in time through a story book in an imaginary town. For the rest of the day, they toured galleries, pubs, and offbeat shops, listened to music and talked non-stop. Their similarities and shared interests on so many levels and subjects became more and more obvious, synchronous, and remarkably compatible.

Early evening, Daniel didn't want the day to end, so he came up with an alternative. "It's almost dinnertime. We're both tired. Instead of going out somewhere crowded and noisy, why don't we spend a quiet evening at the condo I'm staying in? I'll even cook dinner."

"Seriously? You cook, too?"

"Sure do. I love it. Nothing gourmet, mind you, but I know my way around the kitchen."

Once there, they relaxed with a bottle of wine on the deck overlooking the ocean. Ella got a far-off look in her eyes while looking out over the sea, those old memories and fears coming back to haunt her.

"Where are you?" he asked while taking her hand. "You seem like you're drifting away."

"I am. Sometimes the ocean, even though beautiful, brings back memories I'd rather not have."

"Anything you want to talk about?"

"No." Ella looked around at the unfamiliar surroundings, at him, and suddenly felt very uncomfortable, reminded of the loss of Peter and of what the sea could take. And here she sat, letting herself fall for a man whose career was at sea and in the air above the sea and on ships out in the middle of the sea. *My God*, she thought, *what am I doing? I must've been crazy to let this go this far. I have to put a stop to it.* She slipped her hand out from under his.

Tuning in to her thoughts, sensing she was ready to get up and leave, Daniel confronted her. "Ella, I feel you drifting away. You want to leave now, don't you?"

She looked at him with a combination of awe and resentment at his accurate intuition. With her intentions now usurped, she knew he'd try to talk her out of leaving. So Ella just got up, grabbed her purse, and headed for the door.

Daniel ran after her and gently held her by the arm. "You can't just leave. Tell me what's going on. Did I do or say something to offend you?" His crestfallen face showed he was hurt.

Ella couldn't leave him like that. He didn't deserve it. After all, this was her doing, and now it was her responsibility to end it without hurting him more.

Setting her purse down, she cupped his face in her hands. Instantly, he looked relieved by her touch.

But her words betrayed her actions. “I’m so sorry for letting this get out of hand, going beyond what I’m capable of. It’s nothing you did or said; it’s all me. Me and my messed-up life and fears. I’m so sorry. I really do care for you. You’re a terrific person, but I am not capable of being in a relationship with anyone right now. Can you understand?”

His eyes went from showing relief to flashing anger. “No, I don’t understand. We are really connecting in an extraordinary way. I’ve never felt emotion to this degree, especially so soon with a woman. I know you feel it, too. How can you just walk away from it? Hell! How bad could your life have been to make you walk away from something that could be the best thing that’s ever happened to you? If you’re leaving for good, you at least owe me an explanation.”

Ella walked back to the sofa and slumped into it, looking up at him with real sorrow. “You’re right. You’re an honest, good person who doesn’t deserve being walked out on with no explanation. It’s just that I almost never speak of the things that have haunted me. My grandmother and Janie know some, but not all. No one knows the whole truth of what got me in this place in life except me. And I don’t even know all the reasons; there are mysteries about my past I’ve always been too afraid to explore, and my grandmother always urged me to forget the past.

“So even today, at twenty-seven, I’m still in the dark. I guess I’ve wanted it that way. I didn’t really want to know the whole truth, so I kept moving and running and hiding in my career, hoping someday all would be miraculously revealed and healed." She knew the time of reckoning was upon her, having gotten herself in this place of hurting other people, and it was time to end it. But she felt like a great ship that takes miles to slow down, stop, or turn. She couldn't do this on a dime. It would take more than just a day or two.

Daniel sat beside her. "I have all the time in the world to listen."

Unnerved again by his uncanny ability to read her thoughts, she backed off. "I really do want to explain things to you, Daniel, but first I have to get things straight in my own head. Can you give me some time to dig deeper and figure out what's really going on?"

He took her hand. "You promise we'll get together again to talk about this?"

With tears in her eyes, she simply answered *yes,* incapable of saying more. Daniel knew she'd keep her word and so dropped her off at the cottage with a promise to call when she was ready to talk.

****

Janie had turned in early that night after a couple days of hard partying.

Ella slept fitfully with thoughts roiling inside her, trying to decide if she should tell Janie more of the truth—kind of like a trial run for what she'd have to do with Daniel. If Janie was shocked, disbelieving, or judgmental of her, then she'd spare Daniel the truth and let him go with only the barest minimum of details necessary to make sense to him. She cared too much to drag him into her black widow's spider web, into the curse she believed she'd had for a lifetime.

Ella woke early with Janie bursting into her room, dragging her out of bed. "C'mon! Let's talk while we have a great breakfast. I'm starving." While working together in the kitchen, making pancakes, Janie asked, "So how's it going with Daniel-the-Navy-hunk? Everything okay?"

Hesitating, not sure if she really wanted to open the door on this conversation, Ella finally relented, realizing she had to. "No, things are not okay. In fact, I was wondering if you'd mind hearing me out today because I'm about to walk away from him and I owe him an explanation, except how do you explain something you can't fathom yourself, you know?"

"Yes, kiddo, I know. And of course, I'm here for you all day or however long it takes. Why don't we take our breakfast and a pot of coffee out to the patio, relax, enjoy the view and talk?"

Ella sipped her coffee, still unsure about sharing her stories. "Janie, promise me you'll listen with an open mind. I'm not delusional or psychotic, but what I'm about to tell you could make you think I was."

"I know you. I know you're sane. More so than me, I'm sure." They both laughed. Then Janie assured her, "Seriously, my mind is open and willing to help you, even if just by listening."

Relieved, Ella decided to come clean with the part of her history she'd only partially told Hannah, and some she'd never shared with anyone.

****

The Woman on the Widow's Walk

Even after nearly drowning, by the following spring, ten-year-old Ella was inexplicably drawn like a magnet back to the old Victorian house and stretch of beach below it. The memories of that horrible day had faded, and Ella missed her walks on the beach. The first time she ventured back, the air had been gray and dense with fog wrapped around the house like a shroud. An ominous energy drifted out and swirled around her, catching her up in its cloak. Death felt close, and a silent whisper mixed with the wind calling out to her, as if to summon her closer.

Scared, she turned to run, but as she did, the faint image of a woman appeared outside the house, high up near the roof where a porch wrapped around the peak. Her image was almost transparent, seemingly made from air and sea mist. Ella had blinked hard, rubbed her eyes to make the vision disappear, and when she opened them, it had vanished. But the fear lingered and had followed her home, making its way inside her life where she knew it would never let her go.

Without mentioning the image of the woman, Ella had told her grandmother, Hannah, on that day she thought the house was haunted.

Hannah Jameson had adopted and raised Ella after her mother—Hannah's daughter, Cecilia—had died. Even with being devastated by her daughter's death, Hannah had always had a calming effect on her granddaughter with her practical New England heritage and down-to-earth approach to the mysteries of life. After hearing Ella's story, Hannah had been rational: "The house looks haunted because it's been vacant for years with peeling paint, sagging shutters, and dead trees. There's no life inside or out. That's what you're sensing. But it's not haunted."

Reassured, Ella had continued to walk there frequently, feeling she might learn more of the mystery of that terrifying day a year before—intuitively sensing answers lurked in the space where she'd almost died, as if the air was charged with information. Even on the hottest summer days, though, a cold feeling emanated from the house, like whispers of lonely voices looking for consolation. At ten, Ella didn't know what the porch wrapped around the peak of the house was for and wondered why someone would put it there. But she was drawn to it like a moth to light, and on gray, stormy days, from a distance she thought she'd seen the same woman standing up there.

Blinking her eyes and walking steadily forward, Ella wished for it to disappear. As if hearing Ella, sometimes the woman did, but then came back. Her image seemed real, but looked almost transparent, as if floating in on the fog. The woman never looked at Ella. She'd appear, look out over the sea, then vanish. After seeing the same image every day over a few weeks, Ella was sure it was real and was so frightened she finally told her grandmother.

Hannah had looked a little worried at first but calmly explained that the "porch" was called a *widow's walk*, named for women whose men would be on ships at sea for long periods of time. The lonely women would go there to watch for incoming ships and, hopefully, their men coming home. She assured Ella her imagination was getting the best of her, that the image of a woman couldn't possibly be real.

Over the next several months, though, the vision grew stronger and more solid. Hannah saw the increasing fear in her granddaughter and thought more information might help her understand. She thought divulging part of the history of the house to Ella would put her mind at ease. She told Ella how a woman had lived there long before Ella was born. Her husband had been a fisherman and gone to sea, but never returned. The woman waited and watched for years. She grieved and was inconsolable but held out hope he'd return until the day she died. Ever since, there had been rumors of a ghostly image seen on the widow's walk, but no one could prove it was real.

Hannah had added that Ella was old enough to know the truth, but still she didn't want her to go back there. She didn't make her promise, though, as if she knew Ella would have to go back, and so she did. Continuing to see the image most days, her fear mixed with compassion at how lonely and sad the woman must've been, searching for her husband lost at sea.

One day, tired of constant anxiety over the ghostly image appearing and wanting to rid herself of it, Ella decided to face the house and its supposed widow's spirit up close to prove it was not real, that there was nothing to it but her vivid imagination and local gossip. As she climbed up over the rocks and onto the hillside to get closer, gray clouds closed in and a storm approached, but she couldn't turn back after going that far. Her fear grew with every step toward the front porch, and her body shivered with the ocean mist and the dark essence of the house surrounding her. The wind blew in gusts, and the old wood house creaked and groaned, its sadness filling Ella's heart and the space around them.

Standing directly below the widow's walk, shaking and scared, just when she couldn't bear it and turned to leave, she gave one last glance up. The woman appeared. Her head turned and looked straight into Ella's eyes, locking them with her gaze. It was not evil, but full of agonizing grief, void of light and life. Death and mourning saturated the air while the sky darkened and lightning flashed. Their eyes locked for mere seconds, but in them Ella saw a shocking thing, a face terrifying in its impossibility, yet somehow familiar. As if the widow's eyes were mirrors, Ella saw a reflection of herself.

She'd screamed and run away while rain fell in sheets, sliding down the muddy hillside, slipping and falling over wet rocks, scrambling to the shore below. Running at a speed she thought not possible, those eyes seemed to follow her all the way. Ella never doubted she'd get home safe, feeling somehow protected, as if someone were watching over her. She never looked back. She didn't want to ever see the woman again.

****

Clearly shocked, Janie's mouth dropped open. "I can't believe that actually happened to you. Do you really think it was an honest-to-God ghost?"

"What else could it have been? I saw it enough times, and finally so up-close, I knew I didn't imagine it, even though Hannah thought I did."

"That's incredible. Didn't Hannah get worried about you, a child, seeing something so frightening? And what about the woman looking familiar and seeing your reflection in her eyes?"

"If Hannah was worried, she didn't show it. In her no-nonsense way, she said no harm would ever come to me, that I had a guardian angel watching over me. But I never did tell her the part about the woman looking straight at me and seeing myself in her eyes and feeling them on me as I slid down the hillside."

"You never told her the scariest part! Why not?"

"It was bad enough with the near-drowning and the

message I'd gotten; I didn't want her to think I was completely crazy. And I didn't want to worry her more. She already had enough with raising me on her own; she didn't need another burden. She did, however, ask me not to go by there anymore."

"And did you?"

"For a long time, I couldn't; I was too afraid. I'd walk in the other direction. I avoided that stretch of the coast. But after not walking by the house for six months or so, I began having dreams of the woman where I'd see her like I used to from the beach."

"You actually dreamt about her? Why, do you think?"

"I'm not sure. I don't think it was fear because I hadn't walked there in six months or so and wasn't afraid. I don't think I brought the dream on. I think it was the widow. She might've missed me walking by and was reaching out to me. Who the heck knows why? I can't imagine. It's too creepy."

"Ella, do you hear yourself? How could it be the widow coming into *your* brain, *your* dreams? Is a spirit capable of doing that?"

"From what I've read and heard, it's possible if the spirit has a connection to you."

"But you didn't have any connection to her."

Ella's eyes opened wide. She was speechless for a minute, processing what Janie had just said. "My gosh, I never thought about it that way. I never questioned it. Maybe subconsciously I felt connected to her. But you're right—there is no valid connection."

Janie smirked. "None that you know of. You never investigated that whole situation, so you don't really know."

Ella waved away the thought. "No. Hannah would've told me."

"Did you ever ask?"

"No. Like I've said before, Hannah and I both never wanted to ask any questions or stir up the past. But now that you bring it up, I do recall in the dream the widow looked exactly the same as she had up close, and she also seemed familiar. After having that dream for another year or so, I felt differently about the day I saw her. I don't think she was trying to scare me. I think it was the opposite. I might've scared her in the middle of her grief. She didn't expect me to be at the house, so close to her. I started to identify with her sadness and felt truly sorry for her.

"In the dream, I felt myself walking that widow's walk, looking out to the sea through her eyes, searching for a loved one, only to have the sea keep him. I'd wake with such a deep sense of loss that, even though I loved the ocean, I never felt the same way about it again. I loved its beauty, but it also took life and love away, from the woman and from me somehow. I've never figured out why or how that could be, but I feel it as real in my gut as I do sitting here with you."

"It sounds like there really is a connection. Any ideas what it could possibly be?"

Ella's eyes filled with fright at the suggestion. "I don't know and I don't want to know. Not now. Maybe someday."

Janie just stared at her, realizing she was not ready to push the issue, but she thought "someday" was already upon Ella to find out more. But so as not to upset her friend even more, she only stated the obvious. "Man, that's some story. It's troubling, not to mention horrifying."

"Gee, thanks for all those lovely adjectives describing my life. Do you think you can cut me a break now and not badger me about any of this?"

"Sorry about the words. But they're just words. And if I feel those things, I can't imagine how you've felt your whole life living with those memories and dreams. But that's no reason to stop loving or living life fully."

"It *is* when you add all the other reasons to those. If you had my history, you'd be reluctant to get involved in a romantic relationship, too."

Janie choked on her coffee. "Seriously? There's more? Oh, wait a minute. Now I remember when you told me about the near-drowning. You mentioned it was only *one* of the reasons for your weirdness about the sea."

Ella put her head in her hands and rubbed her temples. "I can't believe I let that slip."

"Well, you did, so now you owe me the rest of the story."

Ella stood, grabbed the empty coffee pot and shot back, "I don't owe anybody anything. I'm burned out with all this. Can you understand? I can't talk any more about my past."

Janie grabbed her hand. "Sit down. Listen. I do understand. It's a lot for me to comprehend, let alone for you to dredge up. I get it. But you told Daniel you owed him an explanation. Are you going to tell him everything? If so, you might as well practice on me. Besides, I can't imagine anything scarier than what you just told me."

"Well, *I* can. So let's leave it at that. I'm going to

tell Daniel I need more time to sort through this stuff. I need a break."

Sensing Ella was near a breaking point and might shut down altogether, Janie said, "That sounds like a good plan. Why don't we spend the day together and *not* talk about your past, unless there's something you really want to share."

Ella smiled gratefully. "Oh, you are a good friend. Thanks for the reprieve."

Looking at her watch, Janie announced, "Hey, only four hours 'til cocktail time. Let's get started."

Ella laughed while clearing the table. "Are cocktails all you think about?"

"When I'm on vacation, absolutely. What d'ya say?"

"Too early for me. Let's go into town and grab some lunch, do some sightseeing, and just chill."

****

After a late lunch and margaritas, they strolled around town, relaxed and laughing. Janie needed a new bathing suit, so they hit every beach goods store advertising a sale. Ella dragged behind her, the day's activities catching up to her and tiring her out. In store number four, Janie begged Ella to come into the dressing room to offer an opinion. Janie stood in front of the mirror, checking out all of the vantage points. Ella told her, "You're so petite and athletic. You look good in anything."

"Thank you, girlfriend, but is it too skimpy? What about the color on me?"

Ella stood behind her, looking this way and that, turning Janie around and assessing the suit when she thought she saw a shadow in the mirror. As soon as she looked up, it was gone. “Did you see that?”

“What? Something wrong with this one?”

Ella shook her head. “No, no, never mind. I thought I saw something in the mirror. It was nothing. The suit looks great. Buy it.”

As Janie gathered up her clothes, Ella glanced in the mirror again and thought she saw the faint outline of a face, a smile. “I’m really losing it. Let’s get out of here.”

“What happened? I saw you staring at the mirror. What’s the matter?”

Ella deftly diverted Janie’s attention, so she wouldn’t ask any more questions. “Nothing’s the matter, except we’re missing happy hour.”

Janie yanked the curtain closed. “Oh, no! I’ll hurry. We *cannot* miss happy hour.”

****

The open-air bar near the beach amplified the effect of the drinks on Ella with the hypnotic melody of the ocean. Her skin was drenched in fresh air and soft breezes. With a band playing Jimmy Buffet, reggae, and calypso tunes, along with half-price drinks and Janie’s overenthusiastic palate, Ella was seduced into drinking more than usual. She found herself swaying to and fro while perched precariously on a barstool. Janie danced nonstop, resting only to imbibe margaritas. She tried to drag Ella out to dance, but Ella didn’t think she could stand, let alone dance.

So she ordered a coffee, then another in an attempt to clear her head. Janie grabbed her by the waist, begging her to accompany her to the ladies’ room, feeling woozy. They wobbled on their way to the small restroom in the back of the bar. Ella pushed Janie into a stall, closed the door, and rested herself against a sink. She felt too tired to even wash her hands, but managed it. After splashing cold water on her face, Ella realized the low light and her slightly inebriated state made her feel like she was in a fog. Glancing into the mirror, she winced at the sight of herself—hair frazzled, makeup melting from the heat, eyes not quite focused. "What a mess." Turning the water off, she felt a slight nudge at her shoulder, urging her to look up again. Ella thought it was Janie, so she looked into the mirror expecting to see her, but Janie's reflection was not there.

What she saw was the face of a woman she'd forgotten about long ago, a woman who'd appeared to her when she was three years old, also in a mirror back then. Her face looked briefly at Ella, her eyes filled with love, and then she vanished. Ella let out a gasp, a guttural sound of disbelief, of needing to escape. Janie came out of the stall, disheveled, but she'd heard Ella.

"Are you okay? You sounded really weird just now. Or have I had too much to drink?"

"Both," Ella said. In her groggy state, she blurted out what she'd just seen in the mirror.

Janie slapped the faucet handle and slammed the soap dispenser. "For God's sake, we can't even go out for a good time without your frickin' ghosts following you around. Even I'm getting tired of this." She washed her hands hard as if to take the skin off and slammed the faucet closed. "What the hell, Ella? What the hell is going on with you?"

Ella grabbed her by the arm. "C'mon. We're getting out of here."

"No, I want to stay and party."

"Janie! You've had enough partying for three

nights. We both need to get home before anything weirder and scarier happens. Okay?" Ella's eyes, full of fear, pleaded with her.

Janie looked into the mirror while she dried her hands and saw her out-of-focus image, sweaty face and clothes, and matted hair, and didn't recognize herself. "Oh, my God. I look worse than bad. You're right. It's time to go."

Later, they both fell into their beds in a deep sleep within minutes. Janie slept like the dead. But Ella dreamt of the dead. The image in the mirror that night had unlocked another buried memory. It unfolded in her sleep like a bad fairy tale.

The next morning, she had to talk about it or she'd explode. But talking also meant exposing herself as a liar. The word *liar* jolted her back to the beach when she was nine, when she'd heard: "*Secrets, lies, and murder—yours, all yours.*" *Maybe this is what it meant—to get me to confront my secrets and lies, to expose them.* As she gathered the courage to speak, though, in the back of her mind, she knew this process wasn't over. There'd be more. There was still the word *murder* to fathom. It followed her in stealth, like a dark stranger in the shadows behind every step she took, as if waiting for her to slip up. Then it would pounce. Bringing what? Knowledge? Answers? Death? She pushed it out of her mind to save her sanity.

Ella probed Janie's memory, "What do you remember about last night? Anything?"

"Of course. I wasn't that bad off. Last thing I remember was you acting all weird in the ladies' room, and before that, in the dressing room of the store. Something about seeing things in the mirrors. What were they?"

"I thought I saw a shadow, a shape, or an image, a woman's face very faint, almost not there. I didn't want to believe it, but it jarred something loose in my memory, and I dreamt of my mother, or rather, my mother's spirit."

They sat outside on the patio. Janie poured her third cup of coffee while munching on a bagel. "You told me about her. You have some great memories until you were around eight or so, right? When she got sick? Then she died of some illness. So, what did you dream?"

Even though this felt like torture, Ella had to spill the truth. "I'm embarrassed to admit this, and I'm ashamed because I lied to you, but I think I've been lying to everyone so long I forgot the truth. I made up the story of her dying when I was eight. Remember those delightful memories I shared with you to convince you I had a normal childhood?" She stopped, hating to be exposed.

Janie stopped eating and looked up at her. "Not true?"

"No. The only thing I know of her is what Hannah told me." Ella looked out over the ocean, uneasy again. "This is too hard. I can't do this."

Janie threw her arms in the air. "Oh, c'mon! You can't lay something like that on me and not finish! I forgive you for your little white lie, and I understand why you did it. I'm not here to judge. I want to help."

Ella stared straight ahead. "Okay. From as far back as I can remember, long before seeing the widow…I have felt…I can't think of any other word for it…and it sounds crazy…but I've felt *haunted*. I've actually *been* haunted. Sort of. I just didn't know it at the time, and I forgot about the experience until just last night when I dreamt of her."

"What the heck do you mean by being *sort of* haunted, and what does that have to do with your mother?"

Taking a deep breath as if she was about to go under water, Ella spoke quickly. "I was always told my mother died in childbirth, but that turned out to be a lie, which I found out when I was twelve and needed explanations for all these strange happenings with the widow. My grandmother had to tell me the truth, that my mother actually died when I was two, because starting around age three, I was visited by her, by my mother."

Stunned, Janie gasped and covered her mouth with her hands. "Visited by your dead mother? How do you know that? How could that even be possible?"

Ella looked embarrassed and horrified, but kept talking. "In the dream last night, I recalled what had happened back then. I'd be playing with dolls, having a tea party or something three-year-old girls do, and a woman's image would appear in the tall cheval mirror across the room, just for a few seconds. She wouldn't speak. She'd smile and look on, and I felt happy when she was there. Happy and safe.

"Sometimes I'd sense her presence behind me, looking over my shoulder, again only for a few seconds. She was barely there, just enough for me to get a sense of her as she watched me play. The room would fill with a kind of warm light and love, and then she'd disappear. In my child's mind, it was perfectly normal, and I felt very close to her, like I knew her.

"Of course, when I'd tell Gram Hannah, she'd brush it off as my unusual and vivid imagination. After a couple years, it stopped, but I'd always remembered it. I guess because it was so vivid and unusual. But, added to that, by the time I was twelve and had been seeing the woman on the widow's walk, Hannah became concerned. She started asking questions about what the woman I'd seen in the mirror looked like. I told her she resembled her. I guess that's why I hadn't been afraid. The woman in the mirror looked familiar and comforting. And that seemed to make my grandmother even more worried."

"Can't blame her. This stuff is like out of a gothic horror novel."

"I appreciate your sensitivity. You see why I buried this stuff and never told anyone?"

"I'm sorry. Actually, I'm fascinated. You really had yet another honest-to-God ghost around you?"

"I guess I did, according to Hannah."

"How did she know it was a ghost, and why didn't she freak out about it?"

"She's a down-to-earth person, but she has a side to her that believes in this kind of stuff. Every summer we'd visit her best friend in Marblehead, MA, for a week or so. It's a small coastal town near Salem."

"Oooh. The Salem with all the witch hunts and stuff?"

"The one and only. As a kid, I really didn't know much about it, but Gram and her friend did. They'd get readings at the local tarot and crystal ball places. The summer I was twelve, she became intrigued by my seeing the widow's spirit, so she asked one of the mediums if there was something unusual about her granddaughter. The medium told her, ‘You think the girl imagines things, but she does not; she has a gift—the ability to sense spirits if she chooses to let them in, and there has been a spirit very close to her who comes out of love; no need to be fearful of it; it will move on when the girl no longer needs her.’”

Janie’s eyes opened wide with astonishment. “Incredible. And Hannah believed this and told you about it later?”

“She certainly did. She thought it best to get it out in the open. When we got home from Marblehead that summer, she sat me down, and in her direct way, said as calmly as if she were telling me what she ate for lunch, ‘Ella dear, do you remember that lady you used to see in the mirror as a small child when you were playing? Well, I think I know who she was. Your description of her resembling me makes sense, and the dress you described is exact—it was the dress your mother was buried in. I believe it was your mother, her spirit.’”

Janie drew in a deep breath, slapped the table, and shrieked, “Nooooo!”

“Yes. She told me what the medium had said about wanting me to know the truth, so I wouldn’t think I was crazy.”

“This is amazing. You couldn’t dream up a story like this, not even you, the writer.”

“Well, I suppose I could, but who’d want to?”

“True enough. But what about the spirit on the widow’s walk who scared you half to death? Did Hannah say anything about that?”

“I never told her the whole story of what happened that day, remember? And I never told her about the dreams I’d had for so long, so she just left it at having told me the true story of a local woman who lived there and died before I was born. She told me the medium said I had a gift to sense things like that and was satisfied with telling me she believed my mother had visited me as a child. As far as the widow, she left it at my having the heightened perception to pick up on the widow's grief."

"And you never investigated anything further about the real person you call 'the widow'?"

"No, never. Like I've said, I needed to keep the status quo. I was too stunned by all the information, and frankly, at twelve, I was scared to death of what I might see next or what spirit might come around. I mean, it was a bit comforting to hear the spirit in the mirror was my mother, but it also gave me the creeps. I just wanted to be normal. I didn't want this so-called gift. I wanted to be rid of it, so I never told anyone, and I made up stories like I did with you to appear as normal as possible. But it's catching up with me now."

"You mean with Daniel?"

"Yes, partly. There's even more, though, that relates directly to him and to me being incapable of pursuing a relationship."

"Are you alluding to Peter, perhaps?"

"You certainly have a good memory. Yes, Peter."

"You have to tell Daniel something. Tell him everything you've just shared with me. If all these stories don't blow his mind and have him heading for the hills, well, he's a keeper. Maybe you won't ever have to tell him about Peter. I mean, we all have histories with other lovers, and it's not necessary to divulge all the dirty details of every breakup, right?"

"I guess not," Ella answered, but she felt like a

traitor because she'd even lied about Peter. His was another horror story she'd been running away from since her last year of college. The memories and the talking were overwhelming. She was emotionally spent and tired, but at least she had a plan. She'd tell Daniel everything she'd shared with Janie and hope he'd be scared off by her insane life enough to drop the idea of a relationship. She hoped he'd leave of his own volition, so she wouldn't have to leave him.

Chapter 7

After a couple days of chilling out and rehearsing her stories, Ella met Daniel at his condo. She spoke for a good long time, telling him everything she'd told Janie, including her "gift" for connecting with spirits, that was more like a curse. As she spoke, she kept a keen watch on Daniel, on the look in his eyes and his body language to gauge his reactions, even though he didn't say much, except for the occasional, "Wow" or "That's something," and at times, he smiled knowingly. Ella focused on relaying the facts of her past, hoping he would be scared off. But fear never appeared in his face or eyes, or words. All she saw was understanding, comprehension, acknowledgment, and even agreement. He amazed her, and she'd been so hoping he'd want to walk away. When she finished, he sat silently and just stared at her.

Ella couldn't stand it and paced around the room. "You think I'm certifiably nuts, right? I don't blame you. No one could deal with this, and I'd understand completely if you want to stop seeing me. We can be just friends, if you want, or not."

Daniel laughed, stood, and took her hands in his. "First of all, don't tell me how I feel and what I should do because I'm going to lay out for you exactly how I feel: *A)* I think you're probably more normal than most people. You certainly are brave to have coped with these very unusual circumstances your whole life and still be so functioning and whole. Well, except for not being able to have a relationship, but we'll get to that later. *B)* I don't want to be just your friend; I want to be more than that. And *C)* I want to keep seeing you, as often as possible. I want to spend as much time with you as I can during the rest of this trip, and then we'll figure it out as we go along, depending on what you want, what you can deal with." He smiled the brilliant smile that lit up her world entirely.

"I think you're amazing, incredibly interesting, talented, intelligent, and so beautiful. And you've got this deep spiritual side that tells me your brain, heart, and soul are expansive and loving, capable of the most remarkable experiences. Did you really think, with what you know about *my* unusual upbringing, that these stories of your past would scare me off?"

Ella looked down, fiercely blushing, and whispered, "Yes, I hoped they would."

"Not on your life. In fact, I'm more intrigued."

Pulling her hands away from his and turning her gaze out the open glass doors to the ocean, she searched her heart. It was still afraid because there were more mysteries and obstacles to keep her from getting serious with him, and she told him so.

"I get it," he said. "But I hope you'll get to the bottom of all this. In the meantime, don't you think we should at least hang out together during this vacation since we really do like each other's company? I'd much rather spend my time here with you than with my buddies, who I'll see the rest of the year. Do you think you can handle that much?"

"Even talking about these things is hard for me,

and new. I'm taking baby steps. I do enjoy your company, but I need to keep things on a platonic, friendship level until I get myself straightened out. I can't make any promises beyond friendship."

Daniel leaned in close to her and spoke in a low voice. "Something just occurred to me. From the things I've read and learned about the subject, sometimes when people have these inordinate fears, they can't quite pin down the source of, well..." He hesitated, not sure if he should proceed. "Now you'll think *me* crazy."

Ella couldn't help but laugh. "You're kidding, right? Please, go on. I can't wait to hear this."

"Well, it's possible the source of the problem or fear is not only from this life, but from something that happened in another lifetime."

She cocked her head, her eyes quizzical. "Hmm...it's interesting you'd say that because I remember saying to Janie this fear seemed like something I was born with. It had always been there on a physical, cellular level. That's what made me think I'd never understand or resolve it."

"So you do believe in past lives?"

"I don't know," Ella said, hesitating and shaking her head, questioning her own mind. "Some things make sense, yet are unexplainable—like déjà vu or the feeling of knowing a place or person very well, even though you've never been there or met them before. The experience in the ocean at nine—something wrapping around my legs, dragging me under and feeling a woman drowning—it felt like something I'd actually lived through before, and so did seeing flashing scenes of people who were so familiar they felt like they were a part of my life. And I occasionally have dreams of living in an ancient time. It's so real and familiar, like I'm taking a trip back to some ancient home."

"Exactly," Daniel said, excited. "I think there is so much energy inside us, in our brains, bodies, and spirits. It has to go somewhere when we die. There's too much there for it to just die or dissolve. I've read about, and personally known, many people who've had near-death experiences. And they all say the same thing—that they, their spirits or whatever it is, float above their bodies and see things they couldn't possibly have known. The accounts are too numerous to discount.

"Heck, your grandmother went to a medium who picked up on you having heightened perceptions of spirits. And your experiences at the old house, in the ocean, with the widow, and your mother's spirit as a child—they all point to elements of life that we can't explain, but they're real all the same. Don't you agree?"

Ella sat back at the table, crossing her arms in front of her. "Well, of course I do. Given my past, I know firsthand what you're talking about. Even the 'normal' life experiences I've had seemed to be linked to paranormal or extrasensory things like spirits and past lives which make them more powerful or devastating in my case. I guess I'm at a place where I just don't know how to go on from this point." She stopped talking and glanced at the sea again, searching for reasons. "I still can't find my way with mysteries to unravel and unanswered questions, most especially, *Why*? Why all these experiences centered around the sea? Where are they coming from? What are they related to? And how do I move beyond them?"

Daniel sat across from her. “Look at me and listen carefully. Probably, the first step is trying to recall some of those times and traumatic events. When I was studying and researching spiritual subjects and was exposed to these things, I knew many who tried past-life regressions or hypnosis. There were some amazing results, unbelievable insights that gave them answers, helped them find peace, to heal and move on with their lives without carrying some age-old burden that had no basis in their current reality. There are a couple people here in Key West who do regressions. Would you be interested in having a session with one?”

Doubt filled Ella’s eyes. “I’m sorry. The skeptic in me is not ready for something like that.” But in reality, it was mostly a crippling fear that kept her from being open to it.

“Well, maybe just start with meditation or prayer, if you’re into that. Or maybe reach out to your mother’s spirit, who might come around if you need her.”

“She hasn’t come around from the time I was three, until just the other night. Seeing her image in the mirror brought back those memories. What makes you think she’d come back, and how the heck could she help?”

“With spirit, anything is possible. I dreamt of my mom when I was going through a really hard time after her death. She came to me and just loved me so completely I’ve always felt her close since. And I’ve read a lot about it. In dreams, spirits can give you messages. Not like they’re speaking audibly, but you ‘hear’ the message they’re trying to get across. And you should try hard to remember their words—they are always significant. They communicate with actions, emotions, pictures, and silent messages. As for why she'd come back now? Out of love. And you need her. She obviously loves you, and if your need is desperate enough and you reach out to her, she might just respond. It certainly can't hurt to try, right?"

"I suppose. Reaching out to my mother, maybe. But the regression—I guess I'm just not there yet, not that desperate or brave enough to bare my soul and sensibilities to that extreme of the supernatural."

"Try not to judge it. I don't consider it extreme, but only you know best what's comfortable and appropriate for you. Is there anything I can do to help?"

She looked at him appreciatively and touched his cheek. "No, you've already helped enormously, but I've got to do this on my own."

"Can we hang out together then, while you're on your quest?"

Ella smiled and wanted to just kiss him for his understanding, but she held back. "Why not?"

Chapter 8

Janie was not at the cottage when Daniel dropped Ella off early in the evening. There was a note on the table saying she'd gone out for the day with Eric, the guy she'd met their first night in town, and they'd be partying into the night again. Ella took advantage of the peace and quiet to run a hot bath and soak for a long time before falling into bed. Before she nodded off, she took Daniel's advice and wished for some guidance to be given, for someone, something, even her mother's spirit, to explain the root of her losses and fears.

Ella's sleep was long, deep, and uneventful, no bad dreams but no good ones either. With the first low light just before dawn, coming out of her unconscious state, not asleep but not yet fully awake in the place where clarity and truth are clear, she wondered, *Why did Daniel come into my life, and why am I so afraid?*

With her eyes still closed, half in a dream state, and with her heart open wide and spirit yearning for truth, she saw a picture in front of her eyes, like a play unfolding. It flashed by quickly, but she understood every unspoken word and grasped the meanings behind the words.

A young man sat with her, in her lap as she cradled him in her arms. She was dressed in long robes with a hood draped over her head. It was dark, just before dawn; they were hiding, afraid they'd be seen and their secret revealed. He was maybe eighteen years old and dressed in the garb of an ancient Grecian warrior with sandaled feet and a sword lying by his side. His dark hair curled to his shoulders; his face was kind but very sad. She held him for their last moments together. A thick mist wrapped around them, a cocoon of love and sadness. She heard the sound of the ocean in the distance where ships waited; he was leaving to go to war.

They loved each other more than life itself but could not be together. She had no choice but to let him go. He put a ring in her hand and promised to come back for her. It was a simple, wide gold band with a black Greek key design all around, like a maze with no beginning or end. Placing it on her finger, he said it was a symbol of his undying love and a guarantee he would return. They kissed, their love consuming the air around them until he disappeared into the darkness.

Ella woke abruptly, filled with so much emotion; her heart pounded with love, loss, and grief. She touched her ring finger, expecting to find the ring there, feeling only its absence, and the loss of the love it symbolized. Her heart nearly shattered with not knowing how the story ended. *Did he really leave? What was the secret they shared?* Death swirled around her in that ancient time, as it did now.

In waking, all she knew was he was so real, everything about the dream was real, as if she'd lived it. And it was exactly the feeling she'd had seeing Daniel wave goodbye in her rearview mirror the first night she met him. *How are such things possible, these windows into the past?* It didn't matter how; it was as real as the bed she lay in. Sitting up, rubbing her eyes for clarity, she wondered, *Is it possible I've had a glimpse into where my fear might be coming from about loving a man and losing him to the sea?*

That thought made more sense than any other theory, but it seemed crazy. It wasn't just fear she was dealing with. There were the very real facts she'd never told anyone: of how she'd lost her first lover, Billy, and her fiancé, Peter. Her fate seemed doomed when it came to the men in her life, and she didn't know how to change or fix it. But if she didn't and kept seeing Daniel, Ella knew for sure he would be the next to be lost, and she couldn't bear it.

All those thoughts tumbled obsessively through her mind as she dressed and prepared for the day. Fear surged through every pore in her body, and it had to stop. Having asked for guidance and gotten it—not all of it, just enough to put her heading over the edge, made her feel worse and out of control. Ultimately, the only recourse now was to keep to her original plan to keep her sanity and keep Daniel safe: to run, to move, to leave.

Before making any drastic, irrevocable plans and bringing more bad karma into her life, though, Ella needed solid answers.

She intuitively sensed Hannah knew more than she'd always let on. Ella had never wanted to pursue any details, frightened of what she'd unearth. But it was time to have the courage to face the past, not in a previous life, but the real past in this life, in the here and now.

****

The reporter in Ella kicked in as she detached herself from her own story and approached it as a mystery to be solved in someone else's life. First, she made a list of everything that seemed "off" in her life thus far: Hannah told her she was sure the spirit that had visited Ella at three was her mother. But Ella didn't even know what her mother looked like. Hannah had never shown her a photo and didn't keep any around the house, but told her that Cecilia looked just like herself and that Ella strongly resembled her mother as well. For the first time, Ella realized not having photos around was odd, especially since Hannah had loved her daughter deeply.

Then there was the widow's story, according to Hannah—of a local woman whose husband was apparently lost at sea and she had lived her whole life waiting, sad, and died still grieving. So why then, did Ella see her own reflection in the widow's eyes, of a woman who supposedly was a complete stranger and died before Ella was born? And why did the spirit look familiar?

Ella's logic determined there had to be some connection, especially with the widow coming to her in dreams. And it couldn't be sheer coincidence that nearly drowning and seeing and hearing such odd things happened in the same physical place as the widow and the old house. Ella could rationalize the reason was merely her "gift," that she was open to that kind of connection to souls crossed over. But why did no *other* spirits ever come to her, besides the widow?

Before her emotions got the best of her, Ella continued with a rational list of facts. She needed to know who the widow actually was, her name and connection to her, if any. If Hannah's version were true, there must have been some kind of story in the local paper. Ella, when she first heard of the widow from Hannah, had asked her the widow's name, but she hadn't known it or couldn't remember then. And she knew Hannah would be of even less help now. Her best bet would be to search the Internet first.

Ella had promised herself limited use of technology on this vacation. She had briefly checked her email on her phone each morning, but she didn't work on or use her laptop—no checking her paper's website, no social media, or surfing the Internet. But now she pulled out her laptop and sat at the kitchen table to search the newspaper in Cape Elizabeth. With no name, she searched for articles on ghost sightings or stories. The archives only went back to 2003, and the widow would've died in the mid-eighties or decades earlier. She tried a couple other smaller papers in the area with no luck.

Pulling up the Portland paper was also a dead end. A general search for ghost stories in Maine brought up a few sites with the dozen or so of the most haunted places, including one in Cape Elizabeth, but it wasn't even close to the one she'd seen. *I guess this widow wasn't famous enough to make the paper or the Internet, if there really is a ghost.* After several hours, Ella's frustration grew. *I can't sit around here wasting a couple days surfing the Internet. I've got to get help straight from the source.*

She realized she'd need to look at actual physical files or archives at the paper up there to find pre-2000 stories or obituaries. But she couldn't get up to Maine. She needed a contact, someone who could act like her eyes at the actual paper. Then she remembered the summer she'd worked there after her junior year in high school as an intern, learning the ropes of the news business. Scanning the paper's website, she found the executive editor's name, and sure enough, it was the same man who had been her supervisor in the newsroom way back then. He'd liked her, but probably wouldn't even remember her now. It was worth a shot, though; it was her only shot at this point. She called his office number and, after a long conversation with his assistant, schmoozed her way in to leave a personal voice mail for him.

Within an hour, he returned her call, and he'd remembered her. After sharing old stories and catching up on their present careers, Ella had to stretch the truth a little, saying she was doing a story on ghosts and haunted places in the Cape Elizabeth/Portland area for a travel story and could he help with finding any local stories going back earlier than twenty-five years ago. He said, for the mere price of dinner and drinks the next time she was in town, he'd be happy to oblige and assign the duty to the summer intern who wasn't very busy at the moment. Ella was thrilled and thanked him profusely. She then gave the intern the pertinent facts and dates and let him loose to research.

Several hours later, he called back to say there were thirty or more relevant stories in their electronic database and said he could either scan everything and email PDFs to her, or, if she preferred and wanted to cover the cost, he'd make hard copies and send them to her. Ecstatic, Ella, without having a printer at the cottage and wanting hard copies for proof, said she'd happily cover all the costs, including for next-day delivery.

Next, Ella rounded up every ounce of courage to

call Hannah and get as much information out of her as she could. It was time to ask some tough questions that should've been asked a decade ago.

****

Near Cape Elizabeth, Maine
Hannah Mae Jameson

Gentle breezes made of ocean mist and salt air lightly stroked Hannah's cheek, curling wisps of white hair around her face and calming her mind. This was the best life, the only life she knew—living in a 140-year-old stone cottage that'd been in her family for almost five generations—idyllic with its wraparound porch and long view of the sea. She never grew tired of the endless blue of water and sky merging or the scent of air cleansed raw from traveling thousands of miles right here to her spot on the coast of Maine.

On this porch, she sat in her favorite weather-beaten wicker chair surrounded by climbing roses and the distant thundering of waves crashing to shore, holding a card and letter from her granddaughter, Ella. Hannah had raised Ella since the age of two when her mother died. She didn't know who she missed more—her own daughter, Cecilia, after her death, or Ella, who'd moved to Florida six years ago. Sipping a cup of tea, she read the letter slowly, savoring every word. By the time she'd finished reading, tears ran down her cheeks. Hannah pressed the letter to her heart then folded and placed it in the lovely card.

She was used to Ella often calling her "Hannah" instead of "Grandma," and was comfortable with it. She understood it might've been Ella's way of emotionally distancing herself when she needed to. Because Ella had been so badly hurt over her young life, abandoned by the death of her parents and then lost her fiancé, Hannah worried that Ella may never trust or give herself fully to any loving relationship. But no matter the words, actions, or names exchanged between them, she knew Ella loved and appreciated her deep-down, and this letter proved it.

Her granddaughter's words were warm and kind, recalling highlights of the past twenty-five years—of Ella's childhood, of all the wonderful times they had shared. She was glad Ella had good, healthy memories during a time when so many unusual things happened that could've been traumatic. *I love you like a mother*, the card said. Thankful Ella had taken the time to write of gratitude and love, Hannah couldn't help but feel mixed emotions. Nearly seventy now, sturdy and healthy, Hannah was not ready for the grave, but Ella's letter had the tone of finality, of a goodbye, as if it might be the last time they communicated, as if Ella needed to express her feelings before it was too late. A chill went down Hannah's spine. The two of them had shared an empathic sense of life, people, and a strong intuitive connection to each other. Hannah wondered, *Could Ella be picking up on something about my life or the end of it?*

Carrying the letter with her, Hannah walked down the steps into the garden and breathed deeply of salt air mingled with the scent of her roses, and looked out over the sea to regain her composure. *Heavens, no. It's not about the end of my days. You're acting like a foolish old woman.* Feeling the love coming from the envelope, she realized Ella simply took the opportunity to write a heartfelt letter. In fact, she had a feeling lately something had been off with Ella, that she was lonely or sad. Something was wrong and Hannah had meant to call her on the very day the letter arrived. *Why did the letter seem like a goodbye?* A horrible thought entered her mind: *Oh, my goodness! Maybe it's not my life but hers that's coming to a close—not of her physical life—but possibly of a stage of life where Ella is conflicted, worrying about making a wrong choice causing her to unexpectedly pick up and move someplace even further away where I really never will see her again.*

The thought cut her heart like a knife, along with a strong pang of guilt about the secrets she carried about Ella's past. She always wondered if Ella knew she'd been hiding something all her life, keeping secrets to protect her from more pain. But Ella had never asked or pursued the subject of her mother or father, as if she didn't want to know any more than the surface facts, trusting Hannah would tell her what she needed to know.

But now Hannah wondered if she'd betrayed that trust and if these secrets could be affecting Ella in adulthood. At twenty-seven, Ella had suffered losses and deaths that no one should have to suffer at such a young age. Her granddaughter seemed resilient on the outside—too strong to let anything get her down for long. Only now, Hannah sensed Ella *was* down, and stuck in a life that didn't seem to grow or move forward. *I always thought there'd be a right time. Maybe now's the time to tell her the truth.* Wrestling with the pros and cons, she searched for her phone number, doubting her actions. Then she thought about how Ella's letter had made her feel. *What if this* was *my last day on earth? Or hers? Would I want to die with this secret in me, or would I want her to know the truth?* She remembered Ella's home number was on speed-dial, then picked up the phone, pressed the button, and made the call. There was no answer on the other end, only a voice mail to leave a message, which Hannah never did.

After a couple days of not being able to locate Ella, she finally left a message, but after two more days, a call had not been returned, and she grew more than concerned. *Where could she be? What's happened to her?*

That night, Hannah dreamt, as she often did, of her daughter, Cecilia. She came to Hannah looking as young and beautiful as she was on the day she died. In the dream, her face was surrounded by light and love, and she silently said, *Ella needs you. Find her.*

****

Key West

Ella actually looked forward to calling Hannah and hopefully getting information to help clear things up, even though she was nervous about asking her certain personal questions. She poured water to make a whole pot of coffee and, while waiting for it to brew, found Hannah's number in her contacts list. Positioning a chair to face the open sliding doors to the ocean, Ella sat at the kitchen table with phone, paper, and pen.

Just as she was about to push the call button, though, the phone rang, shrill and loud, scaring her, as if someone knew she was sitting right there, waiting to answer it. Things were getting very synchronous and strange, especially seeing the words on the caller ID—Hannah Jameson.

Ella, shocked but glad, said, "Gram, I was planning to call you this morning at the same exact time when you called me. I can't believe this. Is something wrong? Who died?"

Hannah laughed. "For heaven's sake, no one died. What's wrong with you, Ella?"

"Funny you should ask. But seriously, did you get my letter, and is that why you've called?"

"I got your card and letter and loved every word. Thank you so much for taking the time to think about me and write. You're such a dear. But I had one of those weird feelings of something being wrong, something up with you. I called your condo in Tampa several times, and with no answer, I got more worried. And I'd misplaced your cell phone number, so I called the paper and your editor told me you'd gone on vacation with Janie and kindly gave me your cell number. I'm calling now because I got a strong, intuitive feeling that something is going on with you. You know me and my gut feelings."

"Yes, I do. The propensity for being slightly clairvoyant or crazy or both certainly runs in the family."

"It certainly does. But we're not crazy. We've been blessed with a gift. So tell me, what *is* wrong? I know there is, especially after hearing you were going to call me just now."

Ella hesitated, but it was now or never. "You're right, as usual. In fact, I'm so glad to hear your voice. Thank you for reaching out, because I feel like I'm on the edge of losing my mind." Ella then explained everything that had happened since her experience on the bridge driving into Key West, to the details of Daniel, and memories of the widow and her cryptic messages, then the odd dream of life in an ancient time.

She explained how her fears were so overwhelming she was on the verge of running away from Daniel, from her job, and starting a new life far away.

Hannah listened patiently, responding only with an occasional "Oh, my," or "how wonderful," then "how awful," and "you poor thing." Finally, after hearing the whole story, Hannah sighed from the depths of her soul. "I'm so sorry for everything you're going through, for everything you've been through your entire life. You've had more than your share, and I always thought you'd outgrow sensing the widow's spirit and seeing her in your dreams. And with moving to Florida, I thought you were on your way to healing and moving on with your life. But it seems things have gotten more complicated, haven't they?"

"Yes. Complicated and crazy, and I just don't know what to think or do anymore, except move on and hope for the best next time."

"Do you really think leaving will solve what you're dealing with now?"

Ella thought for a long time. She couldn't con Hannah or herself and knew running away wouldn't work. This would all come back to haunt her no matter where she lived. "I'm just afraid I'll be haunted for the rest of my life and never be able to have a real relationship."

"Would you like to be able to have a true, loving relationship with Daniel?"

"My heart says yes, but I can't figure out how to do it. I'm so afraid of something awful happening to him if we're together. The only thing I know to do is leave and start over. Where is this coming from? It's deeper than losing Peter. Do you think there's anything to that dream I had of losing someone in another time and place, or am I absolutely bonkers? And I don't mean to be disrespectful, but I have a strong feeling there's more to my early years and my parents than what you've told me. If you know the truth, I need to know it. That's why I was going to call you. I have questions for you that I've always been too afraid to ask."

"I guess I always knew this day would come."

Ella poured her coffee and sat down, trying to relax. "I realized that I've never seen a picture of my mother. Why didn't you have any?"

"I have them, buried in the attic. I loved your mother so much, and her death was so sudden. I just couldn't bear to have her smiling, live face looking at me. Then later, as you grew, you looked so much like her, memories of her returned and old wounds reopened. So I guess it was selfish of me, but it was too painful to have reminders of her around. And you never asked, so after a while, it never occurred to me to bring out Cecilia's photos or even talk about her, for that matter. After all, I had you, her daughter, and that was a reminder of her in the best, most loving way."

Hannah grew silent, processing her emotions. She asked Ella to hold on while she blew her nose, and when she returned, Ella heard her sniffle.

"Gram, are you crying? Please don't be sad because of me."

"I'm not sad, and certainly not because of you. I so deeply regret how I handled things. My goodness, I never even told you stories of her as a child or growing up." Hannah cried between words. "I…I'm so sorry, Ella, for all the things I never explained. There are things you should know…" But then she began to sob.

Ella felt terrible for upsetting her so much. "Oh, no, please stop crying. I can't stand hearing you this hurt. It's all okay. Really it is. Someday, when you're not so sad, when this is not so new to you, we can talk more, and you can share those old stories of her."

Hannah blew her nose again and wiped her tears. "Yes, yes, thank you, dear. I can't believe how much this has affected me. It's like losing her again, bringing back the memories and the stories. I didn't expect to be this emotional. I feel so stupid for blubbering into the phone. What a doddering, old fool I am."

"You're no such thing. Now listen, I want you to calm down. Make yourself a cup of tea and rest. There's plenty of time later to talk about the past, when you're more prepared. Okay?"

"Yes, that's good. Let me get everything straight in my head with events and dates and stories. Yes, we'll talk more when I'm ready."

"Good. I'll say goodbye now and let you calm down. I love you."

"I love you, too. Before you go, though, I want to say that you must do whatever it takes to love that young man and have something meaningful with him."

Ella said, "I will," thinking, *I am doing exactly that, and hopefully I'll have more answers tomorrow.*

****

As soon as the package arrived from Maine, Ella tore into it. Janie had come back from her afternoon beach date and joined Ella at the table, eager to help.

Inside was a stack of photocopies of articles and newspaper pages from ghost sightings from the 1800s and later. Ella tossed aside the ones older than fifty years ago. "There's got to be more recent ones. The intern said he found one that was about twenty-five years old." Ella searched frantically through the stack while Janie thought about what she'd just said.

"Twenty-five years old? Well, that wouldn't have been before you were born. Hannah said the widow died *long* before you were born, so we may need to look at some older stories."

"Hmm…I think you're right about that. Let's look at some of these older ones." She handed a stack to Janie to look strictly at the dates to find the right time period.

They pored over the documents for an hour, and finally Janie said, "I don't know about you, but I don't see any story in here that's no more recent than a hundred years ago. And they're from all over Maine, not just the Portland area. None of these could possibly be your ghost."

Ella shuddered. "Ugh, please, don't call her that. This is hard enough, without thinking of her as '*my* ghost.'"

"Sorry. It's just easier to say it that way. So, do you see anything interesting?"

About to give up, Ella reached into the bottom of the stack and pulled out a dozen sheets of paper and spread them out all over the table to scan them quickly. Her eyes darted from one to the next, looking at dates when Janie let out a nervous laugh and said, "Hey, this picture kind of looks like you."

"Will you stop making jokes about this?" Ella glanced where Janie pointed. She stopped and picked up the paper to look closer. "How weird. You're right. But she really resembles Hannah."

"No way. Is there a caption? Who is it?"

The copy wasn't the sharpest, so Ella strained to read the tiny print. She turned pale and dropped the paper. "No, it can't be."

"What?" Janie grabbed it and read the caption under the old photo. "'Cecilia Rowe.' Hey! *Rowe* is your name. Do you think you're related to her?"

Ella stared out to the ocean, seemingly in shock. "No. I don't *think* so. I *know* so. Cecilia was my mother's name. This story is about my mother."

"Whoa," Janie said, excited, and started reading the story. Ella listened, tuning out words and sentences except those that hit her brain with a jolt of recognition, going straight to her heart and tearing at it… "'*The closest thing to a real ghost story in this century …Cecilia Rowe died unexpectedly…cause not known, most likely her heart…but her mother, Hannah Jameson, says she was young and strong, that most likely she died of a broken heart…only married one year…her husband, local fisherman Elijah Rowe, presumably drowned at sea before his daughter…*'" Janie stopped. "This is too unbelievable."

"Keep reading, please, Janie. I can't. It's all I can do to keep from falling off this chair."

Janie took Ella's hand. "It's okay. We'll get through it. You need to know this stuff, right? The truth is finally coming out."

"What does it say about his daughter?"

Janie continued, "'*Elijah Rowe presumably drowned at sea just before his daughter, Ella, was born.*'" She looked at Ella, who hadn't moved and was still staring at the ocean, looking dazed and terrified. Janie dropped the paper and ran to Ella's side, hugging her. "This must be so shocking to you, but it's just words."

"It's not just words; it's my life. Just let me sit for a while and let this sink in."

"I'll get you some coffee or a drink. What do you want? Do you want to sit outside? What can I do to help?"

"Nothing, Janie. It's nice of you, but quit hovering. This is like getting hit with a brick. I'm stunned, and I feel like I'm about to pass out after hearing this new information, afraid of what is yet to come."

"There's more in this article. Are you ready to hear it?" She squeezed Ella's hand with both of hers. "Want me to keep reading?"

"Not really, but I have to learn the truth."

"Okay, here goes… '*Elijah and Cecilia lived in the house at the end of Lighthouse Lane and…*"

Shouting, Ella cut Janie off. "What? No, it can't be. That's the house, Janie! That's the old Victorian house I saw from the beach where I saw the widow!"

"Oh, my God! Are you sure?"

"Of course, I'm sure. That point and the street name have been there a hundred years. So that means the widow was my mother? Does it mean I saw my own mother's spirit?" Ella got up and ran outside, hoping the expanse of beach and sea would swallow up her torment. "This is too much to wrap my head around. My mother is the widow? No, no, no." She held her hands over her face and started to cry. "I just can't deal with this. How the hell do I deal with this?"

Janie followed after her. "Shh. Stop. Ella, let's stop reading and take a break. This paper's going nowhere. We can read more tomorrow."

Looking at the paper as if it were a bomb or the

plague, Ella avoided it as she rushed back inside to the sink where she burst into tears, splashing water on her face.

Janie moved alongside and hugged her. "You're okay. It all happened a long time ago. It's not real anymore. Let's get you calmed down. How about a glass of wine?"

Ella's tears turned to laughs. "Thank God that's your answer to fix anything. Yes, I'll have one. Or the whole bottle."

With sharing a soothing drink and Ella relaxing a bit, Janie tried to make sense of the whole thing. "Listen. I know you're in shock. But look at the good side—this validates a lot of things. At least, now you understand, and you know you're not crazy. The widow resembled Hannah and you because she really *was* your mother. What I'd be upset about is that Hannah knew this all along and never told you."

"I am upset. Even though everything does make sense now, I'm furious with her. The Victorian house on Lighthouse Lane—now I know why I was so drawn to it, why the widow looked so familiar, and why Hannah never wanted to talk about it."

After two glasses of wine, Ella looked at the photo with new eyes. "I can't believe it. My mother." Then she looked at Janie. "I think I need to know the rest of this story now, or I won't be able to sleep tonight."

"I think you're right. You want to read it, or should I?"

"Please, if you don't mind."

"Here goes," Janie continued. "'*After Elijah's disappearance and presumed death at sea, Cecilia could be seen carrying her baby daughter out to the widow's walk, where she'd spend hours walking and watching for Elijah to return to her...these events most likely spawned the accounts of seeing Cecilia's image on the widow's walk after her death...can't be proven for sure, but we think this town now has another twentieth-century ghost story.*'"

The look in Ella's eyes was sad but angry. "I'm so glad the town got a great story out of my loss. And for my own grandmother to never tell me the truth of how and when my father died is unforgivable."

Janie looked shocked now, too. "Yeah, I remember now that you told me he died of cancer when you were about a year old."

Ella choked up a bit and spit the words out quickly to lessen the pain. "Yup. That was Hannah's story. I guess telling the truth to a five-year-old would've been too traumatic. And then, I never asked questions about him, so she just never wanted me to know, hiding pictures of him, too, probably. But why?"

"Maybe the older you got, she saw how you wanted to just be a normal kid, but then with all these weird things happening, she was afraid to add more to your fragile state of mind."

"Yeah, that sounds like her. But it's so much worse for me now."

"I'm so sorry."

"There's nothing to be sorry about. I never knew my parents. I have missed the idea of having them, wondered what it would've been like, how my life might've been different, how I might be different today. But today I sit here and know only one thing for sure—the beautiful sea I loved really took both my parents. The sense of loss started with them and has continued throughout my life, right up until today. I guess I really am cursed."

"No, you're not. This happened so long ago, and now that you know the truth, you can come to terms with it and move on."

"I don't know if I'll ever get over this. My brain is reeling with all the odd events of my life, and I never questioned them: no pictures of my parents around the house, why we didn't socialize much, except with out-of-town friends, and, even though it was easier for me at the time, how Hannah was so supportive of my going away to Boston for college, going overseas to study, and then my first job so far away in Tampa. She'd probably been relieved, thinking the farther away I was from home, the less chance I'd stumble over the truth."

"I get how you feel, and you have every right to be angry and upset. But it almost sounds like your grandmother was trying to protect you."

"Some protection. I actually lived in that Victorian house for the first two years of my life. My mother took me on that widow's walk and poured her grief into me. Then she died of that grief. No wonder I'm screwed up with these deep-seeded fears."

"True, on all accounts. But now you have to decide what you're going to do with the truth. Let it eat you alive or turn it around and use it to have a better life."

Ella stood up and shoved the chair under the table. "I appreciate your advice, but please, I need some time to process this hell of a mess that is my life. Now I understand better what that warning was of '*secrets, lies, and murder*.' Will there be no end to these secrets and withholding of truth and the lies?" Ella got the feeling this wasn't the end, there'd be more, but all she could do was try to deal with the shock of today's revelations. "Janie, please just let me process my anger and grief, if that's even possible. Then I'll decide what the next step is. But right now, I am even more sure that I am cursed, and there's no way I'll let Daniel into my life, or he'll be the next man to die because of his love for me. No way am I going to let that happen."

Janie put her hands up, resigned, knowing Ella couldn't deal with more debate. "You're totally right, Ella, and I understand. You do what you gotta do."

"Well, the next thing I'll do, first thing tomorrow, is call Hannah. Now I know why she got so upset on the phone yesterday. She knew all of this and that the lifelong house of cards she'd built was about to crash down, and she couldn't handle it. The prospect of telling the truth overwhelmed her, and she got so upset she couldn't go through with it. Well, I hope she's recovered by tomorrow because I want answers."

****

The next morning, Ella made the call to Gram Hannah. "I know we only spoke yesterday, but I hope you've steadied your nerves enough to talk seriously about the past, my past."

"I was hoping I'd have a couple more days to prepare, but I suppose it's better to get it over with."

"Good, because I've done some research through the paper in Cape Elizabeth and I've found some very upsetting facts about my mother."

"Oh, dear. You know, don't you? You know she was…" Hannah couldn't spit out the truth.

Ella finished her sentence. "Yes, I know my mother was, *is* the widow I saw as a child and the same spirit who visited me. And I also know I lived in that house, my father died before I was born, and he died at sea, and the grief probably killed her. How could you not tell me any of this?" Ella, raising her voice for the first time at her grandmother, asked, "How could you?"

Hannah's voice cracked. "Please believe me—I thought I was helping you by not telling you everything. I didn't have the forethought to know that what could help you as a child would be so harmful to you as an adult. I can't bear the fact I hurt you so deeply." Now Hannah wept openly. "I'm so sorry. I almost told you the whole truth a long time ago—after Peter. But your heart was so broken then, I couldn't bring myself to add to your trauma. Can you understand that I thought I was protecting you?"

"I just don't know. I guess I have to. My emotions are so conflicted and extreme right now. I don't know what to think. I would like to hear the whole truth, though, the details about my parents and what happened."

"Yes. You deserve that. Is Janie with you? Are you sitting down?"

"Yes, to both questions. Please, just share the truth with me."

Hannah took a deep breath. "Where shall I start? Your parents were only eighteen and unmarried when they conceived you. Your mother loved Elijah dearly, but he was not the marrying kind, although he *did* love her and marry her, being the good man he was. He was a fisherman by trade, from a long line of fishermen and sailors. It was impossible for him to ignore the lure of the sea. Your mother begged him not to go to sea until after you were born. I think she might've had a premonition. But fishing was his only means of making a living, and he had a wife and a child on the way to house and feed. They'd fight bitterly about it, but he went out to sea anyway on his old fishing boat every morning.

"Right before you were born, he left one morning to fish as he'd done all his life, but this time he never came back. They sent search parties out to no avail. There had been a terrible storm at sea late that afternoon and neither he nor the boat was ever found. Your mother waited and prayed and never gave up hope he'd come back. But after two years, something deep inside her knew the truth and she did give up. Grief and loneliness consumed her heart. It shriveled and died long before she did. I loved her and tried to console her, but there was no consolation for this. Not even having you, her baby, helped. I thought she'd put everything into you and come alive again, but she was almost sadder and more depressed knowing you'd grow up without a father."

"So she made me grow up without a father *or* a mother. How thoughtful."

"Ella, don't think or talk like that. Your mother loved you deeply, but what happened to her seemed almost beyond help of any kind. I tried, believe me, to get her help—friends, counseling, medication, talking about her grief, but nothing worked. It was like her heart died along with him. He was her first love, and she never got over it. She didn't intend for her life to end. I think her heart just gave out from the destructive burden of grief and loss."

"That's what the article in the paper said. They quoted you."

"Yes, I know. I felt that way then and still do. I'm

so sorry for you, Ella, for how you became an orphan so young. I also struggled with my own grief for many years which affected my judgment, I guess—losing my precious twenty-year-old daughter. That kind of grief would've killed me, too, except I had you to care for—Cecilia's daughter, hers and my own flesh and blood. In a way, you saved me. I think of you as my own daughter, and I love you so deeply that I never wanted the truth to come out for fear of what it would do to you. I didn't want you to hurt even more than you did growing up with no parents.

"And later, after Billy disappeared, then the loss of Peter…well, because of the coincidences, I just couldn't tell you the truth at that point. You loved those men soul-deep, the way your mother loved your father and to tell you then would've devastated you beyond recovery. I couldn't take that chance or be the reason *you* died of grief, too. So you can call me selfish, but I truly wanted the best for you, and I am sorrier than anything else in life for being so afraid to tell you the truth. I'm so sorry."

Ella closed her eyes, leaned her elbows on the table, and held her head. "I just can't believe you kept all this from me, but I do hear the deep sorrow in your voice and words," she said, realizing what a huge burden Hannah had carried all those years. Now the truth was bringing Ella closer to answers, yet deeper toward fear about a future with Daniel. Hannah stayed silent on the line, so Ella continued, "I actually saw my own mother's spirit on the widow's walk and felt her pain. This explains something I've always been afraid of and never told you." Ella then told her about the day the widow looked straight at her, and Ella saw herself reflected in the widow's eyes.

"Oh, my Lord! I wish I had known. You must've been terrified." Hannah was quiet for a moment, picturing Ella seeing herself in her mother's spirit and not knowing who she was or why it was happening. "I wish you had told me right away. I would have shared the truth then. It could've saved you years of wondering and fear."

"Truth is, we both withheld facts and kept secrets from each other, out of fear, out of concern. What a helluva thing. But it's done now. I don't want you to feel bad about it. I love you, so let's just never withhold the truth from each other again."

"I promise. I just wish I could help you more now with what you're dealing with. In the spirit of truth, you should also know, when your father disappeared and when you were born, I tried to get your mother to bring you to live with me, for both of you to live here at the cottage, but she wouldn't hear of it. She was so sure your father would return, that he had survived and would be found washed ashore down the coast. She wanted to be there when he returned."

Hannah held back tears to no avail. "And I watched while she took you with her on that widow's walk every day and night. I worried for you, an innocent baby having all that sadness poured into your little heart and soul."

Now Ella cried as well, feeling her mother's pain as fresh as it was twenty-five years ago. "I think my psyche still carries the memory and the sadness, both of which still connect me to her. It's weird because I'm sad but also relieved. This explains so much. The only thing I'm afraid of now is there truly is some kind of curse. We keep losing the men in our family to the sea. And I'm terrified about bringing Daniel into my life knowing what could happen to him."

"I don't know what to say, child. The psychic I saw years ago in Salem also said you had some powerful karma to deal with centered on loss and the sea. I didn't tell you then. You were only twelve, and you wouldn't have understood. Now to hear these fears still haunt you, and your mother came to you in a dream…she came to *me* in a dream two nights ago, too, when I couldn't reach you. She told me you needed me and to find you."

"This is just crazy. What's wrong with us, Gram?"

"Absolutely nothing. Our parents and theirs all talked of these happenings, of spirits, of intuition, and of prophetic dreams throughout their lives. Maybe it's hereditary, who knows? Who cares? It's real. There are things just beyond this veil of life here on earth that we don't understand. But they happen. You can't ignore something in front of your face that you see with your eyes, hear with your ears, and feel in your heart. These dreams we have and the so-called psychic ability—I hate that word *psychic*—it's so melodramatic and off-putting for something that is, or can be, a very normal ability. Well, I'll tell you, there's nothing crazy or weird about those things or us."

"Do you really believe that?"

"Yes, I do because it's simply intuition, having a heightened perception of things that most people don't allow themselves to feel because they're afraid. It's being open to experiences of this nature, instead of having a closed mind. Given that, my advice to you is to call on your mother's spirit for guidance like the psychic said, remember? Maybe it would help to reach out. It certainly couldn't hurt."

"Maybe. I'm so exhausted mentally, physically, and spiritually. I just don't know how to go on from here."

"Yes, you do." Hannah's voice grew tough and convincing. "You're the strongest person I know. You *will* find your way. At least you know the source of some of these fears now. Do whatever you have to do to conquer them, so you can live the life you deserve. I'll be praying for you every day."

"Thank you, Gram, for your support. And thank you for telling me the truth."

They both shed soft tears as they hung up.

The only thing Ella's body and mind were capable of doing was going back to bed. She had barely slipped under the covers and laid her head on the pillow when she fell into a deep sleep—and dreamt of her mother.

She saw her face vividly, with a concerned look in her beautiful blue eyes, the same as Ella's. She wore a long white gown and robes that swirled gently around her face and body, as if she floated in the air or on a calm sea. The air sparkled with light emanating from her heart, filling the space with love. Even in the dream, Ella felt her mother's love as surely as if she stood before her in the flesh. Cecilia whispered, *Now the truth's been told. You've lived as I did and have lost as I have—there is more to come: different times and places, names and faces, but the same loss.*

Ella woke in a cold sweat, her heart aching with grief and feeling, no matter how far she ran or where she traveled in life, she'd never escape this sorrow, never move beyond the losses—they were somehow programmed into her destiny.

****

Janie had slept late and found Ella on the patio. "Hey, girl! Are you feeling any better today? Did you call Hannah? How'd it go? And I never did find out the details from a couple nights ago with you telling Daniel about the crazy parts of your life. What happened?"

"Make a pot of coffee. We have lots to talk about." Ella told her about the whole conversation with Hannah and how they'd resolved everything, which pleased Janie. Next, she relayed the conversation from two days ago with Daniel and how well he'd taken hearing about the weird happenings in her life.

Janie could barely contain her enthusiasm. "Wow. It sounds like you've got a real winner there. He didn't run away like you thought he would. You *are* going to keep seeing him, aren't you?"

"I just don't know. My heart says yes, but my logical reasoning says to run as fast as I can in the other direction."

"Why the hell would you do that? This guy sounds perfect for you. No one else would ever understand your life the way he seems to. With hearing those stories you told me, most guys would grab a crucifix and garlic and run away as fast as they could."

"Gee, thanks. You have such a sensitive way with words about my messed-up life."

"It's not as messed up as you think."

"Really? Well, listen to this." She then told Janie about the dream she'd had of ancient Greece and losing a lover, then of the morning's dream of her mother who said they'd had the same losses and there were more to come. "My fears are valid. Can you understand that?"

"I do, but they can't be real."

"But they are, and they affect my real life, and at this moment, I feel like I can't give the sea a chance to take anyone again. That doesn't bode well for a relationship with Daniel, does it?"

"Given he's in the Navy *and* at sea, no, it doesn't. But do you feel no hope for things changing in the future?"

"I feel I was born with a predetermined outcome for my life, and I can't shake the past and how it affects my present."

Getting fired up, Janie stood with her hands on her hips. "Well, that attitude has to stop, or you'll never have any kind of meaningful life. What happened with your parents was so long ago. Then Peter, but you two broke up because you were too young for marriage, right? No death or loss to the sea? So move beyond it like other people do. You deserve better in life."

Ella was not prepared to reveal the whole truth about Peter, so she continued with a predictable reply. "I have a good life. I love my work, and I have a terrific best friend I trust who likes to hang out with me. What more do I need?"

"A life! You need a real life. You think I'm going to hang out with you forever, drinking at happy hour after work, talking about our next assignment? I want a great guy, a husband, a family. Don't you ever think about the future beyond the next few years?"

"Not really, especially not now. I just try to live one day at a time."

"Well, that's a crappy attitude; it's defeatist, so *not* you, and it's ending now. I'm not dismissing what you've been through. It is huge, but you've had years to come to terms with it, especially now that you know the truth. It's time to let it all go and move on, don't you think?"

Ella answered, "*Yes*," but in her head, she knew there was no way out of this curse she was carrying. She couldn't tell Janie the whole story, about Billy after high school or the real truth about Peter. Janie would see Ella as a total basket case with no hope of recovery. Ella wasn't about to live life like that. Her life might be limited in terms of love relationships with men, but she wouldn't be pitied or thought of as a lost cause. If Janie could have hope, then Ella would feign it, just as she'd done her entire life. After all, she was successful, had friends, and good work relationships. She enjoyed life. The rest of it was Janie's dream for herself. It didn't have to be Ella's.

Janie danced around in her chair, happily moving with the rhythm of the calypso music in the distance. "We're going to take a good, long rest during the remainder of this vacation and get your head turned around right. You haven't had time off in years, no traveling, no change of scene." She put her hand on Ella's arm. "I love ya, kiddo. With all this history behind you now, you can get your head straightened out. I want to see you happy."

Ella let her talk on and on, but she knew her life, in its current state, was as good as it would ever get. She'd never tell Janie the rest of her stories, the ones that no one would believe, the ones that had shaped her adult life and frame of reference for living, shrouding her past in a fog of mystery and choking the kind of future Janie spoke of, out of the realm of possibility.

Chapter 9

Daniel called the next morning and invited Ella to spend the afternoon and evening together.

"I can't promise you how much I can talk about the last few days," Ella said, "so let's just get together to relax."

They went to his condo and walked the beach for a while, talking about general things, with Daniel giving her space to offer her thoughts. By early evening, they were both tired and moved to the deck with a glass of wine. After walking in the sun for a couple hours, Ella's drink went to her head, and she found herself giddy and lighthearted—a welcome change from the recent days' events. The setting sun threw otherworldly colors over the earth, immersing them in awe and tranquility. Sea breezes blew all the worrisome thoughts from her mind, and the ocean's rhythm lulled her into a safe state of mind. "I guess it's about time I shared with you what happened."

"Only if you want to."

Ella smiled. "Well, what happened is partly due to your suggestions, I think, so I owe some of it to you."

"You don't owe me anything, except an evening enjoying your wonderful company."

"Okay, here goes." Ella laid out the facts she'd discovered about her parents and childhood, then both conversations with Hannah, and the message from her mother about loss, then finally the dream of ancient Greece with its feelings of deep loss that were similar to how she felt driving away from him the night they met. "I think I'm traumatized by all of it."

Daniel got up, walked over to her, pulled her up from the chair, and held her for a long time. "Ella, you're so brave. I care for you so much. I'm so proud of what you did and how you're handling this. You are the most amazing person I've ever met. I just want to hold you like this, to ease your pain, to help you heal. Will you let me do that?"

His embrace was badly needed and the best she'd ever felt in the arms of a man. Ella relaxed fully into him and finally let go. She cried gently into his shoulder. He didn't say a word; he just held her. Daniel wanted so badly to kiss her, but instinctively knew it would not be a good idea in her fragile state.

Instead, when she let go of him and sat down, he took his own seat and continued talking, encouraging her, "I think you're on the way to healing. Do you feel that way, like you've made some progress?"

"Some. I guess. I'm still reeling, you know?"

"I do. If you just want to chill out the rest of the night, that's fine. Talk about only what you want to. Let's just enjoy this beautiful place and each other. Sound good?"

"Sounds perfect."

"How about some music, a bite to eat, and another glass of wine?"

"Again, perfection. Are you this attentive to all the women you date?"

"I don't date many, and no, I've never been quite this way with anyone before. And that's no lie or exaggeration. You're a first for me, Ms. Rowe."

Ella thought, *And you for me*. But she couldn't admit it out loud to him.

Sensing her hesitation, Daniel tried to reassure her. "Even though these last couple of days were traumatic, I can't tell you how interesting it is to meet someone who's had firsthand experiences like yours. I mean, I saw some crazy stuff growing up, people smoking pot or doing peyote, and I heard some pretty weird stories. But you—you're an educated reporter, someone who relies on facts. You're basically level-headed and have good common sense." He continued to ask her all kinds of questions about her unusual experiences, and she answered honestly.

As she rid herself of most of the details, Ella felt her heart lift, shedding layers of old burdens. It felt good to unload them—first to Janie, now Daniel. Maybe something was changing in her life. But she reminded herself of the new course she was going to chart. Maybe she could talk openly because she was already planning her next move. Something inside her had been jostled and was breaking loose. That meant she was on the right track and had to keep with the plan of relocating to a new place, a new job, and a whole new life…away from Daniel.

Toward the end of the conversation, Daniel, in keeping with the mood of sharing strange stories, said, "You're not the only one to get these feelings and subconscious messages." He then told her about his strong intuition whenever something was terribly wrong in his life or something was about to happen.

With him explaining his stories of his heightened perception, Ella felt normal, like maybe she wasn't all that weird, and she grew very comfortable, thinking she truly could share anything with him—until he told her what happened in the cockpit the week before, as he was taking off and the warning he'd heard about something coming at him and it being fair warning.

Ella asked what day that had been. He revealed it was the same day she'd been driving into Key West. She had felt the sensation of flying just as he'd described it, at around the same time. And then she had heard the same words of warning he had. Even in her far-from-normal life, this was almost too much for her to wrap her mind around. She could have if it had been someone else's life. But to think there really was some strong, cosmic connection between herself and Daniel scared the hell out of her. She stood and walked to the railing of the deck and fell silent for several minutes, too long, lost in what this new information really meant about them.

He followed and stood next to her. "What is it? Have I gotten too weird for you?"

She looked down, then out to the ocean, up to the sky, anywhere but at him. "No—with *my* history, are you kidding? I'm worried it's the other way around."

"What do you mean?"

Ella had shared her stories, thinking their relationship was going to be short-lived, a platonic vacation fling, that he'd run away from her crazy life and she'd run to a new life. But hearing him say he'd heard the same exact words she'd heard had thrown her. She had *not* shared this with him because she thought it too over-the-top; she didn't understand it herself, so how could he? In fact, she wanted to forget about the warning she'd gotten.

He pulled her close to him. "C'mon. You can tell me anything."

Being that close and feeling a kiss was imminent, she thought, *Fine. If he wants to know, I'll tell him all the horrible details. That should scare him off for good.* She proceeded to tell him how she'd heard the same exact words: *Something is coming, and this is fair warning*. She threw in the clincher of having asked what that meant and hearing back, *You'll know when it happens; it won't be long now.*

"And the next thing that happened, within mere seconds, was that I met you. You walked straight up to me at the Sailors Rest, and straight into my life." She searched his eyes for an instinctual response. "What do you think of that?"

His reaction was not what she expected. She thought he'd run for the hills or to his jet for a faster getaway. Instead, he smiled wide, grabbed her around the waist, drew her dangerously close, and said, "I think it's amazing. Unbelievable. It proves my point—our meeting is kismet, destiny. Don't you see? All of this was meant to be. This is the proof."

Ella began to refute his logic, but before she could get out two words, he leaned down and kissed her. It took her by such surprise she didn't know what to do except respond. His mouth was warm and sultry with wine, intoxicating her even more with the emotion behind it. She had expected him to run, not kiss her. She tried to back away, but he pulled her even closer, whispering in her ear, "This is more meant-to-be than anything in either of our lives. You know it. It's happening. Enjoy it."

With that, he kissed her again with an intensity to

draw her spirit into his own. She felt it go there. She lost herself in him. Instead of scaring her, she just let it be, and it felt perfect and safe. He held her tighter and kissed her neck, her face, and then went back to her lips where, instead of escalating, he calmed and kissed her softly, gently with short, sweet touches to her mouth. Then he ended with one long, slow, light kiss as if to seal their bond.

Ella thought she might die, might melt away and slide out of his arms into a puddle of desire. She could not speak.

After the kiss, neither could he.

They sat again, but this time, next to each other in silence, holding hands tightly, looking out to sea, each lost in their own thoughts and emotions. Every once in a while, she'd glance at him; he'd clutch her hand, bringing it to his lips to kiss.

Finally, Ella, having let her feelings calm down and sort out, reverted to her practical self. "Daniel, that kiss was amazing, but let's not make more of it than what it was—a great kiss after a couple glasses of wine and a day in the sun."

Instead of arguing, he let it go. "Okay, fine by me. But, hey, I'm starving. What do you say we get some dinner?"

Ella, who had been expecting a rebuttal, was so shocked her mouth dropped open. "Ah, yeah, sure. Fine. Okay. Dinner. Good."

He got up, and she followed him to the kitchen, her heart trailing behind.

He had gotten Chinese takeout earlier, just in case they ended up there, and warmed it in the microwave. "Sorry. I'm just not up to cooking a dinner from scratch."

"That's fine. Chinese is good. It's been a long day. Let's just eat."

"Why don't you go grab that bottle of wine from the deck?"

She brought it back to the kitchen and refilled their glasses. He lifted his to toast and said, "Here's to us. Whether you're afraid of it or not or whatever you're feeling about it, there is now officially an 'us', so here's to us." He touched his glass to hers. She stood dumbfounded. The buzzer on the microwave screeched, breaking her trance.

Nervous, in a shaky voice, Ella said, "I think the food is done."

Daniel put his glass down and then the cartons of food on the counter. He took her hand.

The feel of him was like the sun bursting through her body. She didn't know how this could be, but there it was.

He sensed everything she was feeling. His eyes filled with and reflected to her the deep, warm yearning he saw. In one swooping motion, while staring into her eyes, he slid the cartons off the end of the counter and into the open trash bin.

Before she could ask what he was doing, he said, "I don't want Chinese food."

Even more nervous now about what would come next, she said, "That's fine. What *do* you want?"

"You. All I want is you."

She put her glass on the table next to his and finally met his eyes. "That's fine, too."

They smiled in unison, big, fat, joyful, knowing smiles, and he led her to the sofa.

"What are you doing? Where are we going?"

"I want to lie down here with you and do nothing but have you next to me, your whole body." He lay down and pulled her next to him.

Relieved he didn't take her to the bedroom, she slid close to him.

"Kissing you is pretty amazing stuff," he said, smiling. "I don't think I could handle any more. More than this is not even appropriate right now, not with a woman like you."

Ella was so flattered and refreshed by him. A true gentleman. She didn't think there were any left in the world. She nuzzled up against him, and he held her tight. "Yes, it was amazing. And so is this, so are you."

"Nah," he said, "I'm really not. I just happen to be totally, completely *into* you, into everything about you. I'm not like this with every woman I date or kiss. Usually that first kiss tells me a lot. If it's not good, with no deeper connection, then that's it for me. I don't see her again."

"Amazing. You really are different. Your parents brought you up right."

"Yeah, there's that and also the 'good karma/bad karma' philosophy I believe in; it keeps me on the straight and narrow. When you do the potentially dangerous kind of work I do, you have to have your wits about you all the time, intuition sharp, brain clear. I can't have my head muddied up with crap like, *Did I lead her on? Will she pursue me? Is she expecting me to call? Did I hurt her? I don't want to hurt her*, on and on. It can really screw you up. So I keep things very simple, honest, and straightforward with women."

"I see. So is that what you're doing with me?"

He rolled on his side, hugged her tightly into his chest to face him, and flattened his whole body up against hers. "Oh, I already did it with you. I already checked you out on my spiritual gauge."

"Really. And where do I fall?"

"Off the charts. On the good end, the spectacular end of the spectrum. I believe you're my good karma coming in for me, and me for you. That's how I can be so sure, so direct. Because I know. My razor-sharp internal radar picked you up, and you're locked onto my sights."

"So I have no choice about this, about you?"

"Oh, you always have a choice. Just don't make the wrong one."

"I wish it were that clear and straightforward for me. My intuition says the same about you, but it doesn't mean I have to follow through. I don't see choices as wrong or right. I see them as acting in my best interest with the facts at hand."

"There's truth in that reasoning. It just doesn't take into account one very critical thing in the decision-making process."

"And I'm sure you're about to enlighten me with what it is?"

Laughing, he cuddled her. "It doesn't take into account…love."

Ella was speechless. Did he just say *love*? He did. Men almost never offer that; they aren't the first ones to bring it up; they avoid it like the plague. It's always the woman who speaks of it first—the dreaded "L" word for a guy, at least, the guys she'd known since Peter. Oh, God, Peter, another horror story.

As if reading her mind, Daniel sat up, taking her

with him. With his gorgeous smile, he calmed her and said, "Your wheels are spinning like crazy. I can practically hear your brain working overtime. You're adorable and even predictable in your wacky compulsiveness."

Even she had to laugh.

Taking her hand, he said, "Don't let a word scare you. It's just a word. The important thing is how we treat each other. And I didn't say it as in '*I* love.' I said, 'Love is something to be taken into consideration when making a decision.'"

Ella couldn't believe how wise he was or how relieved she was.

Daniel stood. "I think we've had enough for tonight, don't you? What do you say to getting a couple sandwiches and cold beers. Then I'll take you back to your cottage for some rest? We've got tomorrow, okay?"

He was wise *and* practical. During these last few days, she'd begun to realize he was truly a gem, a rare, beautiful stone unearthed from the depths of male humanity. And he'd found his way to her. Ella's head still spun with his mentioning the "L" word. In her prior experience and with her fears rearing up at the potential this relationship had, another dreaded "L" word came to mind as it always had in the past at this stage...*Leaving* ...and she'd have to explain it to him soon.

Chapter 10

Daniel had taken Ella back to the cottage and left her at the door with another sultry kiss. Walking into the cottage, the goodness of the kiss faded, giving way to the inevitable fear of getting too close to him. While brushing her teeth, she glanced in the mirror and swore she saw her mother, just for a fleeting moment, reinforcing the warnings she'd gotten, a sign that she needed to let go of Daniel. At their next meeting, she would have to explain the *leaving* part to him, even though it would kill her to do so. This was what she hadn't wanted—for their relationship to go so far that he'd be hurt. But she had no recourse. It had already gone too far.

The next morning, Ella slept later than usual and was yanked out of sleep by the blaring sound of the blender running in the kitchen. She dressed quickly and found Janie whipping up some concoction. "What the heck are you doing in here?"

"Don't worry—no margaritas—I'm actually whipping eggs for omelets," Janie said with a pleased grin on her face. "And I've got a protein shake on the table, if you'd like to share it. It's late and I figured you must've had one heck of a night with Daniel. I have to hear all about it."

Sighing deeply, Ella rolled her eyes. "Do I really have to get into it with you, too?"

"What do you mean by 'with me, too'? Did something happen with you guys?" Pointing a wooden spoon at Ella's face, she accused, "You didn't break it off with him, did you?"

"No, I didn't, but I'm going to."

"You can't do that! Talk to me. What happened? The last we talked he was the perfect guy and you were getting your head straightened out."

"I got *somewhat* straightened out, but not totally. I told him all about it, and he completely understood. He was so empathetic and compassionate, I even let him kiss me."

Janie had been cooking the omelet, and she whirled around as fast as the widow's head had snapped at Ella long ago, and threw the spoon on the counter. "You buried the lead! He kissed you? That's great! But of course, in your world, this is the reason to leave him, right? Please don't tell me that."

Grabbing a chair for support, Ella sat, shrugged, and looked solemnly at Janie while taking a swig of the shake and spoke no words.

Janie knew this was the answer she didn't want to hear. "Unbelievable. You are just unbelievable, Ella. Most women would kill for a guy like him, and you're throwing him away. I *know* you are not that messed up. There is something else going on with you, and dammit, you better tell me because Daniel could be your last chance at happiness, and I'm not going to let you throw it away for the ridiculous excuse of *fear*."

All the events of the last few days coalesced inside Ella's heart, bringing it to near bursting, and she broke down in tears, hiding them with her head in her hands.

Janie hugged her. "I didn't mean it, Ella. I'm sorry.

Please stop crying. I can't stand to know I hurt you." She handed Ella a tissue.

Ella couldn't stop crying, letting all the pain out, embarrassed she was doing it and blurted out, "It's not you. You didn't hurt me." She sobbed even more.

Janie helplessly looked on, feeling useless, not knowing how to console her friend. "Well, I'm sorry about the comment of using fear as an excuse." She wiped her hands on her apron. "I guess you really are pretty messed up, after all."

Hearing that, Ella's sobs turned to laughter.

Relieved, Janie knelt in front of her. "Good, good, keep laughing. That's good medicine. But you know what? I know something better." She stood and raced around the kitchen, opening cabinets and the fridge, dumping the smoothie in the sink, and pouring vodka in the blender with tomato juice.

Ella's mouth dropped open as her eyes darted all over the room, following Janie. "You madwoman, what the heck are you doing?"

"I'm not the madwoman. You are, remember?"

Ella burst into laughter again. "Well, you dumped my protein shake. Now what are you concocting in that blender? Are you going to freeze drinks for tonight?"

"Heck no. I'm making Bloody Marys for right-the-hell now."

"Drinks for breakfast?" Ella asked, looking shocked and concerned. "That's even a bit much for you, isn't it?

"You're seriously asking *me* that? Besides, technically it's time for brunch. *Plus* we're on vacation. Plus, after what you've been through the last couple days, you could use something to bring you in off that ledge."

"You're terrible. I'm okay, just shaken up. Everything built up and the damn burst. Sorry about that. I hate getting so upset."

Janie put hot sauce and a stick of celery in the drink and sat it in front of Ella like a prize. "Here, this is a beautiful, therapeutic drink. Lots of good stuff in that tomato juice, and it'll calm you down." She sat across the table from Ella with her own drink. "I'm sorry. I didn't mean to be harsh with you."

"It's okay. Most of what you said is true."

"Take a long draw of that strong drink. You need to loosen up and start talking. We have to get to the bottom of this. I just keep thinking about the potential with Daniel, and I hate to see you walk away from someone who could be the love of your life, you know…could be *the one*. The way I see it, the *other* Ella is kicking in and calling the shots here. The distrustful, fearful one who's so afraid of some ridiculous curse and losing someone to the God-forsaken sea.

"And of course, the man of your dreams, the perfect man, would have to be a sailor." She took a couple swallows of her drink. "And he's a fighter pilot, to boot. Double the danger. It's the universe testing you, you know, throwing everything good at you with your worst fear factors thrown in to see how you'll react, if you'll have enough guts and good sense to rise above the fear and take what's being given to you. On a silver platter, I might add."

"Again, you're partly right. But all these dreams and messages and spirits are getting stronger, especially after learning the truth about my early life. I don't understand what all this means, how the pieces fit together, and I'm worried they won't stop until something bad happens, because they're linked to my past losses and will directly affect my future."

"Damn these spirits and messages and dreams. Have they ever helped your life? Seems, to me, all they do is hinder you, hold you back from living, from loving. How the heck do you know the difference between them and fear?"

Janie's words riled Ella to defend herself. She was angrier than she'd ever been with her friend and tired of Janie thinking her past issues were all in her head to be gotten over with new information and a simple attitude adjustment. "How do *I* really know the difference? I'll tell you how, if you'll keep quiet about this forever and stop challenging me all the time. I'll tell you what *really* happened to me after high school. And college. And just last night. Then maybe you'll have a better idea of what it's like to be me and walk in my shoes."

Taken aback and a little offended, Janie still wanted to hear more. "Great. Terrific. Can't wait. Obviously, this will take more than talking over brunch. I'll call Eric and cancel our date. You and I can take the whole day to talk—if you want to. Do you?"

"Yes, I really do want to put this to rest for good. I've had it."

"Okay. I'm all ears, but you better call Fly Boy and let him know you're mine today."

****

Ella wore a big straw hat and a long, strapless beach sarong, while Janie donned a no-nonsense visor, short shorts, and tube top with sun block head-to-toe as they walked along the shore for over an hour. Ella, in attempting to explain herself to Janie, hoped to gain better insight at the same time.

"I never told you the real reason Peter and I split up, or about the guy before Peter."

"There was someone before Peter? Someone serious?"

"Yes. His name was Billy. I really loved him. He was my first real boyfriend in high school. In our senior year, we started arguing over me going to college and him staying in Portland to work as a mechanic in his father's garage. I thought he could do better; he was smart and could go to college. The arguing was because I loved him and wanted the best for him. His father drank and was abusive. But Billy worried about leaving his mother with that awful man.

That summer was hot and dry, and his father drank heavily and became more violent. Billy and his mother had taken one too many beatings. His mother fled to the Midwest to live with her sister, but not before making Billy promise to get out of there any way he could. So in an act of desperation, he joined the Navy to escape, to have his way out paid for, and to get as far as he could from Maine and his father. He showed up at my door and said he was so sorry; he loved me, but he had to get out from under.

Within a week, he was gone to basic training, then, sometime after that, shipped out to sea. I went on to college. We wrote, or I should say I wrote a lot, but he stopped after a few months, fearing a future was impossible for us, given the different paths our lives were on. He wouldn't give me his cell phone number, so I kept writing him regularly for a year, not wanting to lose him. I loved him that much. But the sea loved him more and kept him. Eventually he never wrote back, he never called, he never returned. I worried constantly there'd been an accident and he'd died. I hoped he was still alive and safe. To this day, I don't know what happened to him. It crushed me."

"Man, that's so sad. But you did get over it because there were more guys after him, including Peter. And you and Peter broke up amicably, right? So how does that translate into why you can't love someone now?"

They had brought along a small cooler with water and snacks. Ella drank from a bottle of water and said she wished they had brought those Bloody Marys.

"Uh-oh," Janie said. "That means another awful story must be coming on. You *are* going to tell me what *really* happened with Peter, aren't you?"

"Let's sit for a while under this palm tree. I need to cool off, drink this, and yes, I'll tell you the real story, only in the hope that you will, once and for all, forget this notion of me walking off into the sunset with someone, and nothing bad will happen to a love interest again.

"After losing Billy like that, when I met Peter, it was a big risk emotionally, but I went for it. I overcame my fear, just like you keep telling me I have to do now. I decided to have faith that no worse things could happen because I'd already had a lifetime's worth of bad things. Isn't it true that lightning never strikes the same place twice? Well, the lightning in my life had already hit twice, so the odds of it striking a third time were astronomical. This gave me confidence to love and be loved and have hope for a future that included a husband and a family."

****

Peter's Story

"Senior year in college, I spent a semester abroad in Spain in an exchange program. It felt like home to me, as familiar as if I'd grown up there. I loved it: the people and culture, the land and architecture, the traditions and food. I loved everything about it.

"Peter was faculty, an advisor in the program, and wasn't supposed to date students. But our attraction was immediate on every level. The connection was so strong we ignored the rules and had a whirlwind romance for eight months, fell madly in love, and made plans to go back to the States. He would give up the exchange program and teach full-time. I'd finish senior year, and we'd marry after I graduated. I even accepted an engagement ring I couldn't wear because we couldn't tell anyone about it. I didn't want to risk his job until he took a new position and I was no longer a student.

"So everything we did together had to be under the radar, in secrecy, and in out-of-the-way places at out-of-the-way times. I didn't like sneaking around and knew he'd lose his job if we were found out. But I was young and so in love and had never been happier. I felt, finally, the strange dreams would go away; the widow wouldn't have to visit anymore.

"About a month before we were scheduled to go home, I did have another odd dream. My conscience had been nagging at me, and I was worried, thinking this was too good to be true, so I waited for the other shoe to drop. One night as I slept alone, aching for Peter, not knowing how I'd be able to hold out for another month, I had this weird dream sequence as I was waking, in that twilight space, still half-asleep, where truth glares out of your subconscious like the dawn. I saw lots of pictures and people, many children.

"In this dream, there was a man that was familiar. As I got closer to him, I realized I loved him, but he wasn't my husband. The place was Spain. I was wealthy, but for some reason, I had to lie, sneak, and pretend to be something I wasn't. And the man was so good. I couldn't resist him, although there was something forbidden about him. But he loved me to the same degree I did him, maybe even more.

We met one night in a dark underground room lit only by candles. The room was filled with our love for each other, but we didn't embrace, or even touch. We looked at each other from afar. There were evil people lurking in the shadows. We were terrified. Even so, he hid children from these awful men. And even though we knew he was doing something good, I was heartbroken beyond pain, almost to death because there was some kind of deceit and betrayal affecting our choices—not intentional, but necessary for survival. Next, I was standing on a hillside watching from afar as a ship with him on it made its way to open sea.

"I woke fully then, devastated with the heartache of not knowing what happened to this man, but feeling an immeasurable sense of loss. I carried it with me for the next month.

Peter thought it was just because of my guilt about having to hide our relationship and sneaking around, lying to friends. He said not to worry about it. True, it was very similar to our circumstances at the time, but it wasn't real; it had been just a dream.

"But for me it was a waking nightmare, and when Peter and I would get together and talk about our future, about being married, having a home and children, something would eat away at me. I wasn't sure if I wanted children. I had some irrational fear of losing them, and him. I couldn't bear it. Peter would laugh it off. 'Just wait till we get back home to the States,' he'd said, 'and start our future; you'll see all of this was silly.'

"A week before we were to leave to go home, there was one last sail for the students. Peter was a good sailor and taught the class, so he had to take the last sailing trip. But I didn't go because I had a lot to do to prepare for the trip back home."

Janie got a horrified look on her face. "Oh, no! Don't tell me. Please don't tell me something happened to Peter."

With tears welling, tears Ella thought were long dried up and gone, she whispered, "You should feel lucky. All you have to do is hear about it. I had to live it."

"Oh, my God. What happened?"

"I had a horrible feeling as I watched Peter and four students get into that sailboat and go off into the harbor. It was windy, late in the day, and the sun was setting. The kids were drinking and celebrating. The wind began to pick up with strong gusts, and the waves grew high and choppy. Peter didn't drink, but the rest of them did, so they weren't much help in handling the boat. Long story short—Peter was single-handedly trying to get the boat to come about to return to port. The boom swung violently with a strong gust, hit a student, and flung him overboard. The others ran to the side of the boat to jump in and save him. The uneven weight, along with the strong wind and a huge wave, capsized the boat, trapping them underneath. Only one student survived to tell about it." Ella choked up with retelling the truth about Peter.

Janie reached over and held her friend. "Ella, how awful for you. I'm so sorry. I'm sorry for every word of doubt and sarcasm. I had no idea."

"It's okay. You couldn't have known."

"Because you didn't tell me. If you had opened up about this stuff a long time ago, it would've saved a lot of torment. Jeez, I'm so sorry."

"No apologies, please. But you can see how deep this fear or curse goes with me, along with the dreams that coincide with actual events, and now finding out the truth about my parents, my father lost at sea." Ella looked at Janie, worried and fearful. "Honestly, I wonder if it will drive me stark-raving mad. And then to meet someone as wonderful as Daniel and be carrying all this horrible baggage and not wanting to get him involved."

"I get it. I totally get it. I see your hesitancy, your wanting to run to keep ahead and away from any more horrific events, more loss. But, Ella, don't you think maybe now it really *is* over? Maybe Peter was the last of the losses?"

Ella then told her about the dream of ancient Greece and how it had felt so real it could've been a previous lifetime, one where this all started, and about the recent warning Daniel got that was almost exactly similar to the warning she'd gotten from her mother with a portent of more loss to come.

Janie's eyes widened. "It's really hard for me to wrap my head around this. I don't know how you live with these, for lack of a better word, *supernatural* events all the time. This is the stuff weird movies are made of. It doesn't happen in real life."

"Well, it does to people like me and Daniel."

Clapping her hands together, Janie said, "I just realized something! It happens to you guys because you and Daniel are so alike; you're cut from the same mold. You're both unique in your shared extrasensory thing most of us don't have, at least not to the degree you do. So, if any two people can beat this, you can! I think you should ignore every last awful, negative thing in your past. Imagine it as having been written on a chalkboard and now take an eraser and wipe it all away. It's time to write a new story and what better way to begin again than with an incredible connection and love."

"Love? You're using the 'L' word, too? I never said I loved him."

Janie smiled a coy, knowing smile. "Daniel said it, didn't he?"

Ella looked down at her empty water bottle. Exasperated that she let it slip, she acknowledged, "Yes, yes…he said it. But not as in 'I love you.' He used it in reference to us, to something that should be a factor in making a life-changing decision."

Jumping up, Janie did a little happy dance. "Well, hallelujah for Daniel. That guy's got it all together, I'm tellin' ya. Good for him. He's right. A thousand percent right. There's nothing more important than love. If it's been dropped in your lap, you gotta go for it. Be brave. Take a risk. Look at the risks Daniel takes in flying fighter jets and protecting our country. You admire his courage. Well, give him something to admire in you, too. Be courageous and give him *all* of yourself to love, not just the stuff on the surface. I know I'm being redundant, but I'm right—just take it a day at a time—lose the fear, love the man, and see what happens."

Chapter 11

After baring her soul to Janie, Ella was still not sure what to do, but had more hope with Janie's encouragement. Janie had said the same thing Daniel did: *To take their relationship a day at a time*. Maybe it was a sign, an affirmation of something going in the right direction. Maybe they were right.

Janie had gone out with Eric, and Ella had called Daniel, who was ecstatic to hear she'd like to have dinner with him. Dinner led to the next day of lounging on the beach, touring around town, and good food and drink. The day after that, they got together with Janie and Eric, rented jet skis, and had a great time jetting around the harbor. All were exhausted after a day of sun, then drinks, and a seafood dinner. Ella and Janie asked the men to come back to their cottage for a nightcap, ending the day on a high note.

Both men wanted to linger, but both women were exhausted physically and emotionally, and politely said so. Besides, some girl talk was necessary. After Daniel and Eric left, Janie didn't hesitate to ask what she really wanted to know.

"I have to ask you this."

Ella knew what was coming and prepared her answer.

"Have you slept with Daniel? You know, I mean as in *sex*?"

"I know what you mean." Ella swirled her brandy in the bottom of the snifter. Feeling warm and completely satiated, answering truthfully, "Nope. Not yet."

"Whoa. That means you're planning on it, though?"

"You know better than that. I don't plan on anything. I'm doing what you advised, taking it a day at a time. So, what about you and Eric?"

Janie grinned. "No. But I want to, real bad. He's holding back, I can tell. He doesn't want to rush it. But I say, hey, we're only here another week, so why wait?"

"So Eric, for you, is a vacation fling?"

"Pretty much. We talked about it. We both like to party and have a good time, but other than that our interests are not the same. He's an artist and has some paintings in galleries here and there but just kind of scrapes by. So, we do share the artistic thing. But he's happy to stay here forever and really doesn't want anything beyond it. He takes the Jimmy Buffet stuff way too seriously, a true *live a day at a time* kinda guy, which makes for a memorable vacation, but beyond that, he's not what I ultimately want in a relationship."

"Well, at least you both agree, right?"

"Oh, he'd like for me to stay, but I was very clear about my intentions. So, we agreed to just have a great time while I'm here. I'm hoping to get him into bed at his place tomorrow—don't think it'll take much convincing." She winked at Ella. "So what about you and Daniel? I see how you look at each other, how you touch and kiss. This looks to be a match made in heaven, pardon the cliché, but it's nothing like I've ever seen before, especially for you. What's the deal with no physical intimacy?"

"You know my issues. I'm still trying to sort them out. The one-day-at-a-time thing works as long as I don't let myself get too close."

"But you already *are* close. You're in denial about that. Is your fear the main problem?"

"He's a real gentleman. He doesn't want to push me or himself, for that matter. But it's getting to the point where the kissing and hugging are escalating, and I don't know how much longer I can hold out."

"Making love doesn't mean you're automatically committed long-term. Just do it. It'll feel great. You'll be better off for the experience."

"Until the next day."

"Screw the next day. If it feels good and right, do it. Girl, I'd have been all over that guy the first or second night. You're nuts. The man's done and said everything right to let you know he's falling in love with you. Just go for it."

"He and I both believe things happen when they're supposed to. The right time hasn't presented itself yet."

"Well, then, present yourself, honey, in all your glory. And it'll be the right time very quickly." Janie laughed, half in a stupor. "I've had a lot to drink and gotta hit the sack before I fall over." She waved good night and stumbled into her room.

Ella lingered on the patio with the last of her brandy. The ocean was calm. The full moon cast its glistening shadow onto the sea, captivating her as she mused, *How unbelievable for light from the sun hundreds of thousands of miles away to reflect off the moon. Then, that same light travels all the way to earth and illuminates the entire ocean on the darkest night. If you never saw it for yourself and someone told you about it, you wouldn't believe it. Miracles and magic of all kinds happen in this world every day but are ignored, overlooked, or just accepted as commonplace.*

Maybe it was time to finally accept the magic and miracle of Daniel coming into her life out of nowhere and finding his way to her. Maybe it was time to accept it, take a chance, and learn firsthand what love could be like with someone as remarkable as him. Janie was right—intimacy, and even love, could be a day-at-a-time commitment. *Maybe I should give it a try.*

****

The next night, Daniel had told her earlier he'd had a special evening planned, and to dress up. He walked up to her door and was about to knock when Ella, who'd been watching by the window, opened it. Standing in front of him, she looked like a Grecian goddess, tanned and svelte in a brilliant turquoise silk dress. It had a halter top with a deep V-neck, fitted at the waist, flowing into soft folds down to her sandaled feet. She'd put her hair up in a loose knot with softly curled tendrils falling around her face, and she'd pinned a white hibiscus flower behind her ear.

Daniel kissed her delicately so as not to disturb the vision in front of him, stunned by it and intoxicated with the scent of her perfume. "Are you real? Is this really happening?"

Immensely flattered, she whispered, "Yes. And I feel the same way about you." He was in his summer dress whites, setting off his deep tan with those intense green eyes transfixed on her. More handsome than any man she'd ever seen, he was a rare combination of pure, raw masculinity and a genuinely good soul with an open mind and heart. She grabbed the lapels on his shirt and gently tugged him toward her. He slid his arms around her waist and kissed her gently on the lips, then once on the neck, whispering in her ear, "This is going to be some night." And she agreed.

They drove to a beautiful hotel on the ocean where he'd reserved one of the best tables. The night was filled with outrageously great views—of the ocean and each other, great conversation, amazing food, and a bottle of expensive champagne.

Daniel wooed Ella onto the dance floor where the music was slow and the dancing sultry. As he held her in his arms and they floated around the room, Ella knew her life would never get better than this, better than this place, better than Daniel.

With their evening coming to an end, she suggested they finish it with a walk on the beach. Surprisingly, Daniel said no. He had no interest in the beach tonight, he'd said; his only interest was in her, in his "Ella Bella," his new nickname meaning "Beautiful Ella," reflecting his growing affection and admiration for her. Then, without asking, he took her hand, walked her to the car, and drove to his place.

She asked no questions and barely spoke. They both knew what was ahead. It was inevitable, not just because of the strong connection and the deepening relationship, or the over-the-top evening, but because it was something more powerful than either of their personal desires. It seemed their destiny was truly upon them.

****

Once inside his condo, Daniel did not hesitate or ask. He picked her up and carried her to the bedroom.

Stripping each other's clothes off between deep kisses, they fell into bed passionately, as if having waited for this a hundred years. Their bodies fit together easily, as naturally as if they'd been made from the same mold—both slender and strong with long legs and eager hearts, anxious to fulfill a long-awaited destiny. His hands moving over her skin bathed her body in heat, like coming in from the cold to a lovely, warm room—their passion a great fire, bringing her to a fever that only he could break, healing and sending her into another world—a safe, golden place they'd been to before. They made love urgently, then tenderly, almost in disbelief of this new reality. Their passion exploded, moving them into another world—into an ancient place of living—familiar, golden, a place born of love to sustain them forever. There was no death here, only time eternal with love as the way back.

In between kisses, they whispered things in a language only they knew, soft voices coming from the other end of time, reassuring them this was right, this was not new, it was old; it was them finding each other again. They made love through the night, as if on this one night they had to share enough love to last a lifetime. Almost desperately consuming the other, they clung to the idea that this act was a gift they needed to respect, so they'd never lose it.

Ella had no room left in her heart for doubt or fear. The bedroom, the house, the island, her entire world had suddenly turned safe and good, and the good overcame the bad, and it seemed the odds were finally in her favor, at least, on this night, and this one night was all she had to give. She even whispered to him as they fell asleep, "One day at a time, right?"

Daniel, drifting off into the ethers, said, "Whatever you say, my Ella Bella, whatever you want."

****

Morning came too soon, trumpeting through the dark bedroom with such glory they couldn't help but wake. They lay naked in each other's arms until the sun rose all the way, exposing every raw nerve Ella had. Their night had been otherworldly in its intensity, but now was time to face reality. Satiated, having had every need fulfilled and then some, she approached the real day with her real self. It was time to get back to the business of life and that meant Daniel would be going back to work at sea. She kissed him gently and broke free of his embrace.

"Where are you going?"

Standing, Ella pulled the bedcover up around her, leaving him with only the sheet. She did a double-take, seeing him clearly in daylight. *My God, he's an Adonis.* But she shook her head, hoping to shake off his image so as not to carry it with her, not with having to move on with her life. "I'm starving. Aren't you? Do you have anything I can make us for breakfast?"

"No." He grabbed her arm and tried to pull her back into bed. "I'm still hungry for you, though."

She got away from him, laughing, and said, "C'mon. I'm serious. Too much champagne last night. I need to eat before I faint."

"Just fall this way." He tried to pull her into bed again.

"Oh, forget it." She rounded up her clothes and headed into the bathroom.

He ran his hands through his hair and over his face in exasperation. *Guess I couldn't expect more*, he thought. *At least, she's not running for the door.* He resigned himself to the fact that Ella was Ella, what he knew of her anyway, which was a lot given she didn't share her deepest self easily. The night had been the best of his life. He was ecstatic, thinking that what had been coming at him was her, and refused to think any warning could be attached to it. He threw on a pair of shorts and went to the kitchen to make breakfast.

By the time she'd showered and dressed, he'd set the table with fresh fruit, croissants, and juice, and was scrambling eggs. She was thrilled and dug in.

"That's my girl. Eat up."

Ella shot him an odd look.

"What?" he said. "You're not my girl? After last night? Are you kidding me?"

Relishing the nourishment, she acquiesced. "Last night was amazing. *You* are amazing. But we've each got our own lives to go back to eventually. Speaking of which, you never mentioned how long you'd be staying in Key West."

Daniel set two plates of eggs on the table. "Madam, for you."

"Thank you. This looks great." Eating heartily, she continued questioning. "So how long are you here? It's been over a week already, and I would guess you're going back to your ship soon."

"Not too soon. I took a short leave and have more than another week of fun in the sun. How about you?"

"I'm here another week, too."

"This is great! Now we have all this time we can spend together."

"Oh. Well, I guess so."

"You don't sound too enthused. What's up?"

"Well, I just thought I'd have time to do some research on jobs, which I haven't gotten to do yet."

Enjoying his food immensely, he hardly gave her statement a thought. "What is it, a story you're working on?"

"No." She figured she'd better tell him sooner rather than later. "Now please, if I share this with you, don't tell Janie. She doesn't know yet."

"Fine. You have my word." He grew slightly concerned, with a red warning flag going up in his brain. "Continue."

She saluted him. "Aye, aye, sir."

"Sorry. Occupational hazard. I meant continue, please, with this secret, yet another one."

Ella laughed, hoping to lighten the meaning of the message she was about to deliver. "I am actually looking for a new job and thought I'd take this time away from the office to be able to research new cities and line up some prospects."

"New cities?" He got excited, envisioning the possibilities. "Ever think about Virginia? It's a terrific place to live. And the Norfolk area is on the coast. Just beautiful. You'd love it. Would you consider it?"

"Not in a million years have I ever thought of Virginia. And why Norfolk?"

He looked up at her, grinning. "It's a vibrant, thriving city, right on the ocean. Lots to do. But mostly because my home port is Norfolk. That would be convenient for us now that we're, you know, a couple."

"Convenient? Really? For whom?"

"For us. Remember *us*, last night? If we lived closer together, we could see each other a lot more."

Ella put down her fork. "I remember. But I have a

career, too. I was actually thinking of relocating to the West. Maybe Colorado or Arizona. There are a lot of job opportunities there, and they're great places to live."

Daniel looked at his plate. "Except for one thing. I'm not there. I'm not even close." He thought for a moment, then sadness filled his eyes. "There are no naval bases or ships or sailors in the middle of the desert or the Rocky Mountains."

"Daniel, this has been great fun with you, but remember, you said we could take it a day at a time? I need to move forward with my life."

"You and I meeting the way we did, the kismet, the similarities, our powerful feelings for each other, our parallel destinies—what about all that? Do they mean nothing? To continue growing an already solid, one-of-a-kind relationship *is* moving forward in life."

"For you, but not for me."

"Why not for you?"

Ella picked up her plate so forcefully the silverware slid off. She walked to the sink and threw the plate in it with her back to him.

Daniel followed her and held her from behind with his chin on her shoulder. "I asked you a question."

Ella turned around to face him and took his arms off her waist. "Because you're making plans for the future. That's not living for the day. I can't do this with you. Maybe not with anyone. I'm scared, terrified actually, after what I've been through with other men in my life."

"I'm not going to let you run away from something that could be the best thing in our lives."

"You can't stop me."

Daniel moved away from her, sat at the counter, and put his head in his hands. "No, Ella, I can't stop you. But I can plead with you and try to make you understand. I can listen and talk and try to help you figure this out, this inordinate fear you have."

"It's not inordinate, and not a matter of just talking. It's what I've lived through and what I can deal with. I've lost so much love and so many people to this, this…" She threw her hands up in the air. "I don't even know how to explain it. Just yesterday, I learned about my mother dying of heartbreak over losing my father at sea. Then I have this dream where she told me, somehow, her loss and pain were mine, with more to come—that's a great omen, huh?

"I'm seeing clearly how all of these things dovetail with real events and people in my life. I can't wrap my mind around it, yet it hangs over me like a black portent for the future, like bad karma—I *know* you get that. I've lived with this my whole life. And the only way I've survived is to keep moving and changing and not getting attached to any one thing, place, or person. That way, I can't hurt anyone and vice versa."

Tears welled up as she continued. "I've been in Tampa for five years now, and the dreams and visits are getting stronger, like they're catching up with me or like a pre-determined fate is coming in quickly. And now there's this amazing experience with you. I just don't want to get you caught up in a black widow's spider web, in this curse that still follows me. You're too good for that. I care about you too much to expose you to this. So it's time to move on."

Much to her surprise, Daniel appeared very calm. "Ella, this could be very simple. Instead of changing your whole life around because of all these things that you really don't understand anyway, why don't you just change your mind? Change your mind and rearrange it to embrace the things you understand and let go of the ones you don't. Use the things you call '*being haunted*' as gifts, as unique experiences that can benefit your life. And throw out the notion of a curse, like the garbage that it is—no such thing. Think about it that way and, poof, it's gone. And fear? Fear is only a way to make you say 'no,' to keep you from loving and life."

She was truly amazed at his insight and good common sense. Here she was, going off the deep end, and he seemed to have the ability to bring her back from the edge, to calm her down. That was a first. And she even thought he might be right. But it wasn't just a matter of changing her mind. There was the matter of the work he did, the danger he faced every day, and the fact that he did all of it at sea. She explained this to him. Even if she changed her mind, she couldn't change his vocation, and that was the biggest problem.

He poured two mugs of coffee, and they went out to sit on the deck, hoping the expanse of sea and sky would expand her mind and clear her head. "I have to report back to my home base in Norfolk. That's my job. But I'm not walking out of your life, unless you want me to." He took her face in his hands and looked deeply into her eyes. "Ella, do you want me out of your life? Honestly?"

She turned away from him to look out over the ocean and felt herself seeing through her mother's eyes, walking the widow's walk, her mother's pain searing Ella's own heart. Crying softly, she spoke her truth. "How could I *not* want someone like you in my life, someone who *gets* me, and still likes me, who even thinks my wacko life is cool, and gets all this weird stuff that most people run from. We are very similar; we were drawn to each other. I don't deny any of it. I'd like to keep seeing you, to have you in my life; I'd be crazy not to. I just don't know how to, not with what could happen. There's no predicting it; it's too risky."

"Honey, life is risky. But we still have to live it. So why not live it every day as best as you can, with the people you care about most, who make you happy? Do you think being around me and involved with me in a long-term relationship would make you happy?"

She turned to him and threw her arms around him, squeezed him tightly, and cried into his neck. "Yes, yes. You have made me happier in this last week, in just last night, than I've been in my entire life. But therein lies the problem. I don't want to end up like my mother warned, walking a metaphorical widow's walk, waiting constantly for you to come back from the sea, worrying if you went missing. I'd die if anything happened to you. I couldn't bear it."

"Shhh…shhh…" He cradled her head gently. "I'm not going anywhere, at least, not for another week. Let's take this time and spend it together. Let's talk more about this, flesh it out. Even though I understand what you went through and are still going through, I think this fear of losing me is a little irrational. Let's try to get to the bottom of it, and maybe you can change your mind. Maybe it's not as bad as you think."

Ella was worn down by the events of the morning and the night before, the talking, the lovemaking, the memories flooding her psyche, eating up her heart, leaving nothing to give Daniel. He deserved better. He deserved the truth. He'd worn her down, not with battering, but with kindness and compassion and a genuine desire to help her. He didn't know she had already *been to the bottom* of the problem, been there and back so many times, and the result was always the same. Hannah always said time healed and mended the broken heart. But Ella's heart never had. She didn't think it ever would. But if there was ever a time, a place, or a chance, it was probably right here with him.

Ella came back with, "You think my issues are not as bad as I make them out to be? Why don't I let you decide for yourself? For the first time in my life, I shared these stories with Janie just a few days ago. So I guess I'm up to sharing them with you. If you think you want to pursue a relationship with me, then you deserve to know the whole truth. Maybe then, you'll understand. Maybe it'll change your mind about the kinds of bad things that can happen to a man who loves Ella Rowe." Looking intensely at him, trying to gauge his inner recesses, hoping he might back down so she wouldn't have to relive these parts of her life again, she was surprised when he didn't even flinch.

"I think you know I don't back down from danger in any way. You need to make me understand what is making *you* back down from love when I know, in your heart, you don't really want to. That means you need to start talking."

"I'm so worn out, and this could take a while."

"We've got a full pot of coffee and seven more days. Do you think that's enough?"

"It might take another pot of coffee or two."

They laughed, and he leaned over and kissed her sweetly. "No more avoiding the issues. I'll bring the whole pot out here. Make yourself comfortable."

****

Ella proceeded to tell Daniel of all the deaths—of what had happened with Billy, then Peter, and her dreams and recollections of other places and times in life, in Greece and in Spain, where she'd sensed losses and deaths to the sea that coincided with her present life. Together, with her father's death at sea, the valid fear was growing that some kind of bad karma or curse was attached to her and would follow her forever.

Daniel got up from his chair, pulled her to her feet, and hugged her. "You don't have to go on. I'm so sorry for everything and everyone you lost. I understand now. I completely understand your fears and dilemmas."

Ella cried softly. "Do you see why I can't move forward with this relationship? I can't trust again, only to be dealt another devastating blow. I don't think I could survive another."

He held her by the shoulders away from him and looked solemnly at her. "And here you are with me, whose career holds the risk of dying. I've always been hesitant to get involved with anybody, given the inherent risks of my job. Probably my worst fault is that my career comes first. But there's something different this time, about you, about you and me together. There's something so connected, like we're already family, like we knew each other a long time ago and we're finally reunited."

He drew her close and held her. She responded with a tight hold around his back and buried her face into his neck, feeling his pulse beat there. His scent of soap and salty air transported her back in time as Daniel spoke: "I feel like I've lost you before, and I cannot—

absolutely in any way or form—lose you again, not to fear, not to anything or anyone." He squeezed her, as if to force every ounce of love to her surface. "Do you feel that? When we're together like this or making love, I almost feel no boundaries between us. Do you feel it, too?"

"Yes, I do. That's what scares me so much. If I were to let this grow, what would it be when it's even more powerful than it is right now?"

Daniel felt a slight pang of fear shoot through him as well with that thought, having never felt this way before. It was new territory for him, too. And then there was his own karma—the memory of dying at sea, many times, and leaving the love of his life. These issues were so similar to Ella's losses; they seemed directly connected. Not a good portent, like she'd said. But he did what he was trained to do, as if loving Ella was like flying the jet or engaging in aerial combat—he squelched the memory and the fear; he forced the negative feelings aside and canceled them out in his mind, then focused only on the positive outcome. "Our relationship will be magnificent. It will be even more unusual and extraordinary. I promise you, we will have an exceptional life. Together."

Ella sighed heavily. "Oh, God. Don't you get it? If I lost you, I'd lose myself, too. I'd never come back, never recover. It scares the hell out of me." She drew away. "I don't know how to go on from here."

"This is what you can do." He took her face in his hands and kissed her, pouring love all through her. She responded and lost herself in him again. He whispered between kisses. "You can accept this gift of life, of love, of God, whatever you want to call it. Say these words: I accept this love with gratitude and won't give it up. I'll live it a day at a time. And I will be fine. I will be better for it, no matter what the future brings."

Ella, melting in his arms, repeated the words aloud to him, and even believed them, especially when she saw joy spread across his face. But when she heard his next words, she believed him forever: "Ella, these are our vows. I promise, with a love as strong as ours, we will never be apart. When I leave on a ship to fly jets, I promise I will always come back to you. In one way or another, I will come back. In time, all ships must return to port. Ella, you are my home port."

In that moment, his words were truer than any she'd ever heard. But with eyes closed, her spirit lifted into another realm and through the potent energy passing between them, she detected a whisper. As had happened before, it did not emanate from her brain like a thought; it came from outside herself and drifted in. Just as she knew the light from a star took a thousand years to reach her eyes, she sensed this message was spoken long ago in some ancient time and had just reached her ear on this day. It was the familiar voice of a man who had loved her, and when he'd held her, he smelled of the salt air and the sea, and he had said, *I promise I will come back to you.*

She heard the words now, but her lover in that ancient time had never returned. And now the loss of him drifted back through time as well—it still had a home in her heart, a grief so deep and pervasive it would never leave. The pain was not just felt; it'd been imprinted on her, like a brand on the soul, marking her for life and obviously beyond it. There was no getting over that kind of pain. If she tried explaining it to

Daniel, he wouldn't understand; he'd argue his case and rationalize because he loved her.

Picking up on her feelings, Daniel knew it was time to share the story of what truly happened the night they met. "You can't let your fear make you walk away from me, from our relationship. It's not possible. It won't work. We were destined to meet, and it was inevitable we'd be together."

"What makes you so sure of that?"

"I didn't tell you this before because I knew it would scare you to death and you'd never see me again. But I knew there'd be the right time to tell you, and this is it. Before you came into the Sailors Rest that first night, I'd been playing pool in the back room like I told you. But what I didn't say was that I was overcome by this feeling of my fate waiting for me at the door somehow." He then told her about his conversation with his friend right before Ella walked in, how he'd said, *I'll know who this woman is. I believe I'll know her for the rest of my life*. "So, you see, there's no running away from this."

Ella shook her head and couldn't help but giggle. "The weird part you didn't know at the time was that Janie and I had been arguing over who was going to walk in first. If Janie had come in first, you'd be with her right now."

Daniel laughed. "Sorry. It doesn't work that way. There was no way whatever you believe orchestrates our destinies would've let that happen. I'm curious how it worked out for you to take her place."

"Basically, we argued over whether to go in at all. She'd had second thoughts, but I got frustrated, knew we should go in, and finally just grabbed the handle and walked in first."

"See? All of your interactions and actions were guided by something, a feeling, intuition. Something led you to walk into the door first. And when I saw you, I knew my premonition had been right on. And I didn't waste any time introducing myself, did I?"

"No, sir, and you've got the best intuition I've ever seen."

"You have, too, but there's a big difference between us when it comes to that."

"Really? Enlighten me."

"I have no fear. I'm a wide-open conduit for whatever is sent my way. I think it's why I'm a good pilot. But you, your fears shut you down much of the time."

"Not all the time, but I guess I do shut down out of fear. Just like I'm feeling now. Your super intuition scares me. It's like you've got my life all planned out to be with you, and frankly, I want to run away, quickly."

"I don't have everything planned out. I believe in free will and exercising it. Our choices determine our future. So, no, I don't know what the future will bring. All I can do is be completely honest with you and true to myself about my feelings. If you do the same thing, there's no way we can go wrong, there are no bad decisions and no fear."

"All *I* can do is try," she said. "No guarantees. A day at a time, right?"

"Oh, all right, if that's the best I'm gonna get out of you, I'll take it." Daniel feigned a frustrated look, but then he kissed her with all the love in his heart, sealing their promise and their fate.

Chapter 12

Ella and Daniel spent every day and night together. Everything about them meshed with such ease and comfort. Ella felt as though her previous life had been a giant, unsolvable jigsaw puzzle, and here she and Daniel were—the last two pieces, the only match left, fitting together perfectly to complete the puzzle and her life.

Their last night in Key West came too fast. After a day at the beach, they lounged at his condo, sipping champagne on the deck overlooking the ocean. Daniel tried to hide his sadness at leaving her, but Ella felt it, and oddly, maybe to counterbalance him, she remained upbeat. She thought reviewing the high points of their falling in love would help him refocus on something positive.

With them almost finishing the bottle of champagne, Ella's mood was giddy and lighthearted. "Hey," she said with a mischievous look in her eyes. "Do you remember the night we met and that terrible pickup line you gave me about knowing me in a past life?"

Daniel laughed. "How could I forget? Man, did you give me a hard time about that."

She rubbed his arm lovingly. "True, I did. But you were so adorable, trying to explain yourself."

"I didn't feel adorable. I thought I was blowing it

with you, until you came clean with your ruse."

Leaning back in her chair, looking over the water and her memories of that first night, she grew thoughtful. "Yeah. That was fun. But, seriously, I just realized something. We were always so busy dealing with *my* past that we never talked about *yours*, as in past lives. With you being such a believer, you must have some sense of yours, don't you?"

Looking uncomfortable, Daniel said, "I have."

"Well, don't keep me in suspense."

"Honestly, I don't feel comfortable sharing it."

Ella belly-laughed. "You're kidding, right? After what I went through to bare my soul to you? And now you can't even relay a couple of stories to me?"

"I've always kept them to myself because I feel they're really nobody's business but mine."

Indignant, Ella shot back, "So I'm just another nobody?"

He looked at her with love. "You know you're everything to me. It's just that I did have flashes of old memories when we first met, and again, when you told me of your losses, I thought it best not to bring mine up."

"So you never said a word, and still won't. What I overcame to deal with my fears, to allow myself to love you and be with you, and now you won't do the same. Something about your logic isn't right, and it's not who you are, or at least, who I thought you were. Maybe I've been wrong about you. How can I love someone who won't share something so fundamental to his belief system?"

"Don't talk like that. We love each other deeply, and you *do* know me. It's just that this memory has caused problems and heartache when I shared it with someone a long time ago, and with you, it's much more potent than with her. I didn't want to risk losing you over it because it's not important enough."

"It's important to me. I can't have a relationship with someone who is hiding something, treating me like a fragile child who can't handle the truth."

He took her hand. "I don't think of you that way. But you're right about hiding it, and I guess I always knew this had to come up eventually." Daniel ran his hands through his hair, exasperated, not able to form words. His eyes pleaded with her for understanding. "You can't let this affect our relationship."

"If you can't tell me, then there *is* no relationship."

He took a long drink, hoping to relax and lighten his burden. "That's exactly why I didn't bring up the subject of my past lives. Because I thought it would make it a self-fulfilling prophecy, that you would never see me again. I didn't want to risk it, and I still don't."

Ella's eyes searched his. "But if you don't, this relationship is over anyway."

With his head down, defeated, he said, "It'll never be over, not really."

"What do you mean? If I walk away and never see you again, it's over."

"What I mean is that I think our life paths are so interconnected, if you walk away, you'll only have to repeat the process again in the future or in another life until you fix what was wrong, correct the mistakes of the past. There's no walking away from karma. So, I'll say this to you like you did to me when you were trying to push me away—if you really want the truth, here it is." Daniel's eyes, intense as laser beams, stared deeply into hers to make sure she understood every word.

"The recollection I have of past lives is vague, but seems very similar to yours, and your present-day losses. I don't have details of time and place, but my strongest memory, felt in my body as well as my mind, is of dying at sea many times, and the memory in my heart is of leaving behind someone I loved deeply."

Ella pushed her drink off the table, leaned toward him, and gave him a look he'd never seen before, of anger and terror, of dread and betrayal. "What bullshit!"

He jerked back with a pained look on his face as if she'd shot him. "Ella, what the hell are you talking about?"

"You. You're so full of it."

"Full of bullshit? Are you serious?"

"Dead serious. There's that word again—dead—which, because of its implications and your lying, I don't even want to be sitting here with you, let alone see you in the future." She stood, knocking over the chair, and walked to the railing, grabbing it to steady herself.

Daniel was shocked and deeply insulted but forced himself to calm down. "Ella, please, just tell me what's going on in your mind."

She swept her arm out in front of her. "This beautiful, hateful, murderous sea and its curse. If you are in my life, you are subject to it. Your own memories confirm it, so you've sealed our fate. You should've shared this in the very beginning and saved us a lot of trouble and heartache. I can't be with you knowing this; I can't risk you dying because of me."

Now Daniel stood and tossed his chair out of his way, fire in his eyes. He walked to the railing to face her. "That's not how it works, dammit! If I die, it's not because of you. Don't you get that? My life path is mine alone. If I let this old memory control me and direct my life, I'd never have chosen to be a fighter pilot for the Navy. I'd have led a safe, insulated life never going into or near the sea that I love, that is so much a part of my life, my vital being. I'd have lived as an unhappy, unfulfilled, fearful person. Living like that is *not* life, not for me.

"And with the way karma works, if I'm meant to die at sea, I *will*, no matter how or with whom I choose to live my life. It has *nothing* to do with you, Ella. And that's why I didn't want to tell you, to play into your fears and losses and give you one more very large reason not to love me, when I know for certain that you love me."

They stood apart, stunned, looking over the water, calming down and gaining perspective. "The sad thing is, Ella, you've chosen the insulated, safe life, trying to outrun your fears and loss, squirreling away from the world, from love and happiness. And what happened? People you loved died anyway. Did you learn anything or change your life? No. Until me. With me, you are going in the right direction, correcting the past mistakes, conquering your fears, loving and trying to have a good, happy life. But with your reaction just now, I don't know what direction you're going in next."

Speechless, Ella turned completely away from him, unable to look into his eyes.

Daniel, waving his arm out over the vista, mimicking her gesture, said, "In this ocean, I see beauty, majesty, and life because I choose to. If you want to see it as ugly, cursed, and death, that's your choice. If you want to walk away from me, from us and what we could have, that's also your choice. And by doing that, you don't affect *my* fate—you're choosing your own. And it doesn't look very happy or pretty from where I stand. If you want to choose a life that is a living death, go right ahead. But I'm not on board with that. Sorry." Without so much as a glance at her, he calmly turned and walked back inside the condo.

Dumbstruck, Ella heard his words, followed his logic, even agreed with him as hard a pill as it was to swallow, then watched him turn his back on her and walk away. He was right, about all of it. Her initial feelings were justified, but now she felt petty and small. With watching Daniel walk away, she knew he was at the point of walking out of her life completely. Even heroes have their limits, and she'd pushed him to his.

Through the glass door, she watched him sit on a barstool, his back to her, and lean his elbows on the counter to hold his head in his hands. She'd never seen him this upset and didn't know what to do, so she stood still and watched for his next move. After a couple minutes, he swung around to look at her. Their eyes locked, and he held his arms out wide to his sides, as if to send her a message. Was he exasperated, frustrated, fed up with her? Of course he was, but there was something underneath the obvious. She tried to intuit his thoughts…*What are you trying to tell me? Come to me? What do we do now? How do we go on from here?*

No, she realized, *he's asking me if this is the end, the end of us.*

Chapter 13

Without thinking twice, as if the answer was not a conscious choice, but was a part of her heart, Ella knew she didn't want to lose him. Love drew her to him as it had from the beginning, not a schoolgirl crush or a flimsy love based on superficial things. Their love was palpable, a bond that had substance and a life of its own. Ella knew she'd walk up to him and tell him so, and tell him she wouldn't walk away. But she'd also have to say she didn't know quite how to go on from that point, and she was still afraid of what the future could potentially hold for them.

Daniel, relieved, gratefully took her back, wrapping his arms and legs around her as he sat on the barstool, wanting to meld into her and never let go. "Don't be afraid. Nobody knows the future. Fate brought us together, but what we do now is up to us. And I will keep my promise to always come back to you, no matter where my job or life takes me." Kissing her, he poured soul-deep love into her, and felt the love reach her where her fear hid.

Her heart couldn't help but respond. With the power of the kiss, she believed his words, just like the ancient whisper had found its way to her ear. She recalled something Hannah had said in regard to love: *When you listen with your heart, you hear what God is trying to tell you.* With a heart full of love, the message to Ella became loud and clear—love Daniel right now, and leave tomorrow to fate.

"Tomorrow," he said, "we go back to our own lives, but only temporarily, because nothing will come between us, not geography, not even the past."

****

Separating in Key West had been hard, but back in their respective homes, they video-chatted regularly and emailed almost every day, and both were busy with their careers. Ella still explored jobs and relocation out west, wanting to have a backup plan, still not completely sure she would be able to have a long-term relationship with him, given his last revelation and their seemingly ill-fated past. He sensed her hesitation and knew she still looked into relocating, but he believed in consistency and the power of love and a positive attitude, then actually lived it by reaffirming his feelings about her, life, fate, and that he'd always be there for her.

Norfolk was only an hour-and-a-half flight away from Tampa, so he flew to see her as often as she'd let him visit. They'd met in Virginia Beach a couple times, and occasionally in places centrally located between them. Gradually, their visits became more frequent, as often as he could get away.

Janie and Ella worked together on stories almost every day and wound down with drinks regularly after work. Janie was Daniel's biggest supporter, and whenever the conversation came around to him, Janie also consistently said only positive things and alleviated Ella's fears. She bribed people with favors into covering for Ella several times, so she could take more time off to visit Daniel. Truly believing he was the right guy for Ella, maybe the *only* guy for her, Janie never said a negative word or put up with Ella's fears; she just wouldn't hear any of them, and she encouraged Ella to talk only about all the good things in their relationship. After a while, because her best friend never wavered in her belief that this was the love of a lifetime, Ella began to feel the same way, almost by osmosis.

With spending more and more time together over almost another year, Ella realized that, with seeing Daniel regularly and loving him deeply, nothing terrible had happened. Her visions and dreams subsided as love grew between them, and she felt that maybe, just maybe the curse had been broken and her life was turning around. Her fear returned, though, when she knew he was on board a ship or flying over the ocean. She hid from him that her fear never really went away. It lingered in the recesses of her heart and played out in nightmares.

Like Daniel advised, she tried to take each day as it came, grateful for him being safe. But she didn't trust fate the way he did. In her low moments, she'd recall his words that had reverberated through her soul and stung so deeply she'd never stop feeling them. *"If I'm meant to die at sea, I will, no matter how or with whom I choose to live my life."* He'd said it had nothing to do with her, but she knew part of his fate had everything to do with her, and she guessed he knew it, too. This was the one belief they never spoke of in their time together.

Gradually, Daniel had finally won her over with love and consistency, and by not dying. This kind of love was new for Ella, and it turned out to be very healing in so many ways. She felt it singing through her life, buoying it and giving it meaning as never before.

Giving up the job search out west, she admitted she really liked her work in Tampa at the newspaper, and the life she and Daniel were carving out together, more each day. So, the following June, when Daniel suggested they do something special to celebrate the one-year anniversary of their meeting—to go back to Key West in July for a two-week stay—she didn't hesitate to agree.

But after thinking about it, an alarm bell went off. There was something odd about him suggesting a long July vacation when there were other important dates coming up. "We really didn't meet until September," she reminded him. "Why don't we meet then for a long weekend to celebrate our anniversary? Then we could save the two-week vacation to go to Key West in December for the holidays. I've heard it's beautiful around Christmas. What do you think?"

Daniel was quiet, not ready with an answer, not expecting what she'd proposed, and Ella sensed it immediately.

"What's wrong?"

"Nothing, really. It's just one of my gut feelings. I don't know. My intuition is just telling me we need to meet in July while there's still time."

A red flag went up in her brain again. "Still time? What do you mean?"

Hearing the alarm in her voice, Daniel took her hand to reassure her. "I didn't mean it in the way that something's wrong. It's purely my intuition telling me to take a nice summer trip in July when I know for sure I can get leave. We can always go back to Key West for the holidays if it works out—two trips, instead of one. Besides, I have a surprise for you, and I don't want to wait until September."

"Really? What kind of surprise is it that can't wait?"

"Well, if I told you…"

"I know, I know, it wouldn't be a surprise. I guess you have me hostage, and I'll have to agree to a July trip."

"We're in agreement then?"

"Yup. I trust your intuition completely. You make the plans; just tell me where and when."

"Thank you for understanding. You've made me a very happy guy."

Ella's intuition was just as keen, though, and gave her a different signal. Even though he said how happy he was, he didn't completely act it. There was something going on under the smiling face in his psyche, suppressing his enthusiasm. Hoping it was a passing thing, she let it go, and looked forward to their time in Key West in another month.

****

The last week of July, Ella and Daniel flew to Miami, then made the drive to Key West. He'd rented a convertible, and they drove most of the way with the top down, stopping to eat and browse local shops. Ella felt free-spirited and full of love, the warm wind in her hair, sun on her face, and the love of her life next to her, driving to an island paradise for a long vacation. Recalling the last time she'd driven there with Janie and the panic she'd felt—the odd sensation of flying over the water—she wondered now if she hadn't been picking up on a psychic clue coming at her then, of destiny about to meet her, challenge her, and change life for good. But looking over at Daniel driving now, she felt safer and more loved than ever. Only the slightest pang of doubt lingered regarding his wanting to take this trip now and his subdued response to her idea for the holidays. Refusing to let it interfere with this trip, though, she stuffed it down to the bottom of her internal closet. It was one move from life before Daniel that she still used.

****

They had two weeks of pure rest and relaxation ahead. *Idyllic* was the word that came to Ella's mind in the first week. They stayed in the same condo Daniel had when they met, went to the same places, including the Sailors Rest, and relived lots of great memories. They spent hours at the beach, sunning, swimming, sailing, talking, and laughing. Their nights were filled with great food and drink, oceanside walks under the stars, love and lust, with no talk of the future.

But at the end of the first week, Daniel turned pensive at times, quieter than usual, not really present with her, seemingly having other thoughts swirling in the back of his mind.

Upon asking him what was wrong, at first, he said *nothing*, but looking into Ella's eyes, he couldn't help but speak the truth.

"I can't hide anything from you, can I?" he said.

They were on the deck, having a glass of wine before dinner.

"No. And you better get used to it."

He laughed and agreed. "But this is hard to talk about because there's nothing specific, no hard facts, just gut feelings. There are some unsettling things in the airwaves, things I have no control over."

"Like what?"

"My intuition is going at me pretty good about not planning too far ahead. I don't know why. And some Navy business I can't talk about." He ran his hand through his hair, distressed, then stood, took a sip of wine, and looked out over the ocean. "I'm just concerned."

"Is it about your work or something else?"

"Things going on in the world are concerning, which could also affect my duties. But hopefully things will settle down in North Korea. I'm more upset because I think we have to change our plans for Christmas."

Getting worried, she stood and leaned on the railing next to him. "You mean to come here for the holiday?"

"Yeah. And I might not be able to get away at all."

"For Christmas?" Her face filled with shock. "I know time off is never guaranteed in the service, but you said you've always been able to take time off at Christmas, even if just a long weekend. Why would that change now?"

He finally looked at her, serious and sad. "All I can tell you for sure is that I may not be able to get leave then. And it's mostly just gut feelings at this point. But you know how seriously I take my intuition. I'm so sorry, Ella, to let you think it was possible and now to have to rescind it."

"It's okay. I'm more concerned about you and what might happen."

"Nothing's going to happen. It's all hunches. Ignore me. I'm so transparent sometimes. Forget it. Hey, it's July 30th, almost one month shy of our one-year anniversary. What do you say we start celebrating now?"

"Sounds good to me."

"By the way, I have that surprise for you. Close your eyes."

She knew he was avoiding the issue she was worried about, but there was nothing she could do to deter him. So she let him lead her into the living room. Then he left for a minute and came back with a huge bouquet of tropical flowers. They were gorgeous, but she seemed a little disappointed. "This is the big surprise?"

Laughing, he said, "I hid them in the closet since this morning. I think they need water." He reached for a crystal vase he'd bought and hid in a cabinet. "Here, this should do."

"Well, that sure is one beautiful vase, too. You just happen to have that lying around a rented condo?" Suspicious, she took the vase and flowers to the sink, still wondering where the big surprise was. Untying the ribbon from around the flowers, they tumbled apart and something small but heavy fell from the bundle, onto the edge of the counter, then to the floor. It was a black velvet box. "What's that?"

Smiling like a Cheshire cat, he answered, "Don't know. Maybe you should open it and find out."

Cracking the lid just a bit, she saw a ring. A gorgeous, huge, diamond ring. Shocked and trembling, she said, "What is this?"

Daniel took the ring out the box. "What does it look like?"

"Oh, God, a diamond ring. Is this…does this mean…" She fumbled her words, not knowing what to say, hoping he would say something.

He twirled the ring to make it catch the light, and it sparkled brilliantly. "Do you like it?"

"It's the most beautiful ring I've ever seen."

"I'm glad, because I'm hoping you'll wear it. Like for the rest of your life."

Ella threw her arms around him, tears rising. "I can't believe this."

"Believe it." He squeezed her tightly for a few moments, then took her left arm from around his back, held her hand in front of him, and slid the ring on her finger. It fit perfectly, as did his words. "Please say you'll be my partner for life, my Ella Bella. Say you'll be my beautiful wife."

Her first reaction was shock, then extreme joy, and she almost blurted out, "Yes!" But with him putting the ring on her finger, her memory flashed back to Peter, to the ring he'd given her and how happy and eager she'd been then to be his wife. His tragic death resurfaced. Combined with her lingering suspicions about Daniel's work-related future and his past life issues, an overpowering dread descended over her, suppressing the joy and halting her answer, all of which showed in her eyes.

Daniel sensed it immediately. "Babe? You didn't answer, and you look like something's wrong. What is it?"

Looking down at the ring to avert his eyes, she twisted it nervously. "This is so unexpected. I'm just not sure."

"Not sure? About marrying me?"

Hearing shock in his voice, she looked up and saw deep hurt in his eyes. She couldn't bear being the cause of his pain, but she had a heart full of her own. "I certainly love you. It's not that."

"Then what is it? It's your past, right? Losing your father and Billy and Peter, right? And my past memory that freaked you out so badly last year. God, Ella, when are you going to get over all of that and move on with your own life, with us?"

"I'm trying, I really am. I thought I was doing a pretty good job. You are the most enduring, serious relationship I've had, and I'm so happy in it. But we always said we'd take it a day at a time, and now you're asking me for the rest of my life. I wanted to say yes, but when you put the ring on my finger, I immediately flashed back to Peter and the loss overpowered me. Honestly, that memory combined with your vague answers about what's going on in your work possibly affecting our lives…well, every fear button was pressed. I can't control it. I can't change my history, and I can't magically convert it into something positive like you seem to think is so easy. It's part of the fabric I'm made of. In loving you, it's been buried way down deep and pretty much gone, but then something like this happens to stir it up and, well, here I am, making a mess of things again."

The words were painful enough, but feeling all the emotion with them dissolved her to tears. Deep in her soul, she felt she'd let him down. She wasn't good enough; she couldn't do this. What scared her most, though, was losing him for good. With almost losing him a year ago, and with all the anguish swirling inside her, the one thing she knew for sure was that she did not want to lose Daniel.

He took her in his arms and rocked her gently to the rhythmic ocean sounds filling the room. She wept openly, awash with the pain of yet another beginning dying in its birth, another ending she didn't want to happen. Ella wished the sea could swell up into their lives and sweep the past away, as if it were tiny shells on the shore, casting the losses into a vast, fathomless void.

"I get it. I really do." Daniel held her at arm's length, so she'd have to look at him. "If I were an accountant or a businessman or a house painter, you would've said yes immediately. Wouldn't you?"

Amazed, she answered, "Why, yes. You know, I never thought about it that way. But I think you're right."

"It's my work at sea and my past memories of something awful happening that trigger your deepest fears. I understand. And I just threw another cause for concern at you right before I asked you to marry me. That was pretty thoughtless of me. Dumb. Clueless, really."

Ella laughed. "You? Clueless? That's a first. However, it is true in this instance, and very gallant of you to admit."

"I'm so sorry," he said, hugging her. "But if you can forget about that unnecessary conversation about my work like it never happened, and I ask you again, would your answer be different? Do you need time to think about it? I can't change my line of work. When duty calls, I have to go. I know you love me. I accept your history and your fears. But can you stuff them far enough down in that closet in your heart, or wipe them clean off your memory bank, so you can make a good, clear choice, then give me your best, *honest* answer?"

Ella sat down at the counter and rested her arms on

it, holding her left hand up to look at the ring on her finger. Glancing toward Daniel, she saw him scrutinizing her, filled with anticipation, hope, and mostly, limitless love. How could she resist him? It was almost like *he* was a force of nature sweeping into her life, with only goodness. She took a minute to think it through. *I'm well accustomed to squelching those fears and stuffing them down for reasons far less important than the decision facing me now. I love him, and if I want to spend my life with him, it's something I'll have to live with. I have two choices: to have a love-filled life with Daniel, along with the fear of losing him, or, to spend my life alone, loveless, and still be haunted by the losses of the past.* When she thought about it that way, the choice was clear.

"I love you more than life. How can I let you go? I'll just have to live with the downsides. Life is full of them, right?"

Daniel's smile and joy filled the room. "Yes! Right! You're so courageous. I'm so proud of you and can't wait to have you as my wife. I think I know what you're going to say, but I'm gonna make you say it. I want to hear it."

Ella returned his brilliant smile. "I say yes. Yes, I will marry you."

He picked her up, swung her around, and whispered in her ear as he carried her to the bedroom, "Only God knows how much I love you. I thank God, fate, destiny, all of it—for you coming into my life. And thank you, Ella, for loving me."

"There's only one way to respond to that. Make love to me."

He kissed her all over, like a starving man finding

food, taking her in and devouring her.

Ella took him into herself as she had no other man. This love they shared blurred the boundaries of reality, of bodies and spirits. She lost herself in him completely, not being able to feel where she ended and he began. With the heat and scent of flowers and salt air, the roar of the ocean crashing to shore, the world became a place of magic with only one room, one body, one love, and this one night that would be theirs forever.

Afterward, both ecstatic and hungry, they ate dinner on the beach and spent the rest of the night planning their future, talking of a wedding and a home and careers in places he might be stationed. But when they talked about children and family, her heart sank. She shook the feeling off that night, but it plagued her into the next day and night, into her sleep where dreams had a way of bringing fears out of the subconscious into her waking life. Confused about this feeling of deep sadness regarding children and family, for the first time in a year, Ella dreamt of her mother, who took her back to Spain to shed light on her distress.

In the dream, Ella found herself in the dark underground room in Spain that she'd dreamt of before when she'd loved Peter. Even though softly lit by candlelight, soul-deep loneliness consumed her as she watched children she'd come to love run from the room, away from her. She knew they ran to safety and had to let them go. But she was left alone, feeling undeserving of them. Despite logic and reason and knowing they had to go, she was left with a hole in her heart with loved ones leaving, of what could have been a wonderful future, dying before her eyes. The candles went out; the walls became wet with grief and tears, and all hope was lost.

Coming out of the dream in a panic, Ella woke suddenly, waking Daniel, who asked if she was all right. She gasped. "No. Something is terribly wrong. Something is going to happen."

"What do you mean?" Daniel was still groggy and didn't believe her, saying it was just a bad dream.

"It wasn't just a dream. It was one of those premonitions, where my mother's spirit shows me things." She cried softly, covering her face.

"It's okay," he said.

"No, it's not. You don't understand. There won't be any children. They're gone. Everything's gone. The future is like a dark cave underground, and all the light has gone out, and there's nothing more. I feel like something really bad is going to happen."

Daniel held her close, stroked her head, and kissed her. "Nothing bad is going to happen. You're here with me. We're engaged. The future looks bright. It's only your fear coming to the surface. That's all. You'll beat this down. You have a good life ahead, Ella Rowe. Now lie with me and let's sleep peacefully."

But even as he reassured and uplifted her, he felt his spirit sinking a little with fear creeping into his mind. This was unusual for him, which made it all the more valid. Was it just Ella's fears seeping into him, or was there really something to this curse of hers, this premonition she'd just had? If his own intuition hadn't concurred with it, he wouldn't have thought anything of it. But his gut told him something *was* wrong. Even after the last year filled with happiness and love, something finally *was* coming at him; he sensed his destiny coming up to meet him, and it had nothing, yet everything, to do with Ella. Their fate was now a shared one. But he'd have to hide his ominous feelings, especially with the next surprise he had for her.

Somewhat comforted by his presence, she slid down next to him, cradled in his arms and tried to let her fear dissipate, replacing it with his love. It worked for a while, but she couldn't sleep the rest of the night for fear of what a new dream might bring.

After the rough night, they slept late, and over brunch Daniel announced he had another surprise.

"You're kidding. What could be better than this?" she said as she admired the ring on her finger.

"Well, it's not better than that, or us, but it's still going to make you happy. Anticipating your answer to my proposal would be *yes*, I thought you'd like to share the good news and celebrate with your best friend. So, a few weeks ago, I invited Janie to join us and spend a long weekend to help us celebrate, except I didn't tell her about the ring. I didn't trust her not to tell you."

Ella laughed. "Good call. Seriously though, you really invited her down?"

"She's flying in around five o'clock. Just in time for cocktails. You know Janie."

Ella got up and hugged him fiercely. "You are the best! I can't believe this. It's too good to be true. *You're* too good to be true."

****

That day was full of activity as they prepared for Janie's arrival. Daniel couldn't wait to give her the good news of their engagement, but agreed to let Ella be the one to tell her.

When Janie walked through the door that

afternoon, the first thing she said was, "So…when's the wedding? And I better be the maid of honor."

"How did you know?" Ella yelled, then looked at Daniel. "How did she know?"

"I didn't say anything! She must have ESP."

Janie screamed, "I was kidding! Are you two really getting married?"

Ella flashed the ring.

"This is amazing!" Janie ran to her, almost knocking her over with a bear hug. "I'm so happy for you. So happy!"

They talked and partied late into the night, then still riding high emotionally with nervous energy filling the air, they got up early the next morning. Janie rounded up Eric, the guy she'd met and stayed in touch with over the last year, and they all headed to the beach with a cooler full of picnic food and drinks. The day was a golden one, frozen in time by its near perfection. Ella knew days like this were rare and so paid attention to every detail, soaking it all in, celebrating, not only her engagement and friends, but life itself.

Arriving back at their condo late in the afternoon, while the others showered, Daniel turned on the TV to catch up with the latest news. Within seconds, the Key West bubble burst like a bomb. The news anchor, looking distraught, was giving the latest on threats made by North Korea. It seemed every other month they tested weapons or threatened South Korea and the United States with military exercises and using nuclear bombs and missiles. But this time, it was more serious. North Korea had broken a previous agreement with the South and violated its air space, and the president warned that the United States would retaliate.

Daniel slumped into the nearest chair. This could be more than a serious threat; it could mean war. He hoped there would be no retaliatory air strikes. But he'd have to watch the unfolding of events closely. He quickly shut off the TV, not wanting the others, especially Ella, to see the story; he wanted them to have a night free of worry. But as he walked into the bedroom, he found Ella wrapped in a towel, sitting on the bed watching CNN, listening to the very story he had. She turned to face him. In the year he'd known her, he'd never seen a look on her face like that—beyond worried, her eyes filled with panic and fear.

"This is terrible. This won't mean war, will it, Daniel? Tell me this won't affect you."

He scooped her up and lay with her on the bed.

"Don't jump to conclusions. Any number of things could happen next. The world will not stand for this. All options will be used to avoid war. No country wants that. So just sit tight. Forget about it. There's nothing we can do tonight or tomorrow or the next day. Let's enjoy this wonderful time we have together and forget about the rest of the world."

She agreed but knew she couldn't completely get it out of her mind, and it would certainly interfere with any good time they'd planned.

With telling Ella to forget about it, Daniel knew he couldn't. He'd keep his concerns from the others, but his gut told him this might be it—what he'd been warned of a year ago in the cockpit. He'd met Ella soon after and knew their meeting was destined. Maybe the warning was of getting everything he wanted in a woman, in her, loving her deeply, planning a life together, then having to go off to war with the looming threat of his dying at sea.

****

But by being the ultimate host, Daniel was able to quiet those fears. He mixed up perfect martinis and cooked an elaborate dinner of lobster and steak with grilled asparagus and salad. He broke out several bottles of champagne he'd been saving for next week, but thought everyone would be better off being well-buzzed tonight. He'd seen the look on Janie's face when she heard the news. Having been in the Navy, she knew what this could mean for him—he could be deployed by aircraft carrier in as soon as a week and heading off to fly near North Korea to do only God-knew-what. The next few days would tell.

But Daniel wanted everyone to have a good time that night and enjoy each other in this beautiful place to celebrate his and Ella's engagement. They ate while watching the sunset and listening to jazz, then danced the evening away. At one point, Ella surveyed the room. Pushing down her worries, she let her heart nearly burst with joy, watching her best friend happy and having the time of her life, seeing Daniel cooking, laughing, making sure everyone was comfortable and enjoying themselves. He sensed her thoughts, turned to her, and blew a kiss across the room. An eerie feeling came over her—that she'd need to know how to catch his love coming across time and space. She'd have to know how to see it coming when he wasn't in front of her, to feel it reach her when he wasn't there.

Everyone crashed around one a.m., satiated with sun, food, and drink. Daniel had accomplished his goal, and they bid Janie and Eric good night. Facing Ella would not be easy. They both drank more than they normally would, both trying to tamp down the gnawing in their guts, to hush their voices of intuition. It mostly worked until they were alone.

He tried to get her to go to bed, but she insisted on sitting on the deck and finishing the champagne. After a good, long drink, she spoke her truth to him. "I'm a reporter. I keep up with what's going on in the world more than the average person. I know these threats could have very serious consequences for America, for all the armed forces, for you. I respect you can't talk about the details and the Navy, so I won't ask. But don't think I don't know why you wanted this trip now and not at Christmas. It means you won't be here, maybe not even in the country in December, will you?"

"I know no such thing. I told you, I didn't know this was coming. No one did. What I had was an overpowering gut feeling that something might happen to keep us apart. Remember the feeling I told you about in the cockpit last year? I think it might have something to do with what's happening now. But let's not assume anything. This could all be blown over by next week with world sanctions against North Korea. Hopefully they'll back down, and this will be old news in a month. Think positive, okay? Hopefully we'll have a Key West Christmas holiday together in December. Hope for the best, but be prepared for anything. Can you do that?"

Ella frowned, looked to the floor, and shook her head *no*.

"C'mon. This is a real part of my life, and if we're going to be married, we gotta roll with the punches. Don't think about what's going on in the world. Think about us and moving forward." He hugged her tightly and whispered, "You love me, right?"

"Yes."

"You're in this with me for the long haul?"

She hesitated, but with seeing the deep emotion in his eyes, her answer was unequivocally, "Yes."

"You're strong and sensible. You can do this. Let's just enjoy each other. Okay?"

Ella was reluctant to agree until he kissed her passionately and picked her up. "Where are you taking me?"

"Wherever I go. But right now, I see a bedroom in our future."

Feeling high on champagne and with her boundaries down, Ella couldn't help but laugh. She kicked her legs playfully, anticipating his next move, feeling lucky to be loved by him and not worrying about his next move after that and after that and into the months ahead. She'd enjoy this time and every minute she could get with him.

****

The next morning, they woke to find the president giving a press conference on the developing situation, with no definitive response, as yet, from North Korea. They all talked about it over breakfast. Daniel and Janie downplayed it, hoping to assuage the others' fears. But as they moved on with the day, worry filled all their hearts in different ways. Daniel was unusually quiet and frequently checked his email and phone, which was set on vibrate so as not to alarm everyone for incoming calls. Ella rarely let go of him when he was in the room, holding her body close to his. Janie drank a little too much, and Eric talked a lot about nothing, trying to keep everyone's minds off what their minds were really on.

Daniel had arranged for a boat tour around Key West. The sea was calm, the weather perfect. Listening to the guide talk about Key West's harbors and history distracted them for a couple hours. They next went to the Sailors Rest for drinks per Janie's request, but it didn't have the effect she'd hoped for. Despite the island music and drinks flowing, the mood was somber, especially among the sailors there. After one drink, they went to dinner at a casual place close to the condo, then ended the night there. Daniel practically forced martinis on everyone, hoping to elevate their moods. They all drank and avoided talking about the escalating military situation.

Janie asked a lot of questions about the upcoming wedding, but Ella eluded them with non-committal answers, saying it was something they'd think about planning later in the year. But Janie knew the truth. She tried to engage Ella in conversation all night, so she wouldn't turn on the news. Daniel did all he could do to keep from the TV himself, but thought more about keeping Ella happy.

Loading a tray with champagne and fresh fruit, he asked everyone to move out to the deck and watch the moonrise over the water. They all really let go then, drank a lot and enjoyed each other's company, trying to suppress all thoughts of what was going on in the world. At one point, they sat absolutely quiet, mesmerized by their surroundings. A navy-blue ocean and sky blended together at the horizon while the cool, white moon, alone in the dark void, cast her shimmering light like diamonds dancing over the sea waves. The hypnotic silence was broken by the glaring ringtone of Daniel's phone. He'd changed it to ring, so he could hear it on the boat and at the restaurant, and had forgotten to set it back to vibrate. He moved to the bedroom to take the call.

Fifteen minutes later, he emerged with a forced smile. Ella knew something was wrong and asked.

"It's okay. It's nothing. Everything's fine."

She knew it wasn't, but didn't pursue it in front of Janie and Eric. Instead, they finished off the champagne, then had brandy nightcaps. Ella wanted to blot out any thought of that call, and Daniel wanted to quell the dread filling him and so put on a happy face. He played music; Janie and Eric danced and laughed while Daniel and Ella simply watched, laughing with them and clinging to each other like they'd never let go.

Around two a.m., everyone had had enough. Janie and Eric left for his house, and Daniel took Ella to their bedroom. The room was filled with humid ocean air, then grew even thicker with their worry and denial. Ella felt woozy, knowing something wasn't real or right about this night. Her head spun from too much drink, and she wanted to just lie in bed and gather the nerve to ask him again about the call. But Daniel didn't want to talk; he only wanted to make love to her. And so the next hours were filled with only that, with unfathomable desire and love, different from usual. Daniel made love to her insatiably, like he wanted and needed enough of her to last a long time. She responded in kind, but the unsettled feeling stayed with her. She didn't want to sleep, sensing something was about to go very wrong, but by four a.m. exhaustion took over, and Ella fell into a deep slumber.

After she fell asleep, Daniel whispered, "I'm so sorry it has to be this way. But don't worry, no matter where I go, I'll always be here with you. Always." He kissed her forehead, clutching her to himself, burying his tears into her skin.

****

Ella slept like she was comatose, waking up late morning in the same position she remembered falling asleep. With one difference. She rolled over to kiss Daniel, but he was gone. A note lay on his pillow.

Panic and a soul-deep sadness filled her immediately. "What's this?" Before reading it, she knew it was bad news.

My sweet Ella,

I wish I could write more, but there is no time. I must leave unexpectedly. I had no idea this was going to happen, or I'd have told you. After you fell asleep, I got official orders to report back to Norfolk ASAP. Also under orders—unfortunately, I cannot give you, or anyone, any more information than that. You'll know more as I know it and am allowed to give details. You won't be able to reach me for a while, but I'll email and call you as soon as I can. I promise. No goodbyes.

Forgive me for not waking you, for not having the courage to face you with this. All I was capable of when I got the news was of loving you. Sharing the phone call with you would've been the worst thing to do. You were so beautiful and loving. I couldn't bear the thought of ruining the night, of hurting you, of shattering both our hearts. I couldn't do it, not after our wonderful trip, after you saying you'd marry me. I wanted to leave with those good, positive thoughts, not with a sorrowful, hurtful scene. So I must leave now, but I leave you with my ring on your finger and my promise I will return. I love you more than words can say. With all we've been through and our deep love, I feel like we're already married. In fact, I believe we are in spirit. All we need is that piece of paper, and we'll get it as soon as I return.

I'll see you soon, my Ella Bella. Stay focused on the next time we meet. The condo and car are paid for. You and Janie stay the week. Drive back to Miami as we'd planned and return the car to the same place.

My God, I can't believe this is happening, but it is. If I write more and stay any longer, I won't be able to leave. But I must go. Taxi is waiting outside; I really must go. I'm kissing you now. Feel it? Remember my love is always here right where you are, and I carry yours with me. Always.

I'll be in touch as soon as I can.

With all my love to the end of time,

Daniel

Ella clutched the note to her chest. "*No. No. No!*" Screaming those words over and over, she searched the condo thinking she'd find him somewhere. "There's no way he could be gone. Just like that? Gone? No way!"

She flung open the closet door. His duffle bag was missing. His toiletries were gone from the bathroom. Looking to the dresser, there was no wallet. No phone or keys. No clothes. Nothing left of him. She called Janie, crying and screaming into the phone long after Janie had hung up and arrived at the front door.

Janie held Ella like a fortress for her crumbling emotional state and gently rocked her through the morning, sobbing with her. There was no explaining or understanding any of it. There were no words of consolation appropriate to give. There was only the horror of *nothing* when, just eight hours ago, she'd had everything. Ella now lived in the middle of a horrid reality, and Janie knew this would become Ella's life for the foreseeable future.

They didn't stay the week. Ella was in pure agony and couldn't get out of there fast enough. She dropped the car at a local branch of the rental car company, changed her flight to leave with Janie from Key West, and they flew back to Tampa together the next day.

Phone calls to Daniel went to voice mail. Emails went unanswered. Janie tried to talk sense into Ella, reiterating he said he'd be en route to Norfolk and would get to her as soon as he could. But Ella couldn't sit and do nothing. Janie, worried for Ella's emotional state, wanted her to stay with her, at least, until Daniel got in touch. But Ella needed the comfort and security of her own house and so stayed there alone with daily visits from Janie. She went back to work Monday, a week early, just to have something to focus her mind on, other than Daniel. Her only hope was holding on to that phone call, text, or email coming in.

No communication came in the next couple of days, but Janie reminded her that Daniel was probably being deployed for something classified and would be immersed in the preparation of it. From her experience in the Navy, Janie assured Ella that if that were the case, he wouldn't be allowed to contact anyone for a certain amount of time—the military wouldn't want to risk information leaking and would not want personnel involved to get distracted from preparing for their mission. She'd told Ella, "Just think about him and what he's going through. He is completely immersed in this critical situation in every way you can imagine—physically, mentally, emotionally, intellectually, and spiritually. Flying that big fighter jet, he can't have any equivocations or thoughts of anything except his mission. So just love him, think of him with good, positive thoughts, and sit tight and wait. I have a feeling you'll hear from him soon."

Ella hugged her. "You really think so? I hope you're right. And thanks for sharing all that information. I hadn't thought of what he's dealing with. But it also gives me reason for concern."

Janie sat next to her, took her hand, and looked solemnly into her eyes. "Ella, you're my best friend, so I'm not going to b.s. you. For Daniel to get called away so unexpectedly and not be able to be in touch means it's something serious or highly classified. I heard the war stories about the first Gulf War—Desert Storm—and how events happened as quickly and much the same way as this did to Daniel. One week it was negotiations and ultimatums, and the next week we were flying over and bombing Iraq. Things can happen very quickly. You have to be brave now, for him and yourself."

Ella hugged her tightly. "Oh, God! That scares the hell out of me. I can't even think about how awful this might be."

Janie grabbed Ella's hand. "Don't go there. Don't think about the worst because it might not turn out that way. I just wanted you to be prepared for whatever happens. Focus on being strong and courageous because that's what you are. Daniel needs every bit of your love and courage now."

Calming down and thinking about Janie's words, Ella stopped trembling and said, "You're right. I have to think of him and what he needs. Thanks so much for your honesty and your support. I couldn't do this without you."

"No problem. I'm here for you. Now maybe you can get some sleep tonight."

Finally letting go of the terror, Ella felt the tension leave her body, and she said, "Yes, I think I will. I'm drained and exhausted. I'll run a hot bath and hit the bed early. And hope to hear from him tomorrow."

"Or the next day or the next," Janie added, thinking it might be more like a week. If Daniel was being shipped out, he might not be in touch until after his ship arrived at its destination. Also, she guessed that Daniel, needing to be clear-headed and unemotional, wouldn't be able to handle talking to Ella throughout this ordeal.

****

Almost two weeks went by with no word, then one morning an email came in from Daniel, and Ella nearly jumped out of her skin. She opened it, and her heart dropped to her stomach with a glance at how brief it was.

Dearest Ella,

I can't write or say anything about my situation. I'm so sorry, but I can't. All I can say is how much I love you and will keep your love close to me on my next assignment. I can give you a brief call on your cell tomorrow, again, no information, just to hear your voice and say hello and tell you how much I love you. 'Til tomorrow then, around four p.m. your time.

All my love forever,

Daniel

Overcome with joy to get a message, Ella replied immediately with:

My beautiful, brave Daniel,

I love you forever, too. Can't wait to talk tomorrow. I understand everything. Janie's been helping me to fathom what you could be going through. All I can do is comfort you with every drop of love in my heart. Four p.m. tomorrow, then.
Love you always,
Ella

****

There'd been no declaration of war, but Janie knew there must be covert actions going on behind the scenes to hopefully avert war. Ella was so happy when she told Janie about Daniel's email that Janie withheld her opinion of the imminent phone call. Her guess was that Daniel was already on an aircraft carrier in the Pacific or the Sea of Japan, waiting for orders to take off over North Korea. He'd be allowed to call just before his mission, which would most likely be that same day, given the time difference.

Daniel called as promised. Ella was so ecstatic to hear his voice; she nearly forgot the probable reason for the call. It was almost as if nothing had happened. His voice alone soothed and reassured her. At first, he apologized profusely for leaving with no warning, but Ella did not need to hear "I'm sorry." She told him she understood completely; in fact, it was probably better he left that way because it would've been worse, if not impossible to say goodbye face-to-face. Ella only wanted to know what would happen to him next, but the reality of his words drove fear like a stake through her heart: He'd been deployed and he'd reached his destination, but that was all he could say. He was sorry he couldn't say where or why, and asked her not to share anything about him at the newspaper or with friends, except for Janie. She agreed, relieved to know that he was okay. For now.

The call was brief by necessity. There were no words they could say to convey the depth of love and sorrow they felt, so he focused on the positive, as usual. “I’ll be back, Ella. Don’t worry. I will call or email again, just as soon as I’m able. We’ll just have to wait and see what happens. Hopefully this will all blow over soon.”

“I’ve heard that before,” she said tearfully.

He heard her tears. “I know you’re listening to the news speculations; it’s your job. But don’t put too much stock in what you see and hear on TV. Scaring people makes good ratings. Please just hang in there with good thoughts, with prayers, with whatever faith is within you, and mostly with believing, along with me, that I’ll be home soon.”

Ella knew he needed her to be strong for him. Despite wanting to fall apart on the phone, she loved him enough to be supportive. After all, he was the one going to God-knew-where to do God-knew-what. The least she could do was pretend to be fearless and strong and believe what he believed. And she told him so.

“I knew you’d be there for me when I needed it, Ella. And I need you now. Thank you for that and for loving me.”

She heard a slight quiver in his voice and knew he couldn’t sustain that level of emotion for long, not with having to say goodbye, then facing a dangerous mission, so she pulled every ounce of courage from her soul and spoke to him in a bright and cheerful voice. “No need for thanks. I love you. This is what love does. This next step for you is just a bump in the road, just your job, which you are so very good at—the best. You're going to be fine, and I demand that you get your lovely butt back here to me as soon as possible."

He laughed. "I needed that. And I promise I will. I have to go now. I'm not going to say goodbye. I'll just say, 'I'll see you soon, very soon.' I love you, my Ella Bella."

"I'll be waiting for you and loving you every second of every day. Remember that, and come home soon."

"Always remember that all ships eventually come back to home port. And you are my home port, Ella."

"I'll remember. Is this it? Are you going now?"

"Yes, I have to. But be still." He was quiet for a second. "I'm kissing you now." He kissed into the phone and sent his love through the airwaves to her. "Do you feel it?"

"Yes." Her heart nearly burst with love, along with holding back sadness. "Yes, I do."

"Good. I'm kissing you now and always with love. Kiss me back, love me back, then end the call with no goodbyes, not with us. We'll do it together, so there's nothing left hanging between us but love."

"I love you." She kissed into the phone. Then they hung up at the same time.

Janie had been in the kitchen, waiting. She walked into the living room where Ella was talking and saw the call had ended. "You hung up, but you didn't say goodbye?"

"No. We'll never say goodbye."

Chapter 14

Ella's life became purely one of work and sleep, while keeping a keen eye on news reports and press releases from the Pentagon. Mostly, she prayed for Daniel's safe return. There was heightened tension in the Koreas, and threats were made to retaliate against the United States and South Korean forces using nuclear weapons, there and on the U.S. mainland. Ella listened closely for reports of Navy jets flying over, being shot down, or crashing in enemy territory, of POWs but so far, nothing was made public. As activity escalated, the world held its breath, and Ella thought she'd die from not hearing from Daniel. Even though he'd said he'd be in touch as soon as he could, she continued to email him and leave voice mail messages every day.

News came later of confrontations and aerial combat. The North claimed violation of its air space and retaliated with air-to-air missiles. Allegations were denied, but fighting continued. There were casualties on the ground, and Navy jets were shot down over land and sea. Ella felt life slipping from her every time she heard or read news of "aerial combat," "aircraft crashes," and "casualties." Janie tried to calm her with reassurances that "this wasn't all-out war." But in Ella's eyes, she pictured Daniel fighting for his life somewhere in the Far East.

A month went by, and a world war had been prevented. North Korea suffered heavy losses, and through international pressure and sanctions, they finally backed down, with a truce called. Even though Ella was relieved and thankful, she still hadn't heard from Daniel. With each day, she worried more. Janie knew something was very wrong but didn't let on to her friend, hoping against hope they'd hear from Daniel when everything settled down. But Janie knew that, if he were okay, he'd have been in touch by now.

Ella begged Janie to make calls to any of her Navy contacts to get information.

"They won't tell me anything. I'm not next-of-kin," Janie said.

Ella yelled at her, "Well, neither am I! I was only his fiancée for a day before he deployed. I'm sure he didn't have a chance to or think to change his paperwork. My God, he probably still has his deceased mother as his emergency contact and next of kin. What am I going to do?"

"You have to calm down. I know it's hard. I have to be honest with you. At this point, there's got to be something wrong. I don't know why Daniel hasn't been in touch. He might be injured and in a hospital, unconscious or something, but the Navy will not give information to anyone but next of kin. And they won't make his status public until next of kin has been notified."

"But I don't think Daniel has any living relatives—he was an only child. His parents are dead; he has no uncles, aunts, or cousins. So how can I get information about him?"

"You can't. It's too soon. The Navy will try to find

his blood next of kin, no matter how remote, before they'll release information, and then I don't know how it works. Frankly, I've never heard of a situation like this."

Frantic to the point of hysteria, Ella ranted, "This is ridiculous! I'm his fiancée, and I can't find out anything about him. No one official in the Navy can tell me anything. I'm going out of my mind with not knowing. I'm going to try to find some relative of Daniel's or someone in the Navy who'll talk to me. I'll use every resource I have."

"That's good, Ella. It's good to get busy on something tangible that could help."

Ella spent the next week doing Internet searches, then futilely making calls to any Naval personnel who would talk to her. They were all so apologetic and assured her they'd release information to her after they'd notified next of kin, if there was reason to, which there might not be. Those kinds of statements gave her hope he hadn't been killed. But every day that she didn't get a call or email, her heart would break, plummeting her to the depths of depression.

For all Ella knew, even Daniel's buddies didn't know of their engagement since he hadn't asked her until just before he shipped out. She figured the Navy was probably suspicious of her motives with her being a "supposed" fiancée, yet she couldn't provide information about his family. Ella sat every night with Janie going over all the attempts she'd made and asking for ideas. "Put yourself in my place—I'm supposed to marry him, and my status with finding out about what's happened to him is no better than the general public. This is enough to make anybody crazy."

Janie lent support as best she could, but she knew more than likely the worst had happened to Daniel, and more than likely his mission had been top-secret which meant it might not be made public. This meant Ella may never find out unless she got lucky or Daniel turned up alive somehow. But this was something she'd never say to Ella because she was already at the point of losing control.

Ella couldn't focus on her work. She searched for and called every Ellsworth in the Miami phone book where he'd lived, in San Francisco where he'd been born. She looked into every person she thought might have any information about him. Unfortunately, she only knew his buddies by their first names, but Janie set her straight. "Ella, if they can't tell you about Daniel, they're certainly not going to give out information about his crew or his friends." What Janie didn't say was that, if Daniel's jet went down and he'd been killed, most likely his crew was dead as well, or Ella might have heard from someone.

After another two months went by, Ella knew something was horribly wrong, that something terrible had to have happened to him or she'd have heard from him. There were still Navy pilots missing in action, and she prayed he was one of them, that he hadn't been killed, that he was a prisoner of war, anything but dead. Ella and everyone around her never uttered the word "dead" when referring to Daniel or she'd freak out.

Never before had Ella been prone to public displays of emotion of any kind. But now she would burst into tears at work and be sent home. She'd used her vacation and sick time and was afraid she might lose her job. She cried herself to sleep every night and woke with a feeling of death pinning her to the bed, unable to get up and function.

Janie would go by Ella's condo every day and just listen, just be there for her in any way. She'd bring food, but Ella ate only the barest minimum to stay alive. A month later, Janie began sleeping at Ella's every night, not so much concerned with her not eating or sleeping, but for her mental health.

One night, Janie brought dinner and a bottle of wine to try to relax Ella enough to talk some sense into her. "Ella, I'm really worried about you."

"This is killing me. I can't wait any longer. The battle is over. Where is he? I feel like I'm going to explode or just die in my sleep from so much pain. I can't take it anymore."

"You won't do anything stupid, will you?"

"Stupid? Like what? Pick up and go to Norfolk and demand information on him? You know as well as I that I wouldn't get a foot inside the door. I'd start crying or screaming and collapse. They'd drag me off to a mental hospital or jail."

"True enough, so I'm glad to hear you wouldn't do that. But what I meant by doing something stupid is, to be so overcome with grief, you'd take too many of those tranquilizers the doctor gave you, maybe mix them with too much alcohol, not even realizing how much of both you were ingesting. You wouldn't do anything stupid like that, would you?"

"Of course not. You know me better than that."

"Actually, the Ella I'm seeing these days is not the one I know. You're really half out of your mind and hysterical every day. And I don't blame you. I'd be crazy insane if this happened to me. But as a friend, I'm concerned. That's all. I love you. I want you to be safe. So anything I can do to support you, just tell me."

Ella hugged her. "Thanks. I do appreciate you and all you're doing. Just keeping me company and listening is the best thing for me right now." They sat at the kitchen table, sipping the wine. "But there might be something you can do. Do you still know anyone from your days in the Navy you could get information from?"

Janie frowned and lowered her eyes to the table. "I hate to disappoint you, but I don't have any connections with higher-ups, having only served two years. I could make a couple calls, but I doubt I can get any more information than you can. I can't promise anything."

Hope sprang alive in Ella's heart for the first time in months. "Anything at all would help. Thank you so much."

Seeing Ella's face light up, Janie didn't have the heart to tell her she'd already tried to get information to no avail. But she promised to make a few calls anyway.

A week later brought bad news. Janie explained, "The calls I made, the people basically didn't know anything or couldn't say anything. I tried, sorry. But after I explained your situation to one guy, he leveled with me and said it was most likely not a good outcome. Daniel might have been shot down or is missing in action. They'll search a long time for his blood relatives. And if he was shot down over North Korea and still alive, or God forbid, a prisoner-of-war, it could be a very long time, if ever, that he'd be released."

Ella slumped over the table and nearly fainted. "Oh, God! Janie, don't, don't go on about this. I can't think about him being shot down, a prisoner, or dying over there. I can't take it."

Janie walked over to her and held her, crying softly. "You have to take it, Ella. You have to accept that, even if you were Daniel's legal next of kin, you might not ever know the truth of what happened to him, except for 'missing in action,' at least not for a very long time. The last guy I spoke with at naval headquarters, someone I really trust, said with no one hearing anything at all, there is the possibility that Daniel's alive, injured, possibly in a coma and uncommunicative. Then the Navy might wait for him to recover, hoping him to be conscious and coherent enough to find out if he has family or friends not officially listed. But then he levelled with me and said the flip side of that coin is to expect the worst—that he's not coming back." You had to have been thinking this, too, haven't you, Ella, after all this time?"

"Obviously, I want to believe he's alive. But as far as the alternative, I haven't just *thought about it*. I know it. My mind conjures up all kinds of horrible scenarios. I just don't know how to live with this. I try to shut it down, to hide the awful pictures in my mind, so I can survive another day. But there's nowhere to hide or run from it." Ella screamed into the void that was her life now, with a pain so deep she didn't think she'd survive. "If he's dead, I want to be where he is."

Janie moved over next to her. "Stop! Stop talking crazy. Listen. Look at me. You need to stop imagining all these things that are not real yet. It'll drive you crazy." Janie rocked the sobbing Ella in her arms. "Shhh…shhh. He could still be alive somewhere. Maybe it's like my contact said. Maybe Daniel's in a coma or has amnesia. I know for a fact this happens all the time. He could be alive somewhere. Just hold tight to the possibility he's still alive and don't think of anything beyond it."

Comforted by this sound advice, Ella quieted and said, "Okay. I can do that. I just don't know for how long."

"You will hang on for as long as you have to. That's what Daniel would want, right?"

Ella's eyes opened wide, looking surprised. "You know, through all this, I've always thought of myself and what I feel. I've never thought about what Daniel might think and what he might want me to do. Thank you for reminding me because you're absolutely right. He would want me to be strong and to not give up, to have faith, to *move on*, as he always says."

Wanting to lighten the mood, Janie interjected, "Hey! I just thought of something. How about asking that dead mother of yours for advice? Her spirit used to show up when you needed her. Where is she now? Do a séance, see a medium, do whatever works to call her in!"

She knew Janie was joking. "Yeah, right. A séance. You're too much."

"I mean it! Call Mom for help: 555-DUTD—Dial Up the Dead!"

They shared a badly-needed laugh and continued joking about it. After Janie left, Ella thought about her suggestion, but dismissed it, thinking, if her mother was still close in spirit, she'd have come to Ella long before now. Maybe that part of her life was missing in action as well.

****

Spring turned to summer with Ella holding together fairly well, keeping faith that Daniel would turn up. She gave up seeking information and reading the statistics on pilots missing in action who turned into "killed in action," not wanting to know the deadly details anymore. She tried calling every veterans hospital on both coasts, to no avail. Ella moved robotically through her days. Her work became her sole purpose in life. But when September loomed with what would've been the second anniversary of their meeting, her grief reared up again, overwhelming her like a tidal wave taking over her life. The pain resurfaced and nightmares recurred, seeing Daniel vibrant and alive, then seeing a jet crash into the sea.

Becoming more depressed as the months wore on, by Thanksgiving, she didn't want anything to do with the holidays. The previous year's holiday season had been ruined with his deployment, the uncertainty of his mission and welfare, his disappearance. And now there was the lost dream of him returning at all. Ella had to face it. A whole year had gone by. And Daniel was still gone from her world.

The second week of November brought the usual festive holiday preparations. Happy, optimistic people surrounded Ella, and she simply couldn't make it through another holiday without him. Not knowing what to do, how to feel, or how to handle the upcoming seasons of joy, peace, and hope, of which she had none, she asked Janie for advice.

In the past six months, Janie had reconnected with an old boyfriend from the Navy while making calls on Ella's behalf, and they'd fallen in love. They had recently gotten engaged, and Ella was immensely happy for her. In contrast to her own situation, she just couldn't emotionally deal with it. Janie's advice to Ella was to get away from everything for a while.

"In fact," Janie told her, "I think you ought to face the demon head on. Go back to Key West for Christmas. Just like you and Daniel had planned your first year together."

"Are you crazy? Key West? Oh, my God, no. I can't do that. I'd go off the deep end. You're supposed to be helping me here, not sending me to an asylum."

"I *am* trying to help you. I don't know how else you can move beyond this until you go there and retrace your steps, relive your memories, love him, and then let him go. I know I told you to have faith, to believe that he'd come back. But it's been so long. I hate to be blunt, but it's time someone was: more than likely Daniel will never return. The only way I see you being able to live life and not be tortured by grief is to jump in the fire, face the worst possible pain, and realize you can survive it by *letting Daniel go*—back to the sky he loved flying through, back to the sea he loved sailing on. Let him go so you—"

Ella interrupted, anger filling her words. "I know, I know, so I can *move on.* I'm so damn tired of hearing that mantra, from you and from him. I'm exhausted to the point of being nonfunctioning; I'm hurting all over physically, mentally, spiritually, and I am in agony every minute, and it's all turning into more rage than I've ever felt."

"Anger is good. Maybe it's a stage of grief in coming to terms with this. Oh, and by the way, I was *not* going to say, '*So you can move on.*' I was going to say, 'Let him go, so you *don't die from this.*' Because, from where I stand, this situation could kill you in one form or another, and I don't want to lose you. Daniel wouldn't want you to die or give up on living because of him."

Ella couldn't have been more shocked if Janie had punched her in the stomach. She felt all the air go from her lungs as reality pierced her heart. "You're right. He wouldn't want that. God, I didn't realize that's where I was headed—to the end, the end of it, of me."

"All you do is work. Your life holds no interests, no joys. You've deadened your emotions, and from what you just described of how you feel, your spirit seems about to die as well. Next comes the body. You don't look good; you don't look healthy. You don't want to die, do you?"

"No, I don't. But I don't know how to live without answers or without Daniel. And I'm just so angry, at his work, the Navy, losing him to the sea like all the others."

Janie pounded the table with her fist, eyes blazing. "And now *I'm* the one who's tired of hearing *that* mantra for years. Face it, Ella, in all things—weather, storms, land, houses, ships, lives—the sea takes what she wants and owes nothing back. She gives life and takes it. It's not personal, intentional, karma or a curse; it's just nature, how God designed it. You want to fight God, be angry with God over what the sea took from you? Go right ahead. It's your sanity. Just don't expect your friends to sit around and put up with that and watch you waste away. Face your demons, face the fact that most likely Daniel's dead, or you'll be the one to die inside your life. It's your choice."

Ella looked at Janie, stunned, disbelieving this was

her usually light-hearted, jovial friend. "I never heard you talk like that before, about nature, the sea, about God."

Janie, now calm and serious, said, "Well, when I'm desperate, I bring out the big guns."

Ella couldn't help but laugh. "You, *desperate?*"

"This is no laughing matter. And yes, I'm desperate to reach you. Hear it. Believe it. You're a basket case. Ask anyone. See a shrink, a counselor. Ask your dead mother's spirit. And this time, I'm not kidding. If you can't believe anybody here in the real world, and you have access to one beyond it, then hell, go for it. You had spiritual gifts as a kid. You didn't think twice about spirits showing up. Your mother's spirit helped you with those dreams about Billy and Peter. Maybe she can do the same with Daniel. Please, Ella, I'm begging you, do something, *any*thing."

****

Over the next few weeks, Ella went the conservative route, reading lots of self-help books while seeing a psychologist and a grief counselor. She was open to the experiences, and they'd had some good suggestions, but nothing helped her in any significant way, no more than Janie and Hannah had. Becoming more depressed and at the edge of her sanity, she thought of Janie's original advice. She called Hannah to see what her practical grandmother would recommend. To Ella's surprise, Hannah agreed with Janie.

Ella's brain flipped with anger as she yelled at Hannah, not expecting her to agree. "You, too, Gram? It's so easy for the two of you to tell me to do this unbelievably painful thing when neither of you has lost the love of your life like I have."

"Now hold on a minute, Ella Rowe. Stop your victim talk and listen to me. You think I don't know what you're going through? My husband, your grandfather, didn't die in Vietnam, but when he came home, he was so tortured with flashbacks and panic attacks he couldn't function. He was disabled from wounds; he couldn't work as he had before going to war, and eventually he suffered the effects of Agent Orange. He died in the prime of his life, sick and feeble, unable to enjoy life. I had to watch him suffer and then die when your mother was only ten years old. So don't tell me, Ella, that I don't know how you feel because I do." She held back tears. "I know all too well, and I suffer for you every moment you do with Daniel missing."

Now Ella cried softly with her. "I'm so sorry. I had no idea. You never talked about my grandfather. He'd been gone so long by the time I was born, I never even wondered about him. I thought he died of natural causes. You never said. I'm so very sorry, Gram, and I do appreciate your advice. Please, tell me what to do."

"Apologies aren't necessary. Once again, we both kept our secrets; it's nobody's fault. So if you really want my advice—there is nowhere left for you to go for information, at least, not in this world, so maybe you *do* need to look beyond it, to ask your mother for help. Obviously, no help is going to fall into your lap; it's time for extreme measures. And Cecilia's spirit *has* helped you before. So yes, Janie's right. Go back to Key West. Ask your mother for help. Try everything available to you because nothing can hurt at this point."

Even though she doubted it would work, that night Ella lit several candles in her living room and rounded up every kind of talisman she could find. With incense burning and the old photo of her mother from the newspaper on the table, she talked to her; she loved and prayed and begged and waited. Nothing. She meditated, but Cecilia never showed up. After two hours, feeling abandoned and hopeless, she blew out the candles and took a sleeping pill, intending to sleep soundly until noon the next day.

But before pulling the draperies closed, she noticed how black the night was—no moon, no stars, just a black void—like her bedroom was now, like her heart was becoming with sorrow. She slipped into bed sadder than she'd ever been, even more than after Peter's death, sensing death in one form or another moving in around her. Closing her eyes, Daniel's face appeared in her mind, and she could bear no more. She cried and sobbed and tried to let go of every ounce of feeling in her, including love. It was love that ultimately caused this pain. *Why?* she asked of the black room empty of answers. *Why has this happened again?* An hour or more went by with her crying herself into a sleep as deep as the night was dark, with that question in her mind.

Her dreams found a way to reach her then with her defenses down and her subconscious wide open. Ella's mother appeared, looking beautiful, young, and loving. She felt her mother's love all around her, light filling the dream and her mind, easing her pain.

Ella's heart asked the only question she wanted answered. *Where is Daniel? What happened to him?*

A silent message filled the dream space: *Beneath the pain, your heart knows the truth. Release your suffering. Dry your tears, then look. The answers are there.* Her mother's filmy image turned away while spreading her arms wide, as if drawing apart curtains on a huge stage. An idyllic vista appeared, drawing Ella into itself like water to a sponge. She was surrounded by a wide white beach where turquoise seas lay beyond; palm trees swayed gently, framing the edges of the scene. Her senses soothed, filling with floral scents, fresh ocean air, and peace. Warm breezes wrapped her in a blanket of calm; the sound of the waves coming home to shore brought her home to a place she'd not been in over a year—comfortable in her own skin, safe in her life's journey.

Looking into the sun, its heat dried her tears, and the world became clear as her mother said it would. She knew this place. It was made of love and hope, imbuing her with the same. Her mother turned back briefly before vanishing, leaving words in her wake, *Now, go there. Find your answers. Heal yourself.*

Come morning, Ella woke gradually, replaying the dream over and over to remember it in the light of day and to keep the feeling of comfort and peace with her. But as she woke fully, she realized the place she'd seen was an actual place. She knew it; she loved it. It was Key West and could've been any one of the many beaches where she'd spent time with Daniel. Then her mother's parting words came back vividly: *Now, go there. Find your answers. Heal yourself.* Instantly she knew what she had to do, no second-guessing, no making excuses. It was time to face the place and hope her mother was right. She had to believe she'd find answers in one way or another.

The next thing Ella did was call Janie to let her know what had happened and of her plans to go back to

Key West. She asked her to go along, but Janie's schedule was overflowing with making wedding plans, work, and holiday preparations. She urged Ella on though, applauding her courage, saying, "Even if I or someone else went with you, it's still your journey to make alone. I know you can do it." Janie made her promise to keep in touch over the next two weeks and come back for her New Year's gathering.

"I can't promise to be back by then," Ella said. "I'm going to take a leave of absence and spend as much time as I need, to do whatever I have to do."

"That's wonderful," Janie said with tears. "I'm so proud of you, and I can't wait to have my friend back healthy and happy—at least, back on the road to having a real life."

Ella smiled and agreed, feeling her mother's presence and words lingering in her mind and thought, *It'll be a journey all right. What kind? I don't know. Where will it lead? I can't predict. The only thing I know for sure is that something extraordinary is going to happen.*

Chapter 15

Key West

Driving through Key Largo, heading further down the Overseas Highway, Ella approached the Seven Mile Bridge where she'd been so overcome with fear when driving with Janie two years ago. She was calmer this time, feeling nothing worse could happen than what she'd been through since then. If anything, making this trip was going to help her heal, and she continually reminded herself of that.

The Christmas season was one of the busiest in Key West with tourists flocking there for a warm, tropical island experience in the middle of winter. Traffic was heavy; the Seven Mile Bridge had only two lanes with a stream of cars in front of her and coming at her. A quarter of the way across, the sun started its descent to the horizon straight in front of her, turning the world shades of gold.

Awed by the view, she opened the windows to let the warm tropical air bathe her senses. Island music played on the radio, putting her in a kind of trance as she watched the setting sun, now directly in her line of sight. For a moment, it unexpectedly blinded her. She put up a hand to shield the light, but it glared so intensely she saw nothing, not even the road. Panic hit her in the chest. She clutched the steering wheel to keep the car moving straight, even though she couldn't see. The sun burned brighter. In the next second, a horn blared loudly from an oncoming car. Still unable to see, she filled with fear, her heart raced. A loud, shrill sound came from ahead, then filled the car.

She panicked thinking someone had crashed into the side of the bridge. *God help them*, she silently said as the sun's hot white light instantly permeated the interior of the car, and for a moment, she felt as if in another world, released from fear, knowing she was almost there, knowing she was safe as long as she kept the wheel pointed straight ahead until she could see again. The sensation was like the first time she'd driven there, almost like lifting up above her body and flying. A couple seconds passed and she *was* okay.

A cloud moved in front of the sun, her vision returned, there was no tragic accident on the bridge, and the road ahead was clear with Key West in the distance. With her heart still pounding, she realized she might've swerved, prompting another driver to blare their horn at her. It didn't matter. She was safe now and drove the rest of the way feeling grateful, if shaken, having come out of a frightening experience and delivered safely back. *This must be how Daniel feels when he flies those huge fighter jets and lands back safely on the deck of the ship.*

The thought of Daniel, living in the present, threw her. With exhaustion taking over and a now ominous feeling shrouding this trip after just narrowly avoiding an accident, she questioned her judgment. *I don't know if I can do this—if I can let Daniel go.* But she forced herself to get her mind back on driving, pushing all other thoughts out of her mind until she arrived at the cottages where she and Janie had stayed. She checked in, showered, and fell into bed. Grateful to God, fate, luck, or whatever force had saved her today, she wished for only good dreams.

And she dreamt of Daniel—alive, perfect in every way, and filled with love for her. It was so real, when she woke, she thought he'd be sitting on the bed or standing at the front door. But the room was empty; no knock came on the door. Her heart dropped, but as she pulled the curtains open on a brilliant day, she saw the same vista she had in the dream with her mother and felt the same sense of peace and hope. Something was happening; she didn't know what or why or how. But she was here now with nothing but time and memories stretched out ahead of her.

Light, tropical music drifted in from outside. She walked to the patio door, opened it wide to soothing, warm breezes, the ocean roaring onto the beach, all the sounds and sights of Key West comforting her. Walking to the water's edge, she was surprised she didn't feel sad or agonized over Daniel. Miraculously, she was filled with only the best about him—love.

Back at the cottage, she put on a bathing suit, filled a small cooler with cold drinks, grabbed a hat, blanket, and a good book and headed to the beach for the day. After an hour of reading, she cooled off in the ocean and decided to walk up the beach. Everything sparkled with vibrant energy from the sun reflecting onto the water, bouncing off the sand and palm trees.

Watching the waves come to shore, she noticed they left thousands of bubbles in their wake, scattered delicately like lace. It was as if the ocean placed a veil upon the shore, on the head of its bride, kissing it briefly before dying back into the ocean, only to be replaced by the next new wave. *The sea always returns,* Ella realized. *Life remains constant; the bride has her kiss and her union with her lover. It's so simple—a mere cycle of nature—a rhythm of God.* Looking out to sea, she whispered, "Then where is my Daniel? Why doesn't he return like the next wave on the shore?"

No answer came back, but unexpectedly her heart filled with love, and she thought Daniel might, just possibly, return one day as easily as the next ocean wave. Of course, the idea was unrealistic, as Janie had tried to tell her. But somehow, the way the world felt now, in this place where it had once been filled with love, anything seemed possible.

Returning to her blanket, she moved it into the shade and sprawled out to take a nap. She'd been wrong to dread this trip back to where she and Daniel had begun. She felt him close and remembered he'd promised he would always be close, no matter what. Maybe it was only here she could sense his spirit. Maybe she'd stay for good. Even without him physically here, she'd still feel his love. Being here with his memory was better than sadness, better than loneliness. Waiting was better than nothing. As she drifted to sleep, a thought slipped from her active mind into her next state of being: *I'll wait for him forever if I have to.*

That thought got caught in the web of her subconscious, entwined with images of Daniel and questions about his fate, prompting her dreams to shed light on the truth. Dreams could be a double-edged sword for someone like Ella, whose subconscious could stretch across time and tap into souls who needed to communicate. Her dreams could bring answers or more questions, always vivid while cryptic, a kind of torture because they revealed themselves as if they were a solution *but spoken in another language*.

Today, however, her intention just before falling asleep, *to wait for him forever,* tripped a lever deep in her memory. It was ancient, yet a part of her, and it was waiting for the precise moment she'd understand its meaning. Ella was infused into another world where clues to her life lay buried in her past, and she heard a silent whisper. *Your name was Helena, and you lived in Greece*. Then the dream billowed out around her, engulfing her body and soul, and she lived inside it where the story unfolded in quick sequences, in flashes of pictures and words just like when she was nine and almost drowned at sea. Only this time, more details were revealed:

The Ring
Ancient Greece
"Secrets"

Helena was almost four years old when she discovered a baby boy washed ashore, alone, under a small boat. She'd saved his life, but her mother, Kallias, devised a plan to hide the child, and give the baby to her sister, who had been visiting from Athens, because she was barren and childless. Helena's aunt raised him as her own child. But in order to not risk losing him, both women swore Helena and their families to keep the secret forever, that this boy was not of their blood. Then Kallias moved their family to Athens to be near her sister.

Helena and the boy, Matthias, played together and were close from the time she was five, and he three.

Helena felt that, in Matthias, she'd been given a special gift sent straight to her from the gods. They were so close; she wished her mother hadn't given him to her aunt, but she was satisfied at being able to spend much time with him since they lived in the same town. Growing up, they became the closest of friends, adoring each other from as far back as they could remember, and for her, from the time she'd found him cast ashore. Although she could never tell Matthias the truth of how he came to them, he shared Helena's feeling of the two of them being special to each other.

Through the years, he preferred her company over his friends, and often mentioned he never really felt part of his family—he only felt close to Helena. As their friendship and respect grew, he spoke of how they shared a special bond of love different than that of cousins. Every day Helena wanted to tell Matthias the truth—that he was not her cousin by blood, and that his feelings for her were true and shared by herself. But she'd been sworn to keep the secret and said nothing, knowingly betraying him.

Kallias watched their love grow innocently, yet she and her sister were fearful of the closeness Helena and Matthias shared in their teens. They forbade it, and Matthias's parents sent him off to train to be a soldier. Through the next years, even with separation, their love and bond grew as a young man for a young woman. Helena still kept the secret, even knowing Matthias felt guilty about their relationship, keeping it hidden from their families. It broke Helena's heart to watch him struggle with his emotions and not be able to share the truth. But she couldn't betray her mother and aunt. When Matthias finished his training, he had to go away to war.

But a week before his departure, spending his final time with his family and Helena, he overheard Helena and her mother arguing. Helena cried and screamed, so afraid Matthias would die because of their mothers' horrible secret. Helena blurted out that, if her aunt hadn't been so selfish to keep the baby Helena had found on the beach and hadn't lived a life of lies, then Matthias might've been adopted by another family in their town. Then she and Matthias would've grown up as friends, and now they could be free to love each other and be together as a man and a woman should. Matthias wouldn't be forced to go to war so young. Helena shrieked at her mother, "If he dies, it will be your fault!"

Learning then that he was truly not Helena's cousin, he realized his love for her was indeed honorable, pure, and so strong that he wanted to marry her.

The night before he had to leave for war, he and Helena stole off together, hiding under a stone bridge against the cold rocks, their hearts raging hot with love and desire. Matthias told her, "When I return, we will marry and move far from here. I promise." With that, he placed a ring on her finger, a beautiful gold ring, a wide band engraved with the Greek key, together symbolizing infinite love.

"What is this?" Helena asked.

"My pledge to you of my love that will never die and that we will marry." He kissed her, deeply, reverently, and they held each other for a long time, until the ship's bell sounded, calling all aboard. The air was thick with moisture as she kissed his neck and gathered his scent for one last time—of salt air and the sea. Matthias made a last promise, "I will come back to you, my love."

As he walked toward the ship, Helena called out to him, "Come back safely, my love. I will wait for you forever."

For a year, Helena never gave up hope he'd return. But another five years went by, and she hated her mother and aunt for causing the loss of him. She hated the war and the sea for taking him away.

Another year later, a ship returned with soldiers, but Matthias was not one of them. A soldier found Helena's home and told her Matthias had been his friend. He had spoken at length of his bravery and how he talked of coming back to his Helena. But Matthias had been killed and buried at sea.

With grief so deep, Helena walked the earth as death itself and returned to the edge of the sea where she and Matthias had parted. Clouds moved in, darkening the day; a storm raged at the horizon. White-capped waves driven by fierce winds crashed ashore as she walked into them, letting the cold, raging water slam into her legs. Pulling the beautiful gold ring Matthias had given her off her finger, she held it briefly, remembering his love. War had taken him—war with her mother, war with other lands, and Helena realized war didn't only take life away, war destroyed love. She kissed his ring, pouring all her love into it, then flung it and her love far into the sea, into a deep, unknowable world, casting them out to where she imagined Matthias to be.

The water soaked her long gown, helping the waves to twist their greedy fingers around her legs, pulling her under. She fought hard to stay above water and breathe as the surf crashed over her, but the force of nature was too strong that day. She had not intended for the sea to take her down. She was in a place she should not have been, unthinking, uncaring for her safety, thinking only of love and love lost. As Helena tumbled within the raging water and was sucked out deep under the depths of the sea, it seemed the gods watched and knew she had no reason to be a part of the world any longer, so they let the sea have her.

Helena left the world, taking with her a love so great she knew it would carry her beyond the life she'd lived. The love they shared came to her by the sea and had existed only for a flash in the eye of eternity, and the same love would carry Helena into that eternal world, beyond death to wait for Matthias.

****

Key West

Ella woke abruptly on her blanket in the sand, panicked and sweating. She gasped for air as if she were drowning and heard the words again, *Love would carry Helena...beyond death to wait for Matthias*, reverberating through her mind from eons ago. Her first thought was the dream had been of herself and Daniel. She sat up and looked around, disoriented. *But, no, it wasn't. Yet somehow it was, even though the people in the story had different names in a different time.* She'd been asleep so long; the sun was now moving toward the horizon; the sky was drenched in shades of gold and red.

She took a drink of water and walked to the ocean to clear her mind. *How could this be?* Closing her eyes, she calmed her thoughts. *Of course, logically, this was a subconscious reaction to my statement right before falling asleep. It was a cosmic lesson warning me to be careful of what I asked for.* But she'd felt every emotion that Helena had; she knew their story, and almost as soon as it began, she knew how it would end. *Did this mean Daniel was lost to war as well? Was she doomed to perish waiting for him? Was this an omen?*

Then she remembered the dream she'd had when she was beginning to fall in love with Daniel and wanted to run from it. In a flash, she'd been a woman in Greece with her lover putting a ring on her finger. It was all coming back now. She was the woman, the man was the same man, and the ring was identical.

Panic drove her to run up the beach as fast as she could, trying to outrun the scenes in the dream. She ran for a half hour, then turned around and ran back, still trying to drive those memories out of her. With the sun gone, the beach was dark and deserted, lit only by a rising moon. Exhausted and dripping with sweat, she walked into a calm ocean only a few yards from shore, just enough to sit and submerge her body under the salt water, almost tempting fate; instead, she begged for the sea to draw out every memory from her.

Her body was soothed by the seawater, even as her heart hated it. Looking out to its unfathomable depths into the black, invisible horizon, she realized, *This, this sea that is comforting to me now, is a deceiver, taking love and life away from me, since ancient times through today, continuing until when? Forever? You've cursed me; you are a traitor. I hate you.*

Ella flung herself out of the water, soaked, confused, dazed, and dragged herself into the cottage, stripped off her bathing suit, fell into bed and cried. *No wonder my first reaction was to run from Daniel no matter how strong the attraction and love. I was afraid of waiting forever for someone who'd never return. I have done this to myself, again, it seems. But why? Why would I have chosen this for myself?*

****

The next morning, Ella woke feeling hungover, like she'd had a whole bottle of tequila the night before. But it wasn't tequila slamming her; it was reality. If the dream had bearing on her present life, then she wanted to get more than shock and horror from it; she wanted to gain some benefit to help her deal with the losses she faced today, in the present.

After making breakfast and taking it out to the patio, she looked over the ocean again in the flawless morning light, the sun sparkling like a universe of stars on the water. How different the sea was from last night. Instead of dark and foreboding, it flowed pure and gentle, having shed its former disguise. Suddenly she realized everything was a matter of perception, and she saw her dream in a different light as well: *Remove the cloak of darkness surrounding the mystery of those people, and the truth is found. Regardless of who they were and when they lived, the meaning of the story is the same: I'm wasting my life waiting for someone who will never return.* Instantly, the idea of staying in Key West just to feel Daniel close seemed like a bad idea, not if she wanted more out of life. But then she was left with the prospect of a world alone, loveless, and still missing him as part of herself, an amputated limb with no prosthetic for that kind of loss.

Come evening, she walked into town to get dinner. The historic district was lit with thousands of lights,

Christmas decorations adorning every building. It was magical to look at, but the spirit of the season did not register inside her. The only thoughts to come were of how she and Daniel were supposed to be enjoying this together, how much he would've loved it, and she went over an emotional edge. Her first instinct was to run, to leave, but that had never worked. The longing for Daniel would follow. Sitting in a café with a glass of wine reminded her of good times in the same restaurant with Janie, so she called her, explaining everything that had happened from the drive down to the unsettling dream.

Janie tried to talk sense into her. "You're making progress. Hold on. Stay longer. You may be on the verge of a breakthrough if you can just hang tough. See what tomorrow brings."

But it wasn't the daytime Ella was afraid of. It was the night, the long, lonely, dark nights filled with dreams and bizarre stories and people, new but so familiar. She hated her abnormal, weird life, but that thought triggered something Daniel had said about her running from the past: *Instead of changing your whole life around because of things you don't understand, change your mind and your way of thinking about those things*. Now she thought there might be something to that theory; at least, it couldn't hurt to try.

So, Ella flipped her thinking around 180 degrees, to how enlightening the whole thing could be if she let it. If the dream of ancient Greece could be so telling, maybe she needed more information like it. Instead of feeling haunted and afraid, she'd try being open to the experiences and see if they could bring enlightenment. It certainly seemed a better path at this point than giving up, running away, or waiting for him forever.

The reporter in her kicked in. She wanted answers and needed the whole story, not just pieces, to know the next step, to hopefully find answers about Daniel's fate. But so far, dealing with facts and psychologists and books had gotten her nowhere. Her best progress came from realms beyond intellect and facts—from ethereal, spiritual realms; therefore, it made sense to look to those realms for help.

She recalled a sign she'd seen in town for a "Spiritual Counselor." It had stated: "Psychic Adviser / Medium / Palm Reader." Ella rationalized: physical problems require a medical doctor, so spiritual issues might be helped by a *spiritual* healer. She was open and willing to try anything. And from years of reporting and interviewing, of sorting through lies to get to the truth, her '*b.s.*' detector was sharp. There'd be no harm done with a session, and at the very least, she might glean some insight.

****

A neon '*Open*' sign was lit in the window, so Ella walked through the door, chimes announcing her entry. A woman's voice came from behind a room divider. "I'll be right out. Please sit at the table."

Ella did as instructed. The room was dark and windowless, lit only with large candles. A bible sat on a side table, a cross hung above it. Various colored crystals were strewn around. The table was round and covered in a deep purple satin cloth. Within minutes, a woman emerged, dressed casually in a long, flowered-print skirt, tank top and several strands of crystal-laden necklaces. She had straight, jet black hair and was heavily made up with thick black eyeliner and dark red lipstick. Looking to be in her fifties, she was attractive with smooth, tawny skin, despite the heavy makeup. She sat across from Ella, her eyes peering intensely out from under false eyelashes; their deep brown color seemed to reach into Ella's soul.

The spicy smell of incense, thick and exotic, filled the air, creating a soothing, otherworldly feel to the room. The woman smiled with genuine interest and affection, introducing herself with a slight accent as Kara. "And your name, if you wish to share it?" Ella smiled and introduced herself. Kara then patted Ella's hand gently and assured her everything would be fine.

"What may I help you with today, Ella?"

Purposefully giving no details, Ella answered in a general way. "I need direction. I'm at a point in life where I don't know what to do. Just tell me whatever you see, whatever is there, good or bad."

"Well, my dear, I sense that you have spirits around you that you are probably aware of, aren't you?"

"Yes, I suppose I do have a little experience with them. But couldn't you say that about many people?"

"Not really. Not the way I sense them around you. They are active, especially a female. This might be a mother or someone like a mother who loves you very much. Is this correct?"

Ella did not want to divulge any more information than she had to, but was compelled to answer truthfully. "You could be right about that."

"She, her spirit rather, has been visiting you for a very long time. Since you were a child, yes? She is still around you and wishes to help but sometimes cannot reach you. Your grief stands in the way, grief and sadness block your ability to receive information. You seem to be stuck and are unwilling to move forward."

Ella wrung her hands together and looked down at them. "I suppose that's true. But now I feel at the end of my wits, and I'm open to listening to any advice from anyone."

"Are you right-handed?"

"Yes."

"Please give me your right hand, palm up."

As Ella did so, she wondered if this was a mistake.

Kara looked at her with a knowing smile and said, "There is no mistake that you are here today." She pulled a large candle closer to get a better look at Ella's hand. "I see from your life line that you have had a tumultuous life so far. Your birth parents passed away very young, before you were three years old from what I see here. You are very intelligent, and your work involves storytelling somehow. You have a creative mind. I see a very deep but broken love line meaning very strong, connected, soul-deep love with people you've known before.

"But I also see much heartache and loss through love. You almost expect this in life. In fact, something has happened to a loved one very recently." Kara smoothed the lines in Ella's palm with her finger and turned her hand gently left and right to see the lines more clearly. "You have sustained a very great loss of a relationship recently that you were reluctant to embark upon in the first place. True?"

Ella could not believe Kara's accuracy, so she kept answering her questions, eager to find out more. "Yes, it is."

"And this is why you are here today. There is some mystery around this man."

"Yes. What can you tell me about him?"

Kara took both of Ella's hands, closed her eyes, and seemed to go into a trance-like state. Her head swayed back and forth for a minute, her eyes squeezed shut more tightly, wincing. After what seemed like a long time, she opened her eyes and looked at Ella, almost sad. "I cannot tell you for sure of his outcome. I sense an ending but also a beginning. I feel death, life, and great love. But I can sense this about anyone who walks through my door. We all have experienced life, death, and love in some form or another throughout many lives. All I can say about this most recent love is that you are very connected to him and he came into your life to help you resolve a deep issue around love and loss, all somehow connected to the sea. Is this correct?"

Ella, shocked, looked to the ceiling to avoid Kara's penetrating gaze. "This is scaring me—how accurate you are. How can you know these things?"

"I know them because I am open to the truth; I'm not afraid. You can tap into the same things by using every resource available to you, of which there are many in the spiritual realm, to find the answers you seek. I wish I could give them to you, but it is not up to me. You must make this journey on your own. You have been sad, lonely, and fearful for many lifetimes. You are very receptive in the dream state when your defenses are down and fear is dissolved. Answers come to you then, especially memories of times your soul lived before, giving insight to you now. Ask for guidance before you drift to sleep, be open to anything and it will come."

Ella took her hand away. "All you can tell me,

basically, is that I have to do this on my own? I already knew that."

"Don't be upset, my dear. One consolation I can give you is that you will have your answers soon. I see you are here in Key West on a quest for several weeks. You will have your answers long before that. Keep your heart open and answers will come, within the week, or just days. Does that help you?"

Relieved for, at least, one comforting piece of hard information, she thanked Kara. "It helps enormously. I guess I always knew that answers would not be handed to me on a silver platter by a psychic or anyone else. I always sensed that I would have to find them on my own, that this is part of my journey."

Kara smiled a great, wide smile, reminiscent of Daniel's. "You are absolutely correct, my dear. How nice to meet someone who understands these things. Let me leave you with another positive note. You've lived many lifetimes and are blessed with the ability to connect to people and places from realms beyond this time and place if you have the courage." She stopped talking and cocked her head as if someone just whispered in her ear, and she strained to hear their words. "There is something more. There is a spirit, from this lifetime, one you shared great love with, and wanted to marry. Hmm…I'm hearing something like pain, main; no—Spain—did you meet him in Spain? The name begins with…" Kara hesitated. "P. Yes, a man's name beginning with the letter P, like Peter or Padre or Pedro."

Ella gasped, stunned, her eyes widening in disbelief.

Kara asked, "You know of whom I am speaking?"

"I can't believe this. Yes. I did love a man. In Spain. And his name was Peter."

Kara sensed Ella's fear. "There is no need to be afraid. He comes out of love and wanting to help you. He will help you go back to a life that could explain things further, a life in Spain long ago, back to the year…" Kara seemed doubtful. "Could this possible? Yes, the year 1500. Does any of this ring familiar with you?"

Placing her hands over her eyes, Ella replied, "This is so unbelievable. I don't know the year, but yes, I've had brief glimpses of a woman in Spain long ago, loss of a loved one and children. It was all so confusing, but so real. I don't know what to make of any of this."

"The memories you had are real. But there is more to learn. This man you loved in this life died unexpectedly, in Spain. He's showing me a sailboat, an accident at sea, yes?"

Ella nodded, chills running through her. "But how can you know these things about my life?"

"His spirit is around us now. I am simply a conduit of what Peter's spirit is telling me. He will help you go to the place long ago to find the answers you need. But you must *want to know* the answers. You must have no fear, or he cannot help you. It's up to you to decide. I can help you with a regression, if you like. Or you can ask Peter yourself. You have the ability to tap into this, to intuit his thoughts and messages, as you have before with your mother's spirit."

Rather stunned by all these events, Ella said she just didn't know what to do.

"If you want answers, you must *do* something, take action."

Ella realized, in that moment, she could either be open to what Kara spoke of or shut down, and her choice would determine her future. Tired of being tormented by the past, she chose the future. "I want answers; I'm open to whatever they are, and I'll do whatever I have to."

Kara smiled kindly at her. "How brave of you, my dear. This is a good decision." She smoothed the tablecloth and took Ella's hands in hers. "Now, would you like me to assist you with this regression, or would you like to do it on your own—through asking Peter's spirit to help?"

Ella trusted Kara since she'd already received very valid and accurate information about her life. "What does the regression entail?"

"I use hypnosis for you, a kind of deep, meditative state, and I go into the same state with you, to help you go deeper, to see what you see, or what you are afraid to see, like a navigator on a journey."

"Can we do it now?"

"Yes, if you like. I have time. It could take an hour, more or less, depending on you."

Kara had Ella lie down on a chaise lounge on the other side of the room. Kara sat in an overstuffed, upholstered chair next to her. Celestial, angelic-sounding music played softly in the background. When they were both comfortable and relaxed, Kara gave instructions for her to go back further in time and memory as she counted backward from ten. At one, she would find herself in the time and place she needed answers from. Kara counted very slowly, her voice melding with the music, telling her to go deeper, farther back, to look for Peter's image. Ella had never experienced anything so relaxing, feeling not quite there in body, as if her real self was floating in air, guided and protected by the presence of Kara.

She took her back in time to a town on the coast of Spain where she was a wealthy widow named Isabella, who lived with her father. They were Jews in a time when it was dangerous, even life-threatening to be of that faith. After her husband was killed in the Inquisition, she and her father moved far from their home to live on the coast of Spain. They were *conversos*—they'd given up Judaism to convert to Christianity, to survive the Inquisition. But they both lived a lie in that they practiced their religion in secret—they were still Jews, hiding their traditions and ceremonies in an underground room hidden and locked away off their wine cellar.

The other secret Isabella hid for years was that she'd fallen in love with her best friend, and he was the local Catholic priest, Padre Miguel Morales. Their relationship was one secret built upon another, one lie leading to another, until they could not deny their love for each other any longer.

She and Miguel had fallen deeply in love, forbidden love. They had to bury their true feelings and lie about who they really were in order to survive. She carried guilt for many years, for living a lie and for loving him. After several years of hiding, Miguel finally told her the truth—he'd been gathering and hiding Jewish orphans for them all to escape to the New World, so they would not be killed in the Inquisition. Knowing he would be leaving the next day for Santo Domingo and not knowing when he could return to Spain, he unveiled his biggest secret to her, that he was *not* a priest. He was a Jew pretending to be a Catholic priest in order to save as many children as he could. He'd lived a lie for most of his life, had forged and faked his vows to achieve this end, but felt even if he saved one child, it was worth it.

In one night, she found out the man she loved was of her own religion, and because he was not a real priest, he was able to love and marry her, and, he admitted to loving her for all those years. They then consummated their love on the night before he left to voyage to the New World.

Ella, lying on the chaise in a deep state of living as Isabella in another time and place, became unsettled with strong emotions coming to the surface. She watched her lover leave in the predawn mist, finally knowing the truth of him, their love, and their false lives. She had to say goodbye. He planned to take the children across the sea, get them settled in a new life there, then make the return voyage to Spain to collect her and more children. It would be one or two years before she would see him again, but she promised she'd wait and leave with him on the next voyage.

But Miguel never returned, and Ella, now in the present, was reliving the extreme emotional pain and loss of that time, along with the fear that the sea had taken her love. Her heart felt about to burst, and she needed to escape this horrible fate again.

Kara sensed Ella's heartbreak and inability to experience it again in this state. She slowly brought her up through the hypnotic state, slowly counting up to ten for Ella to be fully awake at that point. She brought her through the various stages of memory, slowly back into the present. Ella slowly came back, opened her eyes.

She was still filled with anguish and panic. She sat up and burst into tears. Kara held her.

"Why, Kara? Why did I have to remember this? What good has it done me, except to push me deeper into heartbreak and fearing the sea?"

"There is more to this story, Ella. The important part you could not handle today. But if you have the courage to get to the end of the story, you will learn more and gain greater insight into your present situation."

Standing, getting her bearings back, Ella said, "I don't think I can do anymore. Why would I put myself through more of this?"

"You said you wanted answers. If you really want to know about Daniel, you need to finish this…with me or by yourself."

"I'm kind of in shock right now. It's not something I want to revisit."

"But then there's the question of Daniel."

"Yes, yes, you're right. I just need to let this all settle down and not feel so raw inside before I move on to the rest of the story."

Kara smiled knowingly. "You might be surprised at what you learn, and remember, if you try this again by yourself, ask for help. It's there for you." Kara then stood and said, "I'll leave you with this: You are surrounded by great love here and by those who have passed on. Tap into it. Anything is possible with love." Opening her arms wide, she hugged Ella, who slipped her payment into the pocket of Kara's skirt and thanked her.

Ella left feeling still a little out of her body, unsure of who she really was. With each step, her legs shook, causing her to wonder if she was walking on solid land, and if her body was really hers. She definitely needed more information to ground herself in reality. Tonight she might ask Peter to explain this journey to her. She'd ask and pray and hope for the best. As she walked along the charming Key West streets with their historic houses and lush, mature trees—the town itself a throw-back in time as well—she envisioned Peter and said, *I'm ready to know the truth. Can you help me?*

A breeze blew through the trees. The palm fronds swayed gently overhead and shook a message loose, a whisper Ella heard in her heart…*Yes.*

****

Emotionally wrung out, Ella's sleep that night was deep and calm. Her mind was too exhausted to dredge up painful memories and ongoing mysteries. Upon waking, she decided what she needed was a day off from searching. Maybe if she put everything out of her mind, except enjoying Key West, she'd clear some space for something new to be revealed.

She toured downtown, went out to lunch, and visited the Ernest Hemingway house. Even though she'd seen it first with Daniel, she didn't dwell on missing him. Rather, as she moved through the rooms, she felt immersed in Hemingway's world completely. She sensed his presence lingering everywhere and pictured him eating at the table with his family, drinking at his bar, sleeping in the oversized bed, swimming in the pool his wife had built, and writing in his office.

Serenity and grace filled the house, as did a sense of nature and life, and a vibrant force emanated from the contents, from the walls and floors themselves. Here was a house that had been empty of residents for decades and yet was full of life and its original inhabitants' presences could still be felt there, especially Ernest with his large, grand, creative spirit, where he'd written some of his best works.

A metaphysician Ella had once met on a story explained to her how everything, all matter has energy, even inanimate objects because they're made of atoms and molecules, of moving, vibrating particles. When people use these material objects and live with them, their own energy transfers to those things—chairs, tables, books, jewelry, pictures on the wall, or the very walls of a house itself. Intellectually, it had made sense to Ella, but now, touring this house proved it to be true as she experienced it firsthand. Moving through Hemingway's house now was like walking into the middle of his life as he lived it long ago.

Instantly, Ella realized how, in the same way, it was possible to walk into, or remember one of her lives previously lived. Just as she could sense and feel Hemingway present in his home long after he'd died, it could be possible to *walk into* another life. In the same way, one could recall or sense the people, emotions, and places previously lived because the memories carry over in the energy of everything in and around us—our brains and souls, what we touch, create, emote, what makes us alive. She saw how it could be possible to sense something that might've happened in another life to the same soul, the same spirit over and over.

She'd had the same feeling meeting Daniel, and he with her. And now her feeling of loving, hating, and losing people to the sea from ancient times into the present was all coming together as reality, not insanity.

She knew then that in this house, this town, and her life, anything was possible.

On the tour, her attention was drawn to photos and descriptions of Hemingway's travels around the world, and she was fascinated about the stories of his time spent in Spain. All that day, Spain dominated her thoughts. Sitting on the outdoor patio of a coffee shop, relaxing with a latte, she looked down the street lined with coconut palms and brightly flowering shrubs, where the ocean sat like a prize at the end of the street. It reminded her of spending time by the seaside in Spain with Peter. His loss had been so sudden and painful; she'd buried all memories of him. But now she wondered, *Why didn't he ever come to me in a dream after he died?*

Later that evening, she drew a hot bath to relax before bed. Closing her eyes, thoughts of Peter drifted in and out. She'd stop them when they became too painful. Then it dawned on her. Maybe she never got over his death because she never let herself grieve completely. She'd wanted to pretend he never existed to wipe away the heartbreak. As she slipped into bed, she recalled Kara had said there was more to the story of Spain and to ask for help. Sleep came quickly, and her last conscious thought was of Peter.

Finally, while in the deepest sleep, Peter's face appeared—alive, young, and vibrant, and filled her with love. His words came through time: *I never visited you before because you weren't ready. You remember the Spain we lived in and loved, but to understand more you must go back farther, far back in your memory and walk into the house of that life, after Miguel left for the New World, and you, Isabella, tried to find him.*

Forbidden
Spain, 1502
"Lies and Murder"

Isabella had stood in the dusky light before dawn, the sea air full of mist and salt clinging to her skin, suffocating her heart as she let her lover, Miguel, go to an unknown fate. She watched from a hillside above the seaport, and as he boarded the ship, she prayed and loved him enough to carry him and the children safely across the sea. She had whispered, "I will wait for you forever; this is the strength of my love."

****

However, after two years with no sign or word from Miguel, she cursed the sea for taking him. Maybe they'd never made it to Santo Domingo, either lost at sea or sunk in a storm. If they had survived the trip, maybe he'd be returning within the coming year. Isabella drove herself crazy thinking of the possibilities. Finally, after another year, she had to accept he might never come back. But she never gave up hope, waiting alone, but deep down in her soul feeling God had decided she was not worthy of such love, of marriage or children, and neither was Miguel. Maybe they were being punished for their lies and secrets. But they both had good reasons—to save lives. In the quiet space of her prayers, she'd wonder, *Couldn't God forgive those things with all the good we tried to accomplish?* But in the end, rather than blame God, she blamed the sea which had probably taken them all.

The gnawing of uncertainty in Isabella's heart brought on a kind of madness, a world where she didn't know what was real anymore. Her father had died; the estate was hers. But sitting alone with her memories and sadness turned her into someone she didn't recognize, someone who was willing to give up everything for the man she loved, even herself, her integrity and character. She devised a plan to get what she needed, to find Miguel.

Evenings she'd venture into town near the port and frequent the taverns where sailors and sea captains drank every night in between voyages. Women like her with money and class were not seen there. She was stared at, teased, and threatened. She didn't care. Her goal was to find a captain of a ship who might grant her passage—something unheard of. A woman was not allowed on board a sailing ship, with one exception—the captain's wife. Isabella could think of no better way than to seduce a sea captain to get aboard a ship, so she could sail to the New World and find Miguel, or die trying. She'd lie, bribe, or use her money and her looks to get what she needed to find Miguel because, without him, she had no life.

****

Pedro Cordova was fifteen years older than Isabella and a commander of a sailing vessel who had admired her from afar. He thought it gutsy of her to mingle with the sailors in the taverns. But he didn't become a captain by being stupid or naive. He knew she must have ulterior motives, other than just wanting to have a good time. Women of her caliber didn't act in such a way, not there in the port with coarse, rugged sailors. The woman wanted something in the men she found there, and Pedro wanted Isabella for the many things a man wants a lovely, courageous, daring woman for. Determined to find out what her motives were, he watched her night after night, following her during her visits into town and afterward to her estate. After several weeks, he waited until she left the tavern, then approached her outside, and introduced himself as the captain of a sailing vessel. She said she wouldn't believe him until he offered proof—to show her his ship. He gladly took her aboard and showed her around. This was his first clue of her motives—she needed proof of a ship for some reason.

Isabella felt her hard work had finally paid off. She'd found a captain, an unmarried and not-too-bad-looking one at that. She spent much time with him, playing the game of pretending to be interested in him. She had the feeling he was also playing a game with her.

She invited him to her home and plied him with good food, wine, flirtations which he reciprocated, and conversation during which she got him to admit he was leaving on a voyage to the New World in another month. He kissed her and said, "I'd like to know I have a beautiful woman waiting for me when I return."

"A woman to do what with?" she asked coyly.

Pedro laughed and drank more wine. "You know exactly."

"But I'm not that kind of woman."

"What kind are you then?"

"The marrying kind."

"I never said I wanted a wife. I want the benefits of a wife, though, *all* the benefits, including taking you to bed."

"Just because I am a widow doesn't mean I take any man to my bed, not even a sea captain. I will only share a bed with a husband. And since you don't want a wife, then I guess we have nothing more to talk about."

Laughing and grinning scandalously, he took her by the arms. "Oh, yes, we do. Like what you really want from me. Tell me now or I'll leave."

"I thought we might fall in love, get married. I don't want to spend my life alone."

"You could marry any one of those sailors you drank with. Why did you pick me?"

Isabella faked a most seductive smile. "I like your handsome face, to which I am very drawn. I like that you're a brave captain of a ship, and I would love to sail the sea someday."

"Ah-ha. *Someday*, you say, when you really mean possibly next month, possibly with me?"

She wrestled away from him. "I mean no such thing. I simply answered your question honestly. And now you don't like the answer. You are suspicious." Her anger riled, and she wanted no more of him. "Get out now."

With her angry reaction, Pedro second-guessed himself. Maybe it was possible he'd been wrong. He looked at her again. She was so alluring in the candlelight with her sultry green eyes and glistening hair, her fine silk clothes and impressive house and cellar full of wine, her lovely scent and body that seduced him like a black widow spider. He felt like prey but enjoyed the feeling. No woman of her class had ever treated him this way. And he liked it very much.

Two weeks later, Captain Pedro Cordova asked Isabella to marry him and sail on his next voyage. Overjoyed, Isabella accepted and attended to the details of arranging for a friend to live in her house and take care of the land and animals. At Isabella's insistence, she wanted to be married on the ship, on the voyage and not before. Pedro questioned her motives but was determined to have her as his wife. Voyages would no longer be lonely. When he asked her why the delay, she said, “I’m worried and frightened. I never thought of the danger involved. I want to be well on our way before we marry, just to give me a chance to get used to a new way of life.”

Pedro kissed her. “We’ll be fine. I’ve made the voyage before. I won’t let anything bad happen to you. We’ll marry long before we get to the New World, and hopefully by the time we arrive, you’ll be with child.”

Isabella smiled, but inside she filled with horror. It was bad enough to think of ways *not* to marry him and share his bed, but to think she might become with child if forced to consummate a marriage! It was an impossible idea. She simply couldn’t risk it. Nothing would be more awful than to make the voyage safely, be forced to marry Pedro, be with child, and *then* find Miguel. Her life would still be ruined.

Isabella managed to put off Pedro for one month, feigning illness, seasickness, women’s problems, fear, and stormy weather, everything she could think of. Pedro was gracious the first month, but at the start of the second month, he confronted her. “We must be married soon. I hear the crew snickering, laughing, and talking about us behind my back. What you are doing is not right. I won’t be made a fool of on my own ship. I can’t command these men if I can’t command my own wife. We will be married tomorrow. No more excuses.”

The sun was almost completely below the horizon as Isabella stood alone on the bow of the ship looking west. The sky was magnificent in colors of gold and red she'd never seen before. The sea rolled gently under a soft, warm breeze. With eyes closed, Isabella had a feeling something wonderful would happen. It was the first time she felt she'd find Miguel as she imagined the islands she could not yet see, then imagined Miguel waiting there. The sky gradually darkened and a million stars shown above. It was magical until Pedro came up behind her barking orders about marrying him in the morning.

Instead, her mind searched for one final thing to say or do to deter him, permanently, from marrying her. She turned to him with a believable, but false tragic look on her face. "I must tell you the truth, Pedro. I have kept a secret from you because, I thought, if you knew, you wouldn't want to marry me."

Pedro's suspicions aroused with a vengeance, but he played along. "Nonsense. There is nothing so terrible as to keep me from marrying you."

"This is very terrible, however. You mentioned my possibly being with child by the time we land ashore. But I carry guilt for not having told you that I cannot have children. You will never have children or a family with me as your wife. I'm so sorry. If you don't want to marry me, I completely understand. You deserve a woman who can give you heirs."

His face looked hard as stone, his eyes turning into fiery embers. "I don't believe you. You're making another excuse. You will marry me in the morning." He grabbed her arm. "Come with me now to my bed. I've waited long enough. We will consummate our marriage a few hours ahead of time. I've certainly earned the right." He pulled her behind him as he took big, angry strides on the deck.

"Let go of me," she shouted, yanking her arm away. Something snapped in Isabella's mind with being treated like a piece of property that wasn't even his yet. She hated him, and it showed in her eyes.

He grabbed her again. She fought, but he picked her whole body up. Kicking and screaming and losing her mind, she yelled, "You can't do this!"

"I will!"

"No, no. I cannot be your wife!"

"Why, pray tell?" he shouted as he continued walking toward his cabin.

"Because I don't love you. I don't love anyone but…" She stopped, realizing what she was about to say.

"Who? Who? You damn liar!" He flung her onto the deck like she was garbage.

"I didn't mean I don't love you. I meant I can't marry you."

"So, you used me and lied to me to get on board the ship—for what purpose? To find your lover? Is he a sailor gone to the New World? How dare you use me that way! You are the black widow spider I saw you for long ago. And you know what we do to vermin and liars and criminals on board ship in the middle of an ocean voyage, don't you?"

"No. But I am none of those things you call me."

There was nothing in Pedro's face she recognized. It was filled with such hatred and vengeance; she knew something evil had taken over his words and actions. "You are every one of those things. And we get rid of them before they sicken and destroy everyone on the ship." Pedro picked her up and carried her back to the bow. "I should make you walk the plank, but I'll have no such spectacle or accusations of murder against me." He looked around. No one watched or listened. He had purposefully sent all the crew below earlier to eat and sleep. "When you are missing tomorrow, I shall say you decided to walk on the bow in those fancy shoes of yours and slipped, fell overboard. And I will feign deep grief to the same degree you have pretended to love me."

"But this *is* murder! Don't do this! You are not a murderer, Pedro." Isabella tried to scream, but he covered her mouth with his large hand.

He kissed her cheek hard and groped her breasts. "I am what I have to be out here on the high seas. As you take your last breath, remember a man who trusted and loved you. Remember you lied to him. Take that to your watery grave."

Isabella calmed and stopped struggling, her eyes turning sorrowful. Seeing them, he removed his hand, sensing she wanted to speak. Quietly, resigned to her fate but hoping her honesty would persuade him to let her live, she whispered, "I'm very sorry for what I did, Pedro. I did care for you, even loved you, but I couldn't marry you when I loved someone else more, someone I shared my heart and soul with. I hope you love someone in such a way one day. I accept my fate and punishment for what I've done. I still can't marry you, so do what you must."

Pedro felt vindicated, but was still insanely enraged with being made a fool of. He couldn't have her on the ship with the men knowing the truth and seeing him as weak. In a fit of rage and insanity, he hoisted her over the side to drop her overboard. She was peaceful, with a faraway look in her eyes, as if her spirit was already leaving to go to her heaven, and she said, "If you do this, you will die soon. At the prime of your life when you have everything you ever wanted, you'll die tragically. And I will be the one to have everything you are denying me now."

"So be it," he said as he let her go into the waiting sea below.

Isabella didn't struggle, letting the water surround her like a blanket, breathing it in, knowing it would carry her away to the next place of living. She relaxed as her mind and spirit drifted away to what she thought heaven to be—a place of peace and beauty, of complete love and joy where she knew, eventually, she'd reunite with Miguel.

Chapter 16

Coming out of sleep, out of another world and another life, Ella woke in terror with her heart pounding, unable to breathe, choking, feeling herself drowning, feeling every emotion Isabella had as she went to her death. The dream had been so real, reminding her vividly of Peter dying on a boat, of Daniel never returning from his mission, and of Isabella searching for her lost love. Ella's stomach turned with grief as she thought, *This was supposed to help me? This is torturous.* To live again in Isabella's pain and loss was almost too much to bear. Memories of Helena and Matthias flashed through her mind, linking her next to Isabella and Miguel.

The places and times were distinct and different, but the scents and sounds of the sea and the undying love and loss permeated both. The people, however, all blended one into the other, and Ella felt her present life as an echo coming back from another time, listening with different ears, but the messages were the same. Now it seemed the sea had won again, taking Daniel. But did it? She couldn't go on much longer without knowing positively the truth of his fate.

All morning, she tossed the scenes in the dream around in her head, weighing their validity and relevance against her own reality. "I get it. To wait for someone who may never come back is a waste of life.

And to give up your life, to die for someone who may never come back is also a waste." She thought of Helena and Isabella, and even her own mother, sacrificing life to a loved one who never returned. *Is that what awaits me now if I don't come to terms with Daniel missing? If he's dead, his spirit probably would have come to me by now in a dream, or I'd have some intuitive notion of his death. It's so odd to have no clue, earthly or otherwise. Until something is shown or told to me for certain about Daniel, I can't presume he's dead. I'll do as Isabella and my mother did. I'll continue to love him, search for him, and wait.*

After breakfast, the beach lured her with its silky, blue-green water and golden sunlight shimmering off the sand and sea, lifting her spirits. Finding a perfect spot to spread a towel, she took a moment to look up and down the beach at all the life around her. Up the beach was a mother with two small children who ran in and out of the water, building sandcastles. Behind them under the shade of palm trees was a group of teens—girls flirting and giggling with boys, boys showing off throwing a Frisbee. Down the beach was a young couple who could've been honeymooners, affectionate, kissing, lying close together, oblivious of anything but their emotions and each other.

Normal life is going on all around me and here I sit in the middle of it looking like a normal person, like one of them, but I'm not. At this point in time, it should've been Daniel and me on the beach like that couple. In a few years, we could've been the ones with our kids playing around us. None of that will happen now. She knew she shouldn't go down that road, the self-pity expressway. In her peripheral vision, her eye was drawn to a man walking down the beach away from her. He stared at the oblivious young couple for a long time. She wondered what he was thinking as he watched them. Maybe the same as she had, how happy and in love they were and how it would never be him. Something about him seemed familiar—the shape of his back, his legs, *almost like Daniel.* But the man had a slight limp and his dark hair was gray at the temples. A deep ache churned in her gut, missing Daniel again and wishing for it to go away.

Lying back on the towel, she calmed her mind wanting nothing but to feel peace. With relaxing completely, her body felt as one with the earth below and the air around her. In the surreal, twilight place before sleep, the world became still as death yet vibrant with life. She lay face up on the beach with cool sand underneath and a golden sun above, warming her gently, seductively, like the caress of a lover's hand. The sweet scent of jasmine floated in the air while faraway soft music drifted into her mind, mixing with the sound of water lapping on the shore. The turquoise sea was so clear, brilliant, and teeming with life; it seemed not of this world. Ella realized she was in the scene her mother had shown her; she was happy and at peace. With closed eyes, she let herself love Daniel with all her heart, hoping to let him go; instead she longed to hear his voice just one more time.

In the stillness, she thought she heard the voice of a ghost calling to her. It said, *Ella*, and it sounded like him. The sound came from far above and all around, yet felt close and warm, as if the sun had burst into her heart. She heard it faintly again as a question. *Ella?*

So soothed and filled with love, her next wish was

for Daniel's spirit, wherever he was, to find her, to come close enough to tell her if he was dead or alive.

Then the whisper said, *Stretch your right arm out as far as you can, and open your hand to the sky.*

Ella was reminded of Kara, the palm reader, and thought the suggestion odd, but did so. As her open hand felt the heat of the sun soak into it, she felt a presence at the tips of her fingers like a warm breeze gliding over them, moving down each one, stopping on the diamond ring she still wore, stroking it, then covering her palm—smooth as silk with its gentle touch. The sensation of soft liquid fire ran up through her arm. She remembered Daniel vividly now and, behind her closed eyes, saw his face clearly.

In this deeply tranquil, hypnotic space, even though she knew it wasn't possible, Ella ached to feel his physical presence.

The palm trees rustled, a whisper flowed through them, sifting down to her. *Take me into your open arm and pull me toward you.*

Bringing her arm in toward her chest, she almost felt his body alongside hers, and the heat of him in an embrace.

She wanted to see him then, as he had been so long ago—his sparkling green eyes riveted on her; jaw squared and strong, skin tanned and slightly lined by the rigors of years at sea.

"Open your eyes," a male voice clearly said.

Ella hesitated, not wanting to wake from this almost-dream state.

The voice was closer now, whispering into her ear. "Please open your eyes. It's time."

Curious now, she opened her eyes just a bit, in a

squint, and saw a man standing next to her. He resembled Daniel, but was older and worn-out looking. Blinking hard against the sun backlighting his form, his face was dark in shadow. He smiled; it was similar to Daniel's smile. She blinked again against the glare of the sun. How odd to see an older man who had Daniel's smile and body. Ella thought she was really losing it now, losing her grip on reality.

She shaded her eyes with her hand and closed them, thinking she must be dreaming, hoping the vision would go away and leave her in peace.

Instead, the man spoke loudly then, as if issuing a command, and a bell of recognition chimed in her memory, of Daniel's slipping into officer mode sometimes when asking her to do something. In that same tone, he said, "Open your eyes again, please. I'm trying to decide if it's really you."

Ella opened her eyes. This was very strange. The man who looked like an older Daniel stood now, blocking the sun, and she saw his outline clearly. She moved her hand to where his foot was close to her and touched him. He was solid, real, not a vision, not a spirit. Alarm bells went off. And she was definitely awake.

She sat up. "You're real. Who are you?"

He laughed. "Of course, I'm real." Then he crouched down beside her, coming out of the shadow, and looked straight into her eyes. "Is it really you, Ella? I can't believe it."

His outer form and his hair had changed, but that smile and those eyes were unmistakable.

"I'm Ella. But you're not Daniel; you can't be. He's gone. Who are you?"

His laugh was filled with pure joy. “It’s me. Daniel. Daniel Ellsworth. Remember me?”

“I do, but you can’t be here. I don’t believe it. This is a dream. It’s not real.”

“It’s not a dream; it’s real and I’m here.”

“But how? How can this be?”

“I don’t know, but here we are. Later we can talk about how I got here. But now, I’d love to hold you. May I?”

Ella stood, touching his hand, then his arm. “You’re a real man.”

Smiling broadly, he said, “Last time I looked, yes.”

Searching his eyes for life, she said, “I’ve dreamt about you so often that I can’t believe this is not a dream. I must be dreaming.”

With that, Daniel put his arms around her. “Do my arms feel like a dream?”

“No. But stranger things have happened lately.”

He whispered into her ear. “How can I prove to you beyond a shadow of doubt that I’m Daniel and I’m real?”

Ella backed away. “Tell me where we met and the first words you spoke to me.”

He flashed his familiar brilliant smile. “That’s easy. Sailors Rest. And I said something like, ‘You look so familiar to me. I think I must’ve known you in a past life.’”

Ella pulled him closer and examined his face, his eyes. “Oh, my God. It is you.”

“You better believe it.” He took her face in his hands, so familiar a move, she knew a kiss would be next. But he asked, “May I kiss you?”

Ella leaned in and kissed him tentatively, still not

sure she wasn't imagining this. His lips were warm and familiar, not airy or distant like in a dream; his embrace was solid and real. She recognized his love coming through the intimacy of his kiss. As she gave in to it, she felt she had walked through the front door of a long-forgotten home where love and warmth surrounded her. Inside the safety of his love, she kissed him passionately. It was a kiss that had been waiting for two years, in the air, carried in the storms, breathed through the dark nights of waiting, hoping, and longing. "I love you so," she whispered between gulps of him, his mouth pouring love all through her.

"I will always love you, my sweet Ella. I can't believe I found you."

"What happened? Where have you been? How did you find me?"

Daniel looked around at all the people on the beach. He was uncomfortable. "Can we go somewhere and sit in the cool air so we can talk?" He pointed behind them. "That cottage looks familiar. Are you staying there?"

"Yes. Don't you remember? It was only two years ago I stayed there, but seems like a decade with what I've been through with you gone, and no information about you. Let's go inside. We have a lot of talking to do." She took his hand, and they walked back to her cottage with her still disbelieving. She pinched herself hard; it hurt, but she didn't wake up. *Can this possibly be real?*

"I keep thinking this is a dream, too," he said. "But it isn't, Ella. I found you."

Once inside, she held him as if she'd never let him go. Touching his shoulders, face, arms, and neck over and over to make sure he was solid and real, she practically yelled, "I can't believe it! You're real. You're here. How did this happen? I spent so much time—days, weeks, months, almost two years dying of grief while waking up alive every morning, thinking you were dead. Everyone believed you were dead."

"Oh, God. I'm so sorry. I couldn't help it."

"But what happened to you? The Navy wouldn't tell me anything because I wasn't your next of kin. They searched for any family of yours; I searched for six months and finally gave up. Rather than face the possibility you'd died, I conjured scenarios of you having been hurt, in a coma, having amnesia or PTSD, and sitting in a VA hospital somewhere, maybe wounded so horribly you didn't want to see me."

"I am so sorry for what you went through. I thought I changed my next of kin to you, but somehow the paperwork got mixed up, and my mother was still listed, and I deployed so quickly I didn't double-check anything. A couple of my buddies knew we might get engaged, but I guess they didn't know enough about you to find you, and you didn't know their full names. In fact, my two closest friends were killed."

"How awful. But what happened to you, Daniel? Why were you gone so long? Where were you?"

He wrung his hands over and over, beads of perspiration formed on his face. Looking away from her and down at the table where they sat, he answered. "Most of it, I don't remember—too traumatic, I guess. My mission was highly classified, secret, and had been to fly over North Korea, to bomb air bases. None of us thought we'd get out alive. The only thing I remember while flying over the ocean toward my target was enemy jets coming out of nowhere. Then something hit my wing, and I went crashing toward the sea. Then I don't remember anything. I was told I ejected and floated in the ocean, eventually drifting to shore. But I'd had a severe head injury and broken bones, including a broken leg. I was in a coma, they said, had a blood clot, surgeries, more coma. When I came out of it, I had amnesia. I lost my memory for a long time. I was told I'd been shipped to a hospital in Japan for a very long time until I stabilized, then more recently came back to a VA hospital in California, then back to Virginia. When I was told my name, I eventually remembered, then started remembering other things about the Navy, flying, my buddies. I'm here now, but I didn't know who or where I was for a long time. The only thing that kept me hanging on to life was a deeply embedded memory, almost like I felt it in my body, of someone who loved me so profoundly it was part of every cell in me. I didn't remember you specifically, but I remembered how loved I'd been by a woman, and how much I loved her."

Daniel put his head in his hands, clearly upset. "They said I had post-traumatic stress disorder. I've probably blocked out a lot as a survival mechanism—the rest is just too painful to talk about. Can we leave it at that?"

Ella smoothed his hair off his forehead. "Of course. I don't need to know everything."

Daniel looked back up at her. "Eventually I remembered this amazing love I'd had, but couldn't recall the details. I think my heart remembered what my brain couldn't. Later, after seeing photos of Key West one of the other patients had, I remembered it clearly as a place I'd been very happy. And with no family, being honorably discharged, and not able to fly anymore, I had nowhere to go. So, I came here a month ago. I thought, at the very least, I'd get a good rest, some sun, and maybe something here would trigger more memories. A lot of people with amnesia regain memories from their family and loved ones being around, telling them their life stories, showing pictures. But I didn't have any of that. So, when my gut told me to come here, I trusted it."

"I'm so glad you did. What's weird is that, about a month ago, I got the idea to come here, where we'd met and fallen in love. But I came here to let you go, to stop loving you and move on. But after arriving, no matter what I did or what dreams or spirits visited me, I couldn't let go and knew I'd never stop loving you."

He clutched her hand in both of his as they talked, like he was falling off a cliff and her grasp was the only thing to save him. "I'm so glad you came. Just this past week, I've been visiting different beaches, walking up and down the shore, looking for something, someone I thought was waiting for me. Today I was drawn to the lovers down the beach, and they reminded me of a time when I had the same kind of love, when I kissed and held a beautiful woman, my woman. Then my gut said, *Turn around. Look behind you.* I saw a beautiful blond lying on a towel. Your face and hair, your body, everything about you was so familiar, like I'd just seen my best friend. The closer I walked toward you, a name came into my mind instantly. And the longer I looked, I knew who you were, my Ella, and all the love came rushing back. Memories of us, this room, your friend, Janie, good times, are flooding back to me now as we sit here talking."

She kissed him, wanting to draw every particle of him into her and never let go.

He laughed with complete joy, then grew calm and serious. "Can I make love to you?"

"Well, if this is a dream I'm going to wake up from, I might as well have a damn good time while it's still here."

"I'll do everything and anything you ask of me as long as you do one thing," he said.

"What's that?"

"Believe. Believe I'm real."

"I do," she said.

He picked her up in his still muscular arms and carried her to the bedroom.

His body still felt as if made for hers. Every curve of his muscles was still familiar; every move he made toward her was natural and loving, moving from kissing to touching to yearning and passion so explosive they got lost in each other. They made love over and over through the night with no sense of time or place, only a sense of each other. Any doubt she had of this new situation being real was extinguished quickly with the power of his love. He wrapped around and moved inside her with the familiarity of a long-time lover, ravenous for her, with the adoration of a husband for a wife. She let him devour her, heart and soul. He gave her his spirit, body, and love in their entirety. Everything that made him a man, he gave to her. She loved him, took all of him, and gave it back tenfold.

This was no ordinary love affair. It was a bond forged from a place they'd known before they were born and to the place they'd go when they died. Ella knew she'd love him no matter how long or far they were parted in the future. They sealed their collective fate now as they moved together into a place of their own making, a life far above the confines of earth—like the jet soaring over the sea, not bound to its limitations. They were free.

"Ella, I'm so in love with you, so enduring after all this time. My God, what is this?"

She held him, with his head to her heart. "What does it matter as long as it exists? A name or explanation isn't necessary. Only you and I need to know what we share."

He reached up and kissed her neck, nuzzling into it. "You're so smart, so understanding of so many things, important things in life, complicated things."

Ella smiled, running her fingers through his hair. "Hmm, yes, I'm good at complicated things. Like you."

"Like me, indeed." He raised up on his elbow to look directly at her. "We've started something I don't want to end. I don't want to lose you. Ever." He took her face in his hands and kissed her, moving above her once more, their bodies becoming as one again, and he whispered, "My Ella Bella. My love."

"My Daniel," she said, closing her eyes, feeling miles above the earth, floating in another world, feeling close to what she thought heaven must be.

****

Early the next morning, Ella couldn't sleep with every nerve in her body tingling with the events of the day before throwing her emotions into overdrive. While Daniel slept, she hummed a tune while she worked in the kitchen, fixing a huge breakfast, whipping up pancakes, scrambled eggs, and cutting fresh fruit. In the middle of her cooking frenzy, her phone rang. It was Janie. Ella had planned to call her that day anyway to let her know of the Daniel miracle, so she greeted her with happy notes in her voice.

"Ella? Is that you? You sound so different."

"Oh, my God, Janie. You are not going to believe what happened yesterday."

"And *you* are not going to believe what I found out just this morning. Nothing, absolutely *nothing* tops what I have to tell you. You're going to flip out! Are you sitting down?"

Ella sat. "This is crazy. What the heck are you talking about? What could be so good?"

"Seriously? What the hell is the most important thing in your life? Why are you in Key West?"

"Well, Daniel, of course. But wait till you hear this!"

Janie started talking so fast, Ella couldn't get a word in. "No, Ella, *you* wait. I have news about Daniel! That last naval officer I spoke with about you and Daniel, the one who said he might be alive, but to expect the worst? Well, he called and said since it had been two years and no next of kin had been found, and no one had inquired about Daniel, or come to claim him, that *you* could. Since you are the only person to come forward being his friend, fiancée, his closest thing to a relative, that you could now claim him."

Ella giggled, then started to laugh so hard she couldn't speak.

Janie held the phone out from her ear in disbelief. "Okay. You've definitely gone off the deep end. I tell you that you can find Daniel and you laugh? W-T-F?"

Calming barely enough to talk, Ella spoke in

between gasping for air. "Janie! I don't have to do anything because I already found Daniel. Or rather, he found me on the beach. Just yesterday. He's here. He's alive. He's sleeping in my bed right now. Oh, God, I couldn't be any happier."

Janie fell into the closest chair in shock. "No, I don't believe it. This is too amazing. How? Where? How did he get there? How did he find you?"

Ella grinned from ear to ear. "Oh, Janie, there's so much to tell you." She condensed everything Daniel had said to explain it to Janie. "He recovered enough to remember Key West as a place where he'd been very happy and loved. So, with no family and nowhere else to go, he came here and ended up on the same beach as me. Just yesterday. We've been together all day and night, talking about everything, picking up where we left off. It's wonderful; it's beyond amazing. It's truly a miracle. I'm so happy. I can't believe it."

"I can't believe it either," Janie said with a flatness in her voice.

Getting back to her cooking, Ella said, "Aren't you happy for me? You don't sound so happy."

"Of course, I am. It's just that something seems odd about the whole situation. I mean, I just got a call from the Navy this morning and—poof—Daniel's already found you the day before in Key West. It's like reverse time-travel or a weird horror movie, like it couldn't possibly be real and have happened like it did."

"Well, believe it; it happened. What did the Navy guy tell you about where Daniel was or his condition?"

"That's the strange thing—he wouldn't tell me anything. He said since you were the only one to come forward and you were his fiancée, they would give the information *only* to you, and you could claim Daniel. And I was just so excited I didn't push it. I just took the officer's name and phone number for you to call him."

"Well, now I don't have to call. But that's an odd choice of words he used, isn't it—to 'claim' Daniel? Maybe the last information the guy had about Daniel was that he was in a coma. He must've had an old report."

Janie was glad Ella couldn't see her face and the worry on it. "Well, maybe. The timing just seems too quick. Hey, don't take this the wrong way, but are you sure that guy in your bedroom is Daniel? What if he's someone who looks exactly like him and knew all about you from what Daniel told him before he died, like that guy in the civil war movie, *Sommersby*?"

Ella dropped the frying pan. "Are you for real?"

"Yes. Because with what you're telling me about Daniel, he could be an impersonator. And you are vulnerable right now and gorgeous and a great catch; what guy wouldn't go for you if he could?"

Laughing out loud, Ella shot back, "Now *you're* the one who's crazy. That's the most bizarre thing you've ever come up with."

"Well, this whole thing is bizarre."

"Listen. To put your mind at ease, I know for certain it's Daniel—his voice, his body, the lovemaking. I even asked him where we first met and his first words to me, and he remembered exactly and instantly. That's no impostor."

"I guess not. Sorry. I'm just still baffled about it all, in shock sort of."

"Well, so was I until he explained most of what

happened and how he got here to Key West…and the personal stuff; well, there's no refuting any of that."

"Just be careful. Be a good reporter and keep on your toes. Keep tuned in for anything unusual."

"Stop! You're my best friend. Support me. Be happy for me. Stop questioning the first happiness I've had in two years."

"Okay, okay. I do want you to be happy, but also healthy and safe."

"Hey, Daniel's just coming into the kitchen. Say hello and you'll know for yourself." She handed the phone to him. "It's Janie!"

Daniel grabbed the phone and smiled with genuine joy. "Hi, Janie!"

It surely did sound like him, but all Janie could say was, "Daniel, I can't believe it's you. I just can't believe this. It's like talking to a ghost on the phone."

A serious, odd look moved across Daniel's face. "Well, good to hear from you, too. And I'm very much alive."

"Hey, don't cop an attitude. I was joking. You know me, always kidding around."

Daniel's demeanor brightened. "True. I kind of forgot. My memory's not the best these days. But I do remember your voice and your laugh. Thank you for being such a good friend to Ella through this ordeal. You're the best."

"No problem. I'd do anything for Ella. And I'm so glad you're alive. What a miracle."

"Yes, it is. Well, I have this great breakfast waiting for me and I'm starving. You take it easy, Janie."

"You, too," she said, and then was curious that he didn't say anything about talking again or getting together soon or even seeing her again. *Odd*, she thought. When he handed the phone back to Ella to say goodbye, Janie told her, "He didn't say anything about talking again or seeing me in the future. I'm sorry, Ella, but my gut says there's something not quite right."

A bit irritated, Ella shot back, "You know, with what Daniel's been through and his head injury, things are going to be a bit odd here and there. I'm willing to put up with it. Things will smooth out eventually."

"Sorry. I'm sure you're right. I'm just protective of my best friend. You deserve only the best."

"Thanks, and now I feel I finally *have* the best, with Daniel coming back. Which reminds me, can you call Hannah for me, fill her in and tell her I'll call when I get a chance?"

"Sure thing. And I truly am happy for you, Ella. Call me with updates, or if you just need to talk."

Ella was relieved they'd ended their conversation on a good, positive note. Now she could focus on the only thing that mattered now—Daniel—getting him completely well again and picking up their lives where they had left off before he went to war.

Chapter 17

For the next week, they were inseparable. Every night they cooked sumptuous dinners, drank good wine, and after incredible lovemaking, they sat on the beach, satiated and intoxicated with each other. Mornings, they drank strong coffee and lay in the sun, dove headfirst into the ocean and played like children. Entwined together, they kissed as they rode the waves. "It doesn't get any better than this," Ella said between kisses. "This place, you, us. I'll never be happier than I am now, finding you after I thought you'd died."

"But you will always be this happy if you choose to be."

"As long as you're here, I'm happy."

"You need to be this happy no matter what, no matter whether I'm here or not."

"Don't say such things. I've already lived through your loss; now you're back. Let me enjoy it. You won't ever leave me again, will you?"

"No one can make promises like that for the future. You, of all people, know the future is not ours to predict. We need to live for the moment, enjoy what we have right now and not look to the future."

A bell of alarm went off in Ella's mind. Why, after being reunited, was Daniel speaking of not having a future? *Of course*, she realized, *he's been so traumatized, having his plans, his career, and future ripped out from under him. Of course, he's cautious. He's just trying to protect himself and me, but is he thinking of any future at all?*

"You're not in the Navy anymore. Have you recovered enough to think about what kind of work you might do, or what you'd like to do with your future?"

"A little. I got a bunch of medals, an honorable discharge, but they don't pay the bills. I don't know what I'll do next. I can't fly anymore, but I can still sail, and I still love the sea."

"The damn sea. The Navy and the sea took you away, almost killed you, and now you want to go back. How could you?"

Daniel held her face. "Because it's my life. You and the sea. I love you both. I have full benefits and disability income, but I have to make more of a living; I have to wake up every day being productive, doing work I love. Don't you want that for me?"

Reluctantly she said, "Yes, of course, I do. But I don't want to risk losing you again." Her thoughts drifted back to Peter dying at sea, to the dream she'd just had of Isabella and Miguel—too fresh in her mind to be magnanimous about his wishes. "If you have to work at sea, you better take me with you. If you die, we die together, because I can't survive your death again."

"If you want to work at sea with me, you can. I have money put away, enough to buy a thirty-five-foot sailboat. We can run tours and charters; you can write about your travels. Sound good?"

"Sounds heavenly."

He put his arms out to invite her in. She fell into them, never wanting to move away from his embrace again. As he held her, she opened her eyes and looked around, waiting for the other shoe to drop. This could not be her life; things this good or lucky didn't happen to her.

Going to sleep that night, Ella fully expected she'd wake up the next morning alone, that it would all have been a dream. But with the first light of day entering the room, she found him lying next to her. "I still can't believe this is true," she whispered as he slept. A seed of doubt crept into her heart, but then he awoke, smiled, held and kissed her, ready to enter her body and capture her heart again, taking her away to a surreal world of only ecstasy and love, and any lingering doubt she had, dissolved.

****

Another week went by quickly with them making up for lost time and lost love. They talked about the past and their lives before they met, about their meeting being destiny. They laughed and spent restorative time on the beach, soaking up sun and water, thoroughly enjoying their paradise and each other.

One day, after a swim, they lay next to each other and Ella touched his hair, teasing him about the gray at the temples. "How did this happen?"

"The doc told me it was probably from trauma, prolonged stress. That will do it. And I'll always have this limp. I hope it doesn't bother you."

"Are you kidding? It's you I love. I wouldn't care if you had worse injuries; I'd love you just the same."

"Some women would go running if their man came back with partial memory and other physical things wrong with him, looking and acting differently from the guy they fell in love with."

Ella took his hand and kissed it. "I'm not going

anywhere. I didn't fall in love with your body and face and hair. Don't get me wrong—those are wonderful attributes of yours, but I fell in love with your heart and soul. Falling in love with you was like finding an old, original love that got reawakened—like something clicked deep inside me. I knew who you were and remembered the love already there. Does that sound crazy?"

"No. Those are exactly my feelings about you. They were from the beginning."

"What we have is rare, Daniel."

He looked off into the sky, finding words there. "Actually, I don't think it is. I think everyone is capable of having this if they'd only wake up inside their lives and recognize it, or stop fearing it or running from it or abusing it. Anyone can love this way. You have to believe it's possible first. Because love is what we are and why we're here, all of us."

"Wow. Going to war has made you very deep."

"No. Almost dying and coming back to life is what's made me realize what a gift all of this is." Daniel waved his arm out to take in the breadth of beach and ocean. "This beautiful life and this paradise." He put his arm around Ella. "And this beautiful heart of yours. Sometimes it takes dying to appreciate life and live it to the fullest, even with all its faults and imperfections and fear and pain. It's all a gift to be treasured every day."

"I do. Now that you're here, I treasure every moment."

Daniel turned to face her. "But if I wasn't here, would you still treasure every moment?"

"It was different loving you when you were gone.

It was hard to treasure anything."

"Love makes life richer, true, but if I died tomorrow, I wouldn't want to think you couldn't carry on and have a great life, fall in love with someone else."

Ella sat up and pulled away from him. "Are you serious? We just found each other, and you're talking about dying and me carrying on with life. Why, Daniel? Something doesn't feel right about this."

He held her. "It's okay. Don't get upset. Remember I told you I'd always love you and be close no matter what?"

"Yes."

"But when I was missing, you didn't remember that, did you? You were sad and lonely."

"I was grief-stricken. One day, I was engaged and planning a future. The next morning, you're gone. I was devastated. How could I possibly have felt comforted by your words when I had no indication if you were even alive?"

"I understand what you're saying. It was a unique circumstance. But with what happened to us just a couple weeks ago, with finding each other again, don't you see how quickly things can change? Miracles happen. You have to have faith and keep love in your life, even if it means loving someone different than who you thought you'd love."

Ella let his words sink into her heart. She knew what he meant, but the words still got stuck halfway down her understanding—too large and worrisome to swallow and digest. She wasn't there yet, where he was in understanding. "I just found you, so it's hard to talk about losing you." *Losing you like all the others*, she thought, with memories flooding her brain of lovers in other times and places. It seemed she'd loved and waited and died alone for a thousand years. Instantly she saw the futility, the waste of herself and knew what Daniel was talking about. He didn't want her to throw away her life because that wasn't love—that was a waste of love. And she told him so.

"That's my Ella." He kissed her sweetly and lightly all over her face, almost as if he weren't there, like he was part of the breezes swirling around them.

She kissed his cheek, and he tasted of salt and sea mist, reminiscent of the last kisses in life with the men she'd loved. She kissed his lips to make sure he was real. He was, but the kiss hinted of goodbye, of longing and loneliness. She opened her eyes and watched him fill with sadness. Something was wrong. But in the next moment, he snapped back to his usual, happy self.

"Why did you look so sad just a second ago?" she asked.

Daniel hesitated, blurting out, "Some things have changed with me that we need to talk about. Why don't we go to a nice restaurant for dinner, somewhere quiet where we can talk?"

"Sounds wonderful, but I'm a little worried about what you want to talk about."

"Don't worry—it's not a big deal. I just need to get it out in the open. Honesty in everything between us, right?"

She smiled adoringly. "Always."

****

They went to the same restaurant they'd gone to before they'd made love the first time, and Ella felt its magic working again. She hoped this was a sign of another new beginning for them. On the drive there, Ella spoke excitedly about the new future the two of them would forge. Daniel kept fairly quiet, just listening and nodding. Their table overlooked the ocean with a spectacular sunset brewing in the distance. Sipping martinis, they both relaxed into the night when Ella broached the subject of the talk he wanted to have.

"Ella, things have changed with me since I came back—from war, from losing my sense of myself and my life. I had a lot of time before we met again to think about what I wanted out of life, never thinking I'd find love again. I was alone and figured I always would be. What I'm about to say, don't take it wrong, because I want to spend every day of my life with you. But as far as a legal marriage and the big wedding and all of that, well, I don't want any of it. I don't want to get married legally."

Ella looked down at the table, not wanting to look into his eyes. She didn't know who this man was—he couldn't possibly be her Daniel. She fiddled nervously with her silverware, not knowing how to respond, then threw her napkin on her plate.

"You're angry and disappointed," he said.

Her eyes flashed intense emotion at him. "Did you think I'd be jumping for joy at that news? Of course, I'm angry and disappointed and shocked and bewildered and worried." She held up her hand with the diamond ring he'd given her. "I've never taken this off since the day you asked me to marry you. Now you're telling me you don't want to get married. I'm beyond confused."

He took her hand across the table. "I told you I want to spend every day of my life with you. I just don't believe in the legal stuff anymore. A piece of paper means nothing, not with the kind of love we have. The paper doesn't mean you won't lose your greatest love. You, of all people, know that."

"I certainly do. But I thought, with finding each other, we'd pick up where we left off and continue on with our plans."

"We've both changed with what we've been through. I don't want to make promises that life events will break and have you devastated again."

Ella thought of the dreams and memories she'd had of other times of living with all the loss and pain resurfacing. It was like he knew—like he was in her head and knew everything about her experiences and was trying to prevent a recurrence of the same ending to their current life story. But he couldn't possibly know. Her thoughts spun and swirled in her head with the drink and the odd, disturbing conversation.

Daniel continued, "As long as we're talking about the future, there are other things you should know. I would really prefer not to have children. I love kids and like the idea of doing volunteer work, maybe teaching them to sail or something."

Ella interrupted him. "Daniel, you're scaring me. It's like you're a different person. What has changed your mind?"

"Probably what I went through and not knowing exactly what the future will bring. With the things I've seen, I can't justify bringing more souls, innocent children, into the world when there's so much suffering. Having a family doesn't guarantee happiness or that you won't spend your life alone," he whispered with a soul-deep pain surfacing in his eyes. His words reminded her of Miguel's, saving the children while having none of his own. She struggled to understand what Daniel must've been through to cause such a drastic change in him. But with realizing how similar his words and actions were to the dreams she'd had of Greece and Spain, the coincidences were coming on fast and getting too weird. She had to share these stories with him, so he'd understand her growing fear.

Ella turned serious and ordered another drink for them. "Now it's my turn to share something with you I never intended. But the similarities are freaking me out, and I don't know what to think. If I don't share this, I'd be lying by omission."

When he heard her stories of living in other times and places, Daniel did not look shocked or surprised at all. He was serene and understanding, as if already having a clue about what she was going to say. It unnerved her, but gave her the courage to blurt out the strange things that had happened on this trip before she met up with him—about her mother's spirit showing her to go to Key West, about Kara and the regression, and how she thought it was both their souls that had lived and loved each other in those times. She went on and on, consumed with the memories, as if she were Scheherazade telling stories to save her life.

Daniel listened intently while sipping his drink. Every now and then, he'd be amazed and in awe of her. When she finished speaking, he simply said, "I believe every word is true. You know how I feel about karma and past lives. This explains a lot. I knew there had to be a history with us long before this life, but you, my amazing Ella, you actually got the times and places and names and faces. What a gift you've been given."

Ella exploded. “A gift? Are you kidding me? You think it’s a gift to be tormented with these stories, not knowing where they came from and why I’m learning of them now? It feels more like persecution. And with you showing up alive out of the blue like you were dropped from the sky, with all your extreme changes dovetailing into these stories and their horrible endings, I’m scared to death of what’s going to happen next.”

Daniel got up and walked over to her side of the table. “Stand up. Let me hug you. C’mon.” She did, and they embraced as he whispered to calm her. “You have nothing to be afraid of. Everything is just as it should be. We love each other. That’s all that really matters, right? The past is the past. Let it go and just love me right now.”

Soothed by his deep, committed love as a salve for her soul, Ella quieted her emotions and realized he was right. He had the ability to bring her back to center when she was emotionally skewing off the edge. Experiencing such peace with him reminded her of what she loved about Daniel most and what they truly meant to each other. She had to admit he was right—their love and relationship wasn’t about anything material or plans or even of the future. In that moment, she realized this new relationship with him would have to be taken a day at a time. Things might change eventually, but she didn’t care. Ella was grateful that this amazing, loving man who knew her like no one else had been given back to her. It really was the closest thing to a miracle she’d probably ever know, so she gracefully acquiesced to his love.

Before drifting into sleep that night, Daniel told her, “The only promises we need to make are to love and take care of each other, help people, do good things, be kind and thankful for all we have, to truly take life a day at a time, and enjoy every moment because you never know when it will be your last. Can you do this?"

"I think so," she whispered, but his alluding to their "last day alive" sent a chill down her spine. With all the emotions of the evening, something felt off-kilter again. She was fine with all of it until he mentioned not knowing when their last day alive would be. Something was very wrong, with him, with the situation. She feared Janie might've been right.

Her last conversation with Janie and her suspicions of Daniel burst into Ella's confused and murky brain like turning on a spotlight in a black room. She recalled Janie's telling her about the call from the naval officer saying she could "claim" Daniel. Now those words struck a chord of fear in her, like something terrible might've happened to him, that he'd been incapacitated or worse. Obviously he was alive and well, yet residual doubt and foreboding still rippled from that stone of truth Janie had dropped into her world.

Combined now with Daniel's uncharacteristic behavior, Ella couldn't shake the feeling of something having gone horribly awry. Or maybe something had been wrong about their reconciliation from the very beginning and she'd been so overcome with love and happiness she hadn't seen it.

While Ella watched Daniel in his sound sleep, her mind filled with suspicions. Fear gnawed at her psyche as her body gave way to sleep. In the night, in her deepest slumber, the fear called out like a beam of light through a stormy night, searching for the guidance Ella needed. In the dark space of the dream world, she saw her mother's spirit in the distance and followed the trail of her sparkling light to a place that seemed familiar, but Ella couldn't quite remember where or what it was. Words then filled the space...*Your memory will return as the pictures unfold of a time when Lilah and Martha were daughter and mother, as you and I are. Don't make the same mistakes we did then.*

****

The Stone Cottage,
Maine, 1852
"Love, Lies, Secrets, and the Sea"

Lilah had been born on the first of July 1852 in Portland, Maine, the only child to Henry and Martha Jameson. Her father was a respected doctor, and Martha was a proper society lady and doting mother. Lilah grew up with many advantages: a lovely home, good education, the best clothing, food, and summer holidays at the seaside.

Her father had high hopes of Lilah attending Bates College in Lewiston, Maine, the first college in New England to admit women. When he saw how precocious she was, he shared his dreams for her to graduate college and make a career for herself, advising Lilah that marriage was wonderful, but independence for a woman would be valuable in the world she'd live in as an adult.

Lilah had just turned fourteen years old in 1866, when a devastating fire on Independence Day in Portland destroyed most of the buildings and homes, including theirs. They were fortunate to have a small cottage by the sea near Cape Elizabeth, so Lilah and her mother moved there while her father stayed in the city to continue his medical practice and build them a new home. In the meantime, even though she missed her father, Lilah was very happy living there, especially in the summer. She'd walk for hours along the coast and look up at the Portland Headlight, the lighthouse, high on a cliff, and daydream about a ship coming to port and bringing her a handsome sailor.

Shortly after moving to the seaside, Lilah noticed boys her age would stare, attracted to her bright blue eyes and long blond curls. She met several she liked, but her mother warned her to stay away from them, with most being the sons of fishermen or farmers, saying her father wouldn't approve.

Lilah and her mother went into town regularly for supplies, and on one trip, bored with shopping, Lilah was drawn to walk by the ocean. She was attracted to its deep blue expanse stretching to the horizon, feeling a sense of freedom, especially when watching the boats and tall sailing ships gliding over the water. But she also trembled slightly with fear of something on or under the water. That vast unknown world below the smooth surface scared her.

Some days she'd walk on the docks where the fishing boats came in, inspecting their interiors, wondering how they worked; sometimes, watching from a distance, a fisherman would unload his catch, and she felt oddly drawn to these men. She admired them for their bravery, facing the unpredictable sea every day to make a living, and felt a familiarity with them. Underneath, though, was her own fear of the water and of how those brave fishermen might go out one day and never come back.

On one of her walks, a young man frightened her

by jumping off a boat and up on the dock right in front of her. Lilah was thrown off guard, not so much by the unexpected presence of him but more by how strikingly handsome he was. She couldn't stop looking into his deep green eyes, sparkling with light, contrasting thick black hair, deeply waved like the ocean itself. He seemed just as transfixed on her. Apologizing for scaring her, he introduced himself as Nathaniel and held out his hand.

"My name is Lilah." She shook his hand lightly. "I'm very glad to meet you."

They made small talk about where they were from and where they lived, family and friends. Even though she'd had young men friends at school, for the first time, Lilah felt completely taken with feelings she'd never experienced before. He was sixteen years old and fished on his father's boat. His hands were rough, and his skin tanned from the sun, but she was very attracted to him. They walked to a nearby bench and talked for an hour until she realized her mother would be looking for her. Lilah really didn't want to leave him, and he seemed to feel the same way. He asked if she might meet him again the next day. "Probably not. My mother only comes to town once a week to shop, so we won't be back until next week."

"I'm sad because I'd like very much to see you sooner. You are very lovely, if I may say so, and quite charming."

Lilah blushed deeply with never having been talked to like this by a young man. She guessed his confidence to speak forthrightly came from being two years older than she. With his handsome face and compelling demeanor, she thought he must have many girlfriends, and so brazenly asked him.

Nathaniel laughed. “Many?” His beautiful smile enchanted her. “I don’t have even one.” Sheepishly he looked down at the cap he fussed with, then looked straight at her and said, “Until now, I’m hoping. Can you be my first true lady friend?”

Lilah returned the brilliant smile. “I would be delighted.”

They agreed to meet the following Tuesday afternoon. Lilah would bring a picnic.

****

Throughout the next year, they met regularly. When Lilah turned fifteen, she felt more like a young woman than a girl, and her interest in Nathaniel grew in unexpected ways. They’d walk arm in arm together near the sea and talk of every subject imaginable. Even though he didn’t have the same formal education she did, he was very intelligent and wise. He loved fishing and made a good living at it and loved being on the sea every day. Through the cold winter months, he would meet her near her cottage. They would ride back to his small home where his father, who had met and very much liked Lilah, was more than happy to let them spend time together. Or they’d slip into a shop or the barn to keep warm and whisper to each other in the corner.

Eventually people saw them together and word got back to her mother. A heated argument ensued after Martha found out Nathaniel was a fisherman. Lilah argued all of his good points and how much she cared for him. But Martha’s response was as expected. “You are much too young to know of such feelings. Even if you did, your father and I would never permit him to court you." Lilah accepted her mother's words to keep the peace, but they didn't change her actions. In fact, the more her mother protested, the closer she and Nathaniel became.

By the next summer, they were spending a great deal of time together. He kissed her for the first time on her sixteenth birthday and thought he would go to the moon with delight. She loved this young man and told him so.

"I love you, too," he said. "I have for a long time. But your parents would never approve of me as a suitor. What shall we do?"

"I don't know. I only know I want to keep seeing you. We'll be moving back to Portland soon with our new home almost ready. I won't be able to come down here to Cape Elizabeth on my own. I don't know how we can see each other."

"We'll find a way. I'll go to Portland. My father will let me take his wagon, even if it can only be once or twice a month. During the winter, visits will be longer apart, but it'll be better than not seeing each other at all." Nathaniel grew pensive. "Maybe time and distance will be a good measure of our feelings for one another."

"Mine will only grow stronger, I know it. But we have no choice. In two or more years, my father will want me to attend college. It's always been his dream for me. But if he will not let me see you, then I'll choose you over college."

"No. You can't give up your dream for me. Eventually, you'd resent me for it. It's best for you to go as planned, and we'll see what the future holds. If we really care about each other, nothing will stand in our way."

Lilah kissed him gently. "This is what I love about you. You're so wise, so fair, and have good common sense. I know my parents admire those qualities in a person. Eventually when they get to know you, they'll accept you."

"Then let's live life each day as it comes and see what it brings. For now, nothing much will change. We can keep seeing each other and letting our friendship grow. Right?"

"Wonderful." She put her arm through his, and her head on his shoulder as they walked by the sea, their love growing. But something else grew in her heart—an odd sense of being alone even while she held him close. This thing felt as if it had lain dormant in her until his love broke it free—a whisper of fear—of losing him somehow. As she clutched his arm and watched the sea, everything felt connected. It was as if the sea clung to him as she did, vying for his time, his love, and maybe his life. As Nathaniel spoke of how good the future could be, the fear in her subsided, but in the coming months, it returned uninvited and wouldn't let go.

****

Lilah and her mother moved back to Portland at the end of that summer. At first Lilah and Nathaniel missed each other so much, she could barely stand it. They wrote infrequently because Lilah would have to intercept the mail to keep her secret love from her parents. Nathaniel managed to take his father's wagon up to see her once a month, usually on Sundays. Lilah found it easy to make excuses to get away. She'd tell white lies, rationalizing because her parents had given her no other way. But as the winter came on, Nathaniel could not make the trip as often.

Martha, her mother, suspected Lilah was still writing and possibly seeing Nathaniel, and prayed she hadn't fallen in love with him. But she decided to say nothing, hoping with winter and the distance, their hearts would grow cool as well. Maybe by spring Lilah would be interested in other people and things. Martha tried to get her to go to dances and meet boys her own age.

Lilah went through the motions for her mother's sake, but her heart only grew fonder toward Nathaniel. She only felt the slightest twinge of guilt at keeping secret from her parents her relationship with him. She became comfortable with it, feeling it was the only way she knew to keep him in her life—by living in a world of secrets and lies. Lilah did, however, struggle with an uneasy feeling of her actions coming back to haunt her, of a fateful, tragic end, a payback for the truth withheld. But she had no choice except to lie by omission. She rationalized that her parents played as large a part as she in the deception with their insistence that she never see Nathaniel again. But even with secrets, winter, and distance, by the next spring, their love burned even hotter.

****

Through four years of college, Lilah and Nathaniel continued seeing each other whenever they could, and their love grew more every year. During those years, Nathaniel had built his own fishing business five times over what his father had done. He owned three large boats and employed several crews. He'd amassed a large amount of money, enough to build Lilah a home. He chose a piece of land near a bluff overlooking the sea and built a modest but lovely stone cottage. There was plenty of room for them and hopefully children in the future. He had a plot for a vegetable garden in the back, away from the winds blowing off the ocean. He planted large flowerbeds all around the cottage and rosebushes down the front walk. Inside was a front parlor and living room with a large stone fireplace. The floors were heart pine, and he'd purchased rugs from Portland to make the place warm and cozy. He outfitted the kitchen with a wood stove to cook and heat the house. He would let her choose the furniture and dishes, and hoped her parents would approve.

But when Lilah told her parents of her wonderful beau and how successful he was, they were appalled that she'd lied all that time and had continued to see the same fisherman they forbade to court her. With her betrayal, they didn't care about his success and only saw him as not good enough for their daughter.

Lilah pleaded with her father, "Years ago, Mother asked me to wait until we moved back to Portland and I finished school to see if I still felt the same way. I did as she requested. Next you asked me to attend college, keeping the future open to new experiences and people. I did as you asked again, and my heart grew even stronger for Nathaniel. I've now accepted a position teaching in Cape Elizabeth at the school there because it's close to the lovely stone cottage he's built for us.

"Now you ask me to wait again, to give up more years of my life waiting for the perfect love, the right husband when I've already found him. I'm sorry, Father, but I've done all you asked and now I must do what's right for me. If you'll not give your blessing and consent, I will marry him anyway. I don't wish it to be this way. I want you and Mother to meet him, love him, and be a family together. There will be grandchildren, and you'll want to be part of their lives, but if you continue with your objections, you'll never know them. Is this what you want?"

Her father rubbed his chest, pain shooting through his breaking heart. "Obviously, you've grown into the strong, independent woman I'd hoped. I got what I wished for, and now you will, too. There's nothing more for me to say because you'll do as you want. I still believe your desires and needs will change as you get older, and this man won't make you happy in the long run. Therefore, I don't approve of you marrying him, so there is no need for your mother and I to meet him, now or ever."

Lilah was overcome with deep sorrow, feeling she no longer had parents in this world. But then she remembered Nathaniel and her sadness dissolved. She left her parents' home not knowing if or when she'd see them again, but her new life and great love awaited. The very next day she packed up her clothing and belongings and moved into the stone cottage, looking forward to creating a new life with Nathaniel.

Overjoyed to hear Lilah would be his wife, Nathaniel still saw sadness in her eyes when speaking of her parents' refusal to meet him or grant permission to marry. More than being disappointed, he was angry at how such educated people could act so ignorantly. And more than that, he was sad for them that they'd miss out seeing their only daughter marry and have a life filled with love, a home, and children, as well as her teaching position and a brilliant future. Yes, her parents were the ones to be pitied.

That first night at the cottage, Lilah intended to sleep in the bedroom and he in the living area. They ate a simple meal and planned for their marriage to take place as soon as possible. She'd ask her parents once more to support it and attend, but if they refused, she'd go ahead with their plans anyway. They clung to each other for dear life as they lay in his makeshift bed of blankets on the floor in front of the fire. Kissing with passion that had built up for years, they almost had no choice about what came next. Consummating their love and uniting their bodies was the most natural thing to do. They loved each other completely as man and wife. As they moved together in love, feeling as one person, their passion moved them into an otherworldly place they could never have imagined, into a different kind of love—a bonding of hearts and souls for all time.

Afterward, they felt as blessed as two people could be in this new, grand life. But the fear Lilah had been able to control over the years came back hard. She knew the next morning the sea would call him, and chills went through her body. He told her, "It's natural to be a little afraid of a new turn in life. But you never have to be afraid of us being apart again or of losing me." He took her into his arms and held her close all through the night, but still she trembled.

****

Before dawn the next day, Nathaniel reluctantly pulled himself from their cozy bed. "I don't want to go, but I must. Today could be a big haul and would mean a wonderful start to our new life. Kiss me now for good luck and send me off a happy man." Lilah kissed him and clung to him for several minutes, wanting as much time as she could get. A strong emotion washed over her like a wave crashing on her head—of dread, sorrow, of losing him, and she begged him to stay.

"But I can't, my love. I'm already late; the crew waits for me." He kissed her deeply, wanting to soak up all her love to keep close on his journey. She clutched at him, desperate to know all of this man in one moment's time, feeling his every breath and heartbeat, smelling the salt and sea in his hair, on his skin, and all around him. She walked him to the door, waving and blowing kisses as he rode off and yelled back, "I'll be home with the biggest catch ever. It might be late into the night. Will you wait up for me?"

"Yes!" she yelled to him, her voice traveling on the wind rushing off the sea. "I'll wait for you, always." She wrapped her arms around herself to ease her fear more than the cold, as an odd notion filled her mind, a feeling of knowing she'd watched him leave to go to sea before, that she'd told him some other time she'd wait for him forever. But there hadn't been another time; there was only now.

Then why did she know he'd never return? Why was this agonizing loss so familiar, as if all the events of her life had been directed to this one moment, this one choice? If only she hadn't done so many things wrong to bring them to this place, hadn't kept so many secrets, hadn't let him go so easily. If only she wasn't haunted by the pain she'd caused her parents, she could find hope instead of the dread that filled her as she watched fate unfolding with Nathaniel disappearing from her sight, from her life.

Lilah waited that day, through the night, into the next day and the next, turning into weeks and months. He never came home, and his boat and crew were never found. The red dawn the morning he'd left had warned of a storm approaching. He wouldn't have known until he was far out to sea how bad the storm would get. Then it would be too late. The other fishermen in town hadn't seen his boat that day, but they all struggled to get back to port with the raging storm. When Lilah spoke with them, they relayed their stories with great sadness, knowing full well, with the severity of the storm and with Nathaniel usually taking his boat out further than anyone else, the outcome didn't look good.

They told Lilah not to give up hope. There was always the possibility his boat had found its way much farther down the coast; he may be alive and make his way back. But when Lilah walked away, they talked among themselves, pitying her for they knew most likely his boat had been sunk, and he and his crew had drowned without a trace of them left in this world.

****

Lilah wouldn't know how bad her life could get until she was out in the middle of it, alone, and with child from their one night together as man and wife. Except, in the eyes of the law, they weren't married. She worried to the point of illness that she would lose her teaching position when her situation was discovered. So, once again, she found herself having to keep a terrible secret and to lie for her survival. Being a tall, full-figured woman, she was able to hide her condition, especially through the fall and winter, wearing heavier clothing and cloaks and carrying books in front of her to conceal her thickening waist.

But with constant sorrow over Nathaniel's disappearance, worrying about coping with a baby and no job or salary and parents who wouldn't help her, the baby was born too early. She delivered him herself in the middle of the night using medical books as a guide, and so her secret was never found out. The boy, whom Lilah loved completely the moment she saw him, lived only one day, despite her constant, begging prayers, as if God were telling her, *This is to prove you don't deserve a child or a husband.*

She blamed her son's death on her unhealthy, debilitating nervous condition, daily sickness, and the inability to have a midwife. The only people she told after his death were her parents, wanting to punish them for casting her out and not accepting Nathaniel. If they'd had a proper wedding and she a normal pregnancy and birth, her husband and son might be alive. But her parents were not sympathetic. They were so appalled and disgraced by Lilah's situation, they disowned her.

Lilah continued to live in the cottage where Nathaniel's spirit surrounded her every day, waiting, hoping, praying that, by some miracle, he'd come back. Her life became one of work, of teaching the children, watching them grow, and eventually leave. She never married; she wasn't interested in anyone but Nathaniel. She walked the bluff every day at dawn and dusk, sending out prayers for his return, admiring the sea for its beauty, yet despising and fearing it for taking him away. She vowed to never trust the sea again with her life or her love, and would take those feelings to her grave, embedded as they were in her soul.

By the time Lilah reached her thirtieth birthday, accepting Nathaniel had died, she held deep regret for her secrets and lies, for the courage she didn't have to change her life, a life now set in stone as solid and unforgiving as that of her cottage, as impenetrable as the fortress around her heart. But she lived there for the rest of her life, feeling his spirit surrounding her and his love coming through the walls, remembering daily the promise she'd made that last morning: *I'll wait for you always*. It hadn't been just a promise—it was an unbreakable bond created with love.

During the next twenty years, her parents, aging and sick, tried to reconcile with her, but Lilah had no love or forgiveness left. She blamed them, as well as the sea, for losing Nathaniel because if they'd accepted him, her life would've turned out very differently.

In her late forties, looking back on her life, Lilah saw it as a test she'd failed and wished desperately for life to begin again, for a second chance to make better choices and do everything differently. She prayed for it daily, desperately, and with such fervor that, when she sensed her life coming to an end, she felt as if she were already being reborn. At age fifty, she met death willingly to reunite with Nathaniel in a place where she knew he waited, a place of paradise, of eternal love—a place of starting over.

Chapter 18

Even though it was December, the tropical Key West sun rose fast and hot, slashing through the fog of morning. It shocked Ella out of sleep, dazed, still heartbroken, and still Lilah. Beside her in bed, Daniel slept soundly, and reality slammed her hard. The last images and messages she'd seen before waking were of Lilah's life ending, and Ella could see how similar the events were with Daniel now: *Meeting her own death to reunite with him in a place where she knew he waited, in a paradise, a place of eternal love and of starting over.* Ella panicked. *But I'm not dead; I didn't die to find Daniel. I came to this paradise to let him go. I didn't know he was waiting here. Him finding me should be a chance for us to start over.* Then why, as she looked at Daniel, did she feel none of this was real and they had no future? Why did she feel exactly as Lilah had while watching Nathaniel leave the morning after they'd made love, knowing she'd never see him again?

Covering her face with her hands, Ella closed her eyes to block out the world. She didn't know whether to cry or scream, to run or die. She was losing her grip on reality with these stories of people she somehow lived as before. Sitting on the edge of the bed, she rubbed her arms and legs to calm down, to make sure she was real. Then she walked around the room and looked out to the ocean. *Okay, I'm not crazy; I'm not psychotic. I'm sane and certainly not dreaming. This room, this day, and this man are real, except that both of us could be spirits of lovers back from the dead.* Too much conflicting information exploded through her mind. The lines blurred between the dream state and reality, her mother's words and Lilah's, other worlds and lives, and this world where Daniel had returned.

Looking out over the sea, watching the waves roll into and disappear against the shore, then rematerialize as newly born waves, Ella realized she had witnessed an actual cycle of life, death, rebirth, new life. She'd been asking for guidance and answers throughout this two-year ordeal of Daniel's disappearance. Suddenly, something clicked into place about all of these memories and stories of other lives—they were her clues and her answers, if she would just accept their validity.

Still entranced by the never-ending life and movement of the ocean waves, she thought, *If only there was a way to prove what's been shown to me, just like I can see and touch this ocean. There must be something factual beyond intangible dreams, spirits, regressions, flashbacks and uncanny coincidences.* Kara had given her some hard facts to hang onto, but the reporter in Ella wanted more. Yet with everything she'd been through, she knew there were answers that could only come from spiritual sources. Not every story was born of terra firma—there was a cosmos, a whole universe of other realms. *But even to have just a few tangible facts,* Ella realized, *would validate these otherworldly occurrences.*

As Ella's brain scanned its recesses for anything

remotely factual through her past life stories, Lilah's name jumped to the forefront. The stories of Greece and Spain were from Ella's memory and did coincide with some of her present life and déjà vu experiences. But with this last story in Maine, there were many things about Lilah that were similar to Ella's present life: born in Maine, living near the coast in a stone cottage, and most unusual—Lilah's surname was Jameson—the same as her grandmother Hannah's. It was hard to wrap her mind around what this might mean, or maybe that surname appeared because it *was* so familiar to her real life.

There might be a way to prove it for sure—to reach out to the person closest to her family and life, who could possibly help her with facts—sensible and rational Hannah. With Daniel still soundly asleep, Ella moved to the patio outside so as not to wake him and called her. Ella blurted out and condensed the story of Daniel finding her, everything about his situation and injuries and how their relationship had picked up as it had left off, except for the disturbing events.

Hannah had been forewarned of Ella's situation by Janie, but still she couldn't imagine how the whole Daniel scenario was even possible. She patiently listened to Ella, lending support while hiding her doubts. "It's all quite unbelievable, but obviously it really happened. How are you? Truly, is everything okay with him? Somehow you don't sound okay."

"I'm not okay. At first, I felt it was like a miracle with him being here in the flesh, and we're every bit as much in love as when he left for his mission. But something's different. He's different in many ways, and I can understand why, but other strange things are happening that I don't understand. I'm worried and frightened." Ella then relayed how her mother came to her, warning her not to give up her life for Daniel.

"Oh, my, my," Hannah answered, shaking her head, trying to make sense of it.

"That's not the worst part, though. After that, my mother showed me the lives of two women from the 1800s in Portland, a mother and daughter—Martha and Lilah. But she'd prefaced it with saying she and I were the women in the story and to not make the same mistakes." Ella described the details of Lilah's life and death, concluding with how it all happened near Cape Elizabeth in a stone cottage on a cliff overlooking the sea. "Sound familiar, Gram?"

Hannah took in a quick, sharp breath. "Oh, no, this can't be literal. Surely, it's a coincidence. It sounds as if your recent traumatic experiences possibly got your imagination working overtime, dear. Surely you don't suggest you dreamt of a real person who actually lived in my cottage? Sometimes our brains get signals crossed and the messages are jumbled up. More importantly they're just symbols, representations of other things going on in our lives."

"I understand what you're saying, and I agree. Except here's the scary part—Lilah's last name was Jameson—just like yours. And I'm freaking out. Does it make any sense to you?"

Hannah poured herself a cup of coffee while she thought about it. "Now don't get so upset. Let's look at this logically. There can't possibly be a connection to us. It was just a dream."

"I'm curious about your cottage, though. I always knew it was very old and had been in our family a long time, but who exactly did you and Mother inherit it from?"

"Why, from my father, Robert Jameson, since my mother had already passed."

"Did your father build the house?"

"Heavens, no. He inherited it from his father, Gerald Jameson."

"So your grandfather built it then?"

"No, no. I'm fairly sure he didn't."

"Well, who did? Your great-grandfather?"

Hannah sat in front of the fire, sipping coffee. "Let me think about this. I haven't ever seriously thought about the origin of this house back before my grandfather. It's always just been 'in the family,' you know? And with all of our family, except us, being deceased, well, it's not like we have ten people sitting around at Sunday dinners talking about our heritage. I just haven't thought about it at all, and this old brain needs more caffeine before it works properly," she said with a laugh.

"Hannah, this is serious. Please, try to remember who built the house or how your grandfather came to own it. It would make a lot of difference."

"Why?"

"Because in my story the house was built by a man named Nathaniel. He built it for his bride-to-be, Lilah, but he died, presumably lost at sea before they actually got married. She lived in the house though until she died."

"Oh, my! What a horribly sad story. I can see why it upset you. It's almost the same as your parents' fate. Goodness, you just never get a break from these horrible losses by the sea, do you? But, really, Ella, it was just a dream."

"Gram, you know these things happening with me are more than dreams. And, no, I certainly don't get a reprieve from these losses, and I'm on the verge of a breakdown here. So, please, let's get back to the history of your cottage. Who built it?"

"Give me a minute here and let me figure this out." Hannah grabbed a pencil and paper and scribbled dates, doing the math. "My grandfather Gerald couldn't have built it. He'd have been too young for the age of this house."

"Think back further. How did the house come to be owned by your grandfather?"

All the while Ella spoke, Hannah's wheels were spinning through her memory banks. Something about that name, *Lilah*, rang a bell. "Oh, my God," Hannah whispered. She got up from her chair, dropping her cup to the floor.

Hearing the shattering glass, along with Hannah's very rare use of the Lord's name in vain, unnerved Ella. "Gram? Are you all right? What's going on?"

"Hold on. I'm going outside and need to put on my winter gear. I have to put the phone in my pocket for a minute." Hannah walked toward the front door and put on her coat, boots, and gloves. "I'm okay. It's just that I recalled something about this house. I do remember now that my grandfather, your great-grandfather, inherited this cottage when he was just a teenager from, I believe, a cousin, a woman who owned it and had no heirs except her only cousin, who was my grandfather Gerald. I recall this with remembering my father telling stories of how *his* father said he'd been blessed by the goodness of his cousin with his home, and for us to always appreciate the gift."

"Do you remember the woman's name who left it to him?"

"No, but I do remember seeing something unusual this past spring when I had to have a dying hedge dug up at the front corner of the house. That hedge had been there ever since I could remember, but the time had come to replace it. When my handyman ripped it out, I saw some kind of etching in the cornerstone of the foundation. I didn't think anything of it at the time. In the old days, they'd leave some kind of marking or date when they built a house. So, I immediately forgot about it, and we planted a new, small evergreen bush there."

Hannah was breathless now, walking to the corner of the house, trudging through snow. "Hold on. Let me put the phone down, so I can move these branches and get a look at it." By now the etching was covered with snow. She brushed it off to find dirt stuck into the inscription. Finding a stick to clean out the grooves, she could barely make out the words. On her knees, looking more closely, she gasped, and thought, *Oh, my God, my God, my God! This can't be true.*

While Ella held on, she held her breath, expecting disturbing news. Hannah was taking a long time. She heard the wind blow harshly by the phone.

"What is it, Gram?"

Breathing heavily, Hannah blurted out, "My Lord, this is unbelievable. I just can't…" and her words trailed off into the sound of the wind.

"Can't what? Please, calm down and just tell me what you see."

"There is something inscribed on the cornerstone—a name." Hannah took a deep breath and sank lower to the ground on her knees.

"Can you read it?" Ella started to panic, knowing Hannah must be really upset with what she was seeing.

"Let me pull my reading glasses out from under my coat here, just to make sure I'm reading this correctly." A few moments later, looking closely at the inscriptions, she let out a gasp. "Oh, my. I thought so. There is not one, but two names etched in the stone. Now please, sit down, Ella, and don't get upset. Is Daniel there? Go get him to be with you."

"Oh, please, just tell me!"

In almost a whisper, Hannah read the inscription in the cornerstone. "It says, *'Lilah and Nathaniel, 1874.'* That's when the house was built. I can't believe it. Those are the names in your dream, in your story."

Ella collapsed into the chair and cried. "Yes, yes, they are. How could this be possible?"

As Hannah walked back into the cottage, she thought about the names. "Lilah must have been my grandfather's cousin, and here is actual evidence of this Nathaniel. He must've engraved his and Lilah's names on it the year he built the cottage."

Ella sobbed then, choked out words. "So, it's real. They were real people…your cottage was their cottage. I'm beyond shocked. I'm traumatized…this whole thing is a nightmare."

Hannah tried to calm her. "Now don't get crazy with this. Stay calm and think it through. At least you know the truth now. Isn't that some kind of relief?"

Ella walked out to the beach again and looked over the ocean, hoping the wide expanse of sparkling blue and golden sun would bring clarity. "I don't know. It seems impossible that I could've been Lilah. But she did live there. I can't ignore the truth of your house—written in stone—it can't get any more real than that. But just because I had visions of her life, doesn't mean I actually *was* her—you know—in a past life. That's just too unreal."

"You can say it isn't real, but there are facts you can't ignore: you also have had many of the same fears, a very similar life story, and the loss of your loved ones to the sea. And from those other stories you told me of Greece and Spain, they all have the same patterns, the same themes and losses. It's extraordinary and amazing if you ask me."

"Now you sound like Daniel." She turned toward the condo and saw him through the glass door, still peacefully asleep, completely unaware of her trauma and ordeal. "Oh, God, then there are the questions about Daniel. I just can't figure out what's real about any of this."

Hannah comforted her as best she could. "Remember when you asked me if we were crazy with all these prophetic dreams and spirits and things, and we talked about them? Do you remember what I said about questioning if it was real?"

Ella had to think for a minute. "You said something like, '*You can't ignore something right in front of your face that you actually see, hear, and feel.*'"

"That's right. And I also said that there are so many things just beyond the veil of life on earth that we don't understand. But they still happen. And these things happened to you. Others who are not as open to them might view them as weird or unbelievable or even crazy. But for you, they're extraordinary, believable, and real. No doubt about it. Now take the information you've been given, sort it out, and put it to good use. You've no time to waste."

"What do you mean? What's the hurry?"

"I don't know, just a feeling, and—"

Ella interrupted, "Yes, I know, you and your feelings. But now you've got me worried."

"There's no need to worry. Be strong and courageous, and with Daniel's help, I know you'll get to the bottom of this very quickly. His love will soothe you and help you understand; I do know that much."

But Ella didn't feel strong; she felt near hysteria with what this new information meant. She climbed into a shower as hot as she could stand. Letting the steaming water run over her, she cried until she had no tears left.

Her sobs woke Daniel. He walked into the shower and held her, his heart breaking for her. "I know. I know what you're feeling. I've been there. It's a hard place to be. You don't know what's real and what isn't. Just cry and let it all out. Go ahead. Let it go."

Truly hysterical now, Ella curled up in a fetal position on the shower floor, unable to let Daniel comfort her, and asked him to leave. This was her agony alone, and no one, not even he, could help. Daniel seemed to understand. He stepped out of the shower, closed the door behind him, dried off, and put on shorts. "Honey, do whatever you have to. Cry it out. I've been through this, too. I know how it feels, and I'm here if you need me. We have all the time in the world to talk."

Daniel's words got stuck in her head. What did he mean by saying he'd been through what she was going through? He couldn't possibly know. Looking out of the fogged up, etched plastic shower door, she saw Daniel's blurry image, almost ghostly, moving around in the room. Watching Daniel's shadowy form, she knew it was him, but slowly his form seemed to change. She saw his body shape, but his hair looked long, dark and curly, and then he seemed shorter and stockier.

Looking more closely as he walked to the other side of the room, she thought he resembled Peter, but his coloring was wrong. Now, through her tear-blurred vision, he looked heavier with dark eyes and a Roman nose, a Mediterranean look to his face. Daniel walked to the glass patio doors near the beach, and from the back, his hair now seemed lighter and shorter. He looked out at the sea, and the hazy image of a boat appeared in the distance, a fishing boat. When he turned around, she recognized him as Nathaniel.

Ella pressed her hands over her eyes. "This can't be happening. This isn't happening." Waiting a few seconds, she dried her tears then looked again. Hot water poured over her body and thick steam filled the shower stall, rivulets of water dripping down the door. Through its haze, she saw Daniel across the room, moving from bed to dresser to windows again, and this time he seemed to change ever so slightly as he glided around the room, his form resembling Matthias, then Miguel, and finally Nathaniel. Ella screamed, losing her grip on reality when Daniel opened the shower door.

He tried to calm her. "It's okay. You're okay. You're not crazy. It is me. They're all me."

"What?" she shrieked. "Who's all you? How do you know what I just saw?" She pushed past him and ran out of the shower, grabbed a towel, and looked at him as though he were an alien, a liar, another damn illusion come back to stalk and frighten her. Now anger replaced the tears. She threw on clothes and ran to the beach toward the ocean. Yelling over the crashing waves, she challenged the sea, "You want him back? You want me, too? Then take us. I've had it! I'm done with trying to solve the mysteries of my life. I don't know if that man in there is real or a ghost, or maybe I'm losing my mind. Please! Just put me out of my misery."

She ran into the water, but couldn't get past the strong waves breaking over her body, knocking her down. Panicking, recalling how Helena and Isabella had died, she realized she didn't want to die, especially in the sea. *I'm not them. I can't do this. It won't solve anything.* Stumbling back to the beach, she slumped onto the sand and looked into the sun rising above the ocean. It blinded her for a moment, and in the flash of a brilliant, hot white light, she felt almost rising above the earth, reminding her of how she felt in the car coming across the bridge in the blinding sun—scared to death, but peaceful.

Daniel sat down beside her. "Go ahead. Be angry. Be afraid. Feel everything you need to feel. Then let it all go."

She looked at him incredulously. "I think I'm having a breakdown, and all you can say is, '*Let it go*'? I'm beginning to think you're not real, that I dreamed this all up. Hell, maybe I'm psychotic and have no grip on reality anymore."

Daniel took her hand. His hand was warm, and it was real. She could feel it, but she couldn't trust what she felt or saw anymore.

"Ella, you're not psychotic. There's nothing wrong with your mental or physical health. Everything happening around you is real. And, yes, I'm real."

"But what did you mean about those three men I saw being 'you,' and how did you know I saw them? I have to be hallucinating."

"You're not. I can explain everything. Eventually it will all make sense to you. First, I need to ask you something. I was just starting to wake when I heard you on the phone outside. I couldn't help but overhear you were talking to Hannah. Is there anything you want to share about that conversation?"

Ella looked out over the ocean. "More confusion, more information to make me crazy." She told him of Lilah, Nathaniel, the cottage, and what Hannah had discovered. "It seems a possibility I might've lived as Lilah, in the same house I actually grew up in, which tells me that, most likely, these glimpses into other worlds could be real. What scares me though is why this is happening at all."

"I think, deep in your psyche and heart, you know why. If you add this to all the other information you've been given through various means, what's your best guess?"

Ella felt physically and mentally sick now with lifetimes of emotion running through her, but she answered as honestly as possible, wanting to get to the bottom of it. "If I, or my soul, really did come into life now after those other three times, then it must be to get it right this time—like a 'do-over'—another chance to correct everything I did wrong the other times. In fact, what I remember of Lilah's final moments, she wanted to be reborn, to have a second chance at life."

Ella's mind then flashed back to the words she'd heard at nine-years-old, after nearly drowning: *Secrets, lies, and murder*. "Maybe this life is about how I'll deal with, or not deal with, love lost to the sea. I've uncovered secrets about this life and come clean with all of mine. This curse that I believed followed me?—I don't think it was a curse at all, but more like guilt over feeling responsible for the deaths of the people I loved by keeping secrets, lying, and letting them go. In a sense, it was murder, as Isabella was murdered for lying, and Helena and Lilah caused their own deaths by wasting their lives to wait forever for lovers they truly knew were dead, which is exactly what I was going to do now because of my love for you. My mother knew all, and she tried to warn me not to give up my life for you."

"You're correct on all accounts, and I hope you won't ever give up your life for me or wait for me forever to return when I might not."

"I *am* learning this. But everything is coming on so fast and it's all so new. I'm so scared, and I feel like I'm in the middle of a terrible nightmare that I'll eventually wake up from." She looked at him solemnly. "I don't even know if you're real with what you said about being all those men. If you *are* real, then *you* are the one who's psychotic. Something is very, very wrong, Daniel, with both of us. Don't you see it? We both need help."

"There's nothing wrong. Everything will be logical to you when you see it from a different perspective."

"Yeah, sure, like when I'm dead. Maybe that will be the only time and place I'll understand. Only I don't want either one of us to die. I'm terrified right now."

She buried her face in her hands and wailed, a great, heaving outpouring of grief that filled the air around them, causing tears to fill Daniel's eyes as well.

He put his arm around her, and together they turned the world dark and wet with their suffering. Daniel let out a big sigh. "I can't stand this anymore. This wasn't how it was supposed to be. God. Oh, my God, it wasn't supposed to happen this soon."

"What? What are you talking about?"

"You told me how Hannah kept a secret from you your entire life to protect you, but you felt betrayed and hurt. Now I have to tell you I have a secret I was supposed to keep, but I can't. I can't stand to see you tortured like this, Ella. I love you too much to let you suffer any more than you have, especially now. This was supposed to happen gradually, in order for you to understand slowly over the coming months."

She jumped up and stood over him. "You better tell me what you're talking about. I've had enough of secrets, symbolic dreams, and cryptic messages. What in the hell is going on?"

"All of what we're living now is really happening, and I'm real but not in the way you think."

Ella grabbed the sides of her head and pulled her hair. "Agh! Real is real, or not! Which is it?"

Daniel stood now to face her. Holding her and looking deep in her eyes to connect with her soul, he said, "This is part of the secret: I'm real in this place. But I'm not the flesh and blood man you loved."

Ella's eyes filled with horror, the meaning of his words incomprehensible. She tried to break free of him, but he gently held her arms. Before she could speak, he tried to calm her. "What I mean is, I'm not a ghost, and you're not crazy or dreaming. I can explain everything if you'll just come with me, so I can show you something to help you understand. Will you come with me?"

Emotionally spent, weak, and unable to fight or flee, her spirit caved, and she just gave up and gave in to him. "You promise I'll be safe and I'll understand if I go with you?"

"I promise."

"Where are we going?"

"I'm going to take you to the place you left."

"Left? What do you mean?"

"To spare you more trauma and show you what's happened, I'll show you where you left to come here, to find me." He placed his hands on her face, kissed her gently, and filled her with love. "My poor dear, I'm sorry I have to show this to you now. I wanted more time with you to prepare you. But you're strong and courageous. You can fathom it; you can accept it."

"That's almost exactly what Hannah said."

Daniel smiled knowingly. "Yes, and she's right. Above all else you see and hear, remember that I love you beyond words and always will, and I'll always be close to you."

His love told her his words were true and she could trust him. He then took her to the bridge coming into Key West. They looked on it from the shore but were somehow close to the scene, as if looking down from above. "This is the other part of the secret. There." He pointed to an accident. "You left there to find me, to come to me where I live now."

She saw a car that looked like hers—crumpled against another. An ambulance with flashing lights sat next to it. “What do you mean *I left*? And that car looks like mine. What’s going on?”

“It *is* your car, Ella.” He gave her time to understand, but she couldn’t. She panicked and tried to run away from him.

He went after her and held her in his arms, loving and soothing her. “Ella, look at me. You must believe me.” He put his hands gently on the sides of her head to make her focus on his eyes, then looked intensely at her, almost through her, as if he was seeing their entire lives. Peace and a healing energy poured through her mind and body. Then she saw him for what he was—a beautiful, open, honest, and loving soul. One who would never lie to her, who had always loved her and always would. She saw and felt their bond.

“I do believe you. I believe you love me and will tell me the truth, but I’m so scared. This whole thing doesn’t make any sense.”

Daniel took her into his strong embrace. “You don’t have to be afraid. I’m here, and I’m not going to let anything happen to you. Okay?”

Trembling, she said, “You promise nothing bad will happen?”

“I promise you with all that I am. But you must look now at the bridge. You crashed your car there. Do you remember anything about it?”

“No. I didn’t crash the car. I remember being blinded by the sun, hearing a horn blare and screeching sounds and a flash of light filled the car, very white, brilliant light and being overcome with a peaceful feeling. But then a cloud blocked the sun and my vision returned. I continued driving here to Key West, where you found me.”

"But you actually were in an accident. The light and peaceful feeling, then your vision returning was actually your spirit lifting up out of the accident, so you wouldn't experience it because, all along, you were meant to come here, to find me."

"My spirit? I'm a spirit? I'm not me? I'm dead? What's going on? Daniel, please tell me. I can't believe any of this." Ella went into full panic until he wrapped himself around her, meshing body and soul, a feeling she'd never known before, like coming home to everything she'd always wanted and loved. Infused with it, she came to an understanding that her destiny waited.

Knowing her thoughts, Daniel said, "Remember Helena and Isabella, and finally Lilah, and how they died?"

Shocked, Ella answered, "Yes, but I never told you about Lilah and Nathaniel. How can you know about them?"

"Everything we ever did, every moment we lived is reflected to us here in this place. Our lives are open to view to clearly see everything, good and bad, right and wrong, every love and hate. We gain better perspective here. We understand everything and have the opportunity to fix the mistakes and get it right, if we so choose. And don't forget, I was part of your story, too—in Matthias and Miguel and Nathaniel. You sacrificed your life to find me those other times, to solve the mystery, just as you've done now."

Unbelievably everything seemed to fall into place. At least his reasoning, although hard to fathom, was logical, but almost impossible to accept as reality.

"Don't have any doubts—this is all very real," he

said, reading her thoughts again, "and this is why we're here now. On the routine flight I made right before we met two years ago, I got the feeling of coming in for a landing into destiny, and meeting you was part of it. The rest of it was my being shot down and dying. I did die, Ella, but I came to find you as I promised. I couldn't stand your suffering through another life like you had. It was time for you to learn and grow beyond the loss of me, to grow into the soul you are. I am here now to guide you in this place that looks like Key West, but is actually a paradise made of our memories, a place between life and death, a place made of love."

A small bud of knowledge bloomed through her mind instantly, filling it with truth, and she finally grasped what he was talking about. It started to make sense. She felt lighter, free of a huge burden of the life she'd lived since forever, it seemed. The same sensation she'd had in her car a few weeks ago returned, a feeling of almost floating now in the air with Daniel, and it was familiar and comforting. This recollection brought tranquility, along with the love now filling all the space around them. Every particle of light in the world turned golden, and she felt part of the rising sun, casting brilliant color everywhere.

Daniel said, "It's a beautiful feeling, isn't it—to be part of everything alive on earth and beyond, part of life everywhere?"

In a hushed and reverent voice, she whispered, "Yes. It is. I think I know what's happening. I can see why so much changed about you—not wanting to marry, not wanting children. You're not alive that way, not in body to do those things, and neither am I."

"You're slightly wrong about one thing—we're

very much alive," he said, pointing toward Key West, "just not the way we used to be there when we met and returned before I was deployed."

Ella, confused, said, "Yet I feel alive. I'm still me. But am I still in my car over there?"

"Your physical body is in the car."

"My body must be dying then, or dead, right?"

"Only briefly. You heart has stopped for several minutes. In those moments, what makes you truly alive—your spirit or soul, whatever you call it or believe it to be—left your body, and you came here to be with me. You needed to have closure and to understand the journey of your soul, not just in this life but throughout all our time together. Now it's time for you to go back."

"Go back! Where? What do you mean?"

He kissed her gently to soothe her. "You must go back to your life."

"No! Not now. I've just found you. I want to stay here, to be wherever you are. Isn't this supposed to be our final reward, the place we stay through eternity?"

A faint, watery image appeared in the distance. As it came closer, Ella saw it was her mother's spirit, who asked, *When I came to you in a dream last time, do you remember what I told you?*

Ella thought for a moment and glanced at Daniel when it hit her. *You told me to not give up my life for him.*

Her mother smiled with love and silently answered, *That's right because you've done it before, and what happened?*

It didn't accomplish anything. I came back to do it all over again and nothing changed; I never learned or moved beyond the very first lifetime.

Nodding in agreement, her mother slowly began to disappear, smiling, loving, trailing a message, *Good. Now you know the next step. I'll see you again when it's truly your time, my love.*

Ella called out for her mother to stay, to no avail.

Daniel asked, "Do you know why you can't be with her now?"

Looking sad, Ella said, "Unfortunately I do. I'm getting it. I can't be with her for the same reason I can't be here with you. I'm not meant to stay here. I have to fix what I've done wrong."

"And what's your understanding of that?"

"Even though I lost you, the love of my life, I need to let you go. I need to fulfill the reason I was born—I can have a good, purposeful life, even without you. I need to prove to myself that I will not waste the gift of life because it truly is a gift. I see that now. I see how much time I wasted."

"It wasn't only a waste of time and life."

Ella loved him so completely; she felt she was made purely of love. "It was also a waste of love—not only my love for you, but the love that could've been shared with other people—a husband, friends, children, family."

"And it really wasn't a waste because you've learned and you're here, ready for the next step. I wish we could stay here forever, too. But it's not your time because you're just beginning to fathom the mysteries of your life. Someday you'll come back again, and we'll love each other for eternity. But it depends on what you do next. You have work to do, a life to live. And with your newfound knowledge of your past, you could live and love very differently. If you return to life right now, knowing for certain that I'm not coming back, what would you do?"

Closing her eyes against all she saw around her—the accident, her mother, him—she envisioned a new life, without the fears and grief of the past. She saw a new self, a life filled with love, joy, creative work, and helping others.

Daniel said, "Yes, Ella, you've got it now. Life can be all those things. You deserve them, and the world deserves you."

She turned to Daniel, who kissed her sweetly, reverently, and she asked, "But while I'm still here, I'd like to know how it can be possible for my body to be in my car in that accident that just happened, when we've spent all these weeks together."

"Time is relative. Time here is not measured like it is there. A few minutes there," he said, pointing to the accident, "can be months or years here. And speaking of time, it's time for you to go now. There are people trying to save you there. Go back. Live, love, and remember my love is all around you all the time. I told you I'd never leave and it's true—I'll be with you always."

An all-knowing and accepting presence filled her as Daniel took her in his arms, and they kissed before she left. The air swirled gold and sparkled with light around them, the colors turning more vibrant with the strength of their love until Ella knew for certain they were in a place beyond earth, time, and space.

As he let her go, she drifted toward the accident scene as if made of air, with only their hands clasped together. Moving further away, only their palms touched, then just their fingers, then lastly as they parted, their fingertips touched briefly in the same way they'd connected initially on the beach a short time ago. She felt the same sensation of a warm liquid shoot through her arm and then her whole body.

"I will love you forever, Daniel, no matter where you are."

"And I you. My love is only a touch away all through your life. Reach out and I'll be there for you," he said, as their fingertips touched, then parted.

Daniel's adoring face and brilliant smile appeared to her as she came into consciousness inside an ambulance. With eyes still closed, she heard a strange voice say, "We lost her for a few minutes, but she's back. Her heart is strong. Vitals are good. Let's get to the hospital ASAP."

Another man said, "It's a frickin' miracle she's alive." He leaned over her and whispered close to her ear, "Hold on, lovely lady. You're much too pretty to die."

Ella did hold on. When she became fully awake, she was in a hospital bed. Janie was there when she opened her eyes for the first time since the accident. They held each other and cried, this time with great joy.

Chapter 19

In the days following the accident, Ella was in and out of consciousness, sleeping and dreaming, not knowing for sure which world she was in. Her dreams were mostly about Daniel. She'd see his smiling face cheering her on, helping her to live, loving her. His presence helped her have the courage to fully recover and rejoin the world.

In two months' time, Ella resumed her career in Tampa and rounded out her life with many interests—creative writing, meditation and yoga, and volunteering at the veterans hospital. Peace descended over her life with no longer feeling the need to escape her past or outrun ghosts. Instead of feeling cursed, she felt blessed to be given a second chance.

During the next year, she dated a few men, allowing herself to get close to one but nothing felt quite right for the long term. She had the strong, intuitive feeling that someday there would be someone perfect, destined for her, just as Daniel had been.

She had told only Janie and Hannah everything about her time in another place where she met Daniel and of the things she learned. Janie was blown away and told her she should write a book. Hannah was simply overjoyed Ella was alive and believed every word of what had happened, telling her, "Now it's time for you to go about having the life you deserve."

"I will. I am. My heart is open to new experiences and people. And I firmly believe, as sure as I'm talking to you, Gram, I will find the love I want someday. It'll come when the time is right."

Part of her healing came with doing human interest stories that might help people in some way. Ella's heart was drawn to the veterans coming back from the fighting in Korea and the Middle East, seeing their struggles and losses. If Daniel had lived and she hadn't, she'd have wanted someone to take an interest in him and his story, to befriend and help him.

So, she got approval to do a series of stories on the veterans' lives—what they went through at war, what they faced coming home to their families and friends, their injuries and rehabilitation process, and their feelings about their new and changed lives. Of most interest to her was how their hearts had changed due to their experiences and what their new priorities and goals were in life.

She'd been visiting a large veterans' hospital in Tampa, interviewing whoever was willing to be a part of the series. Every day when she entered the building, the energy of sadness and pain enveloped her, but so did the energy of hope. Hope and optimism seemed to float up around the ceilings—the purest energy rising, looking down for those who wanted to be helped to have happy, fulfilling lives again. Ella envisioned Daniel's spirit up there, being part of the healing process in any way possible. But invariably when she'd think this, a small, silent voice would whisper, *No, he's not there*. She'd be sad for a moment until realizing Daniel would be exactly where he needed to be, in some realm of living and helping.

One veteran in particular was very forthright about everything he'd experienced and how he'd dealt with it. He was in a ward for veterans who had sustained severe head injuries, had been in comas, and were in recovery. He still suffered from PTSD and delayed memory, and was getting therapy to relearn how to walk, speak and write. He was making progress in physical therapy, rehab, and counseling.

After interviewing him several times and getting to know him better, Ella praised him for his bravery and willingness to get back into life. But the soldier said, "Well, thanks, but I'm just doing what feels right to do next. I'm not half as brave as the guys down at the end of the ward. They're not nearly as lucky as me—they're still in comas. After all they went through and suffered, they still haven't come back, and I hear the nurses whisper that they probably never will after all this time. Poor bastards. Poor, brave, selfless men who gave up their lives for freedom. Talk about brave—most of those guys are Air Force and Navy pilots who went in and bombed the hell out of the enemy, and they end up here…as vegetables. Breaks my heart."

"It breaks my heart, too," Ella said, turning around to glance down the hallway of the ward where those men lay hooked up to monitors and machines.

"I wouldn't look if I were you," the soldier warned. "It's not pretty. It's just so sad." He kept on talking, but Ella couldn't hear him, drawn to walk down that hall, to check on every one of them and say a prayer.

After visiting the bedside of several men, her heart heavy with grief and feeling unable to handle any more, she turned away from the last curtain to walk back and finish her interview. But something stopped her. She turned to the last curtain almost against her will. She couldn't leave with, at least, a wish for this man to recover. She thought, *I don't have to look. I'll stand outside the curtain.* But as she started to whisper her prayer, her inner voice told her to look in at him. *It's the least you can do. Give him the respect he deserves.* Ella touched the curtain gently and slowly opened it to get only the quickest glance. The man looked vaguely familiar. She turned around to see if anyone was watching to warn her not to move closer to the patient, but the hall was empty.

She was compelled to get a closer look to see if she might know him—maybe a friend of Janie's or Daniel's she'd met long ago. She slowly tiptoed toward his bed. Her heart missed a beat as she scanned him from head to toe and realized everything about him was familiar. He was tall, thin, with the remnants of well-muscled arms. His dark hair was longish, but had gray at the temples. His eyes were closed, but she knew this face, this body. She'd know it anywhere. Standing next to him now, she whispered, "Can this be true? It's impossible. Daniel's dead. This can't be him." She put her face close to his, knowing every contour, his brows and lips and the shape of his neck. Her knees buckled, and she slid down the side of the bed, covering her face with her hands. "No, it can't be. It just can't be." Standing up again, half-fearful, half-exhilarated, she said, "Daniel?"

He lay still as death, and her heart broke. *Can this really be him?* There were small scars on his face and arms, but it was him. Still not believing it, she flashed back to him finding her in Key West, or what she thought had been Key West last December. But he'd said he'd been killed then, *So how could he be here? How could it be possible for him to lie in this bed?* But then she remembered Daniel explaining to her how vastly different time was in that realm, that suspended place, than here on earth. Still, she doubted any of this could be real. Maybe it was one of her dreams again, a daydream, wishful thinking, a coincidence—it must be someone who looked just like Daniel.

Ella walked back to the front of the ward to the soldier she'd been interviewing, her face white.

"You look like you've seen a ghost," he said, laughing. But Ella didn't laugh. "Sorry," he said, "I didn't mean to joke. It's really sad, right?"

She held out her hand to him, and he took it. "I'm here, aren't I?" she said. "I mean, I'm real and you're real. We're in Tampa in a VA hospital, right?"

He laughed again. "Of course! Hey, I'm the one who's supposed to have trouble with my brain and memory, not you."

"I'm just making sure. It's just that I think I really did see a ghost. I think I know the guy at the end of the ward. He looks so familiar. Do you know anything about him?"

"Only that he was a pilot, shot down, and has been in a coma for a while. If you want to know his name, you could ask one of the nurses. They're real nice and could probably help you out."

"Good idea. Thanks."

Walking down the hall to the nurses' station, she felt as if walking in a cloud, in a dream that could soon be shattered. The nurse looked at the records and said, "Well, I really can't give out his personal information. This says no next of kin has been notified. In fact, none could be found."

Ella had a good rapport with the nurses having spent so much time there. They liked and trusted her, knowing she was on assignment from the paper. "Please," Ella said, "it's really important. After all this time, there's been no family found, and I'm sure I know him. I won't put him in my stories or tell anyone about him. If you could just share his name, I'd be forever grateful."

The nurse shook her head. "I could get into serious trouble."

"How about this?" Ella suggested. "I'll tell you what I think his name is, and you either confirm or deny."

The nurse agreed. "I don't see anything wrong with that."

"I think he's Daniel Ellsworth, a Navy fighter pilot."

The nurse looked at the chart. "My God. His name *is* Daniel Ellsworth. How do you know him?"

Ella showed her the diamond ring she still wore. "He was my fiancé, but he'd been deployed so fast—the day we got engaged—on a highly classified mission over North Korea, and he obviously didn't think to put my name as next of kin. And all his family are deceased. I never knew what happened to him and couldn't get any information about his status—these last couple years nearly killed me." She stopped, realizing she almost literally died on her quest to find him and a chill shook her body.

The nurse touched her arm. "You're shaking. Are you cold? Are you okay?"

Ella rubbed her arms briskly to shake off the chill.

"Yes, I'm as okay as I can be. To find him after two years, after I thought he had long died; this is almost like a dream—a dream I've had before that ended badly." Deep emotion moved her to tears. "I still love him dearly, like my own life, and I thought he was dead."

The nurse got teary-eyed. "And so you kind of died inside, too, right?"

Ella nodded in agreement.

"Oh, you poor woman. I can't even imagine going through that. Well, Daniel has never had a visitor or a phone call or inquiry. And I do know that, if no next of kin has been located after so many years, and then someone comes forward as friend or family, they can claim the veteran."

Hearing the nurse's words jolted Ella's memory back to what Janie had said in their conversation when Daniel had just found her, about an officer contacting her and telling her the same thing about being able to "claim" Daniel. Ella relayed this information to the nurse, questioning the word "claim."

The nurse explained, "That's because it's usually at a point when maybe the veteran has been incapacitated in some way, or is possibly homeless, or on death's door, or the worst—already deceased and their body can be claimed."

Ella had to grab on to the counter to keep from falling over. Now she understood. The officer had probably known at the time that Daniel had been shot down and was in a coma, near death. "Well, I'm the only person to visit or inquire, so I'm officially 'claiming' him. Is there anything I need to do, so you can give me more information on him?"

The woman smiled kindly and moved to a computer. As she typed and clicked and pulled up various websites and records, she talked: "I'll tell you what. You know his name, that he's a Navy pilot; you know where and when he was deployed before ending up here and that his family is deceased. Those facts are corroborated with Navy records. That's good enough for me. And then there's the ring and I sense that you do love him a lot. You've been through enough. So as head nurse, I make the decision that you're as close to next of kin as he's ever going to get, and I can share some of his information with you now. We can do the paperwork with the Navy and hospital later. Afterward, the doctor can give you more details."

Ella hugged her. "Thank you so much. You're a godsend."

"Well, don't thank me too much. His prognosis is not optimistic. He was shot down, severely injured—fractured skull, brain injury, concussion—that's the worst of it. He also had a broken femur, arm, internal injuries, and multiple lacerations. Unbelievably, his body recovered from his injuries, but he's been in a coma ever since. It seems like he just doesn't want to come back. Maybe something in his subconscious believes there's nothing to come back to. The brain is very powerful in controlling the body."

"I understand what you're saying. I'd like to try to give him a reason to come back. Can I see him now? I mean, sit by his bed, touch him, and talk to him?"

"Of course, but you know the rules—be gentle and don't touch any of the machines, buttons, IVs, or tubes."

Ella promised while practically running to the end

of the ward, and opened the curtain. Daniel was lying there, breathing shallowly, alive, just not conscious. She leaned against the bed and took his hand, pouring every drop of love she'd ever had into him. "Daniel, it's me, Ella. Can you hear me?"

He didn't respond.

She kissed his forehead, his cheeks. "It's Ella. I'm here. I found you. Wake up, Daniel. It's time to wake up."

Still no response from him, and there wouldn't be during the coming weeks.

After confirming Ella's relationship to Daniel, his doctor shared his medical history with her. He was direct in not giving much hope, saying the longer Daniel was in a coma, the greater the odds were he'd never come out, and he'd have to be moved to a nursing home at some point. But his case was unusual; it was already a miracle he'd survived his injuries. The doctor told her, "It's possible the shock, along with the head injury, were just too much. Or maybe he hasn't had enough stimulation. Maybe if he had someone talking to him and touching him—sharing memories, favorite music and books—especially if it was someone Daniel loved, it might help bring him back."

Bringing him back, then, became Ella's quest.

****

She visited every day for a month, touching and kissing him, massaging and exercising his muscles the way the nurses had shown her. She told him how they met and fell in love over and over. She knew the books and music he loved, so she read and played the music repeatedly. Ella wore his favorite perfume, and even brought his favorite foods and held them under his nose, hoping his sense of smell would jolt him back. She dredged up memories of all the places they'd visited, the good times they'd shared, and even of the trip to Key West when they'd gotten engaged and he'd been deployed. Nothing worked.

But she kept trying, spending every evening with him after work and daylong visits on the weekend. The nurses thought she was an angel. But Ella said, "No, I'm just the person who loves him." With the nurses, she shared the highlights of their love affair and how quickly Daniel had had to leave. They cried and she cried, but she knew she'd never give up on him.

Another month went by. Labor Day weekend approached, and when Ella visited Daniel, she reminded him of their three-year anniversary. She took off her engagement ring and slipped it on his pinky finger, whispering, "I love you more now than I did then. I'll love you forever, Daniel, even if you never come back. If this is all I ever have of you, it's enough. I will move on with my life as I promised you." With tears running down her cheeks, she left, closing the curtain behind her, resigned to the fact that he'd most likely never regain consciousness, as his doctors had warned. His body and organs would wear out, and it would be over.

Ella closed the curtain behind her as she started to leave, when one of the men down the hall let out a loud cough, but it seemed to muffle another noise, a subtle sound coming from the curtain nearest her. In the now quiet room, she heard it again—a harsh, raspy whisper, like someone had a terrible sore throat. She opened Daniel's curtain again, and looked in to make sure he was all right. His body was still, as usual, but she noticed a slight movement—his pinky finger with her ring on it moved slightly, then his mouth moved as if trying to make a sound. Walking closer, she said loudly, "Daniel? Daniel, come back. Talk to me. It's Ella. I'm here."

But he fell back into the deep place he'd been. She waited a half hour; he didn't even twitch. Ella told the nurses what he'd done, and they thought it was a good sign; although, not wanting to give her false hope, they said involuntary movements were common in coma patients. But they promised to keep a closer eye on him for any further signs of consciousness.

Another two weeks went by with Daniel showing no movement. Finally, on Labor Day weekend, on their third-year anniversary, when she visited she became overwrought with emotion of loving him again and now losing him again. Crying hard, she took both of his hands in hers and leaned in close to his face, kissing him, then whispered, "Daniel, I've loved you for three years, and I'll love you forever. Before you leave this world for good, I want to remind you of the vow you made to me when we first fell in love and I was so scared I wanted to run. I know you remember this. You said it many times. 'I promise, with a love as strong as ours, we'll never be apart. When I leave to fly jets, when I go to sea, I promise I'll always come back to you, in one way or another. In time, all ships must return to port. And, Ella, you are my home port.'"

Crying hard now, tears falling onto his cheek, she begged him one last time, "Remember me? I'm your home port. You must find your way back to me. Please. Please, give me just one sign that you remember, that you love me, and then if you need to go, to move on,

I'll let you go with my love guiding and comforting you. And if you choose to go now, I promise our love will reunite us in another time and place. I'll find you wherever you are."

She waited for a sign, a movement, anything to let her know he'd heard her words and felt her love. Staying with him until the end of visiting hours, with no tears left, Ella held him and said, "You can leave now if this is what you must do. I understand. I'll be devastated. I'll miss you dearly, but I'll keep my promise to live a good life. And I'll always love you." The only thing she couldn't do was watch him die. She wanted to remember him whole and alive. Sobbing, she walked away, pulled the curtains closed while she said goodbye.

As she turned and walked back down the hall, she noticed how still and quiet the whole ward was. It hadn't occurred to her that everyone would've been within earshot and listening. But she didn't care. Looking in on some of the other men, she saw most of them had tears in their eyes and waved at her; some saluted her. At the end of the ward stood several nurses, all crying. They ran to her and each in turn hugged her, saying how brave she was, that she did the right thing because many patients in Daniel's condition don't die unless their loved ones let them know it was okay to leave.

While hugging the last nurse, a loud noise came from down the hall. Something crashed to the floor. Then came a deep choking sound, a guttural cry. Then silence. They all looked at each other, questioning, astonished, then the nurses ran down the hallway, looking in on every patient. Another sound rang out—a bellow, like a bear using its voice for the first time after hibernation. “Aghhhhhh,” a voice flew into the silence. Ella then ran after the nurses, toward the sound, thinking someone was hurt or dying. When she got halfway down the hall, a loud cough sounded again, then a deeply scratchy, parched, croaking shriek was immediately followed by a slowly emitted, carefully formed word—“E-l-l-a.”

Chapter 20

Over the next three months, Daniel made slow progress. The doctors were amazed he'd become conscious, let alone had some memories. The nurses said it was a miracle. Ella didn't care what they called it. He was back. Even though still groggy with traveling between the two opposite worlds of unconsciousness and waking, he was able to piece together memories. Eventually, as he recalled more and more, Ella, unable to contain her curiosity, asked what was the last thing he remembered, and he said, "You. I remember being with you in Key West."

"You mean before the war, before you were deployed?"

He looked at her curiously. "No. I remember you in Key West when you were in the accident and we found each other again. I loved you so much and didn't want to lose you, but I knew you had to go back. I sent you back. To life. And here you are."

"But, Daniel, so are you! Don't you get it? You came back, too. You weren't supposed to—you'd died. At least, that's what you told me at the time. How is it possible for you to be here and *alive*?"

He closed his eyes and was silent for several minutes, maybe sleeping or dreaming, or maybe traveling again between the two states of mind and different places of living, when he gasped and opened his eyes wide as if seeing her for the first time. "I saw the men rescuing you. I heard one say, 'Come back, lovely lady. You're too pretty to die.' In that moment, love exploded through me, and I knew I didn't want to lose you to someone else; I *shouldn't* lose you to someone else."

Ella sat next to him on the bed, holding his hand with both of hers, as if trying to keep his memory there with her. "This is unbelievable. Do you remember what happened next?"

Daniel looked at her with love and longing, like when he'd watched her go away into the ambulance, back to her life. "Something wasn't right about you going back alone and me standing there watching, alone. It just didn't seem right after all we'd been through. We both learned what we were supposed to, both paid our dues, fulfilled our karma, whatever you want to call it. We deserved better. We deserved the love and life together we'd fought so hard for, and sacrificed so much for."

He closed his eyes again for several minutes, returning to the other place and time, letting his memory return. "I remember next asking of the universe, of God or whatever force had put us in that place, 'Can I go back with her?' Because it was all I wanted, and my whole being was filled with love, intense and palpable, like a chord stretched between us, with you lying in that ambulance. It was like we were one person, one soul, and I remember sending this love out to whomever or whatever listened and made the decisions about life and death."

Daniel opened his eyes briefly and told Ella, "I knew then that I was part of that decision and so were you. And because of everything we'd been through and learned and the sacred bond we shared, I knew it was our time to be together. I might not have died, maybe temporarily, and was suspended in a near-death state, as you had been. Maybe God was waiting for me to come to terms with and articulate exactly what I wanted and deserved. And in those moments, I knew it was you, to love and share life with you. The whole world around me then filled with the purest, clearest, golden light I'd ever seen. Every particle of air and every cell in my body was pure love."

Exhausted, Daniel closed his eyes again, seeming to need to rest. Ella said, "It's okay. Sleep. Just don't forget the rest of the story, of how you came back."

He squeezed her hand, then drifted off again. Ten minutes later, as if having gone away to retrieve more memories, he woke and said, "I came back because I heard the kindest voice—the same one I heard the day you were revived—a voice that seemed to come from one end of time to the other, and it said, '*Yes, you may go back with her*.' I'll never forget what it was like coming into the world again. I felt myself moving through time and space, so fast, like watching a movie where a spaceship is going at warp speed until everything blurs and light flashes by with unbelievable colors and sounds. With those words came a new life, a miracle.

"The next thing I heard was your voice; I felt your sadness and tears but also your love. I heard the words 'promise' and 'home port,' and then I remembered you. I sensed you walking away for good and knowing I could die if I chose to. With you gone, it would've been very easy to die. I was so close to the veil between life and death that I could've quickly slipped away. But I remembered the ethereal voice giving me permission to go back to you, to life, and I knew that's what I wanted.

"You had just said goodbye and left. The shock of it and the need to see you, even if for just one more time, jolted me out of unconsciousness, and I woke. I think I waited to become conscious until I knew for sure you were here, that it wasn't a dream and it was really you, in the flesh, who'd found me. Because without you, I wouldn't have come back—life wouldn't be worth living."

Chapter 21

Cape Elizabeth, Maine

Ella and Daniel married a month after he was released from the hospital. Hannah talked them into marrying in Maine at her stone cottage by the sea. "After all," she'd said, "given your history, it's very appropriate for you to join your lives together here, overlooking the sea that will never bring you bad things again. Your long-ago cousin two generations back, who is the reason we have this house today, Lilah Jameson, would be very happy."

Ella replied with a laugh, "We're both very happy!"

****

Two years later, Ella gave birth to a son they named Nathan, and in two more years came a girl, Celia, both named in honor of the souls who'd come before them and enabled them to find their path to a loving and fulfilled life.

Ella worked for the local newspaper and magazines, writing freelance stories. She researched the history of the town, which was a very personal story to her, and eventually became the town historian. She still liked to volunteer at the veterans' hospital whenever possible, to give back the gift of Daniel's life being saved.

Daniel gave up flying, but still loved the sea. He bought a sailboat and ran tours seasonally. They made a modest living, and when Hannah passed away, she left the stone cottage to them. Their children got to grow up and enjoy life on the coast and marveled at the stories their parents told them of how they came to meet and marry.

Ella was living proof that life could come around full circle, with Lilah having lived alone after losing Nathaniel and her baby there, and now, in the present, the stone cottage was filled with love, family, and children.

She still walked the stretch of coast where the old Victorian house stood. The house had been bought and renovated by a young couple with three children. It still had the two huge windows staring down at Ella as she walked, but it now seemed to look upon her with gladness, all new inside and out, with landscaped lawns and gardens, bursting with life and reflecting the care and love of its new owners. She never saw her mother's spirit there on the widow's walk anymore, knowing Cecilia had moved on because there were no more warnings or messages to be given to Ella. Her life was rich and full. Every once in a while, her mother still came to her in a dream in pivotal parts of her life—when she married and gave birth—just to let her know, Ella liked to think, that she was close by in spirit and love.

Ella and her family continued to visit and walk on the same beach where, as a child, she'd had the near-drowning experience. The whole thing was merely a fading memory now, with no hold on her anymore. She spent many hours there looking out over the sea, reflecting on her life's journey. The sea was not a curse anymore. Yes, she'd lost loved ones to it. But Ella recognized the sea was simply the teacher, the main factor that could spur her to action, to remind her of her choices. It was the vehicle by which she'd made her journey.

Not only was the sea a reflection of her own life, she realized, but of the life of nature and mankind as well. Just as each ocean wave died upon the shore then took new life as a new wave, so did the life force of each person—dying in body, only to be born again, and regain new life in a new form. *Just as the ocean is a whole entity and its waves are small parts that assimilate back into itself, so do we,* Ella thought. *We assimilate back into the greater cosmos or wherever life begins. The sea is subject to celestial and earthly forces that are simultaneously destructive and creative, life-ending, and life-giving, so it is with each human soul, each person a part of the collective ocean of mankind and life itself.* Coming to these understandings took time, but brought consistent and lasting peace no matter what event life threw at her. *Just another wave to ride over,* she thought.

Sitting in front of the fire, she and Daniel would sometimes reminisce about their lives, still in awe of the process and events that led them to their present life. Some nights, lingering pieces of Ella's ancient spirit drifted back, a reminder of what it took to bring her round, of how she'd died to find love. Daniel, in his calm and wise way, would tell her not to judge the process. It just took what it took for her to get to the bottom of her life's mysteries, losses, and fears. And he said, "Thank God you did because, if you hadn't been as courageous and strong as you were, life would be very different for us right now. I probably wouldn't even be alive right now. I'd be waiting in that other realm for you, and then we'd have to come back again and try to get it right the next time. And I don't know about you, but I wasn't looking forward to dying at sea again."

He laughed, half-joking, but Ella cringed with the truth of his words. "I can't believe we'd have ended up going through all that loss and suffering again. But I guess that's what would have had to have happened, huh?"

"It certainly is. In one way or another, you just keep coming back 'til you get it right."

She kissed him and they clung together, grateful for the life they made, and the one they'd avoided. "It's still hard for me to wrap my mind around those other people and lives. Were they real or figments of my imagination, something I dreamed up, like a tool to use to help me understand?"

"Maybe a little of both," Daniel mused. "But of course, there is the tangible fact of Lilah and Nathaniel building this house we live in. It's almost like he knew his Lilah would need proof the next time around, and he gave it to her. To you."

Ella shivered. "Ugh, it's still gives me the chills. It just seems crazy. And from our perspective in the present, everything in the past seems like a bad dream."

Daniel put his glass up to toast. "Well, here's to no more bad dreams. Only a good life ahead. Then maybe another even better life, and another…"

Ella interrupted him. "Stop! No more of that. I'm living life strictly in the here and now. That's all we've truly got."

"Right you are. Speaking of living in the moment, kiss me now, then come to bed. I've got an early day tomorrow—up before dawn to get ready for the charter I'm taking out at seven."

Probably because of the conversation they'd just had dredging up the past, when Daniel said those words, Ella instantly moved back in time and heard Peter, Matthias, Miguel, and lastly, Nathaniel saying those similar words just before they'd been lost at sea. Dread washed over her with the same intuition that Daniel wouldn't return. She clung to him all night, loving him and praying for his safety, even asking him if he could change the tour to another day. But it was impossible to reschedule the crew and the trip. "Tourists, you know. They're on a tight itinerary." He held her close. "Hey, you don't have to worry. I know what you're thinking, but those times and sad endings are over. You're probably having a little PTSD yourself, a flashback, you know? It's normal, but it's not real, Ella. You believe me?"

"Yes," she said, looking deep into his eyes, searching for validation, but not truly believing it.

The next morning, Daniel was up before dawn and headed out with his gear. He kissed her and waved goodbye, making her promise to not think about anything other than him having a wonderful and safe sail, making his living and helping people have a great experience on their vacation. "Take a break," he yelled as he drove down the driveway. "You and the kids go to the beach for the day. Have some fun!"

Ella did exactly as he suggested. She pushed the old memories from her mind and concentrated on packing a picnic lunch and organizing the day's outing. They headed to the beach below the bluff where the Victorian house sat and she sometimes felt her mother's presence. Ella felt protected with envisioning Cecilia's loving spirit watching over them.

It was a perfect, golden summer day, not a lot of wind, small waves they could swim in, and just enough heat to make the cool water inviting. After sunning and swimming, they ate their lunch, and the kids ran back toward the rocks to look for whatever treasures they could find. Ella found herself looking over the water, glad for the calm day, for Daniel having an easy sail, imagining him and his passengers arriving back safely later that afternoon. But a seed of doubt sprouted inside the old, dark emotional closet she used to stash the scary things. It was fairly empty now, and those few things only got to her when she let them. On that day, though, she didn't seem to have a choice. The fear grew, and she didn't know its source. But of course, she did: Daniel was out at sea.

Ella checked on the children. They were building a sandcastle. Something prompted her then, just like the old house had way back when she was nine, nudging her to walk toward the sea. As Ella walked the shoreline, masses of tiny shells washed up. She and the children had a huge shell collection. She used them for art projects and to decorate their tables and shelves.

Scoping out the beach ahead for more treasures, she thought she saw something shimmering among the usual array of sea debris. Walking closer to investigate, another wave washed over it and tumbled the glistening nugget further up the sand. Ella looked at the sun. It shone down on this sparkling thing, bringing her attention straight to it. The golden object seemed to reflect a beam of light directly to her eyes, drawing her in.

"Kids, come here. Look, there's something really shiny up there." They ran ahead to check it out. Her son found it first, picked it up, and turned it over in his palm a few times, pronouncing it was "just some old piece of metal."

Her daughter then took it and put it in the water to wash the sand off. "Well, he thinks it's junk, but I think it's pretty." She twirled it around her finger. "I think it's a ring, but it's way too big for me. It looks like a grown-up ladies' ring."

The shiny, golden object looked like a jewel in her daughter's hand. "Can I see it, Celia?"

Taking it, Ella saw it was definitely a ring. A shiver went down her spine as it touched her palm. "This looks so familiar." It was still encrusted with sand and debris. Ella dunked it in the water again, and with the sharp edge of a broken shell, she dug at and cleaned out the engraving around the ring. It looked ancient and was beat up, having been tossed around the ocean for who-knew-how-many years. As the ring cleaned up, she saw it was solid, real gold—it had to have been to have survived the ocean.

Ella recalled a story she'd seen on the news about hundreds of gold coins found off the coast of Israel that were over a thousand years old and had survived beautifully. The scientists had said that real gold was not affected by air and water. She could tell it once had hard, defined edges, but now, probably from being tumbled over sand and rocks, it was smooth and worn. There were no markings or initials. Finally being able to make out the etching encircling it, she gasped. "This looks like a Greek design, a Greek key symbol." She couldn't recall the specific name of the design, but she clearly remembered the look of it.

But it was when she put it on her finger, that a jolt went through her body, not like an electric shock but rather warm liquid fire shooting through her arm up to her heart, just as when Daniel first found her and touched her hand in Key West. Memories flooded her instantly, and she was plunged into a world long ago. A young man lay in her lap. He had on the garb of a Grecian warrior, with sandals laced to his knees. He looked up at her and she knew his face. It was Matthias. He'd put the ring on her finger with his promise to return and marry her. Ella looked down at the ring—it was the very same one.

"This can't be possible." The memory faded as quickly as it had come, but the smell of the sea and salt air remained, as did the grief. She put her hand with the ring on it up to her heart and covered it with her other hand. Closing her eyes, she remembered him, the ring and the very first love of her very first life. Ella looked at the ring again. The sun hit it just so, making it shine like a beacon, leading her heart home. Then she remembered how Helena had walked into the sea, taken the ring off and thrown it deep into its bowels, vowing to hate the sea for taking her love. Ella thought, *There's no way someone else could've put the same exact ring in the ocean, and done it a thousand years ago for it to be this worn.*

It hit her then in her gut, in her whole body and spirit all at once. The sea had returned Helena's ring, her ring, as if saying, *Your pain and suffering are over, and here's proof—your ring and your love have been returned to you.*

She held out her hand with the ring on it, admiring it as it gleamed like new life. It fit perfectly, but of course, it would. It was hers, no matter which face, place, name, or time—it was *hers*.

They packed up and headed back to the cottage. She got the kids cleaned up, and before putting them down for a nap before dinner, four-year-old Nathan asked, "Is Dad coming home soon?"

"He sure is."

Nathan didn't look convinced, and even looked worried.

"What's wrong, sweetie?"

He looked down and drew little circles with his finger on the bedspread. "Well, I know I'm not supposed to watch these stories, but by mistake, I saw something on TV about how boats sink and people die, and Dad is always on his boat. His boat won't sink, will it?"

She tipped his chin up. "Look at me. Believe me. Your father is the best sailor ever, and he'll bring his boat back just fine. He'll be home safe today and every day that he goes out."

"But how do you know for sure?"

"I just know," Ella said, looking at the ring, a shining, golden promise of life returning, just as each wave dies and returns eventually to shore as a new wave.

She tucked both kids in, then went to the kitchen. With the blender on high, Ella hadn't heard the front door open.

Daniel burst into the kitchen, grabbed her around

the waist from behind, and kissed her neck. "See. I'm home, back in one piece, as promised."

Turning off the blender, Ella faced him and hugged him like they'd been separated a lifetime. "I knew you'd come back."

"That's my girl. When I left this morning, you weren't so sure. What changed your mind?"

Glancing at the ring, she said, "Oh, just a promise, a promise the sea made to me." She took his face in her hands and looked into his eyes, glimpsing his familiar, beloved, ancient soul. No matter to which face, place, name, or time it belonged, the soul was *his*.

Ella showed him the ring and explained everything about it. She told him she'd never fear for their fate again, not his, hers, or their children's. The sea held no malice or magical power—it simply existed as part of the grander scheme of life, necessary for survival, as it had been necessary for her own.

Daniel, in awe, said, "After all these years, you're full of surprises, and otherworldly events surround you. Life with you is extraordinary, and so are you. I'll love you forever, you know that, don't you?"

"Of course, and no matter which face or name we have, no matter what place or time we live in—I am *yours*, you are mine, and this love is *ours*. It will never die." She smoothed her hand lovingly over his forehead, down his cheek, and brushed his lips with hers. They kissed differently then, reverently, as if encompassing a thousand years of living—embodying the people, events, lives and deaths of all those they'd been privy to recall.

In that moment of time, and from time eternal, all the knowledge Ella had gained, the experiences she'd had, and all the love she'd given and received coalesced inside her spirit, bringing complete understanding: *The body does not connect us through time and space. Only love does. Love is the key and the lock, the question and the answer, the beginning and end. Love brought him back as it always would, for all lives, for all time. Only where love is, does true life exist.*

A word about the author…

N. Christine Samuelson writes about the eternal bonds of love that transform lives and transcend death. Her storylines reflect the challenges, fears and conflicts, and tragedies and victories that manifest through time and a powerful connection of love.

Extensive travel and personal experiences have inspired the diverse settings, characters, and storylines of her novels. She lives in coastal South Carolina, where the sea is a constant source of inspiration.

Website: http://NChristineSamuelson.com

Facebook: https://www.facebook.com/NChristine.Samuelson

Twitter: https://twitter.com/ncsamuelson

www.ingramcontent.com/pod-product-compliance
Lightning Source LLC
Chambersburg PA
CBHW071515260626
47170CB00002B/381
9781509219797